A Stepney Girl's Secret

Jean Fullerton is the author of nineteen historical novels and a memoir, *A Child of the East End*. She is a qualified District and Queen's nurse who has spent most of her working life in the East End of London, first as a Sister in charge of a team, and then as a District Nurse tutor. She is also a qualified teacher and spent twelve years lecturing on community nursing studies at a London university. She now writes full time.

Find out more at www.jeanfullerton.com

Also by Jean Fullerton

East End Nolan Family

No Cure for Love
A Glimpse at Happiness
Perhaps Tomorrow
Hold on to Hope

Nurse Millie and Nurse Connie

Call Nurse Millie
All Change for Nurse Millie
Christmas with Nurse Millie
Fetch Nurse Connie
Easter With Nurse Millie
Wedding Bells for Nurse Connie

East End Ration Books

A Ration Book Dream
(originally published as *Pocketful of Dreams*)
A Ration Book Christmas
A Ration Book Childhood
A Ration Book Wedding
A Ration Book Daughter
A Ration Book Christmas Kiss
A Ration Book Christmas Broadcast
A Ration Book Victory

Stepney Girls

A Stepney Girl's Secret

Novels

The Rector's Daughter

Non-fiction

A Child of the East End

A Stepney Girl's Secret

JEAN FULLERTON

CORVUS

First published in paperback in Great Britain in 2023
by Corvus, an imprint of Atlantic Books Ltd.

Copyright © Jean Fullerton, 2023

10 9 8 7 6 5 4

A CIP catalogue record for this book is available from
the British Library.

Paperback ISBN: 978 1 83895 759 9
E-book ISBN: 978 1 83895 760 5

Printed in Great Britain by CPI Group (UK) Ltd,
Croydon CR0 4YY

Corvus
An imprint of Atlantic Books Ltd
Ormond House
26–27 Boswell Street
London
WC1N 3JZ

www.atlantic-books.co.uk

To my long-suffering husband Kelvin

Chapter one

ROLLING HER SHOULDERS to ease the stiffness caused by a four-hour journey down the Great North Road, Prudence Carmichael glanced at her watch.

'Not long now, Prudence,' her father, Revd Hugh Carmichael, called over his shoulder as their elderly Austin Seven approached a crossroads.

'Mind that parked car, Hugh,' said Prue's mother Marjorie from the seat beside him.

It was just after four o'clock in the afternoon. Twenty-three-year-old Prudence – known as Prue to her friends – was squashed into the back of her father's car, and had been since the last of their furniture had been carried out of St Stephen's vicarage in the leafy village of Biddenham.

The truck carrying all their worldly goods was probably some way behind them. Although her father rarely drove above thirty miles per hour, the three-ton Bedford truck carrying their chattels was considerably slower.

Well, when she said 'all their worldly goods' that wasn't quite true, because wedged around her in the back of the car were several boxes containing items with which the removal men were not to be trusted. At her feet was a fruit box with her mother's Royal Doulton bone-china tea set wrapped in newspaper, while on the worn leather bench seat beside her was another, filled with gilt-framed family photos. Propped up in the other footwell were the half-dozen eighteenth-century watercolours of hunting scenes bequeathed to the family by some maiden aunt half a century before.

'Yes, my dear,' Hugh said, replying to his wife and setting the butcher's boy on the bicycle beside them into a wobble as he swung the car into the middle of the carriageway.

Just a year short of his fifty-fifth birthday, with a willowy frame, thinning grey hair and light blue eyes behind the thick lenses of his horn-rimmed spectacles, Hugh Carmichael looked as if a strong wind could carry him off.

As always, when about his parish business, he was wearing a loose-fitting two-piece light grey suit over his black clerical shirt, a stiff all-encompassing dog collar fixed with a stud at the back, and a soft fedora.

'And look out for that ARP truck,' Marjorie added, as her husband cut across a three-ton Leyland lorry that was turning in front of them.

Prue's mother was also dressed in her everyday parish wear, which in her case was a smart light blue dress and jacket with navy shoes, gloves and handbag topped off by a modest, feather-adorned hat. However, in contrast to her father's fragile appearance, Prue's mother's full-busted physique wouldn't have looked out of place on the prow of any of Nelson's battleships.

2

'Thank you, my love,' her husband replied, glancing at her over his spectacles. 'I can see the traffic around me quite clearly.'

'I'm sure you can, my dear, but everyone is driving far too fast,' Marjorie countered, as a wagon piled high with barrels whizzed by.

'It's London,' said Hugh. 'Things are different here.'

Prue's father was right.

Whereas the lanes in rural Bedfordshire were dusty, unpaved and dotted with black-beamed houses and low-roofed thatched cottages, and with horse-drawn farm carts ambling along at a country pace, the main artery into East London had goods lorries and military vehicles roaring back and forth, black exhaust fumes hiccupping out behind them. In addition, the road they were driving along was lined with three-storey houses, many of which had shops at ground level. And they weren't just the regular butcher and baker and candlestick maker you could find on any busy street, but clothing wholesalers, fruit importers and several small tailors' workshops, punctuated at regular intervals with public houses.

However, although the shops might have more variety than Biddenham High Street, the long queues of women with prams lined up outside them were all too familiar. Ever since the Government had introduced rationing in January, housewives up and down the country spent hours each day standing in line.

'And dirtier,' added her mother, eyeing a column of black smoke belching from a factory chimney.

'And where God has called me to serve,' Hugh reminded her.

'Indeed.' Marjorie glanced out of the window at two women, their hair in curlers, engaged in a furious argument outside a shop. 'I just wish the Almighty had called you to minister in a place with a few more trees and the odd meadow.'

They travelled on past men and women with ARP armbands and gas masks slung across them and groups of council workmen renewing sandbags against buildings.

'I don't know why the Government are wasting all this money putting up more air raid precautions,' said Marjorie as they passed a team of builders constructing a four-sided brick shelter. 'I spoke to my cousin Jeremy – you remember him, squint in his left eye and one leg shorter than the other, works in the Cabinet Office. He assured me that Chamberlain and Lord Halifax are poised to start peace negotiations again within days.'

'I seem to remember you said that after Munich, Mother,' said Prue.

'Did I?' she said airily. 'I can't say I recall.'

'"Well, that's put Herr Hitler in his place" were your exact words, when you saw the photo of Chamberlain waving a bit of paper on the front page of *The Times*.'

Her mother swivelled around in her seat. 'That was different. The Germans hadn't come up against our army then, but now they've had a taste of our military might they'll sue for peace.'

4

'Well, I'm just thankful Rob's in France not Belgium,' Prue replied.

'But if he was, I'm sure your brother would be in the thick of it,' her mother answered. 'My father was in the military, as was his father and his father before him, so Robert has the army in his blood.' Marjorie frowned. 'And I don't know why you must be so contrary, Prudence?'

'Perhaps I take after Fliss,' Prue said.

'Good God, I sincerely hope not,' her mother replied. 'And how many times must I ask you to call your sister by her given name, Felicity.'

She swung round to the front, leaving Prue to stare at the back of her hat.

'Here we are: Mile End Road,' said Hugh, having just spotted Stepney Green station on a corner to their right.

Gripping the steering wheel with his fine-boned hands, Prue's father pulled it hard to the left and veered diagonally across the staggered junction, causing the driver of an oncoming black taxi to stand on his brakes and blast his horn.

They motored on for another few minutes then Hugh pulled into the kerb alongside a six-foot-high brick wall. Yanking up the handbrake, he turned off the engine and got out.

As he went to open the door for his wife, Prue opened her own door and swung out her legs. Clutching her handbag in one hand and adjusting her gas-mask strap, she stared up at her new home: St Winifred's Rectory.

'Impressive, isn't it?' said her father as he and her mother joined her on the pavement.

'It certainly is,' Prue agreed.

In contrast to the squat, two-up two-down terraced houses and tightly packed tenements they had driven past since they reached Hackney, St Winifred's Rectory was surrounded by at least three-quarters of an acre of land. There were even a couple of mature apple trees in their white spring blossom swaying in the breeze over by the side wall.

In the ordinary way of things, rectories, vicarages and parsonages were often a reasonable size, with two or three reception rooms. But with dormer windows in the eves indicating extensive servants' quarters, the tall casement windows criss-crossed with gummed tape and the solid front door, St Winifred's Rectory seemed more like the squire's manor house than the humble parson's abode.

'Of course, when I was shown the rectory by the churchwardens a month ago, it had an impressive wrought-iron gate,' continued Prue's father, indicating the empty space between the two Portland-stone pillars. 'But I suppose the armament factories need the metal more than we do.' He offered his wife his arm. 'Shall we, my dear?'

Marjorie slipped her arm through his and the two of them headed up the path to the front door.

Prue followed and was immediately struck by the contrast between the bustling exhaust-choked street behind her and the mute pastoral feel of the rectory's enclosed garden.

Grasping the enamel knob beside the door, her father pulled hard. Somewhere in the house there was the faint sound of a bell ringing. After a few moments a bolt rattled back on the other side of the porch door.

The door scraped opened to reveal a stout woman in her mid to late fifties wearing a flowery wraparound apron over her dun-coloured dress, the sleeves of which were rolled back to reveal brawny forearms. A colourful scarf was tied into a turban, concealing all but a few wisps of greying brown hair. In addition, she had what appeared to be a roll-up tucked behind her right ear.

'Reverend Carmichael?' she said, her deep-set eyes fixing on Prue's father.

'The very same,' he replied. 'Mrs …'

'Lavender,' the women replied. 'Dolly Lavender.'

'Well then, Mrs Lavender,' said Marjorie, adjusting her handbag on her arm and looking the woman in the doorway up and down, 'perhaps you wouldn't mind letting us over the threshold.'

'Of course.' The rectory's housekeeper stepped back. 'You must be gasping for a cuppa, so come in.'

They walked in and Mrs Lavender closed the door behind them. Then, as the housekeeper took their coats, Prue looked around her new home.

The broad rectory hall was large enough to accommodate a coat stand and a hall dresser with elegant curved legs and three drawers on one side. An imposing staircase led to the floor above, the polished treads protected by a central strip of worn, dull-green carpet held in place by rods. The dado rail that ran halfway up the walls and separated the white emulsion above from the redbrick emulsion below continued up the staircase, above which were various tired-looking watercolours and faded photos.

There were four doors leading off the hallways on either side and one at the far end down a couple of steps; Prue guessed that led though to the rectory kitchen and scullery.

'Did you have a good journey?' their new housekeeper enquired, hanging their coats on the hall rack.

Hugh removed his hat and handed it to her. 'Tolerable.'

'Well, it would have been,' chipped in his wife, 'had it not been for the army trucks clogging up the Great North Road.'

'Well, there is a war on,' said Prue.

'Still, no doubt St Christopher himself watched over you, and here you all are, safe and well,' said the housekeeper.

'Indeed, we are, Mrs Lavender,' Hugh replied, bestowing a benevolent smile on her.

'It's a right pleasure and no mistake to set eyes on you both – and Miss Carmichael, of course,' the housekeeper said, giving her a motherly smile. 'And it's nice to have a family in the 'ouse again, especially after having poor Father David rattling about in this old pile by himself for half a year.'

Marjorie's ample eyebrows pulled together. 'I thought Father Owen left only two months ago.'

Mrs Lavender glanced over her shoulder then she leaned towards them.

'Officially yes, Mrs C,' she said, in a hushed voice. 'But you know, with his little problem, you might say 'e's been "away" being looked after at one of those special places for people who ...'

She winked and pretended to drink from an invisible bottle.

Marjorie gave her a cool look then ran her index finger along the bottom of a picture frame. She opened her mouth to speak but Mrs Lavender jumped in first.

'Now then.' She rubbed her work-roughened hands together. 'What say you make yourselves comfy in the parlour while I goes and brews you all a nice cup of Rosy Lee?'

Turning, the housekeeper started towards the rear of the house.

'I'm sorry, Mrs Lavender,' said Prue's father, 'but is Father David not here?'

"E is not, sir, just at this present moment in time, so to speak?' the housekeeper replied. 'Got a phone call, 'e did, at half past one, and dashed out like 'e had the imps of hell after him, muttering about an emergency or some such. And I should wonder after the way 'e bolted his dinner down if he ain't been suffering the heartburn all afternoon.'

'Then tea in the parlour it is, Mrs Lavender,' said Prue's father.

'Right you are, sir.'

The housekeeper puffed and panted her way towards the back of the house then disappeared through the door at the far end of the hall.

'Mrs Lavender seems very cheery, doesn't she?' said Prue.

Prue's mother kicked the corner of the hall runner up and glanced at the unpolished tiles beneath. 'Well, let's hope her cooking is better than her housework or I can see myself having several words with her.'

'Now, now, Marjorie; a little charity, if you please,' Prue's father replied.

'Dad's right,' said Prue, slipping off her summer blazer and hanging it on one of the empty pegs. 'I'm sure once Mrs Lavender gets used to our ways everything will be fine. And this rectory is too big for you to run without help, Mum.'

Her mother raised an eyebrow and opened her mouth to reply but the doorbell bouncing on its spring cut across her words.

'I'll get it,' said Prue, thankful for the interruption.

She retraced her steps across the black-and-white hall tiles and opened the door.

Standing on the doorstep was a tall young man dressed in a black cassock. He had a shock of blond hair and a set of cheekbones so sharp they'd cut your finger.

He blinked a couple of times then pulled himself together.

'M … M … Miss Carmichael, is it?' he asked, in a crisp, cultured voice.

'Yes,' Prue replied. 'You must be …'

'David. David Harmsworth.' He forced a light laugh. 'Curate of this parish.'

'Father David!'

His light grey eyes passed over Prue to where her parents stood.

'Father Hugh,' he said, stepping around Prue to greet her father.

'Good to meet you again,' said Prue's father, extending his hand.

'My deepest apologies for not being here when you arrived,' David said as the two men shook hands.

'I understand and don't worry. We've only just walked through the door and the lorry has yet to make an appearance,' said Hugh. 'Was it someone in need of spiritual comfort in their final hours, perhaps?'

'No,' said David. 'The ARP controller called us all in.'

Prue's mother raised an eyebrow. 'Us?'

David rummaged around in his cassock pocket for a moment then pulled out an armband with 'ARP' embroidered on it.

'I'm the ARP warden for this area,' he replied, twiddling it between his long fingers, 'and there was a bit of a flap at the ARP control centre at the Town Hall. I'm afraid it was all very hush-hush so I can't tell you anything further. Not that I'm implying you're a German spy, Father Hugh, but …'

'You can never be sure, can you?' Prue chipped in, earning herself a hard look from her mother.

Her father's thin lips lifted in a benign smile. 'Father David, may I introduce my wife?'

Putting on her Lady Bountiful face, Marjorie took the curate's proffered hand. 'Lovely to meet you, Father David. My husband's told me so much about you.'

'And my daughter, Prudence, you've already met,' her father said.

'Hello,' she said.

He smiled. 'The pleasure's all mine.'

The doorbell rang again.

Moving out from under David's somewhat intense gaze, Prue went to open it.

This time the driver of the removal lorry and two of the four men who'd loaded their entire home into the back of the vehicle some five hours before were standing on the doorstep.

'Right, miss,' said the driver, pinching out his roll-up and stowing it behind his ear. 'Where do you want it, then?'

'Just bring it inside and I'll tell you where,' barked Marjorie, striding across to the door. 'And be sure you don't traipse mud all through the house.'

'No, missus,' the driver replied.

'Madam, if you please,' Prue's mother snapped back. 'I'm the rector's wife not the daily char.'

'Yes, madam.' Touching the peak of his cap, the driver and his assistants ambled off back down the path.

'And take a care,' Marjorie called after them. 'You're handling my family's heirlooms and I will hold you

12

financially responsible for any breakages.' Turning back, she gave her husband a tight smile. 'If you'd excuse me, my dear.'

'Of course,' he replied. 'Father David and I will get out of your way and adjourn to the study.'

However, before they could move an inch, another delivery man arrived with the first of the tea chests.

'Kitchen,' Prue's mother said, glancing at the label stuck on the side.

The removal man tramped off towards the back of the house as another walked through the door.

'Right, Prudence,' said her mother, taking off her jacket and hat, 'I'll take charge of the operation here and I need you upstairs directing the traffic into the correct bedrooms.'

'But which ones?' asked Prue.

'Obviously your father and I will have the largest,' her mother replied, pointing a delivery man towards the back of the house. 'But other than that, you decide.'

'If you don't think it too bold of me, sir,' David said, shooting a glance at Prue, 'perhaps you'll permit me to show your daughter the upstairs.'

Prue's father looked at his wife.

Marjorie studied the young curate for a moment then gave a quick nod as another of the removal men appeared carrying a standard lamp.

'Join me in the study when you're done, Father David,' Hugh said as he opened the door into the front room.

David turned to Prue.

'After you,' he said, sweeping his hand towards the staircase.

Leaving her mother shooing delivery men hither and thither, Prue headed up the stairs with St Winifred's fair-haired curate a step behind.

'Have you been at St Winifred's long?' she asked as they reached the halfway landing.

'Two years,' he replied. 'St Winnie's is my second curacy. I was in a little place just outside Oxford before that.'

'My father was at Trinity College,' said Prue.

'As was I. It seems we have a great deal in common already, Miss Carmichael,' he replied, as they reached the first-floor landing.

He gazed down at her for a moment, then seemed to remember why they were there.

'Here are the family rooms,' he said, indicating a number of doors painted the same dull white colour as the paintwork below.

'And those are the … the facilities,' he added, as Prue popped her head around the two doors at the top of the stairs and discovered the lavatory and bathroom.

'And up there,' he continued, opening a narrow door tucked into the corner and revealing a rough-hewn staircase, 'are the old servants' quarters. Apparently, fifty years ago, this place had six domestics plus a groom to look after the rector's horse and carriage.'

'Is that where you are?' Prue asked, peering up into the dark passageway.

'No, I'm through there.' He nodded towards a door behind them at the far end of the landing. 'It's just a couple of rooms over what were the stables; in times past the housekeeper and gardener lived there but now it's the curate's accommodation., A smooth smile spread across David's lean face. 'Although Father Owen, the previous rector, was a very spiritual man, he was single and as such the parish – how can I put this? – suffered a little from the absence of a feminine hand on the rudder.'

'Well, you certainly have that now,' said Prue, as her mother's voice echoed up from below, berating the removal men for some blunder or other.

'And we are doubly blessed in that regard as I'm sure you'll be an invaluable helpmate to your mother around the parish,' he concluded.

'I will be,' answered Prue. 'That is until I find some gainful employment.'

His fair eyebrows rose. 'You work?'

'I do,' said Prue.

'How very modern,' he replied, with just a hint of condescension.

Prue pulled a face. 'This is nineteen forty, not *eighteen* forty. Unmarried women no longer spend their days taking tea and pressing flowers. Actually, I was the almoner's assistant at St Peter's Hospital in Bedford.'

'Assisting the infirm and afflicted,' he replied. 'What a noble occupation.'

Prue smiled but decided against mentioning it also gave her two pounds fifteen a week.

'Father David!' Marjorie's voice trilled up the stairs.

They peered over the top of the banister and saw her looking up from the bottom of the stairs.

'Would you mind helping the rector in his study?' she asked, with a sweet smile.

'Of course, Mrs Carmichael.' He gave Prue a brief smile and hurried down the stairs.

Prue soon located the large main bedroom which overlooked the back garden and a smaller one next door which, judging by the fairyland wallpaper, had once been a nursery. The next door revealed a further bedroom also overlooking the garden. Next, Prue strode across the faded hall runner and into a bedroom with bright flowery wallpaper and a view over the rectory vegetable plot at the side of the house. Glancing around it from the doorway she opened the remaining door and walked in.

This room wasn't quite as big as the one she'd allocated to her sister but it had the same cast-iron fireplace and sash windows. The view from the windows, however, was quite different.

Walking across the room Prue gazed out on to White Horse Lane. To her right at the other end of the High Street was the solid square tower of St Winifred's, hemmed in on all sides by tightly packed grey-slate roofs. But it was the hustle and bustle going on just over the rectory wall that held Prue's interest.

Women with shopping bags over their arms and their hair concealed beneath scarf turbans stood gossiping on street corners; men in rough cords and puffing roll-ups were easing barrels through cellar hatches and leaning back to take the strain on the rope. And a dozen barrage balloons overhead, glowing pink in the late-afternoon sunshine, tugged at their moorings. Unlike the soft rolling hills and gentle country ways she'd observed from her bedroom window in Biddenham, this scene was animated with purpose and life.

'Where do you want this, luv?'

Prue turned to see one of the delivery men standing just behind her and balancing the brass headrest of her parents' double bed over his shoulder.

'In the room opposite, please,' Prue replied.

'Right you are.' He half turned and then halted. 'Oh, by the way, have you 'eard?'

'Heard what?'

'There's been a special news bulletin on the wireless about 'alf an hour ago saying that the Dutch have gone under and the Germans are sweeping into Holland,' he replied, the roll-up stuck to his lower lips bobbing as he spoke. 'Looks like we're at proper war now, don't it? Room opposite, you say?'

Prue nodded and the man adjusted his hold on the metal frame and left the room.

Although she wasn't supposed to know, the truth was that her father's move to East London wasn't so much to do with the Almighty prompting him as the newly appointed Bishop of Bedford suggesting that he should perhaps think about seeking another living.

Chapter two

WIPING THE SWEAT from his eyes, and with the sound of tools on metal echoing off the corrugated roof of the London and North Eastern Railway's Stratford shunting yard and works main locomotive shed and ringing in his ears, Jack Quinn grasped the spanner again. Taking a deep breath, he bore down on it and prayed that the bolt would turn. For a moment it resisted his efforts, but just as he was beginning to think he'd have to drill it out he felt it budge.

'Grease, Tosh,' he gasped to the fifteen-year-old apprentice hovering at his shoulder.

The gangly youth with a mop of bright red hair sprang forward and aimed the nozzle of the can he was holding, smothering black glutinous oil on the bolt jammed in the Castle Class 4-6-0 train's piston.

It was somewhere close to five in the evening and Jack, along with the rest of the morning shift who'd arrived as the sun came up at 6 a.m., was still hard at it, even though he should have clocked off three hours ago. Not that anyone working on the London and North Eastern Railway took any notice of working hours any more, not since the Railway Executive Committee took command of running the four big railways six months ago.

The veins on his bare forearms raised with the effort, Jack continued the pressure on the bolt until, all at once, it spun around.

'Cor, Jack, you wanna give up all this train malarkey and take up bending iron bars in a circus,' said Bill Brown, his friend, second-in-command on the maintenance team and ten years his senior at thirty-eight. Unlike Jack, who had been determined to become a senior locomotive engineer since his first job as a cleaner at the age of fourteen, Bill was content to be a maintenance worker.

Jack grinned, giving the bolt one last turn and catching it as it fell out.

'Over to you,' he said, handing it to Bill. 'I'm going to have to leave you and Tosh to get the piston back in working order. Old Prentice sent a message an hour ago to join him in his office when I'm done.'

'Good luck,' said Bill.

'Thanks.' Jack glanced across his friend's head at the red streaks lighting up the western sky behind Stratford station. 'And you'd better get a shift on – the light'll be gone in an hour or so.'

'Bloody blackout regs,' muttered Bill. ''Ow do they expect us to keep the rolling stock on the rails if we can't have the lights on to work by?'

'Better than showing the Luftwaffe where to drop their bombs,' Jack replied.

'If they ever do,' Tosh replied.

'Don't worry,' said Jack, wiping his hands on the tatty bit of towel he kept in his dungarees pocket for the purpose, 'the Germans are coming all right, and we'll be one of the first on their list when they do. Now I'd better get myself over to the office before Prentice sends out a search party.'

Leaving Bill and Tosh to their task, Jack stepped over rail tracks, half-dismantled steam engines and damaged wagons to make his way towards the engine shed's entrance.

Stratford's shunting yards and engine sheds lay to the north of the station, covering what had once been marshland. It was bordered by the River Lee in the west and Angel Lane to the east, with Hackney Marshes to the north and the old road to Essex at its southern border.

Founded in the height of the railway boom a hundred years before, its foundry and workshops had once built locomotives and carriages from the ground up. However, the production of both had ceased by the outbreak of the First World War. By the September following the General Strike, when Jack walked through Angel Lane gates, he discovered that the Stratford works dealt only in repairing and renovating engines and rolling stock.

As well as the dozens of specialist repair shops, Stratford was also one of the busiest shunting yards in the country. Wagons carrying grain from East Anglia, fish landed in Grimsby and Yarmouth, coal from Newcastle and timber from Scotland arrived day and night. In addition, rubber from Britain's colonies in India and

Burma and oil from Egypt and Arabia that were unloaded at Harwich, Tilbury and Hull all passed through on their way to their final destinations.

There were already half a dozen locomotives with the apple-green livery of the London and North Eastern Railway gleaming in the sun's mellow rays, their waggons attached and hissing steam, ready for their night run across the country.

Pausing beside the track, Jack waited as a smart-looking D1 4-4-0 Class pulling low-loading wagons covered by mud-coloured tarpaulin passed. Then, crunching gravel beneath his boots, he headed for the main office building, built some fifty years before in the solid but functional red-brick architecture favoured by civil engineers of the time. The wages and personnel departments were situated either side of the corridor while the canteen took up the back. Usually those working in the office could have looked out on to the yard's activities; however, for the past nine months their view had been obscured by a wall of sandbags that covered all but the top six inches or so of glass.

After holding the main door open for a couple of drivers who were leaving work for the day, Jack strolled in. As it was Tuesday the appetising smell of lamb stew drifted into his nose from the canteen. However, Jack ignored it, and headed up the central stairs to the floor above.

The first floor of the building was the command centre of the whole yard. There were windows on three sides of the room, now all interlaced with gummed paper as per Government recommendations to prevent flying glass. The windows that looked out over the yard and sheds had also recently had internal shutters fitted. They were folded back at the moment but had letterbox-sized peek-holes cut in them so that during the blackout those inside could squint through and see the rolling stock below.

Working at the control panels at any one time were a dozen controllers, in the company's regulation charcoal uniform. Each of them was responsible for the rail traffic using a particular route into the yard. They worked closely with the signalmen in the junction boxes to ensure each train ended up on the right track and, more importantly, not steaming towards another locomotive coming in the opposite direction. A couple of them who were between tasks greeted Jack with a nod as he passed them.

Stopping in front of the brown door at the far end, with 'E. Prentice Manager' painted in gold in the middle, Jack knocked and without waiting for an answer, turned the handle and walked in.

Somewhere between his mid to late forties, Ted Prentice was a rotund individual with a little head, stubby fingers and oddly small feet, which gave him more than a passing resemblance to a spinning top. He was dressed, as always, in a pinstriped suit with his pocket watch chain dangling across the waistcoat beneath.

'Quinn,' said Ted, his thinning, over-oiled hair gleaming in the light from the forty-watt bulb overhead.

'Sorry, guv,' said Jack, sounding anything but. 'But I've only just got the duff piston off *Pride of Cambridge*. Have you changed your mind about signing my release?'

Ted shook his head. 'I can't let you go.'

Jack raked his fingers through his coal-black hair. 'For God's sake.'

'I can't spare you, not with the way things are,' his manager continued. 'That's why railway workers are a reserved occupa—'

'Is there anything else?' cut in Jack.

'No. That's it for now, Quinn.' His piggy eyes looked him over. 'Except stop putting in these bloody requests every sodding week.'

Struggling to hold his temper in check, Jack glared down at his manager.

'Well, then,' he said, holding his gaze, 'as I've still got the coupling gear on a tender and a firebox door hanging off its hinges to fix before I clock off, I'd better get on.' He marched to the door, opened it and turned back. 'Oh, and I'll be putting another request on your desk every Monday until you release me to join the army.'

Two hours later, having unjammed the coupling mechanism, tightened the fire-door hinges and spent half an hour scrubbing the soot from the back of his neck in the changing room's lukewarm dribble of water, Jack finally strolled out of Stratford shunting yard's side gates and emerged on to Angel Lane. Crossing the cobbled road, he strolled into the Railway Tavern situated on the corner.

As usual at the end of the working day, the yard's unofficial annexe was full of railway workers ranging from uniformed station guards and ticket collectors to men like Jack dressed in rough corduroys and frayed shirts.

The Railway Tavern was very much like any other East End pub: faded flock wallpaper, scuffed floorboards and mirrors with the names of popular drinks like Whitby Pale Ale and Mackeson Stout painted on them. However, like the etched windows of the establishment, they were partially obscured by the paper glued across them. There was also a piano up against the far wall and a pitted dartboard fixed to the back wall. As most of the Tavern's customers were railway workers, neither got much use.

Making his way through the press of men and the thick tobacco smoke, Jack took his place at the bar. Ruby, the Tavern's blonde and well-endowed barmaid, was there, dressed in a flowery frock and chatting to a couple of young apprentices. She spotted Jack right away and wiggled over.

'Evening, Jack,' she said, giving him a welcoming smile. 'We don't often see you in here on a Tuesday. The usual?'

'Please,' Jack replied. 'I've just spent all afternoon in the machine workshop in this heat – my mouth's like the bottom of a budgie's cage.'

'I know. You'd think it was July not May. It must be close to seventy degrees this afternoon,' she said, fanning her hand in front of her generous cleavage. 'Opened all the doors and it's still like a blooming desert in 'ere.'

Stretching up, she retrieved a pint glass from the metal shelf above the bar and held it beneath the bitter spout.

'And it's not as if we can pop off to Southend beach to have a little paddle, is it?' she continued, pulling on the polished wooden handle of the pump. 'Not with the army covering the shoreline with ruddy barbed wire and landmines.'

'I don't mind missing out standing in the waves if it stops the Nazis landing,' Jack replied.

'The Nazis won't land here,' said Ruby, placing a frothy pint in front of Jack. 'They've got to get through us and the French first, and we'll stop them.'

Jack handed over a couple of coppers but didn't reply. Then, as he raised his drink and took the first sip, a two-tone whistle cut through the hullabaloo.

'Belt up, you lot,' bellowed Tubby Forester, the Railway Tavern's longstanding publican. 'The six o'clock news is coming on.'

'Bloody wireless,' muttered a voice behind Jack. 'Every time the announcer comes on they just tell you more bad news.'

'Yeah,' agreed someone else. 'Last week it was that the Germans had moved into Luxembourg, then yesterday that the Belgians had blown up all their bridges to stop them Nazis. God only knows what it'll be today.'

As the wireless valves warmed up, the closing bars of *Children's Hour* singing out from the Bush radio on the shelf behind the bar grew louder. The pips sounded and a hush settled on the room.

The plummy announcer started with an upbeat piece about the British Expeditionary Force holding Germany between Liège and Maastricht. This was rather undermined by the next item, which concerned the Dutch Government's flight to Britain in the early hours, followed by a report of twenty bombs landing – albeit harmlessly – in some woods outside Canterbury.

Sensing the end of the bulletin, a low murmur started up in the bar before the refined tones of the BBC presenter cut through again.

'And now, in a change to our scheduled programmes, the Right Honourable Anthony Eden, MP, Secretary of State for War, has a special announcement to the nation.'

Another pause, then the minister's voice rang out across the crowded bar: 'I want to speak to you tonight ...'

After reassuring listeners that any enemy aircraft attempting to enter British air space would be shot down by the air defences, he then went on to describe in some detail the German tactic of dropping specially trained and heavily armed parachutists.

'What? We're going to have bloody Germans dropping from the sky now, are we?' shouted someone on the other side of the bar.

The minister continued to explain how the army would be dealing with such troops promptly so there was no need for the population to be alarmed; however, after receiving countless enquires from those not yet called up who were eager to do something to defend the country ...

'Now is your opportunity,' said the minister. 'We want a large number of such men in Great Britain who are British subjects between the ages of seventeen and sixty-five ...'

With his glass poised halfway to his lips, Jack straightened up as he listened to the minister's convoluted announcement. '... and the name of the new force which is being raised will be the Local Defence Volunteers ...'

The minister went on to explain that it would be part time, based in their own home towns and that the men who volunteered would be part of the armed forces when they were on duty. He finished by saying any man interested was to give their name in to the local police station.

Jack swallowed what remained of his drink in one gulp and silently put his glass on the bar.

'You off home, then?' asked Ruby, as the minister launched into the final few paragraphs of his speech.

Jack shook his head. 'To the local nick.'

Chapter three

STOWING HIS LOGBOOK in the appropriate pigeonhole ready for the night warden taking over his patrol, Father David Harmsworth wished his fellow ARP wardens a cursory good evening and strolled out of ARP post number three.

The weather had been exceptionally warm since Easter, and tonight, as David stepped out into the balmy air, was no exception. Somewhere in the darkness, the metallic sound of a harmonica cut through the still air and many of the locals had dragged chairs out into the street and were sitting having a cup of tea or a bottle of beer with their neighbours. In fact, had it not been for the pitch blackness all around, you could almost forget there was a war on.

They greeted him as he walked back to the rectory, his muted torch making a pale pool of light at his feet on the pavement. St Winifred's clock struck half past nine as David reached the rectory's front gate – or rather, the space where the front gate had been before an armament factory requisitioned it for spare metal.

Taking his keys out of his ARP uniform trousers as he went, David reached the front door in half a dozen strides. He stepped through the blackout curtain into the house and, as he expected, a table lamp illuminated the hallway. Mrs Lavender always kept it lit when he was on evening patrol.

However, instead of Father Owen's shabby mac hanging in lonely abandonment on the coat rack, there were several garments he wasn't used to seeing: a red coat with a fur collar, a tan Burberry trench coat, a woman's tartan jacket and a black Crombie with a velvet trim. In addition, instead of the previous rector's misshaped trilby, there were at least half a dozen perky hats with feathers and ribbons on the pegs above.

Furthermore, a Turkish runner had been laid over the black-and-white hall tiles and a hefty majolica vase placed on the hall table. The dirt-layered, nondescript oil paintings that had been hanging on the wall the last time he was here had now been replaced by a series of bright pastoral watercolours.

Taking off his tin helmet and placing it on the hat stand, David walked into the back parlour overlooking the garden. However, the fruit trees, spring flowers and shrubs within it were now obscured from view by the heavy blackout curtains.

Prudence Carmichael was curled in one of the fireside chairs with her stockinged feet tucked under her, reading a book. She was wearing the same summery dress as she had been when he'd left after supper at six fifteen, a light blue cardigan now draped around her shoulder.

Her auburn hair, which had been pinned up when

he'd left for duty, was now unbound and cascaded down as God intended it. So much more feminine, to David's mind, than the modern craze among young factory girls for short hair.

He had wondered, as he'd patrolled the streets checking everyone was complying with the blackout regulation, if perhaps his mind had exaggerated Prudence Carmichael's beauty, but with her face slightly averted and her hair falling over her shoulders as she studied the text, David realised the opposite was true.

But it wasn't just her outwards appearance that stopped him in his tracks.

He prided himself on being an intellectual rather than a mystical follower of the Lord, so had always been more than a little sceptical of his fellow clergy who claimed to have had a divine experience. But as he stared down at Prue, the peculiar feeling he'd experienced that afternoon when she stood framed in sunlight was washing over him again.

Prue smiled. 'Hello.'

'All by yourself?' he asked, stupidly, as she was clearly the only person in the room.

'Yes, my parents were exhausted and went up about twenty minutes ago,' she replied.

'I'm not surprised; you've all had a long day,' he said. 'How's the unpacking going?'

She rolled her eyes. 'Don't ask. Thankfully we've managed to find the essentials but there are tea chests that have yet to be opened in every room.'

'I only brought a couple of suitcases and a tea chest of theological books with me when I arrived in the parish,' he said. 'I can't imagine what an upheaval it must be to bring an entire house.'

'Don't worry, I'm sure we'll be straight in a day or two,' she said brightly. 'I was just about to make myself a cocoa, would you like one?'

'Yes please,' David replied. 'But only if it's not too much trouble. I wouldn't want to impose on your good nature, Miss Carmichael.'

'It's no trouble at all. And Prue, please. We're not living in a Georgette Heyer novel.'

David frowned. 'Georgette Heyer?'

'She writes stories – romances, really – set in the Regency period,' Prue explained. 'Like Jane Austen's *Pride and Prejudice* and *Persuasion*, where everyone called each other Mr this or Miss that.'

'Romance,' he chuckled. 'I'm afraid I tend to confine my reading to biblical texts or theology dissertations, but as it is the middle of the twentieth not the nineteenth century please call me David in the same spirit.'

His gaze tracked every movement of her shapely legs as Prue unwound herself from the chair and stood up.

Sliding her feet into her slippers, she headed towards the door. David followed a step or two behind, mesmerised by her unbound, auburn hair.

She switched on the light overhead and the forty-watt bulb sprang into life, bathing the tidy kitchen in a yellow haze.

David noted a new blue gingham tablecloth, a vase with a couple of freshly cut dahlias in the centre and a complete Crown Derby dinner set stacked on the dresser with a velvet cutlery box on the shelf beneath. In his absence the kitchen had apparently undergone a transformation from a stark refectory into a homely hearth – complete with the lingering smell of this evening's lamb stew hanging in the air.

Taking the kettle from the back of the hob, Prue carried it to the sink.

'And making you a cocoa is the least I can do after you've spent all evening keeping the streets safe,' she said, holding it under the tap to fill. 'Did you have a good night?'

'Quiet,' he replied, leaning back on the kitchen table and crossing his ankles. 'My patrol patch is …' He rattled off a list of streets and shop names for a moment then stopped mid-sentence. 'Forgive me. You only arrived a few hours ago and here I am bombarding you with the highways and byways of Stepney.'

'Don't worry,' she said over her shoulder as she crossed to the long, lemon-painted Welsh dresser at the far end to collect their mugs. 'I intend to go out tomorrow to get my bearings. I will need to find Stepney Town Hall so I can register us, otherwise Mrs Lavender won't have any ration coupons to feed us.'

'The Town Hall is pretty straightforward from here,' he replied. 'I take it you're going to walk there.'

'I'll have to because when my bicycle was unloaded

today, the front wheel had a puncture. Mrs Lavender said she'd get her son to fix it.'

'Well, no matter,' said David. 'A brisk walk should have you at the Town Hall in twenty minutes. I'll draw you a simple map – I know ladies aren't very good with directions.'

She opened her mouth to say something – her thanks probably for his consideration, he guessed, as he studied her shapely legs again – but before she could the kettle whistle cut between them.

'It's very decent of you to volunteer as an air raid warden,' she said, breaking through his thoughts.

David formed his features into a self-effacing expression. 'I felt I should set an example, you know. Lead from the front, and all that.'

To be honest, he wouldn't have dreamed of volunteering had the bishop not waxed lyrical about the initiative. As a favourable bishop's recommendation was the difference between being offered a comfortable living in the Home Counties or a rundown parish in a smoke-clogged, Godforsaken industrial town up north, David had duly signed up.

'Did you hear the Secretary of State for War's special announcement tonight?' she asked, as she heaped three spoonsful of cocoa into each mug.

'About this volunteer civilian force of locals taking up arms?'

Prue nodded.

'I was out on patrol, but Wilf, the senior warden, filled us all in when we got back. But we shouldn't worry,' he went on airily as she stirred their cocoa. 'The British Army is the best in the world and once we give Hitler and his Nazi thugs a bloody nose they'll be clamouring for peace.'

Actually, to his mind, Chamberlain had had the right idea when he came to an agreement with Hitler over Czechoslovakia. If he'd done the same last September instead of letting the hotheads in the Cabinet push him to give an ultimatum, the authorities wouldn't have needed to set up all this ARP nonsense in the first place. After all, half the population of Great Britain probably wouldn't be able to find Poland on a map.

Of course, now Churchill had muscled his way into number ten and Anthony Eden was recruiting the butcher, the baker and the candlestick maker into this Local Defence Volunteer force, the whole population would be rolling up their metaphoric sleeves for a fight, and such views would not be well received any more.

'I hope you're right,' said Prue, cutting across his thoughts once more, 'because my brother Rob's over there at the moment with the King's Own Artillery Company.'

'Mine too,' said David. 'Although with the infantry.'

'Are there just the two of you?'

'Good heavens, no. I'm the youngest of four boys,' he replied, as she handed him his cocoa. 'Charles has the baronetcy and estate to keep him occupied, James is Conservative Member of Parliament for Milton St Oswald and Henry is a colonel in the Welsh Light Infantry; so with the traditional openings for sons of the gentry covered, it seemed natural that I should enter the Church. I tried my hand at banking but after a misunderstanding over Swiss and French Francs, I felt God was calling me to enter the ministry. Do you mind if I join you in the lounge?'

'Actually, David,' she yawned, 'I've been up since six this morning so I think I might take my drink up and get ready for bed.'

'Of course. I quite understand,' he replied. 'You've had a very tiring day. Goodnight.'

'Yes, goodnight.' Cradling her cocoa, Prue gave him a shy little smile. 'See you at breakfast.'

She left the room.

David stared after her for a moment then made his way to the back parlour.

She'd obviously popped back in before heading up as the book she'd been reading had gone. *Worship through Music* was just starting on the wireless, so sitting in the chair opposite the one Prue had occupied, David took a sip of his nightcap.

There were a couple of hymns and the homily was about the evils of drink, a subject which in the usual way of things would have held David's interest but not tonight. Not with the image of Prudence Carmichael's rich auburn hair bouncing on her shoulders and her sparkling hazel eyes dancing in his mind.

Although it was difficult sometimes to interpret God's plan, David couldn't help but think that Prue Carmichael might just be the Almighty rewarding him for his faithfulness at resisting the temptations of the flesh. After all, why else would the maker of heaven and earth have placed such a beautiful, virtuous and Godly woman into his life?

Chapter four

'MORNING, MISS,' said the ironmonger, standing on a stepladder above Prue as she passed his shop.

'Good morning,' Prue replied.

'Lovely one, too.' He hooked a watering can on to a nail above his overcrowded window. 'Hard to believe there's a war on, ain't it?'

Placing her hand on her hat to keep it from slipping off, Prue looked up into the forget-me-not-blue sky above her. 'It certainly is.'

And it was.

Despite the fact that she and her parents had listened to the BBC's plummy announcer informing them that the British Expeditionary Force were standing ready to repel the Germans, with the spring sunshine warming her face, it certainly was very difficult to believe the country was fighting for its very life.

Prue waited for a khaki-coloured Territorial Army truck and a coal merchant's van to pass, then crossed the road and walked alongside St Winifred's boundaries. She reached the church's stone gateposts just as the clock on the church tower showed half past eight.

However, instead of going into the church, where her

father and David were undertaking morning prayers for the parish faithful, Prue crossed at the junction, passed the Fish and Ring public house on the corner and carried on down Spring Garden Place and into Charles Street.

According to David, Stepney Town Hall was no more than a twenty-minute walk away, so she'd set off from the rectory just after eight-fifteen, hoping to be the first in the registration queue when it opened at nine.

Passing mothers pushing prams and a group of soldiers grappling to inflate a silvery-grey barrage balloon on a patch of empty land, Prue continued on until she spotted Arbour Square police station.

Stopping by the sub-post office on the corner of Wellesley Street, Prue pulled out the scrap of paper Father David had written the instruction on, studied it for a moment, then shoved it back in her pocket and crossed the road.

Having been given the eye by a couple of young constables coming out of the front of the police station as she passed, Prue crossed West Arbour Street and then turned left, expecting it to be the main thoroughfare leading to Commercial Road. Instead, she found herself looking down a cobbled street. Like nearly every other street hereabouts, this one was lined on both sides with three-up-and-three-down terraced houses, their front doors opening straight on to the narrow pavement.

The street was deserted, but Prue thought she must be walking towards her destination so perhaps when she got to the end of the street, she would find a cut-through.

Careful not to step on the newly scrubbed half-circles outside the houses, which seemed to be an early-morning feature peculiar to the area, Prue continued on, but halfway down she realised that she was going in the wrong direction. There was nothing for it; she'd have to walk back to the police station and ask directions.

Pressing her lips together, Prue turned and with her high heels striking the flagstones she marched back down the road.

Crossing diagonally as she reached the end, she was just about to step on to the pavement when a flash of something snagged the corner of her eye.

Instinctively, Prue jumped forward, catching her toe on the kerb as a truck swung around the corner. Stumbling, she dropped her handbag and her shoulder connected with a rough, moss-covered garden wall.

There was a squeal of brakes.

'Are you all right?' a deep voice asked.

Placing her hand on the wall to steady herself, Prue straightened up and raised her eyes.

Standing in front of her was a man a few years older than her and a good head taller. He was studying her anxiously, the front wheel of his abandoned bicycle swirling on the pavement.

He was dressed in a pair of worn navy overalls with a cap sitting at a rakish angle on his jet-black hair, which wasn't tamed into conformity by Brylcreem. He had a square face, a blunt chin, and Prue couldn't help noticing that although he must have shaved only an hour before, the bristles beneath his skin gave his cheeks a dark hue.

'Are you, miss?' he asked again, just as Prue realised that she was staring into his dark brown eyes.

'I think so,' she replied, not totally sure she was.

He glanced down the road and Prue's eyes darted along the firm angle of his jaw.

'It looked like a warden's van on its way back to the Town Hall,' he said, turning back.

'Perhaps I should have asked them for a lift, as that's where I'm heading,' said Prue, looking away as she retrieved her handbag from the pavement. 'At least, I'm supposed to be, but I seem to have taken a wrong turn somewhere. I was told the second turning on the left after the police station and then just straight down from their but …'

He smiled and something rather pleasant fizzed through Prue.

'Well, whoever gave you directions forgot Arbour Terrace; the next road is Jamaica Street where you should have turned. But all you have to do when you get to the main road at the end is keep going until you see Christ Church. Cross over and walk through Watney Market, under the railway, then you look right, you'll see the Town Hall.' Scooping down, he caught her lipstick rolling about on the pavement and offered it to her.

'Thank you.'

She popped it back into her handbag and hooked the bag on her arm.

'Are you sure you're all right?' he asked, his gaze flickering over her again.

'A bit shaken, perhaps,' she admitted, 'but no bones broken and I'm sure a walk in the sunshine will soon put me right.'

'Or you could hop on my crossbar, and I'll give you a lift,' he said in a deep voice, capturing her gaze with his again.

Blooming cheek and fresh, too, thought Prue, but even so ….

Suppressing the smile that tugged at the corner of her lips, she gave him a cool look.

'Thank you for the offer,' she said, with more than a trace of her mother's clipped tones. 'But I think I'll stick with Shanks's pony.'

Turning on her heels Prue marched off, praying all the while that she could get around the corner before the giggle bubbling up inside burst out.

'There you are, Miss Carmichael,' said the young woman in a grey suit, behind the desk. She handed Prue three of the Government's buff-coloured ration books. 'All done and legal.'

It was an hour since her close call with the ARP lorry and she was in a large room on the second floor of Stepney Town Hall. Judging by the high ceiling and the wood panelling, it had once been a council committee room but was now the Ministry of Food Stepney sub-office. As such, a long line of filing cabinets now half obscured a series of portraits on one wall and a row of chairs against the other wall were dotted with people waiting to be called forwards. Between the customers and their files were half a dozen desks with a clerk behind each one and it was at one of these that Prue was sitting. Around her the low hum of voices mingled with the snap of typewriter keys.

Prue had arrived just after nine and thankfully there were only a couple of people in front of her at the citizen registration department on the ground floor, so having renewed her parents' and her own dull-green identity cards without too much trouble she had made her way up the sweeping marble staircase to the second floor where all the Ministry sub-offices were located.

'And don't forget to register with your chosen shops as soon as you can, miss,' continued the clerk. 'But have a bit of a shufti first.'

Prue looked.

'Look around,' explained the clerk. 'Cos let's just say some of the shops around here have trouble with their scales.' She gave an exaggerated wink.

'Thank you,' Prue replied. 'But our housekeeper already has it in hand.'

The young woman's pencilled eyebrows rose.

'My father's the new rector at St Winifred's,' Prue explained.

The young woman's face lit up. 'Oh, you mean Dolly Lavender.'

'You know her?'

'Course, her and my mum are old friends,' the girl explained. 'Lived in the same street, they did, when they were girls.'

Prue rose from her seat. 'Well, thank you again.'

'My pleasure,' said the clerk. 'And tell Dolly: Fran says 'ello.'

'I will.'

Prue opened her handbag and spotted her lipstick. The image of a pair of dark eyes formed in her mind.

It was almost an hour since her encounter with the strikingly handsome man on the bicycle, whose image, for some reason, wouldn't leave her head. Especially that quirky smile he'd given her.

Tucking the ration books firmly alongside her purse and snapping the bag shut, Prue stepped away from the chair as someone in the waiting area made their way forward to take her place.

Back on the ground floor, the entrance to the Town Hall was bustling with people. The walls, which probably once had portraits of the great and the good of the borough hung on them, were now adorned with posters exhorting mothers to evacuate their children to the country and urging people to open their doors to passers-by during a raid.

The trophy cabinet which took pride of place in the lobby was empty, as were the half a dozen plinths that stood in alcoves. Probably to save whatever had been on them from being toppled over, Prue thought, because the area was filled from wall to wall with people dressed in various uniforms. Predominantly they were from the navy of air raid wardens and fire service, but she spotted the odd khaki of squaddies attached to the Civil Defence staff, a few of whom lined up at the WVS's tea bar alongside the reception desk.

As she reached the bottom of the stairs she came face to face with a large black-and-white head-and-shoulders portrait of a woman with the words 'ARP looks to you' across the top.

Stopping on the bottom step, Prue studied it for a moment or two then, glancing around, spotted a door at the far end with the words 'War Work Bureau' painted on the frosty glass.

Walking across the floor with its mosaic of St George slaying a fire-breathing dragon, she passed a couple of fresh-faced lads, with the police messenger armbands, leaning against the curved mahogany reception desk and having a smoke.

Pushing open the door, Prue walked in.

Like the Ministry of Food office, the room she was now standing in had the distinctive oak panelling and high ceilings that marked it out as one of the council chambers.

Beneath this was a row of filing cabinets and in front of them was a long table behind which sat a couple of women talking to people perched on chairs on the other side.

Even though it was the middle of the morning, the war work recruitment office still seemed to be doing a brisk trade because although there were three rows of seats, all but a handful of them were occupied.

Prue was about to take one of the spare seats when she caught sight of a large noticeboard with cards pinned on it in rows and the word 'Vacancies' across the top.

Strolling over and ignoring the first two rows of cards, which were advertising for gas fitters, plumbers and other tradesmen, Prue started at the top of the third row.

However, having skimmed over jobs for factory hands, bookkeepers and warehousemen, one card halfway down caught her eye.

Pulling it from the board, Prue pressed the drawing pin back in the cork then, turning, she made her way across to one of the empty chairs. Resigning herself to a bit of a wait, Prue sat down, idly wondering whether she'd have time to pop into the library when she was finished.

Prue let her gaze wander around the room. A young chap with straw-coloured hair in front of her stood up to take a recently vacated place at one of the desks and Prue's eyes alighted on the bicycle clips around his ankles.

Before she could stop it, an image of the man she'd encountered earlier, with his dark eyes and wild hair, popped into her mind.

Pushing it aside, Prue smiled. Perhaps if she did manage to get into the library, she should steer clear of the romance section.

'You've done *what?*' said Marjorie Carmichael, her fork loaded with pease pudding hovering halfway between the plate and her lips.

'I've got a job,' replied Prue, holding her mother's horrified gaze.

It was just after one o'clock and she was seated in the rectory's dining room overlooking the vegetable garden at the side of the house, with her parents at either end of the table and Father David directly opposite her.

Like much of the house, the room where the family took their meals had off-white paintwork and tired flowery wallpaper, punctuated with slightly darker toned squares, showing where paintings had once hung.

Although spacious enough, it had taken the removal men quite a bit of manoeuvring under her mother's watchful eye to get the large Hepplewhite sideboard, dresser and eighteen-seater table into the room. You might not expect to find such lavish fixtures in a clergyman's dining room, but these items, along with the majority of their other furnishings and the generous annual annuity that supplemented Hugh Carmichael's modest stipend, were courtesy of her mother's wealthy maiden aunt, who lived on a vast estate in Lincolnshire.

Prue had walked back into the rectory just as Mrs Lavender was wheeling the lunch across the entrance hall towards the dining room. After divesting herself of her jacket and hat and nipping to the bathroom, Prue slid into her chair just as her father was about to say grace, earning herself a stern look from her mother.

That was some thirty minutes ago and since then, over their lunch of boiled ham and pease pudding, her parents had given each other a summary of their morning, which in his case was the number of the faithful at morning prayers and for her mother was a blow-by-blow account of how, having taken up the reins of the Mothers' Union, she intended it to function.

David had chipped in here and there, mainly to add in a parishioner's name or to express somewhat excessive praise for her mother's proposed changes. Finally, as they scraped the last morsels off their plates, her father had asked Prue about her morning and having reassured them that they were now legally registered with the authorities and Mrs Lavender was in possession of their ration books, Prue had told them her big news.

'I did tell you I intended to,' Prue added.

'Yes, but I didn't expect you to do so quite so quickly,' her mother replied.

'What is it exactly, this job you've been offered?' asked her father, raising his glass of lemonade to his lips.

Prue took a deep breath. 'I'm going to work for the London and North Eastern Railway.'

Her mother's jaw dropped. 'You're going to work on the railways!'

'Yes,' Prue replied.

'Doing what?'

'I'm not sure, exactly, but it's vital war work because it releases men for the army,' said Prue. 'They are desperate.'

'Well, so am I,' snapped her mother. 'In case it's escaped your notice, Prudence, there are still at least a dozen boxes to unpack and a rectory to order, not to mention getting to know members of the congregation. I need you here not gadding about the place.'

'If by "gadding about" you mean helping move troops and goods essential to the war effort from the factories,' said Prue, 'then I'm sorry. But as I did a full-time job in St Peter's hospital, I don't understand your objection to me doing the same here.'

'But the railways?' said her mother mournfully. 'I mean, all that smoke and grime; you'll be filthy by the time you get home.'

'Then I'll have a bath,' Prue replied.

'And besides, what sort of people will you be working with?' her mother went on.

'Railway people, I expect,' Prue replied, holding her mother's gaze.

Marjorie gave her a cool look. 'Don't be tiresome, Prudence, you know what I mean.'

'I don't know what I'll be doing or who I'll be working with, but I do know it is crucial work, otherwise why would the Government classify railway employees as a reserved occupation?' Prue clenched her fist. 'For goodness' sake! Anyone would think I'd joined the woman's parachute regiment.'

'A woman's parachute regiment,' muttered her father, shaking his head dolefully. 'What is the world coming to?'

'I don't think the RAF are actually recruiting women to jump out of planes, Father Hugh,' said David.

'I'm doing my bit,' continued Prue, 'the same as thousands of other women; it just happens to be in

Stratford's shunting yards,' said Prue. 'And as you didn't need my help running the parish at St Stephen's, I can't see why you do at St Winifred's.'

'Because in Biddenham I had women like Leticia Dawkins, the doctor's wife, Daphne Ford-Wilson, head of the local hunt, and Lady Whitbread, who understood the way things should be done in a church. But here ...' She sighed.

'I'm sorry, Mother, but I hardly think putting the church flower rota together takes precedence over making sure food get to the shops and the army has equipment.' Prue rose from her seat. 'And now, as we're all finished, I'll clear some of these dishes and make a start on the washing-up.'

Chapter five

As THE CLOCK on St Winifred's square tower ticked towards seven o'clock on a balmy late-spring evening, Jack strolled on along the gravel pathway between the ancient tombs and the medieval charnel house where the parish once stored their dead.

It was empty now of bleached bones and had been for several centuries, but as a boy Jack imagined the ghosts rising up to drag him into its dank interior. The dead inside would have had a job getting out of the windowless crypt now, as it had sunk deep into the soft earth. A couple of centuries before, steps had been cut down to the door.

Smiling at the memory of his over-imaginative younger self, Jack continued on towards the solidly constructed building along the northern boundary of the churchyard.

It was Friday, the end of the working week, and just three days since he and thousands of other men up and down the country had pitched up at their local nick to volunteer for this new Local Defence Volunteer force.

Pushing open the double doors with criss-crossing gummed paper stuck on the glass in the upper half, Jack strolled into the hall's vestibule. Although the parish noticeboard still had the times of services and various social clubs pinned on it, it also bore a poster reminding people to be like Dad and keep mum and another instructing them on what they should do in an air raid.

In addition, like almost every other church and memorial hall, Scout hut and social club in the area, St Winifred's parish rooms had been given over to the war effort. Even the abandoned shed at Redcoat, the parish school, was being used as a storeroom for household salvage.

The doorway to his left, which led into the smaller hall, was open. Inside, instead of the Stepney Players rehearsing for their next am-dram production, there were three or four St John Ambulance officers, in their black uniforms with white trim, teaching first aid to a dozen or so volunteers. A note saying 'Stepney area ARP command meeting in progress' was pinned on the committee-room door at the far end.

Skirting past a couple of prams with sleeping infants in them parked against the wall, Jack pushed open the door to the main hall and ambled in.

There were a dozen or so men already there, ranging from gangly youths sprouting their first moustaches to grey-haired old hands who predated the invention of the motor car.

On the stage in front of the colour-faded dusty curtains stood a blackboard and easel covered with a baize cloth. On the hall floor in front of the stage was a trestle table with a clipboard and what looked like a Bible on it and a fresh-faced army private keeping guard.

Spotting a friend he'd known since they were both snotty-nosed kids running barefoot around the streets, Jack wandered over.

'All right, Tommy,' he said.

A few months younger and a couple of inches shorter than Jack's six foot, Tommy Lavender had fair hair, grey eyes and a sharp nose that could sniff out an opportunity. In theory he worked as one of the casual porters at Spitalfields Market, but in truth his profession could be described as a bit of this and a bit of that. Be it a wireless, a pram, a new mattress or a tea set fit to set before royalty, if you wanted it Tommy Lavender could find it for you. He lived in Maroon Street with his mother, and had been in the same class as Jack in Redcoat School – when he deigned to turn up for lessons, that was.

'Not so bad. Yerself?'

'I'm all right,' Jack replied. 'It's all the other buggers.'

Tommy snorted a laugh. 'I thought I'd see you here.'

'Why? Cos I'm patriotic?'

'Na, cos you're not one to walk away from a fight,' Tommy replied.

Jack laughed. 'I'm surprised you haven't been called up yet.'

'Medically exempt, me.' Tommy punched his chest with his fist and coughed. 'Asthma.'

Jack raised an eyebrow. 'I didn't know you had asthma.'

Tommy grinned. 'Neiver did I.' He forced another cough. 'When did you sign up for this caper, then?'

'Tuesday. Bout an hour after Eden made the announcement on the wireless,' Jack replied. 'What about you?'

'The following morning on my way to work,' said Tommy. 'Tell you the truth, I was a bit surprised to get my letter telling me to report here for duty in the afternoon post yesterday. I mean, usually it takes the blooming pen-pushers at the Town Hall at least a couple of weeks to send you anything.'

'True,' said Jack. 'But I suppose now we're expecting parachutists to drop from the skies at any second, even the powers that be in the council can't afford to wait until everything had been signed in triplicate before pulling their finger out. How you doing, anyhow?'

As other men filtered into the hall, Jack and Tommy exchanged news about their love lives, which in Jack's case was non-existent, whereas Tommy was very friendly with a widow who lived near the Shadwell Basin.

They'd just moved on to the latest news from across the Channel when the hall doors burst open and a long-limbed army major of about Jack's age, with slicked-back hair and a swagger stick tucked under his arm, marched in. On his right came a regimental sergeant major, with a broken nose, a shaved head and pair of black eyes beneath a shaggy brow.

On his left, and marching half a beat off from the other two, was a rotund chap in a pinstriped suit, with wiry mutton-chop whiskers either side of his bulbous nose and a pugnacious expression on his fleshy face. He too had a swagger stick and a fabric armband with the word

'Captain' stencilled above the letter's 'LDV'. Close behind him marched Mr Smedley, headmaster of Raine's School, who peered out at the world like some insect through his thick spectacle lenses and sported a set of sergeant's stripes on his tweed jacket. Next to him marched Stanley Goodchild, the district commissioner for Cubs and Scouts. He'd dressed for the occasion in his Scout master's uniform and had positioned his corporal's bar just below his King's Scout badge. However, his efforts to emphasise his martial credentials were somewhat undermined by the sight of his knobby white knees beneath his khaki shorts.

The party marched to the end of the hall and while the major and the rotund chap in the expensive suit marched up on to the stage, the hard-bitten sergeant major took up position on the other side of the table from the squaddie.

Coming to a halt next to the blackboard, the major cast his eyes over the men milling around in the church hall. The two dozen or so volunteers were instructed to form themselves into three lines, Jack and Tommy reverting back to their schooldays and shuffling into their time-honoured place in the back row.

As the muttering of male voices stopped, the slender major cleared his throat.

'Evening, men,' he said, his plummy upper-class tones ringing around the metal roof beams. 'My name is Major Dunmore and I am commander of East London Home Defences. This doughty warrior standing before me is Regimental Sergeant Major Murray and the chap standing shoulder to shoulder beside me is Mr, now Captain, Crowther, who has faced the German before at the Somme and Ypres ...'

'Faced 'em from HQ at Arras, according to my old dad,' whispered Tommy, out of the side of his mouth.

'... and who is newly appointed to head up the Stepney, Wapping and Limehouse Local Defence Volunteers.' The senior officer grinned. 'In short, you ugly lot.'

A polite laugh went around the room.

He looked at the man beside him, who stepped forward.

'Evening, men,' he said, as his deep-set eyes ran over them. 'Now let me just say that some of you will no doubt know me from my time as stipendiary magistrate at Thames Magistrates' Court ...'

Jack certainly did know Basil Algernon Crowther VC DSM, who like many of his contemporaries on the bench considered all and any member of the working classes hauled up before him to be guilty.

'How many times you been up in front of him, Jack?' asked Tommy, under his breath.

'Half a dozen,' Jack replied in the same low tone. 'In my misspent youth.'

'Me too.' Tommy grinned. ''Appy days.'

'... if that is the case I want you all to know that none of your past deeds will influence my actions or judgement. From today, you and I are just proud Englishmen defending the land we love against Hitler and his barbaric hordes.'

'Quite so, Captain,' said his superior officer. 'We're all just chaps fighting for our homes and families.'

'Pip, pip, old bean,' whispered Tommy.

Jack grinned by way of reply.

The officer cleared his throat again. 'However, it is incumbent upon me before we commence this evening's proceedings to read you a message from our Prime Minister, Mr Churchill. I ...'

Taking a sheet of paper from his right breast pocket, Major Dunmore read a short speech basically repeating what he'd already said thanking them for stepping forward to join the efforts to defend their country in its time of need.

'Although you are classified as civilians, you will of course be subject to army discipline,' continued the commanding officer. 'Therefore, you will all have to take the oath of allegiance.'

'Will we cop the King's shilling, too?' shouted Tommy.

A wry smile lifted the major's pencil moustache. 'Very droll, don't you think, Captain?'

Crowther's narrow lips pulled into a tight smile. 'Indeed. Cockney humour, sir. Cockney humour.'

The major's good-natured expression remained a second or two longer, then he frowned. 'However, before we ask you to sign up officially and take the oath I'm duty-bound to tell you that on hearing that our Government is recruiting civilians, the German command, contrary to all the conventions of war, have issue a decree that any citizen found bearing arms or resisting the Third Reich will be treated as a terrorist to be executed without trial.'

Murmurs of 'bloody animals' and 'not if we top them first' ran around the hall.

'Therefore,' continued the ranking officer in the room, 'if any man here feels that he would like to withdraw his application to join the Local Defence Volunteers then he is at liberty to leave without dishonour.'

The straightening of shoulders and the tightening of jaws give the major his answer.

'Good show. Captain, if you please.'

The retired magistrate stepped forward and uncovered the blackboard on which was pinned in large letters the oath of allegiance.

The private held aloft the Bible and the entire room raised their right hands then read in unison from the board in front of them. When they'd finished, the major stepped forward again.

'Now, chaps, you will be expected to parade each night and will be assigned a set area to patrol. You will receive uniforms and, more importantly, weapons in the next few days, intensive training by regular army instructors on how to use them plus sabotage techniques to slow the enemy's progress,' Major Dunmore explained. 'Arm yourself with what you can, utilising from your homes. If you have a gun your father brought back from the last war, shotguns you might use for hunting rabbits on waste ground or a firearm you've acquired in any other way, please bring that along and no questions will be asked.

Failing that, knives fastened to broom handles to use as you would a bayonet, long nails hammered through the tops of chair or table legs to use as you would a mace, or petrol in a bottle with rag wicks that can be lit and thrown at vehicles or troops.' The senior officer in the room looked grave again. 'I'll be straight with you, chaps …' Turning over the sheet of paper on the blackboard with the oath written on it, he revealed a map of southern England, the Channel and the northern coasts of France and Belgium. 'Although our valiant boys are fighting like lions, the truth of the matter is the Germans are gaining ground each day. Unless we and the French can hold them in the Low Countries, we estimate they will reach here,' he smacked the tip of his swagger stick on to the stretch of continental coastline opposite Dover, 'in a matter of days.'

The image of his daughter Rachel, with her bouncing pigtails and dark eyes, flashed through Jack's mind as a murmur went around the hall.

'Although paratroopers may well drop from the sky any day now, they will only be the advance party looking to capture key targets like fuel depots, telephone exchanges and the like, ahead of a much larger invasion force. We have to assume that if they reach the French or Belgian coast they will cross the English Channel soon after. Once they land …'

As the men in the hall stood loosely at ease, the major explained to the newly recruited Stepney, Wapping and Limehouse Local Defence Volunteers the part they would be expected to play in defending their homes and families.

Put simply, they were cannon fodder.

Although no one would say it, the job of the beardless youths, arthritic old men and reserved occupation fellas like Jack was to sacrifice themselves to the enemy's advance long enough to allow the regular army to form a battle-line somewhere.

The image of Rachel floated back into his head. Although he'd just signed up as target practice for the invading Germans, he was willing to pay the price to protect her.

'Well, that's about it, chaps,' Major Dunmore concluded. 'Once again, thank you for stepping forward in your country's time of need. Now I'll leave you in the company of your platoon commander, Captain Crowther.'

The major saluted and the retired magistrate returned it, then the three regular soldiers marched out, their steel-tipped boots cracking on the wooden floor.

As the door swung closed behind them, the newly appointed grey-haired commanding officer of the Stepney, Wapping and Limehouse Local Defence Volunteers turned to face his men.

His deep-set eyes ran over them for a moment then he cleared his throat. 'Right, men, let's get to work.'

Three-quarters of an hour later, having been marched up and down the hall half a dozen time by corporal Goodchild, Crowther brought them to a halt. From his briefcase he produced a large map of the area with sections marked off.

The men were told to pair up and they were then given a block of streets or an installation, such as the telephone exchange or coal depot, to patrol. Jack and Tommy were just waiting for their allotted area to patrol when the hall doors swung open and Father David, black cassock swirling around his legs, strode in.

Jack had run into Father David a couple of times, encounters that had left him feeling glad he'd cut ties with St Winifred's and its clergy a while back.

The curate's pale blue eyes skimmed over the assembled men, acknowledging a few with the barest curl of his lip, until he spotted Crowther and his face lit up.

'Captain Crowther,' he cried, bouncing across the room towards him.

The retired magistrate looked around.

'I'm David Harmsworth, the curate here at St Winifred's. My uncle is Sir James Harmsworth,' the priest explained. 'He served with you in South Africa.'

Crowther's heavy features lifted in recognition. 'You're old Jumjum's nephew?'

David nodded.

'How is the old blighter?'

'Do you think Father David's family followed the nobs' tradition of sending the idiot of the family into the Church,' asked Tommy, under his breath, as they listened to Father David's convoluted explanation as to which one of old Jumjum's nephews he was.

'The evidence certainly points to that, doesn't it?' Jack replied. 'Mind you, I have to say I'm a bit taken aback to see him so merry. I didn't think he could smile let alone laugh.'

'Well, perhaps Father David's so full of the joys of spring because of a certain young lady,' said Tommy.

Jack looked incredulous. 'He's got a lady-love?'

'Not as such, but Ma asked me to pop into the rectory the day before yesterday to fix the new rector's daughter's bike and the way he was sniffing around her I'd say she's definitely got 'is sap rising.' Tommy winked.

'Poor woman,' said Jack.

'Mind you, I can't say I blame him cos she's quite a looker, mate.' Tommy ran his hands in two undulating lines in front of him.

The image of the young woman who he'd bumped into earlier in the week flashed through Jack's mind. The new rector's daughter might be a looker but she probably wasn't a patch on that absolute stunner, whoever she might be.

At the time he'd thought he'd seen amusement in her large hazel eyes, but it was a fanciful notion as her hat alone probably cost more than everything he had on his back. And that dress and jacket certainly hadn't come off a stall in the market. Probably some modish establishment with uniformed shop assistants.

Hop on my crossbar! Fancy saying such a stupid thing. Whatever would she think of him? A sardonic smile spread across Jack's face. You brainless idiot! Still, what's the point in worrying? After all, it's not as if you're ever going to see her again, is it?

Chapter six

'AND I HAVEN'T SLEPT since I heard the news, Miss Carmichael,' said the middle-aged woman peering at Prue through the thick lens of her spectacles. 'I don't think I shall have a wink until I hear our Barry's safe back in England.'

It was Sunday, five days since they'd arrived at St Winifred's Rectory, five days of scrubbing cupboards, unpacking boxes, hanging curtains, filling bookshelves and trying to find a place for everything and putting it there.

'I'm so sorry, Mrs ...'

'Jolly,' she replied. 'Ruby. From Matlock Street, up the road.'

It was somewhere close to eleven and the congregation of St Winifred's were milling around in the church hall, holding cups of tea.

Although Stepney's medieval church had escaped the worst of the Victorian fashion for modernisation, they had built a large parish room adjacent to it, which was where Prue was now standing.

Through the serving hatch she could see the good ladies, in their best hats, serving second cups and gathering in the dirty crockery.

Some of the older folk had rested their weary bones on the chairs dotted around the end of the hall for the purpose, but the rest were standing and huddled in small groups.

It had been thirty minutes since the end of the service and as the wives of the churchwardens, verger and choirmaster were clucking around her mother, Prue had been left to her own devices.

So far she'd told at least half a dozen people that yes, Stepney was a bit different from Bedfordshire, and no, she hadn't left a sweetheart behind. She'd also informed them that her older brother was a captain in the army and that her sister, Felicity, worked on a newspaper in Bloomsbury.

'They'd only been married at Easter and … I mean, just last week the papers were saying that our boys were 'olding firm against the Germans and now we 'ear the bloody Hun have marched into Holland.' Taking a handkerchief from the sleeve of her knitted cardigan, Mrs Jolly blew her nose.

'I understand,' said Prue. 'My brother Robert is in France and we're all worried, too.'

'And it's not just me who's worried sick; poor Ella's fair out of her mind, too.' Mrs Jolly indicated a pretty young woman with a newborn baby in her arms chatting to a couple of women. 'Adores our Barry she does. We all do. Always the first up for a lark or a sing-song he was. Jolly by name and jolly by nature, that's our Barry. Ask anyone. They'll tell you.'

'I'm so sorry,' said Prue.

'Can I take the liberty, Miss Carmichael, of asking you to say a little prayer for 'im?'

'Of course,' Prue replied. 'And I really hope you hear from your son in the next couple of days.'

Mrs Jolly gave her an appreciative look, then wandered over to join her daughter-in-law.

As no one else had homed in on her, Prue took a sip of her lukewarm tea.

'I hope you're not feeling too overwhelmed, Miss Carmichael,' said a soft voice just behind her.

Prue turned.

Standing at her right shoulder was a tiny woman with a face etched in fine lines and a pair of soft grey eyes. However, unlike the rest of the women in the room, who were dressed in their Sunday best, the woman smiling up at Prue wore a light grey nun's habit with a pair of stout brown lace-ups. Her veil, however, only reached to her shoulders and the white band of her cowl sat far enough back to allow wisps of her light grey hair to escape.

'Yes, I am a bit,' she replied. 'So many names.'

'I know,' said the nun. 'Parishioners only have to learn your name while you have dozens to remember. It's not fair, is it?'

Prue laughed. 'No, it's not.'

'And now I'll give you another: I'm Sister Martha, St Winifred's lay deacon.' She smiled. 'In the cloth but not in orders, so to speak.'

'Nice to meet you,' Prue replied, offering her a gloved hand. 'I'm Prudence, by the way, but everyone calls me Prue.'

'By name by nature?' said Sister Martha, taking her hand in a surprisingly firm grip.

Prue laughed. 'My parents wished.'

'I'm pleased to hear it. Fortune favours the brave.' The nun winked. 'And don't worry, my dear. It took me months to get to know everyone's name and who everyone was. It must be a bit of an upheaval moving into a new parish, never mind doing it when the country's at war.'

'It is,' Prue replied. 'Although my mother is of the opinion that it'll soon be over now our army's confronting the Germans.'

The old nun raised an almost invisible eyebrow. 'And what do you think, my dear?'

'Given how the Nazis have swallowed up half of Europe in the past three years, I think we'll be doing jolly well if we just hold our ground against them.' Prue gave an apologetic shrug. 'I hope I'm wrong, of course, but ...'

Sister Martha's lively grey-blue eyes scrutinised Prue's face but she didn't comment.

'Have you served in the parish long?' said Prue.

'Twenty years,' the nun replied.

'And glad we are to 'ave her.'

Prue turned to see a young woman about her own height with her dark brown hair pinned up into a mass of curls and wearing a navy maternity dress.

'Miss Carmichael, can I introduce you to Mrs Stapleton?' said Sister Martha.

'Nice to meet you,' said Prue, offering her hand.

'I thought I'd pop over and say hello,' the young women said as she took it. 'And I'm Rosie. Mrs Stapleton makes me sound like my mother-in-law.'

Prue laughed. 'Well, in that case, I'm Prue.'

The young woman smiled, and a memory stirred in Prue.

'And it's true wot I said about Sister Martha,' continued Rosie. 'She set up the church's Bring and Take exchange for mothers to swap the clothes their children had grown out of.'

'Like the WVS?' asked Prue.

'Except,' Rosie gave the nun an affectionate look, 'Sister Martha started ours ten years ago, which with two growing boys at school I'm very grateful for.'

'I'd love to help, if you think I may be of some use,' said Prue.

'There's always room for a willing volunteer,' Sister Martha replied. Her attention shifted to Rosie. 'How's that husband of yours?'

'Stuck in France with the rest of our poor soldiers,' Rosie replied. 'He says it's not too bad but as he's never been further away from home than Hastings on a day trip, I know 'e's missing home and the boys.'

Prue gave her a sympathetic smile. 'My brother's there, too, so I know how you feel worrying about a loved one.'

'Talking of brothers, how Jack?' asked Sister Martha.

Smiling, Rosie rolled her eyes, setting the memory in Prue's head fluttering again.

'You know Jack, Sister,' she said with a light laugh.

'I certainly do.' A soft expression lifted Sister Martha's wrinkled face. 'And so does God.' Something behind Prue caught the elderly nun's eye. 'Oh dear. I can see Gladys Thompson is getting herself into a tizz about something, so if you'd both excuse me I'd better go and pour oil on troubled waters. I live in one of the cottages bequeathed to the Church centuries ago in King John Passage,' she said, looking at Prue. 'Perhaps you'll pop in and have a cup of tea.'

'I'd love to,' said Prue.

'Good.' The nun gave her a girlish smile, wrinkling her nose. 'I think the best antidote to old age is having young people around. Lovely to meet you.' She placed a gnarled hand on Prue's arm. 'I have a feeling you and I are going to be very good friends.'

She gave Prue's arm a squeeze and left them.

'Two boys,' said Prue as the elderly nun made her way across to a red-faced young woman holding a handkerchief to her face. 'Are you hoping for a girl this time?'

'A girl would be nice, but as long as it's got ten fingers and ten toes I'll be 'appy,' Rosie replied. 'The Bring and Take runs on Wednesday afternoon, by the way, and with so many men away some of us at St Winnie's are thinking of starting an afternoon get-together for a bit of a chat.

We're hoping to get someone from the Ministry of Food down to do some demonstrations, if you're interested in coming along.'

'I'd love to, but I signed on for war work at the Town Hall and I start on Monday,' said Prue.

'Good for you,' said Rosie. 'Where have they sent you? My mate Maggie signed on and is a delivery driver at a government food store in Canning Town now.'

Prue laughed. 'I'm afraid I'm not doing anything so exciting. In fact, I'm not actually sure what I'll be doing, although I expect it'll be something clerical as I told them I had experience. Whatever it is I'll find out tomorrow at Stratford's shunting yards.'

Rosie's eyes stretched wide. 'How funny. My brother works there. He's an engineer in the locomotive sheds.'

'Perhaps I'll run into him,' said Prue.

'You might, but it's a big place,' said Rosie. 'And the engine sheds are miles away from the offices.'

'Oh, there you are, lurking in a corner,' said a familiar voice.

'Hello, Mother,' said Prue, half turning to face her. 'This is Mrs Stapleton.'

Rosie smiled. 'Nice to meet you, Mrs Carmichael, and I know the whole congregation are pleased to 'ave you and the rector 'ere.'

'Thank you.' Adjusting her handbag, Prue's mother gave Rosie her very best vicar's wife smile and waited.

A few heavy moments passed then Rosie took the hint.

'Well, I'd better see what those two boys of mine are up to. Lovely to meet you, Mrs Carmichael, and you.' She smiled and the unformed memory shimmered through Prue's mind again.

As Rosie waddled off, Prue turned. 'I wasn't lurking, Mother. I was standing in plain sight.'

'Don't be tiresome, Prudence,' her mother replied. 'You know how important it is to your father that we put on a good face in the parish.'

'Which is why I've talked to dozens of people since the service finished,' added Prue. 'Everyone seems very friendly.'

'Yes,' said her mother. 'But I'm surprised to see so many children.'

'I asked about that,' Prue replied. 'And it seems to be a matter of local pride around here that the time-honoured response to anything official from any authority is to ignore it.'

'How ridiculous!' her mother snapped. 'Still, perhaps it's just as well. Some of the evacuees who came to us in Biddenham were infested with nits and every one of them was a bed-wetter!'

'I'm not surprised,' said Prue. 'I'm sure if I was six years old, taken from everything I knew and packed off to live with strangers I'd have wet the bed, too. And to be honest,' she continued as they watched an infant with a dummy in his mouth toddle across the room, 'with everything happening so fast, if I had children, I'm not sure I would be able to send them away.'

'Well, you might have been able to test that theory if you'd said yes to dear Roland,' said her mother. 'And don't roll your eyes like that, it's terribly common.'

Pressing her lips together, Prue regarded her mother coolly.

They stood in silence for a long moment then Marjorie shifted her gaze across the room to where Prue's father and David, dressed in their black cassocks, were standing.

'You know, Prudence,' she said, 'Father David seems very nice. Kind and considerate. Godly, too.'

Prue's mouth pulled into a straight line. 'Don't.'

An innocent expression spread across her mother's face. 'Don't what?'

'You know very well.'

Marjorie frowned. 'Is it wrong of me to want to see you happily married? And you have to admit,' she glanced back across the room, 'he is rather handsome.'

Prue followed her mother's gaze and studied David as he chatted to a couple of parishioners.

'And incidentally,' continued her mother, 'just so you know, Father David's brother is a baronet, another the MP for somewhere and his other brother is in the army.'

With a mop of blond hair and chiselled features, David was indeed handsome but ... Prue smiled at her mother.

'I think I'll go back and see how the roast is doing.'

'Good idea,' replied Marjorie, giving her a conspiratorial shrug of her shoulders. 'What better way to impress

Father David than with your culinary skills. After all, isn't it said that the quickest way to a man's heart is through his stomach?'

Realising any further protest on her part would fall on deaf ears, Prue turned.

'Just hold your hand still, Rachel,' Jack whispered in his daughter's ear as he cuddled her between his crouched legs.

The sparrow that was the focus of their attention tipped its head a couple of times then hopped on to the little girl's outstretched fingers.

'Don't move or make a noise,' he said under his breath as he felt her tremble with excitement.

It was just after three-thirty on the Sunday afternoon two days after he'd paraded as part of the new LDV in the church hall. Jack was halfway through the four hours he'd been yearning for for the past six days, an afternoon spent with his seven-year-old daughter.

Relishing the feel of his daughter's curls brushing against his cheek, Jack cupped her small hand in his large one while the little brown bird pecked at the crumbs in her palm.

Like him, Rachel's hair was jet black, but although she had his eyes, her colouring and her features were from her mother's Jewish ancestors.

Of course, having signed up he'd been on duty all day yesterday so his day out with his daughter was twenty-four hours later than he'd anticipated which, as Rosie correctly predicted, didn't go down at all well.

However, it didn't matter because when Rachel skipped down the path into his waiting arms all that faded.

They were both dressed in their Sunday best, in his case the seven-year-old navy suit and tie he'd bought from one of the schmutter warehouses in Whitechapel for his wedding. In contrast to his sober outfit, his daughter was wearing a candy-striped lemon and white summer frock with matching yellow ribbons and a knitted cardigan with rabbit buttons.

Having harvested all the bread from Rachel's outstretched hand, the sparrow fluttered its tiny wings and flew off.

'Throw the last bit to the pigeons, Rachel, and we'll get some tea and cake,' said Jack as he handed her the paper bag.

'Can I have angel cake, Daddy?' she asked, shaking out the last scraps of stale bread.

'If they have any, sweetheart,' Jack replied, as the pigeons swooped in around their feet.

She handed him the crumpled paper bag and after stowing it in his pocket he took her hand.

Before the war they would sometimes catch the train to Southend, where they would paddle in the sea, get sticky eating candyfloss and munch cockles from a waxed carton on the train home. Other times, if it were cold and wet, they shared a tub of popcorn while watching the cartoon matinee at the local flicks followed by afternoon tea in one of the steamy cafés along Whitechapel High Street or back home with Rosie and her family.

To be honest, Jack didn't mind what they did on the one day of the week he was allowed to spend with Rachel as long as she was with him.

However, often, when the weather was fair, they would head to Victoria Park, to take a rowing boat out on the lake, feed the ever-hungry ducks and have tea and cake while listening to the musicians playing on the central bandstand.

Of course, when he'd brought her here before the war, the park, which sat on the Bethnal Green and Hackney borders, had looked a little different.

For a start, there hadn't been batteries of ack-ack guns positioned in the middle of the lawns and the low brick perimeter walls were topped with wrought-iron railings, which had now vanished along with the ornamental gate. Melted down, no doubt, and fashioned into tanks or aeroplanes.

'So how's school?' he asked as they set off down the gravel path towards the lakeside café.

'We had gas mask drill *twice* last week,' she said.

'Well, you've got to make sure you know how to do it right,' said Jack.

'That's what Mr Potter said, but we do it all the time.' Rachel rolled her eyes. 'It's so boring.'

Jack suppressed a smile.

74

'But I got the top marks in sums,' she continued, as a couple of women wearing ARP armbands on the sleeves of their summer jackets walked by.

'Did you?' Jack replied.

'Yes, and Miss Williams drew a star in my book,' Rachel replied. 'She said she would have given me a gold one but they've run out.'

'Well, I'm very proud of you, whatever the star's colour,' Jack replied. 'So your new school's not so bad, then?'

She shrugged, setting her dark curls bouncing in their pigtails. 'It's all right, I s'pose.'

'Just all right?' he asked, as they reached the tables set outside the circular café that overlooked the boating lake.

Rachel frowned. 'The teachers are nice enough, especially Miss Kane, but I miss my friends Beattie and Cora from the old school.' Her bottom lips stuck. 'Why did they have to go away?'

Like dozens of other East London schools, Rachel's junior school just off Plaistow Road had been evacuated at the outbreak of war to the country town of Diss in Norfolk.

However, as the much-feared gas attack and heavy bombing hadn't materialised, her mother had fetched her home at Christmas. Sadly, for Rachel, the rest of her school stayed in the country.

'Because their mummies thought it would be safer,' Jack replied, as they joined the end of the small queue.

'I know, but that was ages ago,' said Rachel. 'Why can't they come back now like I have so we can go back to our real school?'

Rachel hadn't been the only child fetched back home for Christmas, so West Ham council had been forced to open a school to accommodate them, meaning that she now attended a junior school with a hotchpotch of local children.

They shuffled forward as the woman in front gave her order to the young woman behind the counter.

'I imagine because their mums still think it's safer for them to stay in the country,' Jack replied.

Rachel sighed and looked down, studying the toes of her tan-coloured summer shoes.

'But I miss them,' she said in a small voice.

Jack studied his daughter's downcast face for a moment then squeezed her hand. She looked up and gave him a plucky smile that squeezed his heart.

'I tell you what, pudding,' he said. 'What about if next week instead of going to see the King's house in London we have an afternoon at Auntie Rosie's and I'll help you write letters to all your friends?'

Rachel's face lit up. 'Will you, Daddy?'

'Of course, sweetheart,' he replied.

The woman in front of them took her order and moved away. Jack stepped forward and the young woman raised her gaze from the till.

With a pile of strawberry-blonde hair piled high under her little white cap and a curvy figure beneath her apron, she was probably half a dozen years younger than his twenty-eight.

'Oh, hello,' she said, her mascaraed eyes running over him. 'What can I do for you, then?'

'One tea, a lemonade and …' He looked down at his daughter.

'Some angel cake,' said Rachel.

Jack raised an eyebrow.

'Please,' she added.

'I'm sorry, pet,' said the women behind the counter. 'We're out of angel cake, but you can have a macaroon, a currant bun or a jam tart.'

Frowning, Rachel considered her options. 'I'll have a macaroon, please.'

'Coming right up.' She picked up the large teapot. 'You having an afternoon out with your daddy, then?'

Rachel nodded. 'We've been feeding the birds and one of them hopped right on my hand.'

'Did it?' she replied. 'Mummy resting at home?'

'No, she's down the Spotty Dog with Uncle Manny,' Rachel replied.

The young woman's gaze returned to Jack. 'Is she?'

'I tell you what, Rachel luv, why don't you go and grab that table over there,' he indicated a free one by the water's edge, 'while I settle up?'

'All right, Daddy.' Rachel trotted off.

The young woman placed Jack's drink on a tray. 'What a gorgeous little girl.'

'I think so,' said Jack.

'Takes after you, then,' she added, giving him a lascivious look.

Jack shoved his hand in his pocket and pulled out a handful of loose change. 'What's the damage?'

'A tanner.'

Jack handed over a shilling.

Sliding out the draw beneath the counter she threw it in and then handed him a sixpenny piece.

'Ta.' Jack returned the coins to his pocket.

'Any time,' she said.

Picking up the tray, Jack wove his way between the occupied tables to join his daughter.

'One lemonade and a macaroon for m'lady.' Placing the tray on the weathered wooden tabletop, he bowed.

Rachel giggled, putting her hands over mouth. 'You are funny, Daddy.'

Crossing his eyes, Jack pulled a face. 'Am I?' he asked in a falsetto voice.

She laughed again and Jack sat on the chair next to her.

Taking a bite from her cake then holding it aloft, Rachel leaned forward and drew a mouthful of drink through the paper straw.

'If I promise not to make you sticky, can I sit on your lap, Daddy?' she asked.

'Course you can, sweetheart.' Jack held out his arms and she climbed on to him.

'That's all right then because Mummy hates me getting her sticky,' she said, reaching across and picking up her cake.

Jack hugged her and pressed his lips on to the soft curls of her hair. 'You can sit on my lap any time you like, even if you smother me in cake.'

Cradling her with one arm Jack sipped his tea while she nibbled at her macaroon, watching the miniature motorboat enthusiasts, young and not so young, play with their little ships.

There was a scrape of metal on gravel as someone sat down at the table behind them.

'You mark my words,' said a gruff voice from over Jack's right shoulder. 'Two weeks and they'll be here, goose-stepping up Whitehall, and we'll all have to learn German.'

'Poxy bloody Hun,' growled another voice.

Jack swivelled around.

'There's kid around, you know,' he said, giving the two old men slurping tea behind him a hard stare.

'Sorry, mate,' said one of them, his rheumy eyes looking at Jack from under the frayed brim of his cloth cap.

They started talking about football and Jack turned back.

Rachel nibbled at her cake for a moment then spoke.

'Daddy ...?'

'Yes, luv?'

'Do you think Germans like macaroons?' she asked through a mouthful of crumbs.

'I don't know,' said Jack. 'Why do you ask?'

She shrugged.

There was a long pause then she spoke again.

'Do you think they will come – the Germans, I mean?'

'I hope not,' said Jack.

'Uncle Manny says they will.' There was another long pause then Rachel turned her face into his chest. 'I'm scared.'

Putting down his tea, Jack wrapped his arms around her and hugged her tight.

'You don't have to be, sweetheart.' He pressed his lips to her soft curls. 'No matter what happens, I will always keep you safe.' She raised her head and looked up. 'You do believe me, don't you, pudding?'

She nodded.

'Good.' Jack forced a smile. 'Now eat your cake because I can see a couple of the ducks over there,' he indicated a pair of mallards waddling about at the edge of the lake, 'and they've got their beady eyes on it.'

Rachel smiled back, warming Jack's soul as it always did.

Wriggling around on his lap she took another long sip of her lemonade then bit into her cake again. Swinging her legs, her eyes returned to the miniature boats being sailed back and forth on the lake.

Jack studied his daughter's button-nose profile and his heart ached with love.

Then he caught sight of his watch on his arm wrapped around her.

'How we doing with that bottle of pop?' he asked, his cheerful tone belying the lead weight in his stomach.

'Almost finished, Daddy,' she replied, closing her childish lips around the soggy straw.

'Good, because we ought to start making tracks if we're going to get you home on time.'

Rachel nodded and tipped the bottle, noisily sucking up the last of her lemonade.

Slipping her off his knee, Jack stood up. He took his handkerchief from his pocket, wrapped it around his finger then dabbed it on his tongue.

Squeezing her eyes tight, Rachel suffered his attempts to clean her then Jack returned his handkerchief to his pocket and took her hand.

'Bus or tram?'

Putting her index finger to her chin, Rachel looked skywards for a moment. 'Bus. But can we sit in the front on the top?'

Chapter seven

Bringing her bicycle to a halt, Prue stepped off and wheeled it the last twenty yards to the Station Road entrance of the London and North Eastern Railway's shunting yards at Stratford. She repositioned the cardboard box containing her gas mask and took a deep breath to calm her nerves.

'Good morning,' she said to the elderly man in the booth. 'I'm starting here this morning and I've been told to report to the main offices.'

'You one of the new women, then?' he asked, the damp roll-up glued to his lower lip bobbing as he spoke.

Having cycled the three miles from home with the sun in her eyes all the way, Prue had arrived at her new place of work just before seven thirty.

She wasn't alone: dozens of men dressed in rough working clothes, their caps pulled low and cigarettes clamped between their teeth, streamed past her into the largest shunting yard and engine works in London.

'Yes, I am,' Prue replied, trying to ignore the odd "ello, darling' and 'give us a kiss' from the railway workers as they rolled by. 'Actually, I'm a bit late.'

'Well, better late than never, as my old ma used to say,'

replied the gateman. 'Follow this bunch down past the engine shed and then turn left and you'll see a two-storey building with sandbags all round it.'

'Thank you.'

'But mind 'ow you go,' the gateman added as Prue took hold of her handlebars again. 'Some silly bugger got too close to the ten-fifty from Clacton last week, and we found bits of him as far away as Liverpool Street.'

Pushing her bicycle before her, Prue joined the stream of workers heading into the vast yard. Walking carefully alongside the railway tracks that glinted in the sunlight, she took in the scene before her. In the far distance she could just about make out Stratford station, but between her and that run-of-the-mill sight of city workers waiting for their early-morning train into town, there was a spectacle straight out of the Victorian age. Instead of the mellow pastel shades of spring flowers and budding trees she had known in Bedfordshire, for as far as the eye could see there were the stark lines and unnatural shades of iron and steel.

In the criss-cross of rails sat engines of all shapes and sizes; some had passenger carriages strung out behind them while others pulled enclosed wagons. Punctuating the scene were raised gantries dotted with signals, their stubby arms ready to instruct drivers either to stop or to proceed.

And the noise! The crash of metal on metal coming from the engine sheds competed with the clackety-clack of locomotive wheels rolling over the rail points and the screech of breaks. But it was the smell – a mixture of coal and oil – that caught Prue's breath.

Glancing around, eyes wide with curiosity, Prue circumvented a massive locomotive with steam hissing from its funnel and workers clambering over it. Finally she reached the engine shed. Spotting the yard offices, she veered off the main pathway and made her way alongside a row of carriages towards it.

After securing her cycle in the rack next to the building and having been told by one of the young girls in the front office that the new recruits were in the meeting room on the first floor, Prue made her way up the concrete stairs and spotted a half-glazed door with a plaque beside it reading 'Training Room'. She knocked, then pushed the door open and walked in.

The room was about the size of a school classroom, with grubby off-white walls, nondescript lino floor and a feeling of boredom hanging over it. Illustrations of train wheels and machine parts were pinned to the wall.

There were three rows of scuffed-top tables with women of various shapes and sizes sitting behind most of them. Standing at the front of the room next to a blackboard was a stout man wearing a navy uniform which looked at least a size too small for him. 'LNER' was embroidered on his lapels.

'Good morning,' Prue said, as two dozen pairs of eyes turned her way. 'I'm sorry I'm late but I took a wrong turn.'

'Well, miss, let me tell you we don't put up with no

lateness on the LNER,' the man replied, his piggy eyes running over her.

'Sorry,' Prue repeated. 'It won't happen again.'

'Name?' he barked.

'Prudence Carmichael.'

He consulted the list on the desk beside him then, taking a pencil from behind his ear, ticked her off.

'Well, Miss Carmichael,' he said, shoving the pencil back where it came from, 'I'm Mr Walters, senior rolling stock supervisor, and you and these other young ladies will be working under me.'

There were a couple of sniggers. The supervisor glared at the assembled women for a second, then his attention returned to Prue.

'Find yourself a seat, and be quick about it.'

Spotting a spare chair towards the back of the class, Prue hurried over to it, put her handbag and gas mask on the floor next to her, and sat down.

'As I was saying before we were interrupted,' said Mr Walters as he turned back to the blackboard, 'although last year the Government set up the Railway Executive Committee to coordinate the railways for the duration, the London and North Eastern Railway is still governed by its Board and ...'

'Don't worry, luv,' came a whisper.

Prue looked at the young woman, with a round face, curly blonde hair and the brightest red lipstick, sitting next to her.

'You ain't missed nothing,' her classmate continued.

'That old bore's just spent twenty minutes droning on about the toff that set up the railways an 'undred years ago.'

'Thank goodness,' Prue replied, in the same hushed tones. 'I took a wrong turn after Carpenters Road.'

'Well, you're here now,' said the young women. 'I'm Maggie, by the way.'

'Prudence, but call me Prue. Everyone does.'

'If I can have your attention,' called Mr Walters.

Grinning like a couple of schoolgirls, Prue and Maggie turned back to the front.

The supervisor cleared his throat. 'Now, ladies, here in Stratford we …'

Heaving a sigh, Prue glanced up at the clock and wondered how soon they would be breaking for a cup of tea.

'Thank you for your attention, ladies. Mr Clark will be coming in now to give you a rundown of your duties,' Mr Walters concluded, some forty minutes later. 'If anyone needs the facilities pop out now and I'll go and see where he is.'

There was a collective sigh as he left the room.

'Fank Gawd,' muttered someone, echoing the sentiment in the room.

There was a scraping of chairs as a couple of girls hurried out to the bathroom and Prue and a few of the others stood up to stretch.

The brunette in front of her turned around and arched her back. 'What a yawn,' she said, shaking out the creases in her flowery skirt.

'I though he was never going to end,' said Maggie, rising to her feet.

'It was a bit long-winded,' said Prue, stretching her elbows back.

'Kate Mulligan,' said the young woman in front of her.

'Nice to meet you, I'm Prue and this is Maggie.'

'Hello,' said Maggie.

The door opened and Mr Walters marched back in, followed by a heavily built, middle-aged man with what remained of his grey hair plastered across his bald patch with brilliantine. He was wearing a baggy set of dirty grey overalls and antagonistic expression on his face.

As the last few women who'd nipped out to the lavatory slipped back in, Prue and the rest of the class resumed their seats and came to order.

'Well,' said Mr Walters as the room quietened, 'this is Mr Clark, in charge of the carriage sheds, so I'll leave you in his capable hands.'

The supervisor walked out, closing the door firmly behind him.

Taking up position behind the desk, Mr Clark surveyed the two dozen or so young women sitting before him for a moment then slammed both hands flat on the desk top.

'I might as well say it straight out,' he said, glaring at them. 'I don't bloody 'old with it. A woman's place is in the bloody 'ome not running about a railway yard pretending they can do the same bloody work as men, because you bloody well can't. However, as 'alf the bloody yard's been called up, we're hundreds of blokes down and you can't run a bloody railway without workers, which is why you bloody lot have been sent here. Thankfully, someone at head office seems to have a bit of bloody sense so they've found something that comes natural to a woman: cleaning.'

'Cleaning?' said Prue, before she could stop herself.

Mr Clark thrust out his jaw and his deep-set eyes fixed on her. 'Stand up, Miss ...'

Prue rose to her feet. 'Carmichael.'

'Well, Miss Carmichael,' he repeated, 'wot did you think you were going to do, drive a bloody engine?'

There was a titter of laughter.

'Well, no,' said Prue. 'But I thought perhaps clerical work of some kind or maybe in the ticket office.'

A young woman with a mass of blonde hair piled on the top of her head sitting two rows in front of Prue swivelled around in her seat.

'Think yourself too good for cleaning, do you?' she asked, looking hard at Prue from beneath her heavily mascaraed lashes.

'You tell her, Gladys,' said an equally brassy redhead sitting next to her.

The space between Prue's shoulder blades tingled.

'Of course not,' she replied, holding their withering gazes. 'It's just that I hear they have women working in the booking office at St Pancras and I thought perhaps—'

'Well, Miss La-di-da,' cut in Mr Clark, mimicking her accent in falsetto. 'This h'aint St Pancras, don't you know, but Stratford, and we don't 'old wiv such fings around 'ere. For your information, everyone working on the locomotive side of the yard started as a cleaner as a lad and then worked his way up to be a wheel tapper, signalman, fireman or driver. Those on the customer side did the same, starting with portering through booking clerk or a guard, but unlike the drivers, firemen and engineers, all our signalmen, booking clerks, station guards and porters aren't a reserved occupation so they've been bloody called up. That means the lads who were working in the cleaning sheds 'ave been promoted, so to speak, leaving us with no one to clean the bloody carriages and engines. Does that answer your question, *Miss* Carmichael?'

'Thank you,' said Prue, feeling embarrassment colour her cheeks as she resumed her seat.

'Now we've got that straight, are there any more bloody questions, before I take you over to the cleaning sheds?' The women shook their heads. 'Good, let's make tracks then.'

'Miserable old bugger. You take no notice of him,' said Kate, as Prue rose to her feet like everyone else.

'She's right,' added Maggie. 'I bet it's being unhappy that keeps him going. Now come on, don't give him something else to moan about.'

The three girls joined the others in the class and made their way down the stairs and out of the building.

Walking behind Mr Clark, they followed him to a hut further down the path.

All of them squeezed into the small entrance hall where a row of shelves containing piles of grey fabric on one side and a row of lockers on the other.

'This here is your changing room and bogs,' he said, indicating the two doors behind him. 'It was the men's so you'll 'ave to put up with the smell for a bit and don't bloody come crying to me if you find the odd bit of fruity drawing or phrase on the wall. We've tried to scrub the worst off, but you might as well get bloody used to it as, mark my words, you'll hear worse round the yard.' His deep-set eyes fixed on Prue. 'So if you're too delicate a flower for a bit of saucy banter you'd better get your bloody cards now.'

No one spoke, but sensing someone's eyes on her Prue half turned and found Gladys regarding her with a sneer across her cherry-red lips.

Prue looked away.

''Ere's your uniforms,' continued the foreman, pointing to a pile of grey fabric on the shelves to the side of him. 'So grab one and get yourselves changed and I'll take you across to the cleaning sheds.'

The women surged forward.

'They've been worn,' said one young woman with round-rimmed glasses and short blonde hair.

'And they're too big,' called another girl of barely five foot holding high a grey boiler suit that would have comfortably fitted an England prop forward.

'What do you bloody expect,' barked Mr Clark, 'some poncy West End fashion? There's a bloody war on, in case you ain't noticed. Now get them on and shove your gear in a locker. I'll be outside. And get a shift on; we ain't got all bloody day.'

He stomped out.

'Right, well,' said Kate, handing Prue and Maggie a set of overalls each, 'I suppose we'd better get on with it.'

They followed the rest of the girls into the changing room. In addition to the pungent aroma of male sweat, the room was filled with battered grey lockers down one wall and benches fixed around the other three walls with clothes pegs hammered into the brickwork above. As the high windows of frosted glass were covered with cardboard as per blackout regulations, the dingy room was lit by three electric strip lights that buzzed softly above them.

With under slips and stockings already flying around them, Prue and her two new friends found themselves a corner and started undressing.

'Just like being back at school,' said Prue as she set her handbag down on the bench.

'Not very stylish, are they?' said Maggie, holding her crumpled grey uniform aloft.

'What do you bloody expect,' said Kate, mimicking their miserable supervisor, 'some swanky West End number?'

Putting her foot on the bench behind her, and glad that she'd decided to put on her stout lace-ups instead of heels, Prue turned up the bottoms of her trousers then she whipped up her hair and secured it under a silk-scarf turban. Kate had removed the buckled belt from her dress and Prue followed suit, securing the excess folds of boiler-suit fabric into her waist.

Someone banged on the door.

'Get a move on!' bellowed their supervisor.

There was a flurry of activity as women gathered up their belongings, so turning back her cuffs and tucking a stray lock of hair beneath her scarf, Prue picked up her clothes, found a free locker and slid her things inside. Having turned the key, she tucked it into her brassiere. Hooking her gas mask over her shoulder, and with the grubby clock hanging above the door informing them it was just nine o'clock, Prue left the changing room.

'See, Sid. Good as new,' said Jack, as Sidney Watts, the fireman on the *Spirit of the Fens*, ran his hand along the piston of the 4-4-0 locomotive that Jack and his team had been working on since they arrived that morning.

'That it is,' said Sid, a lanky chap with a haphazard set of teeth, as he straightened up. 'Just as well we're off to the seaside again.'

Jack didn't have to ask why because all week trains packed with troops and armaments had been streaming through Stratford's shunting yards heading for the south coast.

'Seems to me things are going from bad to worse,' added the fireman, a sombre expression dragging his thin face down further.

It was just before twelve on the Monday after his visit to Victoria Park with Rachel and he was halfway through his ten-hour shift. Today he and the team had been assigned to the boiler repair shop which faced out on to the scrublands and the River Lee, and as the news from Europe was that Amiens had been overrun by a panzer division, he couldn't help thinking that Sid was not wrong.

Although as they went about their daily lives, people did their best to convince each other that the news couldn't get any worse, each morning the country opened its newspapers over their marmalade and toast and read of yet another calamity.

Of course, it wasn't reported as such it was all: 'Our troops halt the Nazi advance' or 'New Plan to thwart German tanks', but people weren't idiots; they knew the truth behind the headlines.

'Mind you,' Sid continued, 'us and the French will stop 'em before they reach Paris.'

Although that was the common feeling amongst many, Jack wasn't so sure. In fact, with the Germans going through the countries of the near Continent like a knife through butter, if the French army and the British Expeditionary Force didn't halt the Nazi advance – and soon – anyone in Dover with a decent set of binoculars would be able to see a swastika flying in Calais.

'Best get on,' said Sid. 'This bugger won't fire itself.'

'Me too.' Jack stepped back. 'And bring us back a stick of rock, will ya?'

Sid grinned then heaved himself into the locomotive's cabin.

Grabbing his canvas tool bag from the gravel between the sleepers, Jack left Sid banking the firebox to build up steam and made his way out into the bright May sunshine. The factory whistles that signalled the end of the midday break had sounded ten minutes before in the far distance, reminding Jack's stomach that it had been idle since just after dawn.

Taking a couple of deep breaths to get the smell of oil and smoke from his nose, Jack started across the busy yard towards the main offices.

There were half a dozen trains either waiting their turn to enter the main station or pulling out ready to journey east to Ilford, Romford, Walthamstow and beyond or north to Stoke Newington, Stamford Hill and Chingford.

However, in addition to the usual traffic at this time of day, the shunting yard was alive with elongated goods trains packed with food and raw material thundering through the busy intersection in all directions.

His stomach rumbling, Jack picked his way across a series of rails. Passing the tool shop on the way and after waiting for a seemingly endless coal train to clickety-clack past, Jack finally made it into the yard's main building.

Stowing his cap in his back pocket, he pushed open the main door. He strolled past the almost empty offices on either side of the corridor and headed towards the double doors at the end. However, as he reached them, they swung open, and Tosh and Bill strolled out.

'For Gawd's sake, Jack, we thought you'd lost your way,' said Bill.

'Got stuck talking to Sid off the *Spirit of the Fens*,' Jack replied. 'You two done?'

'Yeah,' said Tosh. 'It's boiled beef stew today; least that's what's chalked up on the board. But if you ask me some milkman's missing his 'orse.'

Jack laughed. 'Well, that's all right then, cos I'm hungry enough to eat one. Have you finished sorting out the brakes on the guard's wagon?'

Bill nodded. 'Yeah, we filed the completed chit in the office before we had our grub. We're just off to the carriage shop to check some couplings on a sleeper that were reported as dodgy.'

'Good. I'll join you when I'm done,' said Jack.

Tosh and Bill strolled off and Jack continued on, wafts of boiled cabbage and a wall of voices hitting him simultaneously as he walked into the canteen.

With whitewashed walls and three dozen or so scrubbed tables lining the length of the space, the Stratford shunting yard dining hall was very much like thousands of others up and down the country.

The kitchen itself was situated behind the long counter at the far end and connected by a hatch to the handful of women in blue gingham overalls who were serving.

Of course, it was only the shunting yard's blue-collar workers and the junior typists and filling clerks who used this canteen. The administrators, supervisors and secretaries dined separately in the managers' restaurant on the floor above. Well, that's to say they used to. Now the posh canteen upstairs had been given over to the war effort and the Red Cross had set up a first-aid centre in it.

Acknowledging a couple of mates with a nod as he went, Jack made his way over to the small queue and picked up a tray.

Many factory workers had to make do with sandwiches or find themselves a greasy-spoon café close to their place of work, but despite Tosh's grumbles about the food, Jack always ate in the yard's canteen.

The Government's Price of Goods Act the previous November had been an attempt to stop prices in the shops rocketing before rationing came in on New Year's Day, but unfortunately those advising the bods in Whitehall hadn't taken into account the fact that as soon as war was declared the price of everything went up by a quarter.

Although Rosie had insisted that he come to live with her and Mick when he found himself without a roof over his head, Jack knew the seventeen shillings he gave her each week had barely covered the cost of his keep when he'd first moved in five years before let alone now.

Knowing each week that a further twelve shillings of his three-pound-ten-shilling wage was already spoken for elsewhere, Rosie refused to take any more from him, so Jack made a point of having his main meal of the day in the canteen to ease his sister's weekly housekeeping.

'Do you ever go home, Jack?'

He looked up to see May Flannigan, a motherly woman with frizzy grey hair and a ready smile, looking across at him from the other side of the counter.

'Doesn't seem like it, does it?' He smiled. 'So what have we got, Mrs F? Lobster? Grouse? Or perhaps pâté de foie gras?'

'It's beef stew or beef stew,' she replied.

'Well then, I'll have some beef stew, please.'

After loading his bowl, and adding a sizeable wedge of bread and a mug of tea to his tray, Jack looked around. As he was one of the stragglers, there were plenty of empty tables so he selected one by the window and ambled over.

Someone had left a copy of that morning's *Daily Herald* on the table so Jack spread it out above his bowl and skimmed the headlines, which read: 'The French Resistance is Stronger', followed by an account of how Britain's ally was attacking the advancing Germans ferociously.

He'd just got halfway through his stew and was reading how the Germans were fighting like gangsters, when the double doors to the canteen swung open and Knobby Clark, the cleaning sheds' supervisor, lumbered in. Never someone you'd ever describe as cheery, today his fleshy face was extraordinarily downcast even for him.

He collected his dinner from the serving counter, then, looking around, he spotted Jack and made his way over.

'Right, Jack,' he said, as he placed his tray on the other side of the table.

'Not so bad. But you don't look your usual 'appy self, Knobby,' Jack replied.

'Can you blame me?' Knobby replied.

Jack looked puzzled.

'Don't say you ain't 'eard about our new recruits?' Knobby replied.

'Oh, you mean the women who started work today?' said Jack.

'Yes, the bloody women,' growled Knobby, his jowls quivering. 'It ain't right. They should be at home, cooking and tending kiddies, not 'ere doing men's work and dodging between rails.'

'Well, I wouldn't advise anyone to dodge about between trains,' said Jack, as Knobby picked up his spoon. 'But as the cleaning sheds are well away from the fast tracks and through lines, they shouldn't interfere with the work in the yard too much.'

'Not interfere!' gasped Knobby, looking at him incredulously. 'When have you ever known a woman not bloody well interfere?' He jabbed his spoon at Jack and a globule of gravy dropped on to the newspaper between them.

Out of the corner of his eye Jack saw the canteen doors swing open again.

A look of horror spread across Knobby's face. 'Talk of the bloody devil.'

To be honest, with hundreds of men working in the shunting yard, it would have been a miracle if Jack hadn't heard about the couple of dozen women who had arrived that morning. Truthfully, although he maintained to Rosie that he wasn't looking to get entangled in a new relationship, he couldn't deny that he was as interested as any man with blood in his veins to see what the new carriage cleaners looked like. Cradling his mug of tea in his hands, Jack half turned to get a better look at LNER's newest employees.

Queueing up in front of the counter were half a dozen women dressed in baggy grey overalls with their hair sensibly secured under an array of colourful scarves. They were a variety of heights and sizes and stood chatting to each other while they waited to be served, but as Jack's gaze ran along their ranks it was caught by the sight of a young woman third from the back, standing slightly taller than her companions.

A faint memory stirred in his brain; however, before he could retrieve it Knobby's voice cut across his thoughts.

'Bloody women,' he muttered. 'Neither use nor ornament.'

That patently wasn't true, because despite being swathed in a shapeless overall, the thin leather belt secured around the young woman's waist highlighted her trim figure.

Her friend beside her said something and she half turned towards Jack, allowing him a glimpse of her well-proportioned features. The memory niggled again, Jack's mind sifting through possibilities, then the young woman laughed.

'You mark my bloody words,' continued Knobby, 'no good will come of it.'

A broad smile spread across Jack's face.

With his gaze fixed on the young woman, he swallowed the last of his tea then placed the mug next to his empty bowl.

'Oh, I don't know, Knobby,' he said, rising to his feet. 'Perhaps the yard would be better if it had a woman's touch.'

'Cor, I think my blisters have got blisters,' said Kate, looking at the palms of her hands as she stood next to Prue in the queue.

'Me too,' said Maggie. 'And my back aches like billy-o. What about you, Prue?'

'It would be easier to say what doesn't ache,' Prue replied, rolling her shoulders to ease the tightness. 'But I expect we'll get used to it after a week or two.'

'If we live that long,' said Kate. 'Supervisor's a real blooming slave driver.'

After a morning brushing train corridors, washing soot from windows and scooting out all manner of rubbish from under the seats, Prue was more than ready to eat whatever the jolly-looking woman ladled on to her plate.

During the course of the morning, she'd discovered that Maggie, who was two years older than her, lived in Poplar with her parents, four brothers, two sisters and elderly granny. She was engaged to her childhood sweetheart who, despite never having been in anything larger than a two-seater boat on the boating lake at Southend, was currently serving on a destroyer in the Royal Navy. In contrast, Kate, who was just eighteen, lived only a little way away from Prue over her parents' draper's shop on Mile End Road. She had a brother in the Army who was stationed on the East Coast of Scotland, presumably to stop the Germans coming across the North Sea from Norway. Kate wanted to join the ATS like her older sister Milly, but as her mother went into hysterics every time Kate mentioned signing up, she had volunteered for war work instead.

They showed the usual surprise when Prue told them about her family and where they lived, but once she'd assured them that she wouldn't be shocked to the core if one of them said something colourful, they returned to discussing the latest *Broadway Melody* film starring Fred Astaire, annoyance at the BBC for not playing more American songs and the worrying rumour that the War Ministry was considering bringing in clothes rationing.

The girl at the front of the queue moved off with her tray and Kate and Maggie shuffled along. Thinking about the five-carriage train they'd been assigned to clean after lunch, Prue did the same.

'Fancy meeting you here.'

Prue turned and found herself looking up into a pair of deep brown eyes. She stared blankly up at the owner of those eyes for a moment then realised who he was.

'Oh, it's you,' she said, staring into his disturbingly handsome face.

He raised a well-shaped eyebrow. 'I'm glad you remembered your knight in shining armour.'

Actually, over the previous week she had remembered him a bit too often for her liking, if the truth was known. She'd almost convinced herself that her mind had exaggerated the breadth of his shoulders and the blunt chin, but now with him standing in front of her she realised if anything she'd underestimated these elements.

Prue gave him a cool look. 'More like scruffy overalls.'

A quirky smile. 'Snap.'

Prue stared at him a moment longer then laughed. 'Yes, we both look very glamourous, don't we?'

'Well, I'll never win a beauty pageant, but on you I've never seen a set of overalls looking so fine,' he said, his dark gaze holding hers.

Before she could stop it, her heart did a little dance.

'Oi, Jack!'

He turned and Prue's eyes flickered briefly down to the spray of dark hair visible between his unfastened collar before following his eyeline to a youthful lad standing in the doorway with a shot of red hair and wearing navy dungarees.

'Sorry, guv, but the *Eastern Belle*'s just pulled into number three shed with a cracked piston,' he shouted across the canteen. 'Prentice wants us to get her back into action for the night run to Harwich.'

'Right, Tosh, I'll catch you up,' Jack shouted back. His attention returned to Prue. 'Duty calls. See you around.'

Touching the peak of his leather cap, Jack smiled again then turned and strolled across the canteen, Prue's eyes following his rolling gait all the way.

'*Who*, may I ask, was that?'

Blinking, Prue turned to see Kate and Maggie looking eagerly at her.

'Jack,' Prue replied.

'Jack who?' ask Kate.

'Is he a train driver?' asked Maggie.

'Or a fireman?' added Kate.

'Maybe he's a signalman, Kate, and all alone in his little signal box,' laughed Maggie.

The blonde-haired girl in front of Kate turned around. 'Well, I'd keep him company.'

'Me too,' agreed someone behind Prue.

'He's got a touch of that Tyrone Powell about him,' said Maggie. 'And he likes you?'

Prue rolled her eyes. 'No, I don't know what he does or anything about him and yes, I grant you he is very handsome, but right now after a morning working my fingers to the bone scrubbing muddy floors and polishing filthy windows, the main object of my desire is something hot and meaty out of that pot of stew.'

Chapter eight

Y OU'D THINK SHE MIGHT have realised they were gone when it got a bit breezy,' said Kate, lifting up a pair of cream-coloured frilly knickers she'd pulled out from the back of the carriage seat.

'No need to ask 'ow she lost 'em,' said Maggie, pointing at a limp, unravelled Durex lying among the empty cigarette packets and newspapers strew on the carriage floor.

It was just after three-thirty in the afternoon at the end of her long first week. Prue and her two friends, along with the rest of the morning shift of cleaners, were working their way carriage by carriage along a nine-coach passenger train that had arrived in the cleaning shed. As it had been scheduled for the last train to Norwich that day, Mr Clark had told them to leave it until last. Having been scrubbing, polishing and hoovering their way along it for almost an hour, they were, thank goodness, now on the last carriage.

Although it was five days since she'd started at Stratford's shunting yard, Prue still collapsed into bed exhausted and aching at the end of each day. She had also, after days of walking around looking like Pierrot in a too-large overall, got to grips with the uniform. She had managed to bag a couple of smaller boiler suits, which after a bit of tucking in here and turning up there, plus a stout leather belt, meant the stock uniform more or less fitted her.

However, despite this and having to put up with her mother's censorious looks across the dining table each night, Prue was more than happy with her current lot in life, and she was also learning a great deal – and none of it about cleaning.

Prue felt her cheeks. 'I can't believe that …'

'Someone would have it off in a train?' asked Maggie.

'Well, yes,' said Prue.

'Believe me, ducks,' said her friend, scooping the slither of grey rubber up in her gloved hand, 'when the urge 'as 'old of you you don't care where you are. I can see you don't believe me,' she continued, seeing the sceptical look on Prue's face, 'but mark my words, you'll find yourself alone with some big handsome man some time and you'll know well enough what I'm talking about.'

Infuriatingly, an image of that Jack whoever-he-was flitted across her mind.

It was infuriating because, truthfully, she'd only seen him in passing a couple of times during the last week and although he'd given her that quirky smile of his each time, she wouldn't regard him as someone she knew.

'Even so,' said Kate, 'you'd think she'd have the decency to take her drawers with her.'

Prue pulled her thoughts back from their wandering and raised an eyebrow. 'Especially as you can't find a decent pair of drawers for less than three bob, even in the market.'

The other two women laughed.

'Right,' said Maggie, as she picked up a ripped KitKat wrapper. 'Let's give this a quick runaround with the hoover and a bit of a polish and we'll be done.'

Dragging the old vacuum cleaner into the carriage by its fabric flex, Prue plugged it in then ran it across the floor while Kate dabbed a bit of beeswax on the woodwork, leaving Maggie to tie up the canvas sack of rubbish.

Ten minutes later, the three of them clambered down from the last coach.

One of the stubby shunting engines that darted back and forth repositioning goods wagons and passenger carriages ready to be coupled up to locomotives had just rolled into the shed, filling the place with steam and the sound of metal grinding on metal.

As it was now the end of the afternoon, the twenty-plus carriages Prue and the rest of the morning cleaners had made ready for use earlier in the day had already been put back into service, so the vast metal-framed shed was all but empty.

Gathering themselves together and stepping over the railway tracks, the three women made their way out, joining another cleaning team of three along the way.

Outside, the late-afternoon sunlight was bathing the stark greys and silvers of the shunting yard in a mellow glow, dotted with the odd starburst of brilliance as the sun's rays hit a rail.

In the far distance the evening trains from Liverpool Street were filling up with factory workers heading home, east to Manor Park and Seven Kings or northwards to Dalston and Highbury.

Keeping their ears and eyes peeled, they walked on the wooden causeways that were the pathways across the multitude of criss-crossing tracks, pausing occasionally to let a locomotive puff by. Finally, they reached the path to their changing room but as Lena from the other cleaning team pushed open the door, something snagged the corner of Prue's eyes.

She raised her head and found herself looking at the face that popped into her mind with maddening regularity.

'Afternoon,' Jack said, smiling down at her. 'Just finished?'

Prue wiped a lock of hair from her damp forehead with the back of her hand. 'How did you guess?'

He gave a rumbling laugh. 'How're you getting on, then?'

'Not so bad,' said Prue.

'I bet you discovered muscles you never knew you had,' he said. 'I know I did when I started in the yard as a lad.'

'What do you do now?' she asked, her eyes running over the afternoon bristles on his chin and cheeks.

'I'm an engineer,' he replied. 'Spend all my days in a stifling workshop keeping the rolling stock rolling.'

Somewhere in the distance a church clock started to strike the hour.

'What's the time?' she asked.

Jack raised his bare arm and Prue's gaze flickered over the soft dark hair covering it.

'Just four,' he said, glancing at his watch.

'I'd better go; I'm supposed to be meeting someone,' she said.

An odd expression passed across Jack's face. 'Some fella, I suppose?'

Prue laughed. 'No, my mother. And I'll never hear the end of it if I'm late. Bye.'

She turned but she'd only taken a couple of steps when he called after her.

'I'm Jack Quinn, by the way,' he called after her. 'And you are …?'

'Prudence Carmichael,' she called over her shoulder as she disappeared through the door.

A slow smile spread across Jack's face.

There were a couple of reasons for this. The first was because although he'd caught sight of her several time over the past week, he'd never found himself in a position to be able to speak to her. In fact, if he hadn't spotted her and her friends crossing the tracks as he came out of the brass foundry, he would have missed her again.

Secondly, she could have told him to sod off when he asked her name, but she didn't. Well, perhaps she wouldn't have used those actual words. Young women named

Prudence, who dressed in expensive suits and spoke with a country lilt instead of a cockney twang, didn't as a rule tell people to sod off so … Jack's smile widened. Who says an oil-covered engineer with a daughter, an ex-wife and a less-than-spotless past couldn't win a fair lady?

Beneath his cassock David Harmsworth re-crossed his legs and glanced at the grandfather clock ticking away the minutes opposite him.

Four-forty. Annoyance rippled through him but, reminding himself that the meek were blessed, he damped it down.

He was in Tredegar Square, some mile and a half from St Winifred's, and sitting on a less than comfortable chair with a saggy wicker seat in the Archdeacon of Bow's hallway and had been for the past twenty minutes.

Pressing his lips together, he glanced at the oak-panelled passageway, his eyes flickering briefly over the prints of biblical and pastoral scenes displayed there. His gaze ran unseeing up the stairs and finally came to rest on the opaque bowl lamp above him that dangled by three gilt chains from the ceiling rose.

It lingered there for a moment then returned to the clock opposite him and his annoyance started to bubble again. Before it could fill his chest, the door next to him clicked open.

David stood up, formed his long features into a benign expression, and turned as the archdeacon stepped out.

As the bishop's deputy, Leonard Alton-Banfield spent his days either ensuring that the clergy in the diocese were adhering to the Church's cannon laws or disciplining those who weren't.

He was in his early forties, with a reasonable amount of light brown hair for his age and pale grey eyes that were rarely troubled by emotion. Although somewhere near the five-foot-ten mark, his elongated limbs gave the impression that he'd started life a good deal shorter, and that someone had stretched him on a rack.

'Ah, David,' he said, as if he'd forgotten he was sitting in the hall, offering him a soft, slender hand. 'Sorry to have kept you waiting.'

'That's perfectly all right.' David gave his clerical superior an ingenuous smile as he took his hand. 'I'm sure you have many calls on your valuable time.'

'Shall we?' The archdeacon stepped back, and David walked past him into the room.

Leonard's office was at the front of the house, facing south, so the late-afternoon sunlight streamed through the bay window catching particles of dust in its beams.

The heavy desk with a leather top was opposite the door, with a wall full of books behind it. A Persian rug covered most of the floor and although faded was of some considerable quality. Apart from the swivel chair behind the desk there were two upright chairs like the one his rear had suffered on for the past half an hour.

An image of an elderly couple graced one of the shelves, but there were, of course, no photographs of children anywhere because the archdeacon had decided to forgo marriage in order to serve God.

'Do take a seat,' said Leonard as he slipped behind his desk.

Tucking the folds of his black barathea beneath him, David sat on the firmer of the two chairs on offer.

Although Father Hugh was his teacher and mentor of his day-to-day ecclesiastical training in parish work and Church religious ceremony, the person whose job it was to confirm him a fit and proper priest to take on the cure of souls in his own parish was sitting across the table from him now.

The man who decided whether David ended up stuck in an impoverished living ministering to a bunch of country yokel or standing in a pulpit each Sunday with a wealthy patron sitting in the front pew was Leonard Alton-Banfield.

Settling himself in his chair, the archdeacon smiled across at him.

'Perhaps before we start, we might share a moment of prayer together,' he said, steepling his long fingers together.

David smiled his acquiescence. Clasping his hands together on his lap, he bowed his head and closed his eyes.

In his clipped, cultured tone, the archdeacon requested wisdom and discernment while images of Prue's slender thighs, briefly revealed by a puff of wind that morning, replayed behind David's closed eyelids.

Mumbling amen along with his spiritual superior, David looked up.

'Now, my dear boy, how have you been?' asked the archdeacon, pressing a Bakelite doorbell fixed to his desk.

'Very well, thank you,' David replied.

There was a knock on the study door.

'Come!'

It opened and the grey-haired, bespectacled head of the archdeacon's secretary appeared around the door.

'Tea if you would, Miss Lamont,' he instructed. 'One sugar for Father David, if I remember correctly.'

'Please,' said David.

She nodded.

'And how are you settling in with your new incumbent?' asked the archdeacon as she closed the door.

'I am very much enjoying working with Father Hugh; he is a most Godly man,' David replied, 'and of the same mind as myself regarding Church traditions, liturgy and obligations.'

'Excellent,' said the archdeacon. 'And after living a bachelor life with just you and Father Owen, you must find it a little strange to have a family in the rectory.'

'A little, but there are blessings too,' David replied. 'Mrs Carmichael has taken a firm hand of the rectory's domestic arrangements and improved them no end.'

'And what about Miss Carmichael?'

The memory of the faint swell of Prue's breast above the neckline of her light blue dress returned to David's mind.

'Although I only see her in passing most days,' said David, forcing a neutral tone into his voice, 'she is a very pleasant young lady. Full of laughter and with a ready smile. She's also very good with children and the older members of the parish. Everyone, in fact; and she sings, too, in a most joyful manner, as she goes about her tasks. I even found her dancing a quickstep with an imaginary partner in the kitchen while a piece of popular music played on the wireless. And Prue ...' The archdeacon raised an eyebrow. 'But as I say, I only see Miss Carmichael in passing.'

Leonard scrutinised David's face for a moment, but just as he opened his mouth there was a knock at the door and Miss Lamont came in balancing a tray with two cups of tea, each with a single rich tea finger in the saucer.

Placing the tray on the end of the archdeacon's desk, she put one teacup at the side of the blotting paper in front of her boss and the other before David.

The archdeacon smiled his thanks then, as she left the room, turned his attention back to David.

He chewed his top lip for a moment and then spoke again.

'I wonder, David, if living under the same roof as a laughing, singing, dancing and smiling young lady has perhaps caused the unhealthy practice you have previously struggled with to rear its head again, so to speak?'

Swallowing a mouthful of tea, David replaced his cup in its saucer.

'It has tried,' he replied, forcing himself to hold the other man's piercing gaze. 'I continue to follow your advice and find regular immersion in cold water most effective at strengthening my resistance against self-gratification.'

The archdeacon nodded sagely. 'I'm relieved to hear it, my boy. As St Paul himself says in his Epistle to the Corinthians chapter seven, verse seven, "for would I that all men were even as myself", which, as he tells us in verse eight, is unmarried.'

'Indeed, undoubtedly the perfect, pure status to serve the Almighty.' David's broad forehead creased slightly as a devout expression glided across his long face. 'However, I am mindful, Archdeacon, of the following verse, which instructs those who cannot contain their passions to marry rather than burn – in Hell, presumably.'

Frowning, the senior cleric chewed his lip for a moment. 'I had hoped, David, that you would follow my own path.'

'That was always my intention, but alas, the spirit is willing, but the flesh is weak.' David hung his head. 'I'm afraid, Archdeacon, I'm not blessed nor can match your devotion.'

There was a long silence.

'Very well.'

David looked up.

'But I counsel you to choose wisely,' continued the senior cleric. 'As we are told in Proverbs that, "whoso findeth a good wife obtained favour of the Lord".'

Deciding not to correct the misquote, David smiled.

'That, Archdeacon,' he said, as the image of Prue bobbing down the stairs with her summer dress floating around her returned to his mind, 'is exactly what I intend to do.'

Chapter nine

JACK PRESSED HIMSELF against the stout trunk of an ancient elm and peered through the undergrowth.

'Can you see 'em?' asked Larry Briggs, crouching behind a holly bush a little way away.

'Not yet,' said Jack, screwing up his eyes against the sharp sunlight filtering through the foliage above.

'Well, I hope you can, lad,' said Smudger Smith, from somewhere just over Jack's right shoulder. 'Cos even with my glasses on, I can't see that bloody far.'

It was Saturday and he and a dozen or so men from the Stepney and Wapping Local Defence Volunteer platoon were in Epping Forest near … well, he couldn't tell you exactly where as the last place he'd recognised them passing through was Woodford. After that it had all became a bit of a mystery tour.

Despite the constant reassurance from the plummy BBC announcers and the daily special broadcasts by members of the Government, it was clear that the powers that be were preparing for a German invasion. If anyone doubted it then the King's call today for the whole country to take part in a day of national prayer tomorrow would have dispelled any illusion that this conflict was going to end by negotiations. After all, you don't call on the Almighty for help unless things are looking pretty bleak.

Finally, after a couple of hours bobbing about in the back of an army truck, they had pulled up outside a dilapidated country house that the army had taken over for training purposes.

This was the second day of their intense training regime – the first, a week ago, was mainly square bashing – and today they were tasked with searching out German paratroopers. It was now close to three in the afternoon and after spending all morning being lectured about undercover warfare they were on a mock exercise to capture said paratroopers.

Jack was determined to show the mouthy retired major in charge of the 1st Thames LDV Company, which his platoon was a part of, that although they might not be regular soldiers they too could fight for their country.

"Ow are we s'posed to find them and disarm them if we can't even see the buggers,' asked Larry, his lower lips stuck out in a juvenile sulk. 'I've been kneeling here so long the damp's seeping through my trousers.'

'Damp!' barked Smudger. 'You want to be up to your knees in mud for weeks on end before you start complaining, lad.'

There were a handful of reserved occupation volunteers like Jack in their mid-to- late twenties in their platoon, but the rest were either like Larry, all knees and elbows with a half-broken voice, or like grey-haired Smudger, who'd fought the Germans in the trenches the last time Europe was at war. Also, Jack's Local Defence Volunteer platoon, like all the other platoons stumbling around in Epping Forest's undergrowth, were all wearing their own clothes with just an armband with 'LDV' stamped on it.

This wasn't so bad for Jack because he'd turned up in his heavy-duty railway trousers and a very old jacket, but the office workers in their ranks were looking in horror at the mud splatters on their smart suits.

'Ow,' said Larry, snapping his hand from his pretend weapon. 'That's another blooming splinter.'

They didn't have any guns either and, although they were assured they would arrive within days, dashing around with a roughly shaped plywood gun had its own hazards.

'Splinter,' scoffed Smudger. 'You wait until you've got rats—'

'There they are,' cut in Jack, his eyes fixed on a shape moving through the trees. 'There's two of them hanging about on the top of that mound.'

'Let's go, then,' said Larry, starting to straighten up.

'Get down, you idiot,' hissed Jack. 'If I can see them then they can see you and if that was the real enemy, you'd be dead.'

'I'm not scared,' countered Larry, the sulky lower lip making another appearance.

'Well, you should be,' Jack shot back. 'If they were really German soldiers, they wouldn't be a bunch of civilians like us but crack troops who dealt with resistance with a bullet in the head.' He glanced up for a second. 'Plus, they are higher up than us so we'd have to go uphill to reach them, which would slow us down, giving them the advantage. And if we go charging in straight on, we'll have the sun in our eyes blinding us, too.'

'But we'll look right chumps if we just sit here,' said Smudger.

'We're not going to sit here,' said Jack. He looked around and recognised a chap called Berriman. 'Oi, you lot,' he called in a low whisper to Berriman and another couple of men who were crouching in the vegetation. They looked at him and Jack beckoned them forward.

'What?' asked Berriman.

He was about Jack's age, with a shock of blond hair and baby-blue eyes that made him look like a heavenly cherub. However, the scars across his knuckles told a different story.

'I've got a plan,' whispered Jack. 'What're your names?'

'Cohen,' one of the youths replied. 'Benjamin Cohen.'

Jack looked at his companion. 'Roy Rudd.'

'Right,' said Jack. 'Listen up, boys. This is what we're going to do ...'

Careful not to step on any dry branches lying in his way, Jack tucked himself behind a spreading beech.

'Can you see them?' asked Berriman as he joined Jack.

'Yes,' said Jack, pointing through the scrub. 'Sitting on that fallen tree.'

119

Berriman looked across to the clearing where two regular squaddies, their guns leaned against the trunk, were chatting and smoking.

The tree had obviously been felled in a storm as the roots had been wrenched out of the earth in one piece with the earth still trapped between its dying tendrils and forming a solid mass nine foot high.

'Cocky pair, aren't they?'

Jack grinned. 'They won't be.' He looked at his watch.

'How long?'

'A couple of minutes.' Jack glanced through the spring saplings at the two soldiers again. 'It would be one in the eye for that bloody major of theirs if we can get one of their guns,' said Jack. He looked at his watch. 'Right. I'm going to make my way into position so as soon as I move—'

'Don't you worry about me,' Berriman replied.

Leaving him in their hiding place, Jack placed his wooden gun on the floor and then ducked back into the greenery. Picking carefully each time he put his boot on the forest floor, he skirted around the other side then crept forwards, shielded from the two lounging squaddies' vision by the tree's upended roots.

Holding his breath, Jack listened to one of them question their sergeant major's legitimacy and bemoan the canteen food for a moment then he unbuckled his belt and wound it around his hand.

Suddenly there was a rustling in the trees and a couple of blackbirds soared up, squawking a warning.

'What's that?' asked one of the soldiers.

'Some of the old LDV duffers trying to sneak up on us,' the other replied.

'But probably forgot to bring their glasses so they can't see where they're going,' added the first.

They laughed.

'Still,' said one of them with a heavy sigh, 'we ought to show—'

Jack leapt forward and swinging his belt over the squaddie's head, tightened it around his throat and yanked him backwards across the fallen trunk.

Wearing a startled expression, the other soldier's head popped over the top of the trunk for a split second before it disappeared backwards too.

The soldier, a solid individual, clawed at the belt closing his windpipe as he struggled against Jack's grip, but twisting the belt tighter, Jack rolled his captive on his front and knelt on his back. Finally he released the belt from the soldier's throat and used it to secure his hands behind his back before pulling him to his feet.

By the time he'd frogmarched his prisoner around to the other side of the tree, Berriman was securing the second soldier in the same way.

The two men grinned at each other then Jack let out a two-tone whistle and the other four men walked through the treeline into the clearing.

Jack picked up one of the untouched rifles and shouldered it.

'Right,' said Jack, as Berriman did the same, 'let's take our prisoners to HQ.'

Twenty minutes later, Jack and the rest of his LDV patrol, all with their shoulders held proud, marched the two forlorn regulars into the backyard of the operational headquarters. In the corner, sitting on a low wall and looking somewhat dejected, were several other members of the Stepney and Wapping platoon wearing white armbands that indicated they had been captured or killed during their search for the paratroopers.

With a dozen pairs of regular army eyes on Jack's patrol, he marched them straight ahead to the foldable camp table where a huddle of khaki uniforms were poring over a map.

Major Cuthbertson looked up as they approached.

The senior officer in charge of the afternoon's exercise was a portly gentleman whose stomach was putting a considerable strain on his Great War uniform buttons; he had a grey moustache any walrus would be proud of.

As Jack brought the captured squaddies to a halt in front of him the major's face took on an incredulous expression.

'What the devil?'

Jack snapped a salute.

'Two paratroopers captured and detained,' Jack replied.

'Captured and detained!' blustered Cuthbertson. 'But these are regular soldiers trained for this sort of thing. I don't …'

A slim man who looked a dozen years older than Jack and with the star and crown of a lieutenant colonel on each shoulder stepped out from behind the dumbstruck major.

'Good show, Private …?'

'Quinn, sir,' said Jack, saluting again.

'You and your men are to be commended on your initiative,' said the lieutenant colonel.

'Thank you, sir,' said Jack. 'Just doing our duty.'

'Would you mind telling me how?'

Jack explained how he'd deployed the patrol and ambushed the two squaddies.

'I guessed they wouldn't think much of us LDVs, so we'd be able to get the jump on them and catch them off guard,' Jack explained.

The lieutenant colonel's hard grey eyes studied him thoughtfully for a few moments then he spoke again. 'And what would you have done, Quinn, if they'd not surrendered?'

'Kept twisting the belt until they did, sir,' Jack replied, holding the other man's unwavering stare.

The hint of a smile lifted the corners of the senior officer's lips then he stepped back.

'Carry on, Major,' he said.

The major pulled himself upright and cleared his throat.

'Well, yes, good work, Finn,' said the old soldier. 'Dismissed.'

Jack saluted again then turned to the men behind him. 'Right, lads,' he said, rubbing his hands together. 'I think a celebratory cup of Rosie Lee all round is in order, don't you?'

The men behind him started to fall out and Jack turned towards the two soldiers who his patrol had captured.

He grinned. 'No hard feelings, mate.'

He slapped the nearest one lightly on the upper arm and much to Jack's satisfaction got two resentful glares by way of reply.

Chapter ten

STRAIGHTENING THE Windsor knot at his throat, Jack studied his reflection in the mottled mirror on the right-hand door of his wardrobe.

The suit was good enough, if a little shiny at the elbows and knees, but it's not as if he had occasion to wear one very often.

His bedroom sat over the kitchen, located on the handkerchief-sized landing in the crook of the stairs overlooking the backyard. It was the smallest of the three, with Rosie occupying one of the front-facing bedrooms and her two boys the other. To be honest, it had been a bit of a squeeze getting his few sticks of furniture in, but he wasn't complaining. If Rosie hadn't offered to take him in, he might have ended up on the streets or in the Salvation Army's hostel in Whitechapel with all the other poor homeless souls.

He'd treated himself to a two-bar electric fire, which he'd fixed into the old cast-iron fireplace, which meant he was able to escape with a book in the evenings and give Rosie and Mick a bit of privacy.

Picking up his comb from the dressing table next to the wardrobe, Jack raked it through his hair in a vain attempt to bring it to order. He could have used Brylcreem, but he got enough axle grease on his bonce at work and having soaped it all out at the Municipal Baths yesterday evening, he wasn't inclined to put more on again.

Picking a speck of fluff from his lapel, Jack gave himself a final onceover then opened the door and stepped out.

The sound of Rosie trying to get her two sons and herself ready for church drifted up as he descended the narrow stairs. Pushing open the door he walked into the back room.

With cream-coloured antimacassars on the back of the sofa and chairs, family photos lined up along the mantelshelf and a collection of china safely out of the way of little fingers in the glass cabinet, Rosie and Mick's parlour had a homely feel to it.

Rosie was sitting on the sofa with five-year-old Russell, her youngest son, on her lap. Eight-year-old Michael, a look of utter concentration on his face, was attempting to tie his shoelaces.

Jack's sister looked up at he walked in, and her mouth dropped.

'Where are you going?' she asked, pulling up her son's sock.

'To church with you.'

Her eyes flew open. 'To church! You?'

'Don't I look respectable enough to be seen with?' he asked, glancing at the mirror suspended over the fireplace.

'But I thought you said you'd never darken the door again,' said Rosie.

'Well, there's been a lot of water under the bridge since then.' He raised an eyebrow. 'Besides, the King asked me to.'

'The King!' Rosie snorted as Russell scrambled off her lap. 'I would have thought after spending all day yesterday running around Epping Forest, you'd still be in bed.'

Jack formed his features into a guileless expression. 'I would but I can't go against a royal command, can I?'

Rosie gave him a sceptical look. 'What about breakfast? And aren't you going over to take Rachel out?'

'I'll get myself a bit of bread and dripping while you're getting the boys ready and I'm not picking her up until one thirty so I have bags of time,' he replied. 'When are you leaving?'

'In about ten minutes.'

Leaving her dealing with her two boys, Jack headed towards the kitchen.

Holding her hymnbook in front of her, Prue sang the last verse of 'O God, Our Help in Ages Past', along with the rest of St Winifred's congregation. Well, that wasn't strictly true as alongside the usual hundred or so regular members of the congregation in the pews were at least double that number who had responded to the King's appeal.

Prue was in what was traditionally designated the clergy family's pew at the front, just in front of the pulpit.

Warbling to the right of her was her mother, who, along with her best hat, was wearing the sage-coloured dress and jacket she'd bought in Selfridges for Rob's graduation from Sandhurst last July.

Prue, mindful of the sombre nature of the day, had plumped for her maroon dress with a modest square neckline and bishop sleeves, plus her small black saucer-shaped Tam hat which sat neatly on the back of her head.

On her other side, and looking a little uncomfortable, were the two churchwardens and their wives, who had had to move forward from their usual places behind Prue and her mother to accommodate the swell of people.

In front of them, the men and boys of the choir, in their white surplices and piecrust cassocks, were giving full throttle to the old Isaac Watts anthem.

Sitting opposite in the ornately carved seat, both dressed in their embroidered vestments, were her father and David, who had just conducted the hour-and-a-half-long Sunday service.

A blast from the organ signalled the final note, the singing ceased, and the congregation sat down. Rising from their seats, Prue's father and David took their positions in the centre of the chancel.

Raising his hand, the rector gave the final blessing then as Cecil Granger, their organist, struck up a chorus the choir filed out and lined up before them. Pausing in line until an altar boy had retrieved the cross to carry before them, they then processed out to the vestry.

Sinking to their knees, the congregation sent their supplications and appreciations heavenward, then rose and started to make their way towards the open doors.

'I hope the tea women have set out enough cups for the multitude,' said Marjorie, smoothing her gloves up her forearms.

'I'm sure they have,' said Prue. 'And not everyone will stay for tea.'

'Even so.' Her mother gave her a sweet smile. 'Would you mind slipping through the vestry and popping over to the hall to check?'

As she'd predicted, Nellie Well and Ivy Mulligan, the ladies in charge of the after-service refreshments, had the whole thing well in hand, even unearthing some flowery crockery that clearly hadn't see the light of day since the old queen died. In fact, when Prue had arrived five minutes before, the hall was already filling up with parishioners.

Having greeted a great number of people as they arrived, she was now standing, with a cup of tea in her hands, to the side of the serving hatch next to a stirrup pump and a red fire bucket poised ready for action.

Her mother had taken up position just inside the door a few moments after Prue had arrived to greet the familiar and not so familiar faces as they filed in.

She was now deep in conversation with Mrs and Dr McMasters, who lived in one of the Georgian houses in

Stepney Green. Prue's mother had registered the family with Dr McMasters when they first arrived.

Her father and David, now divested of their colourful vestments, were just in their black cassocks, with cups of tea in their hands and socialising on either side of the stage.

Taking a sip of tea, Prue smiled as she watched a handful of toddlers, dressed smartly for the visit to church, playing a game of their own devising.

'Good morning, Miss Carmichael.'

Turning, Prue opened her mouth to return the greeting only to have the words evaporate off her tongue.

Standing behind her and gazing down at her with those liquid brown eyes of his was Jack Quinn, with Rosie Stapleton beside him.

Unlike every other time she'd seen him, today Jack was dressed in a navy double-breasted suit, a bright white shirt with a light blue tie knotted at his throat. Although she guessed it was off the peg, it couldn't have fitted his tall well-built frame any better had it been hand-sewn in Savile Row. The ascending buttons drew attention to the breadth of his chest, and although the shoulders were only lightly padded, they didn't need to be any firmer because Jack's own were more than sufficient.

She stared up at him for a moment then recovered herself and shifted her attention to the young woman beside him.

'Hello, Rosie. Lovely to see you; and call me Prue, please.'

'Well, Prue, I'd like you to meet my brother Jack,' said Rosie.

'We've already met.' Prue shifted her gaze on to him. 'Haven't we, Jack?'

His smile widened. 'That we have.'

'Several times, in fact,' she continued, holding his gaze. 'The first time was when your brother offered me a lift on his crossbar.'

Shock flashed across Rosie's face.

'After I gallantly helped you when you were almost run down,' Jack added, amusement tugging at the corners of his lips. He offered her his hand. 'It is nice to be formally introduced, Miss Carmichael.'

Prue took his hand, and as his long fingers closed around hers a not unpleasant tingle ran up her arm. Taking her hand back, Prue turned once more to his sister.

'Have you heard from your husband?'

She shook her head. 'It's been over a week but don't they say no news is good news?'

'They do,' said Prue. 'And I shouldn't worry; we've not heard from my brother for a while either.'

'I expect they're both busy giving those bloody Germans what for, if you'll pardon my French,' said Rosie.

Prue laughed. 'Don't worry, I hear much worse than that at the shunting yard. How are those lovely boys of yours?'

'A proper handful, that's for sure.' Rosie's attention shifted to something behind Prue, and she rolled her eyes. 'See what I mean?'

Prue followed her gaze to see Rosie's youngest son having a tug of war with another little boy.

'I'd better go and pull them apart,' she said. 'Scuse me.' And she hurried off.

Thanking his nephew Russell for calling his mother away, Jack turned back to Prue.

She was, of course, not as he'd seen her two days before – wearing her baggy grey overalls with a grease-smudged face – but dressed in a simple yet stylish maroon dress that showed off her hair and eyes to perfection.

Although, to be honest, if she were dressed in a sack, she would still be the most captivating woman he'd ever laid eyes on.

'I haven't seen you here before,' said Prue, looking up at him with those lovely hazel eyes of hers.

'That's because I don't come,' he replied. 'I used to as a boy, I even sang in the choir, but, well … Let's just say, me and God fell out. I only came today because the King asked me to.'

Amusement hovered around her lips.

'Plus, I know Rosie is worried about Mick,' he added.

'I'm sure she is,' said Prue. 'We're worried about my brother, too. For all the headlines in the newspapers shouting about the BEF holding the line against the Germans, I think it's pretty grim across the Channel.' She gave him an uncertain look. 'I know we're not supposed to say as much but …'

'You're right, though, it is pretty grim and going to get

a whole lot grimmer before too long,' he said. 'There's no point pretending otherwise.'

'One of the young women whose husband works on the docks was telling me earlier that there's been a call for some of the Thames' seaworthy boats to assemble at Margate,' she said.

Jack had heard that too.

'And given that each place the British Army was reported to be fighting in was near to France's northern coast, it doesn't take a genius to work out what's really happening on the other side of the Channel.' She heaved a heavy sigh. 'Still, we must hope God heeds our prayers.'

She gave him a plucky little smile then her gaze flitted past him for a second.

'I'm sorry but my mother needs me. Perhaps I'll see you at work some time this week.' She raised an eyebrow. 'Or even sitting in the pews next week?'

He laughed.

Giving him a sideways look, she turned and headed across the hall, Jack's eyes following the fluid motion of her walk all the way.

Having sorted out her quarrelsome son, Rosie returned, dragging the reluctant youngster along with her.

'You didn't tell me you knew the rector's daughter.'

'I only just found out myself, Rosie,' Jack replied, without taking his eyes from Prue. 'I've only seen her at work and when she was nearly run over by an ARP van.'

'And when you asked her to jump on your handlebars,'

Rosie said, giving him the exasperated look he'd put too often on his mother's face.

He grinned.

'Well, you're lucky,' continued his sister as Russell fidgeted beside her, 'because Prue Carmichael doesn't strike me as the sort of person who worries about who you are or where you come from. Not like her old trout of a mother.'

'She's very lovely, too,' said Jack.

Rosie gave him hard look. 'I've seen that look in your eye before, Jack, but don't you go getting no starry-eyed ideas about her.'

Looking down at his sister, Jack gave her an innocent smile 'I thought you said Prue Carmichael wasn't the sort of person who "worries about who you are or where you come from".'

'She isn't,' Rosie replied. 'But she's the rector's daughter, Jack, and a paid-up member of the Church of England, which refuses to give communion to, marry or baptise the children of divorcees, in case you've forgotten.'

Watching Prue crouching down to talk to a small girl about her dolly, Jack mulled over his sister's words. 'I can't argue with what you're saying, Rosie, because you're right but the only thing I can say in reply is you've never seen *this* particular look in my eye before.'

Chapter eleven

WITH THE SUN just skimming the rooftops in front of her, Prue stuck out her left arm and swung her bicycle around the corner into Whitehorse Lane just as a green traffic light was replaced by an amber one.

It was Thursday at about three thirty and, after nine hours of scrubbing, hoovering and polishing, she had collected her three pounds two-shilling wages – four shillings less than the male cleaners earned – and had cycled out of the Stratford's shunting yard half an hour ago.

As shopkeepers reduced the price of their perishable goods at the end of the day, the street that wound its way from Mile End Road to Stepney Green High Street was filled with women, dressed in summer dresses and perky hats, pushing prams and carrying bags.

The ARP were out in force too, with wardens in their navy battledress mingling with fire guards dressed very much like Prue dressed at the yard. As Prue coasted past the Beaumont Arms public house, she was overtaken by an army truck with an old howitzer rattling along behind. Sitting in the back beneath the canvas hood were half a dozen ack-ack squaddies in khaki, who whistled and cat-called to her and a couple of other young women as they shot past.

Prue pedalled on, but instead of turning right into the rectory driveway she continued on until she reached the church hall.

Dismounting, she stowed her bike in the rack, securing it with a chain, took her gas mask and handbag from the basket, and pushed open the door.

Inside the main hall, a dozen rows of chairs were set out with a space down the middle and assorted members of St Winifred's Mothers' Union, in a profuse display of hats, parked upon them.

Presiding over the afternoon's meeting was Prue's mother, flanked by Mrs Hanson, the branch secretary, pen poised to record the proceedings for prosperity. On the other side of Prue's mother was a middle-aged woman in a tweed skirt, plain blouse and toffee-coloured cardigan, with half-lensed spectacles perched on the end of her nose.

Prue's mother looked up as she walked in.

'Prudence, darling,' she said, smiling benevolently over the heads of the women of the parish. 'You're just in time. I have a seat for you here.' She jabbed her finger at the front row. 'This is my youngest daughter, Prudence,' her mother explained to the woman in tweed beside her. 'She does terribly important war work, Mrs Shaw. Don't you, my darling?'

'Just doing my bit,' Prue said, settling herself on to the empty seat at the end of the front row.

Tapping the gavel on its block lightly, Marjorie Carmichael rose to her feet and the room fell silent, but as she opened her mouth to speak someone tapped Prue on the shoulder.

'I expect you could do with this,' whispered Sister Martha, offering her a cup of tea with a Rich Tea biscuit balanced in the saucer.

'Thank you,' Prue replied in the same hushed tone.

The nun tiptoed back to her seat as Prue's mother cleared her throat again.

'Well, we're all suitably replete after our refreshments,' she said as her cool gaze travelled over the audience. 'So I'd like to welcome our guest speaker for this afternoon: Mrs Shaw from the welfare department, who is going to tell us about the marvellous work they do at the council.'

She started clapping and the audience joined her in the applause.

Mrs Shaw stood up and, pushing her spectacles back up her nose, faced the audience.

'Thank you, Mrs Carmichael, for the invitation to speak to St Winifred's Mothers' Union and for your welcoming introduction,' she said. 'I'm afraid I've not so much come to inform you of the work the welfare department is doing but, as I understand the Mothers' Union's central aim is to care for families and children in particular, I've come here to ask you for help. You have no doubt read in the papers about the German advances and our heroic little boats who are still plucking our boys from the beaches of Northern France.'

Murmurs of 'God bless 'em' and 'all blooming heroes' went around the room.

'But they aren't the only ones escaping across the Channel,' Mrs Shaw continued as the noise settled. 'We have refugees arriving from the Continent on every boat with only the clothes they are standing up in and they are overwhelmingly women with children or carrying babies in their arms. At the moment the Government is housing them in Public Assistance accommodation like old workhouses and evacuated schools across the capital, but London County Council has instructed individual boroughs to find billets for them.' She picked up a sheet of paper lying in front of her and peered at it. 'The Government is offering a sliding scale of payment towards the costs of housing.'

Another murmur went around the room.

'Refugees will be expected to keep their accommodation clean and give a hand with general housework and cooking,' Mrs Shaw went on. 'So I'm here this afternoon to ask if any of you can offer accommodation to these poor souls. We would, of course, prefer to keep families together, but if you can only squeeze one person in then please fill in a form.' She held up a wodge of paper. 'And I can start allocating refugees as soon as I get back to the office.'

Her hand holding the forms returned to the table and her shoulders slumped.

'If you could only see their ragged condition when they arrive,' she said, her eyes moist as she looked out across the heads of the women. 'Children with no shoes, who have walked miles and slept on the roadside to reach safety. Hollow-eyed women who haven't eaten for days so they could give their children the little they had with them. And when they come ashore they just sob.' She sounded as if she might do the same herself. 'And the stories they tell, I just …' Taking a handkerchief from her pocket she blew her nose. 'I'm sorry.'

Feeling tears pressing at the back of her eyes too, Prue opened her handbag and, taking out her fountain pen, she stood up.

'We have three unused room that used to be the servants' quarters, haven't we?' she said, looking at her mother as she walked to the table.

Despite a slight flush spreading up her throat, Marjorie gave Prue a sugary smile. 'Well, yes, I suppose we should lead by example, Prudence, but—'

'It might be a bit of a squash, Mrs Shaw, but we could take families at the rectory, so,' Prue pulled a council form towards her and took the top off her pen, 'where do we sign?'

'Thank you, Miss Carmichael,' said Mrs Shaw as she tapped the pile of completed forms into a tidy collection. 'You and your mother being the first to offer accommodation to those poor souls really made the difference.'

'I'm glad we could help,' Prue replied. 'Especially as we have three largish rooms in the loft standing empty.'

It was now almost ten to five and although the afternoon meeting should have finished long before now, there had been so many people filling out the council forms it had run over by forty minutes.

'Well,' Mrs Shaw said, tucking all the papers in her worn leather briefcase and snapping the lock, 'I'll be in touch in the next couple of days.'

Grasping the handle firmly, the welfare officer headed out of the hall, stopping to say farewell to Prue's mother who was instructing the women doing the washing-up about drying the cups properly through the open hatch.

Satisfied that those in the kitchen knew how to use a tea towel, Marjorie made her way over to Prue.

'Well, that went well, don't you think?' Prue said, as her mother reached her.

'Well, certainly not as I anticipated,' her mother replied with a frown. 'I thought she was going to tells us all about the local orphanage, not bully us into taking in people we don't know.' She turned to face Prue. 'I mean, they might not even speak English.'

'They probably won't,' said Prue. 'But it'll give me a chance to use my schoolgirl French.'

'But I don't understand why people are fleeing to England?'

'Well, in case you missed it, Mother,' said Prue, giving her a hard look, 'the Nazis just occupied the whole of Belgium and the Netherlands. And surely if we in the Church can't step forward to help then there's not much hope, is there?'

'No, I suppose not,' conceded her mother. 'Perhaps it wouldn't have been so bad if it had been a couple of young women who could have made themselves useful around the house. But families! Children running around and shouting! How will your father be able to concentrate on writing his weekly sermons?'

'I'm sure Father will manage,' said Prue. 'I also think we should think about setting up something to make them feel welcome.'

Alarm flashed across her mother's face. 'And am I supposed to take that on as well as everything—'

'Take on what?'

Prue and her mother looked around to see Sister Martha, dressed in her usual unassuming grey outfit, standing alongside them.

'Oh,' Marjorie said, looking a little startled. 'I didn't realise you were still here, Sister.'

'Yes, Flo Wallace was getting tearful about her Billy,' said the nun.

Prue's mother looked puzzled.

'Her son,' Sister Martha explained. 'He's her only child. She'd all but given up hope of having any when she was blessed with Billy. I took over her tea towel and let her sister Doris take her home. But you sounded upset about something, Mrs Carmichael.'

'It's just this refugee business piled on top of everything else.'

'Bless their hearts,' said Sister Martha.

'Just so,' Prue's mother replied automatically. 'But

as I was just explaining to Prue, after making sure I maintain a comfortable home for the rector and ensuring the necessary tasks such as church cleaning and the laundering of the altar linen and vestments, I have no time left to organise the sort of welcome committee Prudence is suggesting.'

'Yes, I can see how it might be a problem with everything you do, Mrs Carmichael,' said Sister Martha. 'But perhaps – with your permission, of course – I could take on the task of welcoming the refugees.'

'I suppose that might be all right,' Prue's mother conceded.

'And I'm keen to help too, Sister Martha,' said Prue.

The nun's attention shifted to Prue and her wrinkled face lifted in a smile. 'I know you are, my dear. Perhaps if you're free some time on Monday you can have that cup of tea I promised you and we can put our heads together.'

'I'll come straight from work so I should be with you at about four, if that's not too late,' said Prue.

'Perfect.' Sister Martha's gaze returned to Marjorie. 'You must be very proud of your daughter for being the first to offer to accommodate refugee families. I doubt you would have had half the number come forward if she hadn't stepped up first.'

Marjorie's benevolent vicar-wife expressions slid back across her face.

'Indeed, and trust dearest Prudence to beat me to it just as I was just at the point of standing up myself.' She cast a benevolent glance Prue's way. 'She will make a wonderful vicar's wife one day.'

'If she marries one,' said Sister Martha. 'Now, if you'll excuse me, Mrs Carmichael, time's getting on and I said I'd drop by to see Mrs Conner's new baby this afternoon.'

The elderly nun turned and made her way out of the hall.

'Not marry a clergyman,' snorted Marjorie, watching her go. 'Who else does she think you're likely to marry?'

An image of Jack Quinn, with his collar open, looking down at her with his dark eyes materialised in Prue's mind and lingered there until her mother's voice cut through her thoughts.

'Especially as we have such a handsome and suitable young cleric living under our very roof,' she said, casting a simpering look at Prue.

Chapter twelve

As **THE SIX O'CLOCK** factory hooter signalled the end of the working week, Jack, having showered and changed into a clean shirt, ambled through the main gates with the other stragglers from the early shift. Rosie and the boys were out having tea with a friend, so Jack had decided to wet his whistle before making his way home, leaving his bicycle in the yard rack next to the changing block.

Seeing a couple of khaki-coloured Bedford trucks with a dozen squaddies in the back heading towards him, Jack paused at the kerb with everyone else. As the lorry full of grey-faced, dejected-looking soldiers trundled past, cheers and shouts of 'well done, lads' and 'you've done us proud' went up from the crowd.

As the last belch of diesel smoke and fumes engulfed him, Jack crossed the road and walked into the Railway Tavern. Although the bar was packed with railway workers, dotted among them was the navy of the air raid wardens and auxiliary firemen, the air-force blue of the observation corps and the khaki of the LDV.

After a quick exchange of pleasantries with Ruby behind the bar and ordering a pint of best, Jack made his way to a quiet corner and found himself a seat. Picking up the evening newspaper that someone had left behind, he skimmed the front page, which had the banner headline 'Thousands Home' above an image of smiling squaddies resting in a field.

Jack took a long pull of his pint and flicked to the next page as someone sat down in the chair opposite. He looked up and smiled.

'Hello, Freddie,' he said, folding the paper away. 'I didn't know you were around again.'

'Just got back from my holiday in the country, ain't I?' He winked and slurped the froth off his beer.

Freddie Fouke was a wiry individual with a face full of sharp bones and a mouth that stretched halfway to his ears. His holiday in the country had actually been a three-year spell at His Majesty's pleasure in the Wakefield House of Correction.

Jack had known him since they were snotty-nosed infants playing barefooted in the dirt. However, whereas Jack's mother Ellen had fed and clothed him, Rosie and his older brother Charlie had made sure they attended school each day, Freddie's mother liked the bottle a bit too much. As his father had exited the stage when Freddie was just a babe in arms and his mother was propping up a bar most of the time, Freddie had more or less brought himself up. As Ellen would sooner go hungry herself than see a child starve, Jack often found himself sitting alongside his friend at the supper table.

Having been drawn into the lesser ranks of the Highway Gang after leaving school, the pair had watched each other's backs during the many knife fights with rivals. After the terrible fight with the Cable Street Mob, which left him with a scar on his left forearm, Jack had come to his senses and applied for his apprenticeship at Stratford. In contrast, Freddie had taken up with Jack's brother Charlie, who ran the Shadwell Gang, and along with keeping other gangs from encroaching on their turf, Freddie helped run the gang's protection racket.

However, despite their paths diverging, the two men remained friends.

'They let me out early.' Freddie took another mouthful of beer. 'So how's tricks then, me old son?'

'Not so bad,' said Jack.

'And that pretty little daughter of yours?' asked Freddie.

'Prettier each day but growing up much too fast.'

'What about Alma?'

'Enjoying life as a factory owner's wife more than she ever did as mine,' Jack replied. 'And Rosie and her boys are in the pink, before you ask, but you could have come down our house to see how the family are so, as you must have been lurking around somewhere waiting for me to walk out of the yard gates, I'm guessing you're after something.'

The corners of Freddie's mouth drew back in an extraordinarily wide grin. 'I never could slip one by you, Jack, could I? But it's a bit—'

'If it's dodgy I ain't interested, you know that,' cut in Jack.

'I know, I know,' Freddie replied. 'But it sort of depends on wot you class as dodgy.' His gaze slid around the bar for a second or two, then he sat forward.

'They let me out early for my special skills,' he continued in a softer tone.

Jack gave a low laugh. 'You mean putting people in hospital.'

'The very same.' Freddie shuffled nearer. 'Now I can't fill you in on all the gen, but you, my son, have come to the attention of someone with a bit of muscle and brains in high circles.'

Jack's eyebrows rose. 'Have I?'

'You 'ave, old mate, but if you breathe a word of wot I'm about to say you'll get to see the green fields of Yorkshire on your way to a prison cell.' Freddie took another gulp of beer. 'A couple of months ago some army bugger with scrambled egg on his hat and half a dozen pips on each shoulder put together what you might call a secret little gang made up of ordinary blokes like you and me, blokes who, if the Germans do cross the Channel and overrun us, are willing to do whatever it takes to resist them.'

'Sign me up,' said Jack.

Freddie leaned back in his chair and his grin returned. 'I told the controller you'd say that.'

Jack's mouth pulled into a hard line. 'I've got a half-Jewish daughter, Freddie; why wouldn't I do anything it takes to keep her, and thousands like her, from the Nazi murders?'

'Sweet. The section controller will be in touch in a couple of days, but for now just carry on being your same old law-abiding self.' Freddie finished the last of his beer and placed the glass on the table. 'But remember: not a word.' A grin lifted his lean face. 'Your old mum was right, wasn't she, Jack, when she warned you that one day I'd lead you into trouble.'

Chapter thirteen

'AND WHAT'S YOUR NAME?' asked Prue, crouching down in front of the little boy sitting on his mother's lap. Lowering his head, the child studied his toes in reply.

'I'm sorry but Jan little understand English and he no say words,' his mother said. 'Not since …'

It was just before midday on Saturday the first of June, and a number of women from St Winifred's were still hard at work in the two church hall meeting rooms.

Thankfully, East London's newly formed Local Defence Volunteers wouldn't be using the larger room for their training session until that afternoon, so Prue and Sister Martha had set out chairs in the hall so families who hadn't yet been allocated a billet didn't have to wait in the corridor. It also meant that the women who were offering tea and sandwiches didn't have to push the trolley around with them, a hazard given how many children there were milling around.

Although she might not yet know all their names, one thing Prue had discovered almost immediately was how open-hearted the women of the East End were, which is why she'd been there since eight o'clock that morning.

Sister Martha had set out her Bring and Take children's clothing in the smaller meeting room, which was just as well as Mrs Shaw's phrase 'the clothes they are standing up in' was never so aptly employed.

However, Prue and Sister Martha, who were sitting at one end of the long committee table, were now processing the last few families ready to go with the St Winifred's parishioners who were offering them a home.

'I understand,' said Prue, smiling up at the mother. 'You've all been through so much; I'm not surprised the children are confused and frightened.'

The young woman had given her age as thirty, but with dark circles under her eyes and her downcast expression, she looked almost a decade older. She had two children: the little boy of three on her lap and a girl, Anya, who clung to her mother and watched Prue with wide pale blue eyes.

Casting her gaze past the little group, Prue looked at Mabel Webster, who was trying to elicit a smile from the baby perched on the lap of the mother Sister Martha was currently dealing with.

Sensing Prue's gaze, the motherly middle-aged woman looked around then, waving the infant and his mother goodbye with a wiggle of her fingers, she came over.

'Mrs Webster, this is Mrs de Koning,' said Prue. 'And this is Jan and Anya.'

'Nice to meet you all,' said Mabel, giving them a warm smile. 'I've got a nice little room all ready with a box of toy and some kiddies' books, too.'

'You are kind person, Mrs Veb ...' Tears sprung into the young mother's eyes. 'I'm s ... sorry.'

'That's all right, luv,' Mabel said, putting her arm around the exhausted mother. 'Now let's get you home so you and the kids can settle in proper.'

Taking the toddler in her arms, Mrs de Koning rose to her feet, her daughter glued to her side.

Mabel offered Anya her hand. 'Why don't you hold on to Auntie Mabel?'

The young girl pressed closer to her mother.

'I've made a coconut cake for you and your mum and brother. Would you like some, Anya?' Mabel asked.

The child didn't react for a moment then nodded and shyly took her hand.

'And I believe there's a dolly on your bed that needs a bit of a cuddle, too,' Mabel added. 'So shall we go and see her?'

Anya nodded again.

'Thank you, Miss Carmichael,' said Mrs de Koning as the small party set off.

Prue gathered her paperwork together and slid it into a folder to take back to the rectory. Standing up, she put her hands in the small of her back and arched backwards.

She caught sight of the clock over the door. Twelve-thirty!

'Goodness, the LDV patroon will be arriving soon; I'd better go and set the hall straight,' she said. 'Would you mind finishing off the paperwork?'

'Not at all,' the nun replied. 'This is the last one anyway, so I'll see you in church tomorrow.'

Leaving Sister Martha writing up the council's forms, Prue went through into the hall.

Bless them! The three women who had been doing the refreshments all morning were gone but they'd not only tidied up the kitchen but had also swept the floor. However, two dozen chairs still sat higgledy-piggledy in the centre of the room.

Taking a deep breath, Prue grasped the nearest one to her and carried it across the floor to where the unused chairs were stacked. She repeated the process a couple of times, but as she was about to drop the third chair on top of the stack the main door creaked, and footsteps sounded on the parquet flooring behind her.

Expecting to see Sister Martha, her heart did a little double step when she found Jack Quinn in the doorway looking across at her.

He was dressed in brown cords, white shirt with a navy tie and a pale blue lightweight zip-up jacket with an LDV armband. But all those things Prue noticed just in passing because it was Jack's face that her gaze and mind fixed on.

They stared at each other for a moment then he smiled that quirky smile of his. 'Let me help.'

It had taken Jack's brain a couple of seconds to catch up with his eyes when he pushed open the door and saw

Prue heaving chairs about. Despite him and God not having seen eye to eye for a while, he felt he owed the Almighty a small prayer of thanks, for having spent all week trying, unsuccessfully, to casually run into Prue she was now just twenty feet away from him. Letting the door swing closed behind him, Jack strode over.

'I can manage,' Prue said, stacking the chair on top of the others.

'I'm sure you can,' said Jack, picking up the seat nearest to him. 'But it'll be quicker if I help.'

'True.' Prue picked up another.

'How's it been in the cleaning shed this week?'

'Busy.' She wiped a stray lock of hair from her forehead with the back of her hand. 'No sooner had one line of carriages been taken off than another half a dozen arrived.'

'It's been the same in the workshop; hardly had time to eat,' he said.

'Oh,' she said, pausing for a moment. 'I wondered why I hadn't seen you in the canteen.'

Jack smiled inwardly. 'So how did it go this morning with the refugees?'

'Very well,' she replied. 'But it took a lot longer than I'd thought, which is why the hall hasn't been put back in order. Your Rosie was a godsend, making pots of tea and helping out with the children.' A sad expression clouded her lovely face. 'You should have seen them, poor little mites; what they must have been through doesn't bear thinking about.' Her expression went from sorrowful to angry in the blink of an eye. 'It's unforgivable to make children suffer like that.'

She shot him a self-conscious look. 'Sorry.'

'That's all right. I feel the same myself,' he replied, as an image of Rachel flitted through his mind. 'It's the children we're fighting for, as far as I'm concerned.'

She strolled across to a chair by the serving hatch.

Jack watched her for a moment then he headed for a couple of seats behind the door.

'Has Rosie heard anything about Mick?' asked Prue, as he carried the two stacked chairs.

Jack shook his head. 'But one of the Southern Rail firemen hauling goods through the other day said there were hundreds of trains steaming down to the south coast every day picking up exhausted soldiers, so hopefully ...'

'I'm praying the same for Rob.'

Unease coiled in Jack's chest. 'Rob?'

'My brother.' She forced a smile then turned and headed back down the hall as Jack picked up another chair.

He reached the row of the stacked seats a little ahead of Prue but as she lifted her chair to deposit it on the top it slipped from her hand.

They both grabbed at it. Prue caught it a split second before Jack did so his large work-hardened hand closed over her small soft one.

Prue raised her head and gazed up at him.

Something he couldn't quite read flickered in her eyes for a moment then the door burst open.

'Oi, oi,' shouted Pete Sullivan as he strode into the hall, with Willy Mace and Stan Poplin a pace or two behind. 'Wot youse two after doing then?'

Prue removed her hand and Jack straightened up.

'I'm helping Miss Carmichael, the rector's *daughter*,' he replied, glaring at his fellow LDV recruits as he placed the last chair on the pile, 'tidy up the hall.'

Pete's face lost its cheeky grin.

'Sorry, miss,' he said, whipping his tweed cap off his head. 'No offence.'

'None taken. And as we've just finished, I'll leave you boys to it.' Smiling politely, Prue looked at Jack. 'Thanks for your assistance, Jack.'

'My pleasure.'

She maintained her civil expression for a moment longer then turned and headed towards the door, Jack's eyes following her all the way.

'Cor,' said Willy, as the door swung closed behind her. 'She's a real looker, ain't she?'

'Too right,' agreed Stan. 'Pity she'll probably end up married to some tight-arsed vicar.'

Jack smiled. Perhaps not.

Balancing on the stepladder, David held the poster of a pair of hands holding a gas mask and reminding the populace to carry their gas masks as 'Hitler Will Give No Warning' against the green baize of the church-hall noticeboard.

'Hello, Father,' said a familiar voice beside him.

'Afternoon, Sister Martha,' he mumbled through the two drawing pins held between his lips.

'I didn't know you were on duty today, Father,' she continued, her grey eyes flickering over his navy ARP battledress.

'Just finishing.'

She cocked her head on one side. 'And isn't that the poster you put up last week?'

'Yes, but I'm just repositioning it. Have you finished dealing with the refugees?'

'Yes, I've just sent the last family off with Mrs Farmer,' the elderly nun replied.

David formed his features into a sympathetic expression. 'Poor souls.'

'They are the fortunate ones who escaped,' said Sister Martha. 'And we must pray daily for those now suffering under Nazi occupation.'

'Indeed we must.' He glanced across her head. 'Is Miss Carmichael not with you?' he asked casually as he pressed the drawing pins home.

'No, she's tidying the hall, ready for the LDV platoon to parade,' Sister Martha replied.

He knew that, of course. Because a couple of LDVs had just wandered by, including that swaggering Jack Quinn.

'I expect she'll be along presently,' added the nun. 'Have a nice afternoon.'

'You too,' David replied, climbing down from the ladder. 'And see you tomorrow,' he called after her as she headed for exit.

Waiting until she'd disappeared through the door, David scaled the three steps to the top of the ladder again then reaching up removed the drawing pins and popped them back in his mouth.

The sound of heels echoed down the corridor, so David stretched up and pressed the poster back on to the place he'd removed it from just a moment before.

'Hello, Father David.'

'Oh, Prue,' he said, looking surprised. 'I didn't realise you were still here.'

Wearing a pale-blue flowery summer dress and gazing up at him, Prue looked utterly Heaven sent.

'I've just finished putting the hall back in order.' She frowned. 'Wasn't that poster already on the noticeboard?'

'I'm just repositioning it.' David pressed the drawing pins in place. 'Are you going back to the rectory?'

'Yes, lunch should be ready by now,' she said.

'If you give me a moment, I'll walk back with you,' he said.

Hopping down from the ladder, he stowed it in the caretaker's cupboard next to the kitchen then opened one of the hall's main doors.

Prue walked past him into the bright June sunlight and David fell into step beside her.

'So,' he said, as they set off along Stepney High Street, 'how did it go this morning?'

'Well, for a start we were told to expect ten women and twenty-seven children but when the council coach from the processing centre at Crystal Palace arrived there were

157

a dozen women and thirty-one children. Thankfully …'

As they strolled side by side and Prue ran through the events of the morning, David contented himself with enjoying the shape and form of her lips as she spoke.

'Those poor children,' he said, when she'd finished running through which member of the congregation was housing which family.

'It was seeing the little children that tore at my heart,' she concluded. 'Some mothers hadn't eaten properly for weeks so that they could feed their children.'

'Dreadful,' said David.

'Even carrying their little ones on their backs for miles to get to safety,' she went on. 'And all the while being shot at by enemy aircraft as they tried to escape. I was almost in tears listening to some of their stories.'

'You have such a compassionate Christian heart,' said David, gazing adoringly down at her.

'Well, you'd have to be made of stone not to have been moved by some of the things I heard this morning,' said Prue. 'I'm just glad we have space for three families.'

'As our Lord himself said, "suffer the children to come unto me".' David's eyebrows rose. 'And exactly how many are we to be blessed with at the rectory?'

Stopping to let a woman pushing a pram enter one of the shops, Prue looked skyward for a moment. 'Ten at the moment but Mrs Leitner is expecting.'

'We'll have quite a houseful then,' said David, thankful that as his room was over the old stable he was unlikely to hear them.

'We certainly will,' Prue laughed. 'Mrs Lavender collected them earlier.' A fond smile spread across her face. 'She made a batch of Chelsea buns first thing as a treat for the children, so I expect they'll have already started to find their feet, so to speak, in the rectory.'

'I think you've done a marvellous job galvanising the ladies of the parish into action,' said David.

'Well, needs must when the Devil – or in this case Hitler – drives,' Prue replied as they reached the corner of the High Street opposite the Ben Hur Cinema.

Although she'd already stopped, David took her elbow to prevent her stepping in front of a milkman's horse that was plodding back to the depot with its empty float.

'You know, Prue,' he said as they crossed the road, 'you've been so busy since you arrived at St Winifred's you haven't had a chance to properly look around the church so you might not be aware of the fact that some parts of St Winifred's are a thousand years old. And that it has some unique ecclesiastical treasures.'

'A couple of people have mentioned it,' she said, as the rectory came in sight.

'I wonder if you'd permit me to take you on a guided tour of our dear church's gems? When you have a day off, perhaps,' he added smoothly, as they stopped in front of the rectory.

She hesitated for a second then smiled. 'I'm sure that would be very interesting.'

'Splendid,' he replied. 'Just let me know when you're available and I'll be there.'

Sweeping his arm gallantly before her, Prue walked up the path to the front door with David, already imagining a couple of hours alone with Prue, half a pace behind her.

Stopping beside Prue, David pulled on the doorbell.

There was a pause then the door opened, and they were greeted by a solemn-faced Mrs Lavender.

'Whatever is the matter, Mrs L?' said Prue as she stepped over the threshold. 'Has one of the children had an accident or something?'

Pressing her lips together, the housekeeper shook her head.

At that moment the study door opened and the rector, grey-faced and looking all of his fifty-plus years, walked out.

'Thank goodness you're home, my dear,' he said, hurrying towards her and taking both her hands. 'Robert is missing in action.'

Chapter fourteen

'ARE YOU READY, NICOLAS?' Prue shouted at the boy clutching the rounders bat some ten feet away from her.

With his eyes fixed on the ball she was holding, the ten-year-old tightened his grip and nodded.

It was the first Wednesday in June and Prue was in the rectory garden. It was somewhere close to three o'clock on a gloriously sunny afternoon.

It was also four days since the refugee families had arrived at the rectory. By the time she got home on that Saturday lunchtime, Mrs Lavender had already settled them in their rooms and had sat them around the kitchen table with bowls of parsnip soup in front of them.

As the aim was, wherever possible, not to split up families, and as the servants' rooms in the eves were a fair size, Prue had opted to accommodate three of the families.

Although they must have been totally exhausted by everything they'd been through, the latest residents of the rambling Victoria rectory, along with many of the other refugees dotted around the parish, had attended St Winifred's Sunday service. At the end, one of the mothers had stood up in front of the congregation and given a short speech in broken English thanking everyone for all their kindness. Her words had Prue, and several other sitting in the pews, in tears.

As this was Prue's first day off since then, she'd decided that in order to help the children feel more at home she'd organise a friendly game of rounders while their mothers put their feet up and enjoyed the sunshine.

Although slender Ingrid Haas, with her fine-boned, Nordic colouring of palest blond hair and ice-blue eyes, was the exact opposite of Mrs Leitner's darker colouring and maternal curves, their recent shared experiences had torn away any barriers there might have been; they were now just mothers grateful that their children were safe.

Aiming at the bat, Prue threw a slow, under-arm lob down the pitch.

Nicolas, captain of the red team, swung the bat and the tennis ball shot off towards the back wall, whizzing past the outstretched hands of eleven-year-old Ernie Leitner, who dashed after it.

Seeing a chance to score, Nicolas flung the bat behind him and charged off across the lawn.

'Run,' shouted twelve-year-old Leah Leitner as she picked up the bat.

Nicolas didn't need to be told.

As Eva scrabbled around among the hyacinths, hellebores and daffodils, he ran around the croquet hoops on the improvised field, skidding on to the last one just as

Eva sent the ball spinning towards Nicolas's sister Freda who was manning it.

'*nog een punt voor ons!*' shouted Nicolas.

'Another point,' corrected Freda crossly as he jumped around.

Sticking his thumbs in his ears, Nicolas waggled them at his sister and poked out his tongue.

'Nicolas!' shouted his mother, who was sitting in one of the deckchairs by the French windows alongside Mrs Leitner.

Nicolas stopped his jumping and trotted over to take up his position ready to bat again.

Freda threw the ball back to Prue as Leah stepped forward. Something blue flashed in the corner of her eye and she looked to see the head of the third family they'd given shelter to in the rectory: Johanna.

Fifteen-year-old Johanna had walked thirty miles cross-country to the coast carrying her ten-month-old brother Peter on her back and holding her ten-year-old sister Eva by the hand.

Trudging along bomb-damaged roads and fields carrying her brother, and with very little food, had stripped her natural slenderness down to skin and bone.

Thanks to a combination of a few good nights' sleep and Mrs Lavender's hearty meals, some of the haunted look had gone from her eyes, but two months ago, the lanky teenager had been preparing for her end-of-year exams in a family home in the town she'd known all her short life. Now, when barely out of childhood herself, she was to all intents and purposes an orphan, in a foreign land and responsible for her two siblings. Prue knew that Johanna's troubles wouldn't be fixed by a boisterous game of rounders in a rectory garden.

Wearing one of the flowery dresses that had been donated, Johanna stepped out on to the patio and smiled a greeting to the two women sitting in the deckchairs. Peeking into the old deep-bodied pram under the pink blossoming cherry tree to check on her brother Peter, Johanna tucked her skirts under her and perched on the edge of the garden bench nearby.

Prue straightened up.

'Hey, Johanna, you're just in time.' She beckoned the youngster over. 'Come and take over from me.'

Johanna hesitated for a moment, then stood up walked across the lawn.

'How did this morning go at Toynbee Hall?' asked Prue when she reached her.

'Goot,' Johanna replied. 'The principal, Mr King, says if I pass the English test next veek I can join the evening classes for the school certificate in September.'

'I'm sure you'll pass with flying colours,' said Prue.

'Thank you for minding Peter.'

Prue smiled. 'Any time. He's a poppet. But forget about him now and concentrate on stopping our blue team from getting whitewashed.'

The young girl's fine eyebrows pulled together. 'Vhat is this vitevashed?'

'Being beaten in a game,' Prue replied.

'Ah,' said Johanna, nodding sagely. 'Like "making mincemeat".'

'Exactly.' Smiling, Prue handed her the ball, then strolled over and took the seat the young girl had just vacated.

'It's goot to see da *kinderen* er ... blij ...' Mrs Haas frowned and looked at her companion and said something in rapid Dutch.

'Happy,' Mrs Leitner supplied.

'Ah, it's goot to see da *kinderen* happy,' beamed Mrs Haas, her pale blue eyes bright. 'Sorry, my English no goot.'

Prue smiled. 'That's all right; I understand what you mean.'

According to the short summary of the family she'd been sent from the Crystal Palace reception centre, Ingrid Haas' husband Peter was a journalist who had elected to stay but had squeezed his family on to one of the last westbound trains out of Antwerp before the Germans swept in.

'You must feel,' Prue added, putting her hands on her chest, 'glad to see your children laughing and playing.'

Mrs Haas nodded.

'And how are you, Mrs Leitner?' asked Prue.

'I am very vell, thank you, Miss Carmichael, and thank God.' Stroking her pregnant stomach, Mrs Leitner looked skyward. 'And ze kind midwife who called zis morning said zi little one is also. Which is a blessing.'

It certainly was; sadly, two of the pregnant women in the group allocated to St Winifred's care had miscarried on their journey to the coast.

'And call me Prue,' she added. 'Everyone does.'

'Then you must call me Dora. How is your mother?' she asked, as her son caught a ball mid-flight.

'Bearing up and keeping busy,' Prue replied.

While her father had spent the previous Saturday afternoon in his study in prayer, her mother, devastated by the news of Robert, had been struck down by one of her nausea headaches and taken to her bed. Thankfully, by the early evening when Prue took her some tea and sweet biscuits, she was able to keep them down.

However, as Prue was getting ready to attend the morning service in her mother's stead, Marjorie had appeared at the top of the stairs, in a dress and jacket and her Sunday hat, and informed them that Jesus had told her in a dream that Rob was not dead so they should carry on serving Him at St Winifred's as they had been called to do.

'It is the best vay,' Dora said. 'I am trying to do the same but it's hard when the children keep asking ven is Papa coming.'

'He's a professor, your husband, isn't he?'

Dora nodded. 'Of physics at the University of Amsterdam. Enrich was at a conference in Utrecht when the Nazis occupied the city. I waited for a veek hoping and hoping he vould come back to our apartment, but ven the panzers rolled into Brussels I grabbed ze children and fled. I only hope ...' Tears welled in her eyes and she pressed her lips together for a moment, then a sad smile lifted her lips.

'You know my Enrich was a penniless student when I meet him. My mama was already negotiating with the *shadchanit* – the matchmaker – for a suitable young man but I knew as soon as I set eyes on my Enrich he vas the one for me. Vat do you call it?' she said softly. 'Love at first sight.'

Before she could stop it, the image of Jack Quinn standing next to his abandoned bike and looking at her materialised in Prue's mind.

Dora pulled her handkerchief from her sleeve and dabbed her eyes. Reaching across, Prue placed her hand on Dora's arm but given the tales of beatings and murders the refugees told, platitudes were worse than useless, so she said nothing. How could she? With the Germans sitting all along the north French coast the very same fate might befall England if, or more likely when, Hitler decided to send his army across the Channel.

Dora marshalled herself and forced a smile. 'But he vould be happy that we are here safe and vell in your lovely house with ze children playing in the garden.'

A cry to the side of her heralded Peter waking from his afternoon nap.

'I'll get him, Johanna,' Prue called, rising to her feet.

Red-faced and groggy with sleep, Peter was sitting up by the time Prue had taken the few short steps to his pram. Unclipping his harness, she lifted him up and gave him a quick peck on the cheek.

'Hello, young man,' she said, settling him on her hip. 'You've had a nice long nap, haven't you?'

'No actually,' said a voice behind her. 'I've been polishing Sunday's sermon.'

Prue turned to see David, with his clerical shirtsleeves turned back, standing in the French windows.

Prue smiled. 'Look, Peter,' she said, rocking back and forth. 'It's Uncle David.'

Although he wasn't sure he liked being referred to as Uncle instead of Father, David smiled. He could do no other really, as the sight of Prue holding a baby, much as the Virgin Mary must have held Jesus, only confirmed to him that Prue was truly sent from above. After all, one of the requirements of a clergyman's wife is that they organise the children's activities in the parish.

'Say hello,' Prue added, waggling the baby's hand at him.

Feeling more than a little foolish, David wriggled his fingers back. The sticky-looking baby stared at him, unblinking.

David had been grappling with a knotty passage in that week's lectionary reading, a particularly bloody passage in the first book of Kings. This endeavour would have been onerous enough but was made twice as difficult by the screaming and shouting coming from the garden. It seemed that while his little studio flat over the old stables prevented him hearing the thump of juvenile feet on the stairs, his small study overlooking the garden wasn't proof against noise from outside.

The baby regarded him in what could only be described as mild hostility for a moment then wriggled in Prue's

arms. She lowered him to the floor, and he crawled off across the grass.

'Isn't he a darling?' said Prue, a doting look in her eyes, as they followed the child across the lawn.

'Yes, a real pet,' David replied. 'I thought perhaps as Mrs Lavender is at the Afternoon Club on Wednesday and your mother isn't at home, you might be making tea today.'

Prue glanced at her watch. 'Goodness. I was having so much fun I've forgotten the time. I'll put the kettle on right away. Tea, ladies?'

The two women sitting in the deckchairs nodded a Prue headed back into the house.

The thin-faced blonde one started to rise. 'I help, mis

David raised his hand and an unctuous expression across his face. 'That's quite all right, Mrs ...'

'Haas,' said her darker companion.

'Mrs Haas,' he continued, raising his voice would understand. 'You stay here.' He jabbed hi downwards. 'And enjoy God's bountiful sun help Miss Carmichael.' He mimed pouring te

David hurried into the house after Prue an lighting the gas under the kettle.

'How can I help?' he asked.

'If you wouldn't mind getting the dresser. Lay them on the second shelf.' dark wood tea trolley. 'I'll fetch the gla for the children from the pantry.'

He did as she asked.

'Your desire to help those less fortunate than yourself shows that you have the tenderest of hearts,' he said, sliding the crockery on to the middle of the trolley's three shelves.

'Thank you, Father David,' she said, making her way back to the pantry.

'I hope you don't mind me asking, but is there any news yet regarding your brother's whereabouts?' he asked, as she placed six lime-green Bakelite beakers on the shelf next to the cups and saucers.

Straightening up, Prue shook her head.

A peal of children's laughter came through the window and Prue gave a sad smile. 'Hearing the terrible accounts of what's going on just across the Channel from Dora, Ingrid and Johanna makes me remember why Rob and the Expeditionary Force were sent to France in the first place. It's just …'

Tears welled up in her eyes.

Reaching out, he placed his hand on her arm. 'You know, if there's anything – anything at all – I can do, Prue, you just have to ask.'

'I know,' she replied, looking up at him through watery eyes. 'It's just …'

A fat tear escaped and rolled down her cheek. She snatched her handkerchief from her sleeve and pressed it against her lower lids.

Seizing the moment, David stepped forward and was about to slip his arm around her to comfort her when the doorbell rang in the hall.

'Oh, it's probably Mr Granger. He rang earlier wanting to discuss the hymns for Sunday,' said Prue, shoving her handkerchief back where it came from. 'You keep an eye on the kettle and I'll answer it.'

Mentally damning St Winifred's crusty organist to hell, David forced a smile. 'Of course.'

Prue hurried out.

David heard the front door open, followed by lots of excited female chatter, before Prue appeared in the doorway, her arm linked through another young woman's and grinning from ear to ear.

'David,' she said, her eyes filled with happiness as she looked across at him. 'This is my big sister Felicity.'

Placing her hand lightly on the pile of fish-paste sandwiches she'd just made, Prue sliced diagonally through them, then, sliding the knife beneath the four triangles, she lifted them on to the large oval plate alongside the others.

'Goodness, that's enough to feed a village cricket team?'

Prue turned and found her sister lolling in the kitchen doorway.

Felicity had shed the jacket of the rather fetching dark green suit she'd arrived in, revealing the cream-coloured blouse beneath, and swapped her high heels for soft house shoes. Like her sister, she had an abundance of dark auburn hair, but where Prue's still sat in waves

171

on her shoulders, Felicity's curls were trimmed in a bob which highlighted her sharp cheekbones.

While Prue's turned-up nose, soft, rounded cheeks and oval face favoured her father's side of the family, Felicity's countenance was pure old D'Apremont from her mother's. In fact, with her aristocratic looks and bearing – she stood a couple of inches taller than Prue – had she been presented at court as many of their mother's forebears were, Felicity would have had the other debutantes grinding their teeth in envy.

However, according to their mother, Fliss had betrayed her class and noble ancestors by embracing socialism. She had compounded this heinous sin, as their mother described it, by taking a job as a junior reporter on the *Workers' Clarion* in Bloomsbury, thereby leaving the bosom of her family to live like a gypsy – their mother's words again – in Pimlico.

Prue smiled at her sister. 'You should be able to squeeze a cuppa out of the pot I made for Father David.'

'Where is your dishy curate?' Fliss asked, taking off the knitted tea cosy and pouring herself a tea.

'In the study sorting out Sunday's hymns with St Winnie's organist,' Prue replied. 'And he's not my anything.'

As she cut several more slices of bread, Prue told her sister about the rectory's newest house guests.

'Poor souls,' said Fliss, when she'd finished. 'Having to flee your home like that.'

'Have you unpacked?'

Felicity shook her head. 'I've only got a few things and thought I could do that later.'

'Is the room okay? Because you can swap it if you like,' said Prue, scraping butter over another slice of bread.

'No, it's just fine,' Fliss replied. 'And it's not as though I'm living here. What's going in this round?'

'Jam for the children,' said Prue, pointing the butter knife at the pot of raspberry jam on the table.

'What about Mother and Father?' Fliss asked as she picked up a buttered slice from the pile Prue was making.

'Dad's visiting someone in the parish and Mother went out about an hour ago muttering something about finding a florist.'

'She'll be lucky,' said Fliss.

'That's what I told her,' said Prue. 'Every rose bed and tulip field in the country's been ploughed up and replanted with wheat and potatoes. We'll have to dig up the rectory flower beds and lawn before too long so we can do our bit for Dig for Victory.'

'Have you mentioned that to Mother yet?' asked Fliss, pulling out a chair and sitting down.

'Not yet,' Prue replied. 'By the way, she was wondering why you hadn't come as soon as you heard about Rob.'

'I would have but as so many passenger trains have been given over to the military for moving troops, I couldn't get a ticket until today. And then it was so crowded, there wasn't a seat to be had for love nor money. Thankfully, a couple of people got off at Rugby, so I managed to squeeze into a corner seat.'

'It was a pity you were in Birmingham, or you could have just jumped on the tube,' said Prue.

'Yes, I was covering a Women's Co-op northern AGM,' her sister replied. 'How is Mother?'

Prue sighed. 'Convinced Rob is still alive and battling on. Dad just keeps himself busy with Church things.'

'Things are still up in the air since Dunkirk,' said Felicity. 'I guess Mother's already been in touch with Jeremy?'

'As soon as we got the news,' Prue replied. 'He said the Red Cross are sending lists of the dead and those taken captive everyday but, thank God, so far Rob's name hasn't appeared.'

Having spread fish paste on her sandwiches, Prue returned to the stove and relit the gas under the oversized kettle.

'Have you heard from Lydia?' asked Fliss.

'She telephoned to say she would come and see us but ...' Prue shrugged. 'You know Lydia.'

Felicity rolled her eyes. 'Honestly, the woman is as shallow as a saucer. What does Rob see in her?'

'You mean other than the fact that she's the House of Beaumont's top model?' asked Prue. 'I honestly can't think.'

They laughed as Prue spooned tea into the large brown teapot. 'And well done again on getting promoted to senior editor.'

'Sales of the *Workers' Clarion* have shot through the roof since the war started.' Fliss's cherry-red lips lifted in a cynical smile. 'Also, the two main feature writers were called up last month.'

'Even so, it was well deserved,' said Prue. 'That piece you did about "A Workers' War" was brilliant.'

Her sister raised a well-shaped eyebrow. 'You read it!'

'Of course.'

Felicity looked puzzled. 'I thought Mother refused to have the *Clarion* in the house.'

Prue winked. 'I sneak it in.'

'See, I knew you were a rebel,' said Fliss. 'And well done you, too, for rolling your sleeves up and getting a job on the railways. I can see you now, standing on the footplate and driving the eight-thirty into Liverpool Street.'

'I'm afraid I'm not doing anything so exciting,' Prue replied. 'They only employ women as cleaners, so I doubt I'll ever be driving a train.'

'Such a bourgeois attitude,' scoffed Felicity. 'When he was in Russia, Giles saw dozens of women driving trains.'

'How is Giles?' asked Prue, as the kettle whistled.

'Oh, you know, all fire and anger for the cause, as ever, but with a big, soft heart beneath it all,' Felicity replied. 'He would have come, you know, even though he's an atheist ... but he couldn't as he's got some very important meeting somewhere tonight. He offered to put it off, of course, but I wouldn't hear of it. He even drove me to the station to make sure I got the train.'

'Is it with the Ministry of Work Production?' Prue asked, pouring the scalding water into the pot.

Felicity frowned again. 'I'm not sure. Actually, he was a bit vague about it, to be honest. But he's had his best suit pressed and he was planning to get a haircut and shave at the barbers, so perhaps it was with Beaverbrook himself. Anyway, he said he'll be counting the days until I get back.' A fond look stole over her sister's face. 'He's such a darling.'

Stirring tea leaves around in the pot, Prue didn't comment.

'Well, I think we've enough sandwiches to feed an army,' said Felicity, placing the last set of jam sandwiches on the plate. 'So perhaps we should take them out to the ravenous hordes in the garden.'

'We certainly have,' Prue replied. 'You start loading up.' She indicated the three-tier mahogany tea trolley. 'I'll fetch the cake from the pantry?'

She started across the room towards the larder door but halfway across she turned. 'I've missed you, big sister.'

Placing a plate of sandwiches on the top of the trolley, Fliss looked up and smiled. 'I've missed you, too.'

Chapter fifteen

'AND AS YOU'LL no doubt notice, Miss Carmichael, although the tracery of St Mary's window looks sixteenth century,' said David, pointing to the top of the stained-glass window, 'they were, in fact, carved just a hundred years ago.'

'Fascinating,' said Prue, holding back a yawn.

It was just after three in the afternoon on the Saturday after her sister had arrived. She was in St Winifred's church and had been for a full hour and, as they hadn't yet finished admiring the architecture of the south wall, she was likely to be there for some time still.

Unfortunately, when David had pressed her over lunch about showing her the historical wonders of St Winifred's, her mother had jumped in and said that Prue was free that afternoon. As there was no way she could argue otherwise without being rude, Prue had agreed.

Not that the church wasn't absolutely lovely, because it was. With the bright June sunlight streaming through the gummed tape criss-crossing the church's stained-glass windows to dapple the interior in colour, it was beautiful. The interior was much as you'd find in any village church. A wide central aisle flanked by solid rows of pews led to the chancel, which had a Lady chapel on one side and the vestry and an enormous multi-piped organ on the other. The north transept housed various memorials to the parish's past rich and famous. The south had plaques commemorating long-gone battles stretching back two hundred years, with ragged and threadbare regimental flags hanging above.

With over a thousand years of history, St Winifred's had many features that stretched back into antiquity. These included the Saxon rude stone behind the altar, the twelve medieval Stations of the Cross depicting in gory detail the Lord's last journey through Jerusalem and the thirteenth-century lepers' hole halfway up the wall of the sanctuary. Even the worn tiles underfoot bore testimony to the thousands of worshipers who had knelt in the sacred place to offer up their prayers and supplications to the Almighty.

However, throughout the church there were also items that those who'd worshiped down the ages wouldn't have recognised, such as two shiny new stirrup pumps flanking the porch door, a white tin chest with a cross and 'First Aid' painted on it in red and a white canvas stretcher rolled up and half hidden behind the Mothers' Union banner in the Lady chapel.

'And this,' said David, taking Prue's elbow and guiding her along, 'is the memorial to Sir Simon d'Arbour and Lady Catherine.'

Prue dutifully looked at the stone-carved couple wearing Tudor ruffs and lying recumbent on their marriage bed, with their dozen or so children depicted around the side.

'Who's this, then?'

Prue straightened up and turned to see Felicity standing behind them.

Mercifully, seeing Prue being boxed into a corner over the ham salad and pickles at lunch, Fliss had expressed her desire to explore the mother church of Stepney, thereby extending Father David's invitation to include her, too.

Like Prue, she was wearing a cotton summer dress, but whereas Prue had a broach in the shape of a butterfly pinned to her chest, Fliss sported a round badge with hands clasped together across the world and 'Workers of the World; Socialist Party' around the white border.

'I was wondering where you'd wandered off to,' said Prue.

'I was talking to Olive and Elsie over there.' She indicated two women wearing wraparound aprons and scarf turbans who were on their knees scrubbing the tiles in the Lady chapel. Her attention returned to the memorial.

'Sir Simon d'Arbour and his wife,' David repeated, moving slightly and pressing his upper arm against Prue's. 'His father was granted the church and lands during the Reformation and built a country house hereabouts, long since gone I'm afraid. He was a favourite at Queen Elizabeth's court.'

Under the pretence of reading the plaque beneath the tomb, Prue stepped forward.

'Munificently, he granted the Church a parcel of land which provides funds for St Winifred's to this day,' said David as she studied the Elizabethan lettering.

'While the rest of the wealth he'd amassed by the sweat of his servants and tenants was passed down to his family,' said Felicity.

A frown ruffled David's high forehead. 'I think you're being a trifle unfair to Lord d'Arbour. By all accounts he was a most generous lord of the manor, Miss Carmichael.'

Felicity's finely plucked eyebrows drew together. 'Was he?'

'Indeed,' David replied smoothly. 'Providing an ox for the village to roast on May Day and endowing the parish school.'

'Huh,' said Fliss. 'Let them eat cake!'

David looked puzzled.

'Marie Antoinette,' explained Prue. 'She was supposed to have said, "Let them eat cake" when she heard that the people of Paris were rioting because there was no bread.'

'I'm afraid history was never my subject.' A benevolent expression lifted David's thin face and his attention shifted to Prue's sister. 'I think, Miss Carmichael, perhaps we would do well to keep in mind St Paul's teachings in his many Epistles that one's place in life is ordained by the Almighty and not for us to question.'

Felicity's gaze flickered over the ancient memorial then back to David, but as she opened her mouth to speak Prue cut in.

'And this must be St Winifred's chapel,' she said, heading for the arched opening between the fifth and sixth Stations of the Cross.

'Indeed it is,' said David, as he and Felicity caught up with Prue.

He led them into the square chapel containing a small altar and a stained-glass image of the haloed St Winifred, dressed in a nun's habit and kneeling in prayer with a spring of water behind her.

'I see you're admiring St Winifred's window, Miss Carmichael,' he said, as Prue gazed up at the colourful depiction of the church's patron saint.

'I am,' said Prue. 'Even with the air raid tape stuck on, it's so vibrant.'

'Sadly,' said David, his expression mirroring the word, 'you're not seeing St Winfred's chapel at its best as the saint's statue has been moved down to the crypt for safekeeping.'

'Well, can't we go and see her?' asked Felicity.

'I suppose so,' said David. 'But the stairs down are medieval and a bit worn in places so—'

'Don't worry.' Felicity slipped her arm through her sister's. 'Prue and I have tackled a few uneven stairs in our time, so lead on.'

'As you wish,' he replied. 'I'll just go and get the key.'

With the hem of his cassock gliding over the tiles, David hurried towards the vestry door.

'He's keen on you,' said Felicity to her sister.

'Don't be ridiculous,' Prue replied.

'Believe me, he is.' Felicity smiled conspiratorially. 'Didn't you see the look he gave me when I asked to tag along this afternoon?'

The vestry door opened and David reappeared. 'This way, ladies,' he said, just a trace of pomposity curling his top lip.

Arm in arm, Prue and Felicity made their way to the small door and after a bit of jiggling of a large, ornate key, David opened it, switched on the light, and they descended.

'Thankfully,' he said, flicking another switch as they finally reached the bottom of the stairs, 'when the church was renovated fifty years ago the builders sensibly fitted electricity.'

Prue blinked into the dimly lit space beneath the church then looked around. The ancient vault was at least three-quarters of the size of the building above, perhaps a bit more, and lined on either side were coffin-sized niches, which thankfully no longer provided resting places for long-dead parishioners but rather for broken church furniture and dusty cardboard boxes.

A couple of antique pews had been pushed against the far wall alongside a dozen or so metal folding chairs, presumably to make space for the crypt's new occupants: half a dozen four-foot-high plaster statues.

Leading them past the Virgin Mary with the star-spangled halo and St Peter holding a set of keys, David stopped in front of a statue of a nun wearing the same brown habit as the nun in the chapel window.

'And here,' he said, with a blissful sigh, 'is our dear St Winifred.'

Prue dutifully regarded the statue of a young woman tucked in next to one of St Thomas à Becket, complete with a sword cleaving his skull. The artist who had modelled the church's patron saint had given her a very young face and she stood with her hands clasped together and eyes downcast in an attitude of prayer.

'I understand that the church used to have one of the bones from her forearm,' added David, 'housed in a gold-encrusted *reliquiae* behind the high altar but, alas, it was lost during Cromwell's reign as Lord Protector three hundred years ago.'

'Forgive me for asking,' said Prue as she studied the saint's tranquil features, 'but wasn't St Winifred a Welsh saint?'

'Indeed she was,' said David, 'but legend has it that on her pilgrimage to Rome some time during the eighth century she stopped in Ossulstone, as Stepney was called then.'

'And why has she got a red band around her throat?' asked Felicity.

'She was beheaded by a suitor she spurned because of her desire to become a nun. Miraculously her head attached to her body.'

Felicity laughed. 'I bet Anne Boleyn wished she'd known that trick.'

She wandered across the cluttered space to study an enormous gilt-framed oil painting of Abraham sacrificing Isaac. David's mouth pulled into a hard line.

'It's a beautiful statue,' said Prue.

His attention shifted back to her, and his urbane smile returned. 'It is, which is why on the very day Chamberlain made his radio broadcast telling us we were at war, our blessed saint was moved.'

'And where does that lead to?' she asked, indicating a rusty iron gate through which could be seen a dark, unlit passageway.

'It's a tunnel to St Winifred's twelfth-century charnel house,' he replied. 'The stone structure by the north wall of the graveyard. You must have seen it.'

'I thought that was a tomb,' said Prue.

'I'm not surprised; it's sunk a few feet into the ground over the years.' David smiled. 'Don't worry, there are no bones in there now. They were cleared out long ago.'

Prue's eyebrows rose. 'I'm surprised it's still standing.'

'Well, those medieval builders constructed St Winifred's and the charnel house to stand the test of time.' His gaze drifted upwards to the stone ceiling ten foot above their heads. 'The vault is some twenty feet below ground and has survived for almost a millennium, so I doubt even a Nazi bomb could destroy anything within it.'

Prue glanced around.

'You're probably right.' Looking up at David in the muted light of the forty-watt light bulbs dangling above, she smiled. 'But I do wonder if with Hitler poised to march across Europe there might be a better use for St Winifred's crypt than storing statues.'

'What a ridiculous idea,' said Prue's mother, staring at her as though she'd announced she intended to run naked around the parish boundary.

Prue gave her mother a cool look across the worn hearth rug. 'I don't see why?'

'Because it is …' Looking heavenward, Marjorie heaved a dramatic sigh then lifted the cup she was holding to her lips.

It was just after four and the three Carmichael women were sitting in the back parlour having afternoon tea. Thankfully, they seemed to have declared a truce around all things political, thereby, for once, saving Prue the task of refereeing.

A century ago, the room they were sitting in would have been the lady of the house's parlour. Here, with the dew on the rectory lawn sparkling through the French windows, she would have discussed the day's menus with the cook and instructed the head parlourmaid on her duties. Now, however, with a pair of saggy chintz sofas facing each other on either side of the fire and a solid teak wireless in the corner, it served as a family lounge, leaving the larger front parlour for more formal occasions.

David had finished showing them the wonders of St Winifred's about half an hour before and the sisters had left him talking to the verger about the Sunday service and strolled arm in arm back to the vicarage.

They arrived to find their mother having a somewhat animated conversation with Mrs Lavender about the meat for a forthcoming visit from the bishop and his wife.

Naturally, the thought that she would only have a plate of vegetables to set before the rector's ecclesiastical superior had frayed her mother's temper, however Prue's suggestion that they set up a bomb shelter in St Winifred's crypt had tipped it over the edge.

'But the crypt is perfect,' persisted Prue. 'And it would comfortably shelter a hundred and fifty people, probably a few more at a push. I can't see why you would object.'

'Need I remind you that St Winifred's is a holy place?' said Marjorie.

'I don't see what—'

'It's bad enough,' interrupted her mother, 'that a place dedicated to the worship of God is cluttered with first-aid boxes and buckets of sand, without having people traipsing through there every night in their pyjamas.'

'Well, I think it's a jolly good idea,' said Felicity, green eyes twinkling as she grinned at Prue from the other end of the sofa.

'Well, you would, wouldn't you?' snapped their mother. 'You'd think anything was a good idea if it upset me. And besides, it's quite unnecessary because along with building dozens of those awful-looking brick street shelters, the council has leased a number of basements under warehouses in readiness. Apparently, there's one that can house thousands of people somewhere.'

'Well, I still think it's a jolly good idea,' chipped in Felicity. 'Giles says that Hit—'

'Giles!' interrupted her mother. 'Is this the same Giles

who deems it proper to sit down to dinner without a tie? The same Giles who believes that a group of unshaven Bolsheviks should be running the country? And the same Giles who wants to do away with God's ordained order and make us all peasants?'

Felicity frowned. 'You know that Giles doesn't believe in God, Mother.'

'Doesn't believe in God,' scoffed Prue's mother. 'What sane person doesn't believe in God?'

'Well, he doesn't,' Felicity replied, tucking an escaped strand of auburn hair behind her ear. 'And just because he doesn't conform to an outdated bourgeois dress code and is fighting for workers' right doesn't mean—'

'You know something, Felicity,' Marjorie said as she crashed her cup back on to its saucer, 'between your crackpot philosophies and Prue's ill-thought-through plans, I seem to be developing one of my heads.' She stood up. 'Perhaps, before I add dyspepsia, too, I'll go and have a little lie-down.'

Giving them both a look-what-you've-done glare, she glided out and shut the door firmly after her.

Prue's hazel eyes and her sister's green ones stared after their mother for a moment then they turned to face each other.

Straightening her skirt, Felicity leaned across and picked up the teapot and pulled a sour face. 'Shall I be mother?'

Prue laughed. 'Please.'

The door opened and Mrs Lavender shuffled in.

'The lad from the newsagent's has just shoved the early-evening edition through the door,' she said, offering Prue a copy of the *Evening News*.

Taking it from the housekeeper she skimmed the front page then turned it so her sister could see blazoned across the top, 'Sirens go off in Seven Counties'.

Prue raised an eyebrow. 'Looks like I'll have to find some way of setting up St Winifred's air raid shelter after all.'

Chapter sixteen

Handing over tuppence, Jack took the ice cream from the pimply youth in the refreshment booth and stepped out of the queue.

'There you are, Rachel,' he said, handing it to his daughter as he joined her.

'Thanks, Daddy.'

Closing her eyes, she gave it a lavish lick and Jack smiled.

It was just after three in the afternoon on a very hot and sunny Saturday afternoon in June.

Even the grey waters of the Thames to the right of him sparkled and the rough stone of the Tower of London's curtain wall glowed in the mellow sunlight bathing the whole country. To be honest, with cobbled pathways running between the ancient fortress and the capital's river awash with Londoners like himself enjoying the balmy weather, it was easy to forget that thousands of German troops were sitting just across the English Channel.

Well, that was if you didn't raise your eyes to the dozens of cigar-shaped barrage balloons glistening and tugging at their moorings, the ack-ack guns set up between the ancient cannon and the embankment wall and the navy and khaki uniforms surrounding them.

He'd been at his ex-wife's house on the dot of eight to ensure he didn't miss a precious minute of his day with Rachel. They'd been back at Rosie's by nine, where Jack had a mid-morning cuppa while his daughter slurped on a lemonade, received a dozen hugs from her aunt and played a game of ludo. They headed off after that, but as he and Rachel reached the bottom of Stepney High Street and turned into Whitehorse Lane, the large Victorian house on the corner drew his attention.

Although Jack chided himself for acting like a moonstruck youth rather than a man of twenty-eight with a daughter, as he walked past St Winifred's Rectory he couldn't but hope that Prue Carmichael might appear. Of course she didn't, so they caught a number twenty-five bus to Aldgate for Saturday-morning story time in Whitechapel library.

With Rachel excitedly recapping on a story about a young girl of her own age who was sent to live with a grandfather up a Swiss mountain, they popped into Woolworth's so his daughter could spend some of her pocket money. Two hair slides and a sherbet dip later, they jumped on a number fifteen bus this time, getting off at Watney Street Market for their midday meal. Jack would have preferred to squeeze into the pie and mash shop between Maypole Dairy and the Congregational Church, but its distinct liqueur-lavished dish was made using water from stewed eels, and the pies weren't kosher either. Although Alma herself wasn't exactly frum, he didn't want to give her an excuse for making his visits difficult so they'd found a spare table across the road in Pollock & Sons Fish and chip shop instead.

'So how has school been this week?' he asked now as he led her towards an empty bench facing the river.

'Not so bad,' she replied, shifting from side to side to get comfortable on the wooden struts. 'I got nineteen out of twenty for my maths test.'

Jack looked suitably impressed.

'I see you've got my brains,' he said, as Rachel scooped a large dollop off the top of the cone with her tongue.

'Mummy says I take after her,' she replied through a mouthful of ice cream.

'You certainly have her looks.'

She did. One day his daughter would be a stunner and break dozens of hearts, including his when he walked her down the aisle.

'What have you been doing, Daddy?' she asked, twisting the cone to slurp up a drip.

'Oh, the same old thing,' he replied, stretching his arm out along the back of the seat. 'Fixing old engines and getting filthy in the process.'

She rolled her eyes. 'Not work, but going out like Mummy and Uncle Manny. They're always going out to have a drink with people or to a fancy club up the West End.'

I'm sure they are, thought Jack. After all, Mummy and Uncle Manny don't do a twelve-hour shift grappling with clapped-out machinery.

'To be honest, Rachel, after a day at work I'm happy just to get home and listen to the wireless with a cup of tea in my hand. Although I do have the odd pint at the pub from time to time. Why are you sad?' he asked, seeing her crestfallen expression.

Making a play of nibbling the cone, she shrugged.

'Come on, sweetheart, tell me,' he coaxed.

Popping the last inch of cone in her mouth, she looked up. 'Mummy's happy now she's got Uncle Manny. But you haven't got anyone, Daddy.'

'I've got Auntie Rosie,' he replied.

'I don't mean Auntie Rosie. I mean a special lady friend who you'll be happy with too,' his daughter replied, looking up at him with his mother's soft brown eyes.

An image of Prue Carmichael, as she'd stood in the canteen queue the day before, loomed into Jack's mind, wearing a shapeless grey boiler suit as if it were a couture gown and looking even more beautiful than when he'd last seen her. But that was not a surprise really, because he thought exactly the same every time he laid eyes on her.

However, Rosie was right. His ex-wife was his biggest hurdle. Well, not his ex-wife as such but the fact that he had an ex-wife at all. Logic told him to put Prue from his mind, but the problem was his heart was increasingly not listening.

'And you won't unless you go out and meet people,' continued his daughter, bringing him back to the here and now.

'I meet lots of people at work,' Jack replied. 'Hundreds, in fact. Every day.'

Rachel rolled her eyes again and let out an exasperated sigh. 'That's just men, Daddy.'

'No, there are ladies working in the yard at Stratford now,' said Jack, as the image of Prue floated back into his mind.

Rachel's eyes flew open. 'Are there?'

'Yes, about two dozen of them,' he replied, happy to move the conversation on to a safer subject.

'Are they driving trains or engineers like you?'

Jack shook his head. 'They aren't allowed.'

Rachel frowned. 'Why?'

'Because some people think that women aren't strong enough or clever enough to do the same things as men,' he replied.

'Do you think that, Daddy?'

'I certainly don't.' Jack laughed. 'I'd say women have the edge on us poor blokes in the brains department. In fact, I'd go so far as to say that a woman can do or be anything a man can.'

A self-satisfied look of superiority that only a seven-year-old could muster spread across his daughter's face. 'That's true. And when I grow up I'm going to be a train engineer just like you.'

'Well then, you need to keep working hard at school, especially at arithmetic,' said Jack.

'Just like you did.'

Jack looked puzzled. 'Like me?'

'Yes,' continued Rachel. 'Mummy always says you were the top of the class so I'm going to work hard like you did.'

The memory of his erratic attendance and belligerent attitude in the classroom flitted through Jack's mind.

'Well, sweetheart, I'm not sure I'm the best example of a hardworking—'

'Don't listen to him, Rachel,' a voice said, behind him. 'Your dad was one of the best pupils Redcoat School's ever had.'

Jack turned in the seat to find a familiar figure dressed in a light grey habit with a shoulder-length coif standing behind them.

He stood up and smiled. 'Sister Martha.'

To be honest, when he'd told Prue he and God had fallen out it wasn't strictly true. It wasn't so much that he and the Almighty didn't see eye to eye as that some of those sitting in St Winifred's ancient pews had been less than welcoming, but he was happy to make an exception in Sister Martha's case.

She had been an almost daily visitor to their home for months, comforting his mother after his father had his brain knocked out of his head when a ship's block and tackle broke loose. He might have no time for the so-called faithful of St Winifred's, but God had chosen a worthy ambassador in Sister Martha.

'Hello, Jack.' The elderly nun's piercing grey eyes shifted on to his daughter. 'And your lovely daughter, too.'

Rachel jumped down from the bench. 'Hello, Sister Martha.'

'Hello, Rachel,' the nun replied. 'My, haven't you grown since I last saw you?'

'I'm four foot three and a half now,' the young girl replied, standing tall.

Sister Martha looked astonished. 'Goodness, at this rate you'll soon be as tall as me.'

'Are you just out for a stroll?' asked Jack.

'I am. It seemed a sin not to be out enjoying God's lovely sunshine,' the nun replied. 'Do you mind if I join you?'

'Course not,' Jack replied.

He and Rachel resumed their places on the bench, shifting up a little to make space for the newcomer.

'So how are you, Rachel?' Sister Martha asked.

With the sun warming his face and his arm stretched along the back of the bench, Jack listened to his daughter recount an argument with her best friend, a trip to Uncle Manny's elderly mother that was 'dead boring' and the fact that Auntie Rosie was teaching her to knit plus a retelling of the story she'd heard that morning in the library.

'Well, you and I have something in common, Rachel,' said the nun when his daughter had finished, 'because I loved the story of Heidi when I was your age, too.'

His daughter smiled, then her gaze shifted past him to a crowd of youngsters climbing on the antiquated cannons aimed at the river. 'Daddy, can I go and play on the cannons?'

'You can as long as you stay where I can see you,' he said.

Hopping off the bench, she dashed towards the group of potential playmates.

'And don't scuff your shoes or your mother will have something to say about it,' he called after her.

'Such a lovely girl,' said Sister Martha, as they watched Rachel dash across the cobbles.

Love swelled Jack's chest. 'I think so. But then perhaps I'm biased.'

'And I wish I had her young legs, too,' added the nun, watching Rachel clamber up on to a Victorian cannon.

Jack raised an eyebrow. 'Oh, I don't know, Sister, I reckon you could still catch some nipper if they gave you a bit of cheek.'

She looked around. 'You mean like you used to?'

They laughed.

'It was good to see you in church a few weeks ago, Jack.'

'Oh, well,' he replied, forcing himself to hold her sharp eyes, 'I thought I ought to, for Rosie and the boys' sake.'

'What about you, Jack?'

'Me? I'm overworked and underpaid like everyone else but,' he replied, 'I suppose I should be grateful I'm not being ordered around by Nazis.'

She smiled and studied the barges being dragged along behind a stumpy tugboat for a moment, then her gaze returned to him.

'I hear you saw Freddie Fouke recently,' said the elderly nun.

'As it happens, I did run into old Freddie,' he replied casually, remembering their cryptic conversation. 'Had a chat about what we were up to and our nearest and dearest, you know.'

'Anything else?'

'School days mostly. Just this and that,' he added, resisting the urge to shift under her razor-sharp gaze.

A granite-like expression he'd never seen before stole over her wrinkled face.

'Well, when you chatted about this and that, he told you that the section intelligence officer would be in touch, didn't he?' she said.

Jack's brain span for a moment, then he looked the elderly nun in the eye. 'Yes, he did.'

The corners of her thin lips lifted slightly. 'And now they have.'

Jack stared at her in astonishment.

'You'll get a letter in a day or two and do exactly what it says.' She stood up. 'And I don't know why you're looking so surprised.' Her smile widened. 'Didn't you say yourself that a woman can do and be anything a man can?'

Chapter seventeen

'SORRY, PRUE, I soon out vay,' said Ingrid Haas, her forehead creased with worry lines as she stirred the enamel pot on the stove.

'You're not in my way at all,' said Prue, rinsing the vegetable knife she'd used to scrape the parsnips. 'They aren't back from church yet. And it's an hour until dinner's ready.'

It was just before noon on the second Sunday in June and although it was stupid of her really to expect to see Jack in church that morning, Prue couldn't help feeling a twinge of disappointment when she spotted just Rosie in the pews. However, he wasn't there, so having had a quick chat with a couple of people and knocking back a cup of tea, she'd decided to return to the rectory to make sure all was prepared as they were hosting special visitors for Sunday dinner: Bishop George Poppleton and his wife Agnes.

'That smells delicious,' she added as the meaty aroma wafted up. 'What is it?'

'Hazenpeper,' Ingrid replied. 'It's er ... *konijn* ... how you say?' Putting her hands by her ears, she waggled them.

'Rabbit?' said Prue.

Ingrid nodded.

'Well, it smells scrummy,' Prue replied. 'And I'm sure those little rascals,' she indicated the Haas children sitting at the kitchen table, 'will agree.'

Spooning out some of the stew, Ingrid took a sip then said something in Dutch to her son, who shot out of the room and clattered up the stairs. A few moments later he reappeared with Eva hot on his heels followed by Johanna carrying baby Peter in her arms.

The young girl gave Prue a quick smile before settling her brother into the highchair.

Leaving Ingrid draining red cabbage over the sink, Prue went through to the dining room.

Taking the embroidered linen placemats from the sideboard, she positioned them around the table then opened the canteen of cutlery.

The pips heralding the twelve o'clock news sounded from the lounge across the hallway, so Prue hurried through. Tucking the skirt of her pale blue flowery dress beneath her, she sat on an armchair next to the wireless cabinet to listen.

The announcer repeated the sobering news they'd all awakened to this morning – that the Germans had bombed Paris – followed by the equally gloomy news that Russian troops were massing on Lithuania's border. He finished off with an upbeat announcement that the navy were now evacuating hundreds of British troops from the ports in Western France.

Praying that her brother Rob would be among them, Prue stood up and switched off the wireless just as the signature tune of *Music Makers' Half-hour* blared out.

By the time she returned to the kitchen those sitting around the table were finishing off their meal.

Refilling the kettle, Prue had just put it on the back burner and relit the gas when she heard the front door open and the sound of her parents' voices in the hall.

The gas rings were now free, so Prue retrieved the pots of peeled vegetables she'd already prepared from the kitchen dresser, but as she placed them on the stove her mother, wearing a navy shot-silk dress and jacket with a sapphire and diamond broach pinned on the collar, walked in.

There was a scrape of chairs as the children around the table got down and carried their plates to the sink. Depositing them in the basin they dashed for the door, shouting and bumping into Prue and her mother.

'So sorry,' said Johanna, giving them both a contrite look as she gathered the dirty crockery on the table together.

Prue laughed. 'Children will be children. And leave the washing-up, Ingrid,' she continued. 'We can do it together afterwards.'

Ingrid cleared the table, put the plates and bowls to soak in soapy water as Johanna lifted her brother out of the highchair and both women left the kitchen.

Giving them a quick hello and her practised rector's wife smile as they passed, Prue's mother joined her daughter at the cooker.

'Where's Mrs Lentil and her offspring?' she asked, as footsteps thumped up the stairs.

'She's visiting a distant relative of her husband in Stoke Newington,' Prue replied. 'And it's Mrs Leitner.'

'Well, I suppose we should be grateful for small mercies,' her mother went on. 'I dread to think how we would cope with someone else cooking another set of meals in the kitchen.'

In the past week the new arrivals had settled into the usual domestic routine of any family, with the children being packed off to school after breakfast and the women busying themselves in the house and everyone, much to Mrs Lavender's delight, pitching in with the chores. Cooking was another matter.

As they were cooking more or less the same things, Ingrid and Johanna had sensibly decided to combine their rations for their main meals.

However, Mrs Leitner cooked her family's kosher meals separately. This meant that there were now three cooked meals each day in the rectory.

'I thought you'd all got lost,' Prue said, throwing salt into the saucepanful of chopped carrots. 'I was expecting you back half an hour ago.'

'Well, it's not for want of trying, I can tell you,' said Marjorie, raising her voice above the thunder of small feet overhead. 'Not only did everyone want to say their bit to the bishop, but Mrs Poppleton seemed to be on a mission to speak to each woman and pull a funny face at every infant in the hall.'

'I thought she was very friendly and thankfully not like Dad's previous bishop's other half who could barely bring herself to acknowledge you,' Prue replied.

'True,' her mother acknowledged. 'Mrs Chalfont was a bit of a cold fish, but at least she had some appreciation of her husband's position, not like …' She jerked her head towards the door. 'I only just managed to talk her out of clearing away the empty cups and helping with the washing-up. And when I saw her changing that baby's nappy on her lap! Well, honestly.'

'Well, I think the card she sent when they heard Rob was missing was very kind,' said Prue.

'It was,' conceded her mother.

Prue's lips lifted at the corner. 'Where are the bishop and his wife now?'

'Having a sherry with your father, Father David and Felicity, in the lounge,' her mother replied. 'Who I thought, by the way, was coming back to help you but instead stayed and spent the whole time after the service trying to turn the congregation into communists by handing out pamphlets about fair pay and workers' rights, whatever they are.'

Prue smiled. 'Fliss is a socialist not a communist.'

'Well, as Russia is hand in glove with Hitler, I'm pleased to hear it,' Marjorie replied. 'Naturally, like any rational, intelligent person I always vote Conservative, but to my mind politics has no place in the Church of England and vice versa.'

Wrapping a tea towel around her hands, Prue opened the oven door, pulling out the tray of sizzling roast potatoes.

'I'm not sure if the meat will stretch to all of us,' said her mother, eyeing the joint cooking on the shelf. 'I don't want the bishop or his wife to think we're penny-pinching.'

'I'm sure there will be plenty,' said Prue. 'And I think Mrs Lavender did very well to get such a large leg of lamb, especially as every time I walk by the butcher's all I see in the window is offal.' She set the tray of potatoes down on the table.

'Aren't they a little pale?' Marjorie said, peering at them.

'That's why I'm basting them, Mother,' Prue replied through tight lips, as she ladled hot fat over the knobbly chunks.

Small feet thumped down the stairs again and there was a shriek of utter delight from the hallway.

'Hello, sweethearts,' warbled a woman's voice. 'What're your names then?'

Marjorie heaved the heaviest of sighs. 'How long until dinner?'

'Once I put the potatoes back in the oven, I'll get the veg going, so about twenty minutes,' said Prue, carrying the tray of potatoes back to the oven. 'Why don't you go and hold the fort with Dad and the Poppletons.'

'Well, it seems to me, Father Hugh,' said George Poppleton, slicing his spoon through the roly-poly and custard before him, 'that you and your good lady wife have slid into your places at old St Winnie's without causing the slightest ripple.'

'We feel as if we've been here for ever,' said Marjorie, smiling genially down the table at the bishop. 'And it's such a beautiful church, isn't it, Hugh?'

It was just after two thirty and Prue along with her sister, parents, David and the bishop and his wife were sitting around the extended table in the rectory's dining room.

The spiritual head of the dockland hamlets of Stepney, Poplar, Wapping and Shadwell was a lean individual with a light-bulb-shaped head and seemed to have only two facial expressions at his disposal: utter delight or grave concern.

In contrast, Agnes Poppleton was pleasantly plump, with a jolly round face, and despite Prue's mother trying to guide her towards the more well-to-do members of the congregation during the tea that was served in the hall after the morning service, she kept darting off to pull funny faces at a niggling baby or crouch down to ask any little girl about the doll they were clutching.

Also, whereas Marjorie had pulled out her special navy dress and jacket for the important visitors, the bishop's wife appeared to have dragged the first thing that came to hand from her wardrobe so was wearing a Royal Stewart tartan skirt teamed up with a colourful floral blouse.

Naturally as the honoured guest, the bishop sat at the top of the table with his wife to his right with Prue's mother on his left; Prue's father sat at the opposite end.

Originally, Prue had placed herself and her sister alongside their mother, but on returning from church her mother had switched the seating. This meant that Prue now sat between the bishop's wife and David, whose knees had an annoying habit of straying across and touching hers.

The conversation over lunch started quite well, with Prue's mother telling her guests about the parish they'd come from and them expressing their sympathy again at the news about Rob, followed by an assurance that he was in their prayers daily.

However, there had been moments to enliven the conversation thanks mainly to Agnes Poppleton. After she'd listened intently to Prue telling her about her new job on the railways, and much to Prue's mother's consternation, the bishop's wife listened equally attentively to Felicity explaining how the Socialist Party of Great Britain intended to dismantle capitalism.

However, soon after that it had reverted to what Prue had come to expect when sitting down with clergymen: the Church. Now, after an hour of discussing liturgy, vestments and the various incumbents in the diocese, Prue was repeatedly struggling to suppress a yawn.

'Indeed, it is,' agreed Prue's father. 'St Winifred's is such a spiritual place.'

'You can feel the presence of the Almighty as soon as you walk in,' added her mother. 'You know, Bishop, I sometimes feel I should take St Luke at his word when he writes in Acts, "Put off thy shoes from thy feet: for the place where thou standest is holy ground."' Hugh's attention shifted to David, who was sitting to his right. 'Of course, much of the credit for me finding my feet so quickly must go to Father David, who has spared no effort these past weeks to set out the lay of the land, so to speak.'

The bishop nodded sagely. 'I would have been surprised to hear otherwise as the archdeacon speaks very highly of Father David.'

David lowered his head meekly.

'And your intersessions today were excellent, too,' the bishop added.

'I'm glad you approve, sir,' Father David replied. 'I'm very conscious that I am praying to the Almighty on behalf of the congregation so I did question whether I should include mention of what's happening in Paris and Europe.'

'I think it would have been odd if you hadn't,' Prue replied. 'After all, it's splashed across every Sunday newspaper and was the main topic on everyone's lips this morning.'

'That may be true,' said David, turning to look at her. 'But I'm never sure about concentrating too much on worldly cares when perhaps I should be focusing St Winifred's flock on the heavenly realm.'

'That's all well and good,' Prue replied, shifting around in her chair, 'but to my way of thinking there's no point ignoring what's going on across the Channel, especially as it's very likely to affect all of us directly before too long. To do otherwise would be just plain—'

She felt a stabbing pain in her ankle and looked around to find her mother glaring across the cruet set at her.

Pressing her lips together Prue turned her attention back to her pudding.

'Actually,' said Agnes, putting her spoon in her empty bowl and half turning towards Prue, 'I agree with you, Miss Carmichael. I'm sure God's not ignoring all the terrible things going on in the world at the moment so neither should we.' She cast her eyes around the table. 'And while, with its long history and beautiful fittings, St Winifred's is a very lovely place, without people it is just a pile of stones and mortar.'

Stretching out his bony hand, the bishop closed it over his wife's plump one.

'As always, my dear, you take us to the heart of the matter,' said George Poppleton, giving her an adoring look.

'The Church is the people who we are called to serve,' continued Mrs Poppleton. 'Their burdens and concerns should be our burdens and concerns.'

'So true, Mrs Poppleton, so true,' said Marjorie, putting on her devout face.

'And after the Nazis bombed Paris one of the things everyone is worried about is whether we'll soon be in for the same,' said Prue.

'I fear we may be,' said Mrs Poppleton.

'Which is why,' said Prue, feeling her mother's eyes boring into her, 'I proposed that we set up an air raid shelter in St Winifred's crypt.'

Agnes's pale blue eyes lit up with joy. 'What a splendid idea. Don't you think so, George?'

'I do, my dear, I do,' the bishop chuckled.

'It's a good idea, of course, in principle,' said Marjorie, a flush inching its way up her throat. 'But—'

'I don't see why not,' chipped in Felicity. 'It's only full of junk.'

Prue felt David bristle. 'I don't think the statues of our beloved Winifred and the other saints we have placed in the crypt for safekeeping can be described as junk, Miss Carmichael.'

'But they can be boxed up with other church valuables and slotted into the empty burial shelves,' said Prue, smiling from David to her mother and back again.

'I suppose that would be possible,' conceded David. 'But where are people to sit or even sleep if they are caught there for some time? What about the amenities and refreshments?'

'Just you leave that to me,' said Prue.

'What talented daughters you have raised, Mrs Carmichael,' said the bishop's wife, beaming at Marjorie. 'One who is working towards eliminating poverty and another who is seeking to protect her fellow man from Nazi bombs. You must be so proud of them.'

Prue's mother forced a smile. 'Very.'

Mrs Poppleton grabbed Prue's hand and squeezed. 'And you, my dear, must promise me that you will telephone the bishop's lodge as soon as you've set up St Winifred's shelter so I can visit.'

Prue smiled at the motherly woman sitting next to her. 'Perhaps you'd like to officially open it.'

'That would be wonderful,' trilled the bishop's wife. 'Perhaps we could get the local newspaper along. It might encourage other churches in the diocese with crypts to do the same.'

Smiling, Prue rose to her feet and cast her gaze around the table. 'Now, as everybody seems to have finished their dessert, who's for coffee?'

'So thanks to Mrs Poppleton St Winifred's going to have its very own air raid shelter after all,' said Felicity, folding a six-panelled skirt and placing it in her weekend case.

'It is,' Prue replied, looking across her toes at her sister. 'Although goodness knows how.'

After enjoying their after-dinner coffee, the bishop and his wife departed back to their residence five miles away in East Ham just after three. As the front door closed, their mother, stating that the strain of entertaining the Poppletons had given her one of her heads, had gone upstairs to lie down.

She'd surfaced at four thirty, just as Prue and Felicity were setting out the tea things. Having polished off a plateful of ham sandwiches and several slices of Battenberg cake, Hugh and David headed off for the six-thirty Evensong service, with Prue, her mother and sister following a short time later. That was some three and a half hours ago, and Prue was now sitting with her legs stretched before her up and her feet crossed at the ankles on her sister's bed.

'I'm sure there'll be tons of leaflets and things about it at the Town Hall,' Fliss replied, pulling out a pair of knickers from the top drawer of the dressing table and tucking them down the side of the case.

'I'm sure there will be,' Prue replied. 'And I hope we'll see more of you now we're living nearer.'

Felicity shrugged. 'I might if I got a warmer welcome from you-know-who.'

'That's just Mother,' said Prue. 'Ignore her. That's what I do when she gets on her high horse.'

'I wish I could, Prue, but she makes it quite clear she abhors everything I believe in,' her sister replied.

'Even so, at the moment with Rob ...' Prue gave her sister a meaningful look.

Felicity heaved a sigh. 'You're right, of course, but Mother won't be able to stick her head in the sand for ever. There's a revolution coming whether she likes it or not. As Giles said in his speech to the Socialist Women's Guild last week, "This time the workers of this land won't wait for their oppressors to construct a land fit for heroes; this time we'll build it ourselves."'

'Have you spoken to him?' Prue asked.

'Giles, you mean?'

Prue nodded.

'Briefly when I telephoned on Friday, but he couldn't really talk as he was hurrying off to a meeting,' Fliss replied. 'He said he'd call back but it must have slipped his mind.' Laying her underslip on top of her skirt, Felicity laughed. 'Honestly, that man would forget his head if it wasn't screwed on. Anyway, never mind me and my love life, what about you?'

As it did annoyingly often, an image of Jack Quinn flashed through Prue's mind.

'I haven't got a love life,' she said, shoving the image aside.

'You will have if Mother has anything to say about it,' Felicity replied. 'She's got David in her sights for you.'

'David!'

'Of course,' laughed Felicity. 'After all, his family are well-to-do and he's a man of the cloth, so everything Mother always looked for in a prospective husband for you.'

'For us,' corrected Prue.

'Not me,' Felicity huffed. 'As far as marriage goes, she's written me off. No, you're the one she's determined to have follow in her footsteps. She's picked a very willing target in David Harmsworth: he's only got eyes for you, that's for sure.'

'I'm sure that's not true,' Prue replied.

'I'm sure it is. You should have seen his face when I invited myself on his tour of the church,' said Felicity. 'It was as plain as the nose on your face he was planning to spend the afternoon soft-talking you between the pews.' Clasping her hands together over her heart, she formed her features into a doe-eyed expression. 'Oh, Prudence.' She fluttered her eyelashes. 'Although we will have but a draughty vicarage, my paltry stipend and a lifetime of parishioners knocking on our door day and night, do say you'll be mine.'

'You're just terrible, Fliss,' Prue laughed.

'At least he's not bad looking, not like Reverend de Pole—'

'Or Roly-poly, as he was known to his friends, and with good reason. Roland was the most tedious and self-opinionated man God ever put on the earth,' said Prue, all but shuddering at the thought of the last curate her mother had tried to fix her up with.

'But his family did own some ancient pile in the wilds of Westmoreland, and he was the nephew of the Bishop of Flintshire,' added Felicity, 'so Mother naturally thought otherwise. Anyway, I don't blame you for not setting your cap at David: he is a bit of a wet fish.'

'Fliss!'

'Well, he is,' her sister protested. 'Handshake like a lettuce leaf. He's got a weak chin, too. Take a bit of advice, sis: go for a man with a firm chin.'

The image of Jack Quinn swam back into Prue's mind, reminding her of his granite-like jawline.

'Prue!'

'Sorry. My mind wandered off for a moment,' she replied, dragging her brain back to the here and now.

Felicity raised an eyebrow. 'On to whom?'

'No one,' Prue shot back.

'You've always been a terrible liar.'

Prue bit her bottom lip for a moment then spoke again. 'There's just this chap ...'

'Do tell.'

'There's nothing to tell,' said Prue.

'He's good-looking?'

'Yes,' Prue replied, as the image of Jack in her head smiled.

'Is he someone at church?'

Prue shook her head. 'At work, but it's nothing. '

Fliss raised an arched eyebrow. 'Are you sure? Because the look on your face a moment ago said otherwise.'

Prue forced a light laugh. 'Honestly, Fliss, it's nothing, and even if it weren't, it couldn't go anywhere because ...'

'Because he's a train driver or a fireman, and Mother wouldn't approve?' said Fliss.

'Jack's an engineer, actually,' Prue replied. 'And no, she wouldn't.'

'Does it worry you?' asked Fliss. 'That he's an ordinary working man who hasn't got a Home Counties accent or a bunch of wealthy inbred relatives.'

Prue frowned and shook her head. 'Of course not. In fact, I admire him for working hard to become one of the top locomotive engineers at Stratford.'

'Then forget about what Mother thinks,' said Fliss, rolling up a pair of stockings. 'You're over the age of consent so you can do what you like with anyone you choose. And if you choose engineer Jack, well, don't worry about what anyone else thinks because your happiness is more important. And,' a mischievous twinkle crept into her sister's eyes, 'I bet he's got a stronger grip than Father Lettuce-leaf downstairs.'

The memory of Jack's hands and the muscles of his bare forearm as he effortlessly carried one of the railway's oversized spanners loomed into Prue's mind.

'Yes,' she agreed, an odd sensation bubbling through her, 'I'm sure he has.'

Chapter eighteen

SPRINGING FORWARD, Jack swung his left arm around the man's throat and threw him to the ground. His victim braced himself against the soft turf but spreading the man's legs wide with one of his, Jack pinned him to the ground. Grasping his chin, he yanked his target's head to the side and shoved his newly issued fighting knife upwards to connect the razor-sharp point with the soft area just below the left ear.

'Break!'

Jack released Jim Faraday, a stocky farmer from Kent, and they both stood up.

'Well done,' bellowed Sergeant McPherson, a sharp-faced, battle-scarred Glaswegian standing to the side of the half a dozen men in a mismatch of working clothes and, like Jack, scruffy boiler suits.

It was just after four on the third Saturday afternoon in June and Jack was in the grounds of Coleshill House, a grand Georgian Palladian-style house. The square country pile, which Jack estimated would have taken up one side of Arbour Terrace, was situated almost a hundred miles from East London.

There were dozens of tall casement window arranged

on three floors plus the smaller dormer windows of the servants' quarters in the roof, a brick-built chimney at each end and another two centrally. Leading up to the double-doored entrance were a set of steps almost as wide as Rosie's house.

However, whereas when they were planned in the last century the spreading pastures had been designed to have a herd of deer grazing on them with the odd peacock for colour, now the grasslands were dotted with camouflage-painted First World War tanks, sandbag-enclosed machinegun posts and other military paraphernalia.

Instead of marble statues lining the paths where the house's occupants and their guests would have wandered, there were army trucks and cars in various states of destruction. The box-hedge maze now had sections dug out as it formed part of the woodland assault course and the pond had camouflaged rubber dinghies floating on it.

Jack was with two dozen men like himself who had received a set of instructions and a travel pass in the post that week. As with everything else connected to these auxiliary units – as he'd discovered they were called when he arrived – the instructions were layered in secrecy. Having dashed out of work as soon as the five o'clock end-of-day hooter sounded, he'd headed across London to Waterloo. Jumping on a train to Southampton, Jack disembarked at Coleshill and arrived in the village high street just as the shopkeepers were starting to put up their shutters for the night. As instructed, he'd given his name to the grumpy postmistress at the town's post office then loitered by the post box with a farm labourer from Eastbourne and a car mechanic from Rye for twenty minutes before an army lorry appeared to collect them. Having been shown to his billet – a rickety-looking bunk in the stable block – he'd been given a hot meal.

After they were fed and watered, he and his fellow resistance fighters or, if they fell into Nazi hands, terrorists, were given an introduction to the course. Hailing from the city, Jack was a bit of an oddity as nearly every other man who'd signed up for this covert army were either farm hands, cattle men or estate workers from rural areas adjacent to the south or east coast. However, it seemed that the beaches exposed at low tide along the banks of the Thames at East London were judged to be as vulnerable as those in Kent, Sussex and East Anglia, and so it was decided to initiate an auxiliary unit to cover Wapping, Shadwell and Stepney.

During the initial briefing Jack was surprised to discover that, rather than just a foot soldier in the organisation, he had been designated patrol leader and, in addition to Freddie, he would be expected to recruit two or three more members – preferably men with talents such as housebreaking, forgery and lock-picking. An easy task given that, like Freddie, half those he rubbed elbows with while enjoying a pint had such skills.

The next day they had been marched into the ballroom; however, what had once been the glittering social centre was now given over to more deadly pursuits, and over the course of the next two hours Jack was instructed on the correct use and maintenance of both the Enfield rifle and the American Winchester. He was also issued with the hunting knife he'd just held at Jim's throat, a garrotte made of piano wire with wooden handles, a knuckleduster and, last but not least, a 0.32 Colt pistol, ammunition and holster, which had the New York Police Department stamped into the leather.

'Remember, chaps, hesitation will kill you as surely as a bullet, so as soon as you gain the upper hand strike.' McPherson looked at his watch. 'Right, that'll do for now, so you've just got enough time to clean up before grub's up in the mess at six, but I want you back in the library for eight. The guvnor'll be here this evening to speak to you all. So don't be late. Dismissed.'

'Right, men!' bellowed McPherson two hours later as Jack scooped up the last of his spotted dick and custard.

The rumble of male voices faded.

'If you'd like to grab yourself a tea or coffee and a slice of fruit cake and follow me to the library …'

It was now just before eight and Jack was sitting at one of the long refectory tables in a dining room which you could have stored an E4 0-6-2T Class engine in. Around him were the couple of dozen men, who, having scrubbed themselves clean in the stable-block showers, were wearing their LDV or ARP uniforms with the odd civilian suit dotted among them.

A few moments later, cup in hand and with a wedge of cake in the saucer, Jack wandered past the blind-eyed marble statues that stood in niches up the staircase and the oil paintings of the house's past residents and through a solid oak door at the far end.

As you'd expect from its name, the room they were assembling in was lined with bookshelves but it also had a couple of dozen straight-backed chairs arranged in neat rows in front of a small mahogany desk and two easels. One of them had the same map of Southern England and East Anglia that Major Dunmore had shown them at the first meeting of the Local Defence Volunteers.

As the room settled down, Jack found himself a few rows back from the front and sat down next to a ruddy-faced man with a crop of straw-coloured hair about his own age. McPherson took his place next to the map and a hush fell over the assembled men.

Behind Jack the door opened again, and McPherson snapped to attention, bringing the men in the room to their feet. Two men marched to the front of the room: a middle-aged man with dark hair wearing a colonel's uniform followed by an unassuming-looking major of middling height and the obligatory officer moustache.

Every man in the room saluted, but the colonel waved them away.

'We don't do all that saluting malarkey here,' he said, his somewhat deep-set eyes surveying the room. 'The name's Gubbins. And they tell me I'm in charge of this bally place. Isn't that right, McPherson?'

'Aye, so I've been told,' replied the sergeant, in broad Glaswegian.

'Gentlemen, welcome, welcome,' he said, a smile lifting the officer's salt-and-pepper scrubbing-brush moustache. 'I must apologise for not being here when you arrived yesterday evening, but I've been wrestling with the damn pen-pushers in Whitehall to get you chaps more equipment. Before I go any further, I'd like to introduce you to Major Beyts,' Gubbins continued. 'He will be in charge of your training from now on and believe me, you'll be in good hands because ...'

Over the next twenty minutes Jack discovered that although this was the first training weekend for the men for the newly formed auxiliary units, they weren't the first group of freedom fighters that Gubbins and Beyts had been involved with.

Both men had cut their teeth fighting the IRA in the Irish War of Independence, gaining valuable experience by being at the sharp end of guerrilla tactics. When, after Munich, it was clear that it was a case of when not if Hitler would move against Britain and its allies, both men had worked with the Secret intelligence Service's D section and despite opposition from some in Government, pulled together so-called observation units who had been trained in sabotage. When war was declared, both men were posted to Norway where they organised the units of ordinary men and women to disrupt and kill the invaders.

Now back in England, Gubbins and Beyts were

determined to use their considerable skills in terrorism on their native soil.

'... so you see,' said Gubbins, as he rounded off his little speech, 'you men have been selected to be patrol leaders of small tight-knit groups of men to fight what many would consider to be a dirty, no-holds-barred war, a war that breaks all the recognised conventions, but one that is necessary unless we just want to stand on Dover cliffs and wave a white flag at Hitler and his thugs sitting across the water from us.'

A grumble of angry voices went around the room.

'But there isn't much time,' continued the commander. 'Now, while we are preparing, the Germans are sitting all along the north coast of France and could be making their landing craft ready to launch. As we speak, squadrons of Heinkel and Junkers could be firing up their engines ready to drop SS commandos on our green and pleasant land. You men have a lot to learn and not much time to do it, so I hope none of you are hoping to get any sleep this weekend.'

Giving them a grim smile of approval, the commander nodded to the man standing beside him.

Major Beyts stepped forward. 'Thank you, Colonel.'

Giving the men assembled before him a last look-over, Gubbins marched out of the room.

'Now, I know many of you are in LDV platoons and have been told that your job is to hold the line while the regular army regroups for a counterattack,' said Beyts, and another rumble of agreement went around the room.

'As the guvnor said, this will be dirty work, killing work, and not just the enemy but sympathisers, too, and I'm sad to say it, but in my experience in any population that is occupied there are traitors. People who will betray you and those you love to curry favour with the enemy.'

Images of Rachel, with her Jewish heritage writ large on her pretty features, flashed through Jack's mind.

'However,' continued Beyts, cutting across the raw fear tearing at Jack's heart, 'when you see the enemy goose-stepping up your High Street and a Nazi flag goes up over the local Town Hall, your job will be to disappear into something like this ...' He turned back the map to reveal a line drawing of a cylindrical underground hideout covered with shrubbery. 'Ready to emerge under cover of darkness to run amok among the enemy with the weapons and explosives we will be supplying to your local intelligence officer.'

Jack raised his hand.

Beyts' substantial eyebrows rose in acknowledgement. 'Yes?'

Jack stood up. 'Quinn, sir.'

'All right, Quinn.'

'Well, sir, begging your pardon,' said Jack. 'But I'm not sure where I'm expected to dig a hole ten feet deep in London.'

There was a ripple of laughter and Major Beyts' moustache lifted at the corners again.

'I'm afraid you chaps from the smoke are going to have to hide in plain sight by becoming absorbed into the general population when the Germans roll in,' Beyts replied. 'Your intelligence officer may have already identified places where you can hide explosives and firearms; if not, you'll have to scout the dumps for yourself. As Colonel Gubbins said, we may just have days to prepare so all of us at HQ are working on a wing and a prayer and our native wit. That's just what you'll have to do, too. Do you think you can, Quinn?'

As the stark reality of what was being asked of him dawned on Jack his stomach clenched.

Could he recruit men who would, in effect, be signing their own death warrants if caught by the German invaders? Could he withstand torture if captured? And could he stand resolved in the face a German hangman? For King and Country probably not, but for Rachel ...

Shoving aside all his base fear and anxiety, Jack looked his commanding officer square in the eye. 'Yes, sir. Us East Enders have been living like that since God was a boy.'

Chapter nineteen

'COR, YOU JUST FINISHED?, said Jimmy Ross, the sallow-faced supervisor in the lamp repair shop as he let the canteen door swing closed behind him.

'About ten minutes ago, thank goodness,' Jack replied, as he reached him.

It was the last Monday in June and over a week since his weekend at Coleshill House, and according to the clock in the clerical office he'd glimpsed at on his way in it was a quarter to two.

'Well, you're just in time as May's starting to clear away,' Jimmy replied. 'It's Irish stew, in case you're wondering.'

'I'm not,' said Jack, grabbing the handle. 'I'm that hungry I'd sink my teeth into a pair of old boots if they had a bit of gravy on them.'

Jimmy laughed and Jack strode into the canteen.

As the midday meal break ended in a little over ten minutes there were only a few stragglers dotted around the tables. However, although his vitals had been gnawing at him for over an hour, all thought of food vanished as he spotted Prue sitting alone at one of the tables by the windows reading.

Praying she wasn't at the end of her break, Jack headed over to the serving counter.

'Any chance of a little something left for a late one, Mrs F?' Jack asked, pulling an overly sad face.

'Course there is, ducks,' said May, wiping her hands on her apron.

Stratford canteen's longest serving cook and general bottlewasher went through to the kitchen.

Jack turned and found Gladys standing behind him.

'Hello, Jack,' she said, as her eyes slid over him. 'I'll always have a little something for you.'

Jack didn't reply but his gaze flicked past her to where Prue sat, her head bowed over her book.

Gladys glanced around and her scarlet mouth pulled into a hard line. She opened her mouth to speak but before she could the canteen door swung open and the redhead who she hung around with popped her head around the door.

'Oi, Gladys,' she hissed, 'old Clark's heading over here and if he catches us still hanging about, we'll cop it.'

Annoyance flickered over Gladys's powdered face.

'Gladys!'

'I 'eard you, Pat,' she snapped, her eyes still on Jack.

'Any time,' she said to Jack, giving him a lascivious look. She sauntered out of the canteen just as May returned with a bowl of steaming stew.

Jack thanked her then carried his tray over to where Prue was sitting. He gazed down at her for a moment, enjoying the sprinkling of freckles that a vainer woman would have disguised with powder. Cutting short his speculation of what it would be like to press his lips on to hers, Jack plucked up the courage to speak.

'Was it the butler?'

Prue looked up and smile, setting his pulse racing in response.

'Can I join you?'

'Of course,' she said, closing her reading matter.

Placing his tray on the table, Jack took the seat opposite. 'Well, did he?'

'No, it was the Nine Tailors.' She laughed, holding up a copy of a book of the same title. 'But you'll have to read it to find out how. You're late today.'

'I've been grappling with a firebox all morning,' he replied, oddly pleased that she'd realised he was usually earlier. 'Did you have a good weekend?'

'Not bad,' Prue replied. 'I went to the library on Saturday morning and my sister telephoned in the afternoon.'

'Any news on your brother?' he asked when she'd finished.

She shook her head and sadness clouded her face.

Jack picked up his cutlery. 'I'm sorry.'

'Well, we're not the only family waiting for news, and besides,' she forced a bright smile, 'don't they say no news is good news? And we have such a houseful these days to keep me busy ...'

As Jack worked his way through his meal Prue told him about everything: her sister being a reporter on the *Workers' Clarion* and being sent to cover this year's

TUC conference, what the refugees staying at the rectory were up too and her plan to set up English classes in the rectory..

'So you can see,' she concluded, smiling across at him as he scrapped up the last morsel from his bowl, 'we have plenty to keep us from dwelling on things. What about you? Did you get up to anything exciting this weekend? Maybe tripping the light fantastic up West?'

'Wot, me dancing with my two left feet?' he replied, thrusting his size-ten boots out from under the table.

Prue raised an eyebrow. 'That's not what I heard from May in the canteen. She said you were a regular Fred Astaire at last Christmas's works bash at the Regal.'

Oddly pleased that Prue had been talking about him, Jack gave a short laugh.

'Well, maybe you were cheering on the Hammers at Upton Park, then,' she continued.

'They were playing away,' he replied, scooping the last of his pudding into his spoon.

Planting her elbows on the table Prue clasped her hands together then rested her chin on them.

'Well then,' she said, a teasing smile playing across her lips as she looked across the table at him, 'what did you get up to this weekend?'

Placing his spoon carefully in the empty bowl Jack studied her for a moment.

'Nothing much yesterday, but on Saturday I did what I usually do,' he replied, watching closely for her reaction. 'I had a day with my daughter, Rachel.'

Prue's lovely hazel eyes opened wide with surprise. 'You're married.'

'I was.'

A sympathetic expression replaced her playful one in an instant. 'I'm so sorry, Jack, I didn't—'

'I'm divorced,' he said, his heart hammering in his chest as he held her gaze. 'Five years ago. When Rachel was two. She lives with her mother in East Ham.'

Staring across the light blue Formica tabletop at him, Prue didn't speak.

'Miss Carmichael!' Breaking his gaze from hers, Jack looked around to see Knobby Clark striding across the canteen.

'Sorry, luv, I know you've got five minutes yet, but some bloody idiot's chucked up on the bloody three-ten to Norwich. I've sent your chums to clean up but it's due out in ten bloody minutes, so you'd better get over to the shed and give them a hand.'

'It's all right, Mr Clark,' she called back. 'I'll be there right away.'

Swallowing the last mouthful of tea, she stood up.

'Don't worry, I'll take them back,' said Jack, as she started gathering her used crockery.

'Are you sure?'

He nodded.

She gave him a grateful look. 'Thanks.'

'See you around?'

Her gaze travelled over his face for a moment then, giving him a little smile, she hurried off.

Jack stared after her.

There was nothing he could do about his less than spotless past. And he wouldn't even if he could, because of Rachel. He'd been married, had a daughter and was now divorced, and that was the truth of it. Perhaps even for Prue, who seemed completely devoid of any pretensions, falling in love and marrying a divorcee was too much to countenance, but one thing he did know. As Tommy Lavender correctly observed, Jack wasn't one to give up without a fight.

"Ow you doing?' asked Maggie, hanging around the end of the compartment door.

'Not so bad,' Prue replied, wiping the newspaper over the soap-smeared window. 'What about you?'

'Me and Kate have finished,' Maggie replied, smoothing a stray lock of blonde hair from her eyes and leaving a dirty streak across her forehead. 'So do you need a hand?'

It was now two hours since Prue returned from her meal break. Thankfully, the mess Knobby Clark had summoned her back to help with wasn't as bad as he'd made out. Someone had been ill, probably after travelling in the old, bone-rattling Victorian carriage for miles, but as they had had the foresight to lower the window, a couple of buckets of water thrown on the outside of the door had done the trick. Since then, she and her two friends had been working their way along the eight carriages allocated to the eight-thirty to Clacton tomorrow morning.

Prue shook her head. 'I've only got the windows in the next compartment to polish so why don't you and Kate make a start on the next carriage, and I'll catch you up.'

'Right, if you're sure, only ...' Maggie frowned.

'What?'

'It's just you've not been your usual chirpy self since you came back from dinner,' said Maggie.

Prue looked puzzled. 'Haven't I?'

'No,' Maggie replied. 'And as me and Kate noticed that too-handy dirty-old-man Piggot lurking about by the paint shop, we thought perhaps he'd tried it on with you like he did with Ivy last week. That's all.'

'No, he didn't.'

'I'm glad to hear it,' her friend replied. 'But if he does, you make sure you knee 'im in the nuts. That'll cool 'is blooming ardour.'

Prue laughed. 'I'll remember that. And honestly, Maggie, I'm fine.'

'Righty-o then, see you in a jiffy.' Maggie rolled the compartment door closed and Prue returned to her polishing of the windows.

Running the screwed-up newspaper back and forth, she'd just stretched up to reach the final smear when she heard the compartment door slide open again.

'Almost done,' she called over her shoulder.

Sweeping down the edge of the glass pane, Prue turned but instead of Maggie or Kate she found Gladys, cigarette held between her cherry-red lips, filling the compartment door.

Prue dropped the newspaper into the bucket containing her mop, brush and cleaning cloth. 'Can I help you?'

Blowing a stream of smoke towards the arched roof, Gladys ran her overly made-up eyes over Prue for a moment, then she threw herself on to the seat.

'Jack Quinn,' she said, thumping her dirty boots on the seat opposite, which Prue had recently cleaned. ''Ow do you know 'im?'

'Why?'

'Just asking,' said Gladys.

Prue matched her frank stare. 'Not that it's any of your business, but if you must know his sister goes to my father's church.'

A leer spread across Gladys's powered face. 'Handsome bugger, though, ain't he? Sort of man any woman, even a vicar's daughter, would want to get under the sheets, and between her legs. You know what I mean, don't you? Solid under 'is fly buttons and with plenty of go.'

Several images of Jack flashed across Prue's mind before Gladys's voice cut across them.

'Or perhaps they don't learn you that stuff in Sunday school,' she added.

Prue matched the other women's unblinking stare for a moment then picked up her two buckets and made to leave the compartment, but Gladys didn't move her legs.

'He's divorced, you know,' Gladys added, blowing smoke up into Prue's face. 'With a kid, too. Not the sort of man Mummy and Daddy would welcome with open arms at the vicarage, is he?'

Resisting the urge to cough, Prue gave her a cool look. 'Don't you have some carriages to clean, Gladys?'

Gladys glared up at her for a moment then, taking a long drag on her cigarette, she stood up and flicked her cigarette past Prue on to the window she'd just polished.

Giving her a scornful look, she sashayed back along the corridor towards the open carriage door at the far end.

Putting down her buckets, Prue returned to the window. Picking up the lipstick-stained butt, she released the leather sash to lower the window then flicked it out. Closing it again she extracted the newspaper but then paused.

Idly gazing through the window at a stub-nosed shunting locomotive backing a tender loaded with coal to the back of a newly cleaned train, Prue pressed her lips together.

She was a bit surprised, of course, to hear Jack's admission. A little shocked even, but when she took all the other things into account, like the way she'd seen him teaching the young apprentices, jumping in to help anyone if he could and the fact that unlike most of the other man in the yard he didn't make a suggestive comment to any of the women working there, Prue was astounded to discover that him being a divorcee didn't seem to matter as much as she thought it would.

Chapter twenty

'JUMP,' SAID JACK, holding Rachel's hand as she hovered on the backboard of a number fifty-eight tram.

It was the last Sunday in June and the tram had just pulled alongside the kerb at the bottom of Green Street by the wood and corrugated iron of West Ham's football ground.

Rachel leapt down on to the pavement beside him and the conductor rang the bell. With sparks snapping from its arm scrapping along the powerlines above, a solitary sixty-five tram slid past on its way to Barking Broadway. Standing outside the closed Boleyn public house, Jack waited for it to pass then holding Rachel's hand tightly, walked her across the road and into Central Park Road. However, as they turned into the residential road a deep frown furrowed Rachel's brow.

'What's the matter, pudding?' Jack asked.

'I don't think it's very fair, is it?' she replied.

'What isn't?'

'Those men being put in that camp just because they come from Italy,' she replied.

After picking her up that morning he'd returned to Rosie's for Sunday lunch, after which he and Rachel had headed off to Victoria Park with a bag of crumbs for the ducks and a handful of loose change for tea and cake in the lakeside café as usual.

However, on arrival they found that the army had requisitioned the west side of the park and set up a makeshift compound with four or five wooden cabins sitting next to each other against one side. Within the tall industrial-strength wire fencing, a hundred or so men shuffled around while soldiers patrolled the perimeter. The unhappy captives were Italian or their families came from that country, and they had been rounded up since Italy threw in their lot with Hitler a month ago.

'No, neither do I,' Jack replied.

'I mean, it's not their fault that horrible man in their country has joined the Germans, is it, Daddy?'

'No, it's not,' he agreed, as they strolled.

They continued on for a moment then Rachel started to drag on his arm.

'Daddy, can I ask you something?'

'Anything you like,' he replied.

'Yesterday, after we came out of synagogue, I heard a man talking to someone about ...' Rachel stopped and looked down.

Jack hunkered down in front of her. 'What did he say, Rachel?'

'He said the Germans put Jews in camps like the one in Victoria Park and when they come over here, they'll do the same thing.' She looked up, her eyes moist with unshed tears. 'Daddy, I don't want to.'

Jack's mouth pulled into a hard line, and he drew in a deep breath.

'Listen, Rachel,' he said, looking intensely in her eyes, 'I promise I would die before I let anyone put you in any sort of camp. Do you believe me?'

She nodded then gave him a plucky little smile that tore at his heart.

Gathering her to him, Jack hugged her as the lump clogging his throat threatened to unman him. He held her close for a long second then stood her away from him and somehow forced a bright smile. 'Now, let's get you home before Mummy thinks we've got lost.'

Rachel nodded and Jack stood up.

Taking up her hand once again they walked on, turning into the last street on the right. Unlike Arbour Terrace, this street had double-fronted detached houses on both sides, with manicured front gardens and net curtains behind the criss-crossed gummed tape at the windows. There was even the odd modest Hillman Minx and Austin Sixteen parked against the kerb. However, outside the house he and Rachel were heading for there was a notable space where Uncle Manny's cream and burgundy Salmson C4C was usually parked.

Unhooking the gate, Jack pushed it open and his daughter trotted down the crazy-paving path with himself half a step behind.

Pulling on the doorbell, Jack waited. After a pause a shape started to form itself behind the bevelled half-circle of glass at the top of the door and then it opened.

Standing on the doorstep in a pair of high heels, and her dark hair swirled on the top of her head, was Alma.

As always, his ex-wife was dressed as if she was heading off up West somewhere for dinner with a duchess. On this particular afternoon she'd chosen a natty little Lincoln-green two-piece, probably from one of the swanky lady's outfitters in East Ham High Street. Under this she wore a light green silk blouse tied at her throat with an oversized bow and a string of pearls laying over it. He should have known from the start that a two-up two-down railwayman's cottage in Leyton would never satisfy Alma Goldstein née Abraham.

Her gaze flickered briefly over Jack then her attention shifted to her daughter.

'Hello, darling,' she said, a joyful smile spreading across her powdered face. 'Have you had a nice time?'

'Yes, Mummy, we went to Auntie Rosie's for dinner then I played with Michael and Russell,' Rachel replied.

'Did you?'

'And then we went to Victoria Park and saw—'

'It sounds as if you've had a very busy afternoon,' cut in her mother.

Taking the slender Continental cigarette from her lips, she blew a stream of smoke out of the side of her mouth.

'Now come and give Mummy a big kiss,' she said, bending down and offering Rachel her powdered cheek.

Her daughter did as she was bid.

'Inside you go, sweetheart, and take your things off,' said Alma, standing upright again.

Rachel turned towards Jack and waved. 'Bye, Daddy, see you next week.'

'Nine o'clock on the dot,' said Jack.

She stood looking at him for a moment then turned and trotted into the house.

He watched her until she disappeared into the interior of the house then his attention shifted back to the woman on the doorstep. 'Could I have a word with you, Alma?'

Uncertainty flickered across Alma's face for a second then she gave him a tight smile. 'I suppose so.'

'Inside, if you don't mind,' he added.

She stood back and Jack strolled past her and into the front room on the right.

Like everything else in Alma's life, the small parlour he'd just entered was furnished with fastidious care and no thought to the expense.

The carpet was several shades of light to medium grey with a stylised swirl pattern that complemented the lime-green velvet three-piece suite that probably came straight from Heal's front window. There were a couple of armchairs upholstered in the same fabric with gilt arms and legs, plus a footstool to match. The mirror-surfaced coffee table in the centre of the room had a large onyx ashtray, cigarette box and matching ball-shaped lighter.

'So,' sighed Jack, looking dispassionately at his ex-wife as she closed the door, 'you've started going back to shul again.'

'Well, yes, I have because ...' She took a long drag on her cigarette. 'I wasn't going to say anything yet but as you're here you might as well know: I'm expecting.'

'Congratulations,' said Jack. 'I take it Rachel doesn't know.'

She shook her head. 'I'll tell her in a few weeks.'

'I suppose Manny's hoping for a boy.'

'He hasn't said in so many words,' she flicked ash into the half-filled ashtray, 'but doesn't every man want a son?'

'I'm quite happy with what I've got,' said Jack.

'Anyway, what was it you want to have a word with me about?' she asked.

'Rachel,' said Jack. 'If the Germans do invade, then I'm coming to get her.'

His ex-wife's immaculately made-up eyes opened wide. 'You're what?'

'I'll come to get her, Alma,' Jack repeated. 'It's the only way I can keep her safe.'

She looked confused. 'Safe from what?'

Why was he not surprised his daughter knew more about what was going on across the Channel than her mother?

'In Poland the Germans have closed the Jewish school, confiscated Jewish businesses and made all Jews wear white armbands with the Star of David on them,' Jack replied. 'And the same will happen here when they arrive. If Rachel is with you she'll be classified as a Jew, but as my grandfather was Portuguese, I can explain away her dark colouring. I'll even put a crucifix around her neck and take her to St Winifred's if needs be. Anything to save

238

her from whatever cruel and twisted answer Hitler has to his Jewish question.'

'I'm not sure Manny will like the idea,' said Alma.

'I don't care,' said Jack. 'I'm her father. And he'll have enough to do to protect you and his unborn child from the Gestapo without worrying about someone else's child. I'll see you next week when I pick up Rachel.'

He retraced his steps to the door, but as he reached it, he turned.

Alma was staring at him with a stunned expression on her face.

'We both know that if it hadn't been for Rachel we would never have married and that we haven't always been kind to each other, Alma,' he said, 'but when the Germans do land on our shores I will do my best to help you and Manny if I can.'

Although the watch on his wrist showed it was close to ten o'clock at night, because of the introduction of double summertime at the outbreak of war the long thoroughfare that ran south from the Highway was abuzz with porters and warehousemen hoisting barrels and crates from merchant ships moored on Shadwell Basin and London Dock into the trapdoors high above.

However, as Wapping station came into sight and the stench of the river filled his nose, Jack turned away from the bustling wharves and into the shady cool of Colemans Street.

The narrow passageway that wound its way through to Wapping Wall was flanked on both sides by warehouses. However, the tall brick buildings packed with merchandise were punctuated halfway down by the Boatman pub, which looked as if it had been hammered into place between them.

Although the Prospect of Whitby and the Town of Ramsgate might claim to be the oldest pubs in the area, judging by the low-slung black beams keeping up the red-tiled roof and a saloon door that even an average-sized man had to stoop to pass through, Jack would lay a pound to a penny that the Boatman could give them both a good few years.

Reaching around under his jacket, he made sure his fighting knife was secure in his belt, then he placed his hand on the worn brass plate and pushed open the door.

In contrast to the hectic streets outside, the low-ceilinged bar of the ancient alehouse was an oasis of calm. Like the exterior, the long narrow interior was from a bygone age, with scattered sawdust over creaky floorboards worn rough under countless hobnailed boots. Although customers no longer had their beer placed in front of them on a plank balanced across two barrels, the Boatman had a plain oak counter rather than a polished mahogany one and there were no artistically shaped Victorian wrought-iron holding glasses above it.

There were a few scruffy individuals loitering against the bar chatting to the hard-bitten barmaid as she polished glasses. There were two old men snapping dominos down on one of the tables and three more of a similar age and dress playing cribbage at another, but other than that the bar was, as usual, practically empty. A stranger entering the premises would be forgiven for wondering how, with so few customers, such a place stayed open, but then a stranger wouldn't know that its owner's business had nothing to do with beer.

Legend has it that a hundred years ago the Boatman was the haunt of a gang of river pirates. Jack didn't know about that, but he did know that these days it was the favourite watering hole of Johno Murray, the longstanding leader of the Greenbanks Gang.

For that reason, and with Jack's brother Charlie heading up the Shadwell Mob in those days, it was a place he had only been in a couple of times when the rival riverside crews called a truce to parley.

It was even more empty tonight because, like every other Tuesday evening, Johno was in Chin Loe's illegal gambling house three miles away in Limehouse.

Of course, while he was away Johno had no intention of allowing the mice to play. Casting his eyes through the cigarette smoke, Jack spotted the man left to oversee Johno's interests, his son, Georgie Murray.

A year or two Jack's junior, Georgie Murray had the same tight weasel face and wiry russet hair as his father. Unlike his old man, who made Joe Louis look like a flyweight, the heir to Johno's illegal empire was slender to the point of looking half starved. However, his lack of weight and girth hadn't held him back in his life of crime.

Like half the population living around the docks, the Murrays were Irish, but whereas most of their countrymen filled the pews in St Mary and St Michael's and St Patrick's Catholic churches each Sunday, the Murrays were Protestant. Originating from Belfast, they were also fiercely patriotic, as the Union Jack and photo of the King behind the bar testified.

Jack made his way past the empty tables and handful of customers, Georgie's shrewd amber eyes fixed on him all the way.

'Cor, Jack Quinn,' he said as Jack stopped in front of him. ''Aven't see you in these parts since I can't remember when? 'Ow you doing?'

'Well, enough. Yourself?'

'Mustn't grumble,' Georgie said. 'Drink?'

'Wouldn't mind,' Jack replied.

Georgie let out a two-tone whistle through his front teeth and raised his half-empty glass. Jack took the chair opposite him as the barmaid waddled over with a pint of brown in each hand.

'Cheers.' Jack took a sip and Georgie did the same.

'Now then,' he said, smacking his lips and putting his drink back on the table. 'Wot brings you down t' this neck of the woods?'

'I have a little proposition for you,' said Jack.

Georgie raised a scraggly eyebrow. 'I fought you weren't in with the Shadwell outfit any more.'

'I haven't come down 'ere about my old crew but Hitler's,' said Jack.

'Bastard Germans,' Georgie ground out, a florid colour appearing on his cheeks. 'Killed our ma and baby sister, they did, with their bloody Zeppelin. Visiting her sister in Deptford she was when one of those fucking airships dropped a bomb on her. I owe 'em a reckoning so I do, Jack, so let me 'ave it.'

'Before I do, I have to warn you that …' As they drank their pints Jack gave Georgie the caution that Freddie had given him then he offered Georgie a place in the auxiliary unit he was pulling together. 'You'll have training, but your particular skills will make you an invaluable member of the team.' Jack grinned. 'After all, no one else I know can get in and out of a house without so much as disturbing the dust on the mantelshelf.'

Georgie's narrow chest swelled with professional pride. 'Well, it ain't for me to say, you know, but I have 'eard that some calls me the top 'ousebreaker in London Town.'

'I don't doubt it,' Jack replied. 'So you in, then?'

'Course I'm in,' he replied.

Jack swallowed the last mouthful of his beer and stood up. 'Good. I'll be in touch. But remember: not a word. To anyone – not even your old man.'

Chapter twenty-one

As HE SHOVED the completed docket for the 2-4-2T Class locomotive he'd been working on all morning in the appropriate pigeonhole outside the ground-floor offices, Jack's stomach let out an almighty growl.

It was hardly surprising really as it was now almost one and he hadn't eaten anything since a hurried cup of tea and some cold toast at eight o'clock. However, instead of heading towards the canteen at the far end of the corridor, Jack swung around the corner of the stairs and took them two at a time to the top.

Stopping outside the yard manager's office, he knocked and then walked in.

As ever, Ted Prentice was wearing his shinny navy suit with his rapidly vanishing hair doing its best to cover the pink roundness of his knobby skull.

He looked up as Jack walked in. 'You should wait until I tell you to enter.'

'Tosh said it was urgent,' Jack replied, closing the door behind him.

The chair beneath Prentice creaked as he leaned back. 'It is but—'

There was another brief knock and the door swung open again.

'That's a relief,' said Wally Unwin, strolling into the room followed by Harry Kemp. 'I through I was in for a bollocking, but if you're here it must be something else?'

'Doesn't anyone bother to wait before they burst in?' said Prentice, glaring at the three engineers.

'Did you fix that old relic in the Boiler shop?' Harry asked, who at five foot ten was one of the few men in the yard who came close to Jack's six foot one.

'After practically sweating blood I did,' Jack replied.

'You've got my sympathy, mate,' grumbled Harry, his dungarees straining across his beer-belly as he shoved his hands in his pocket. 'Since the likes of Crewe and Swindon are making aeroplanes and tanks instead of repairs on engines and wagons, it's us who has to keep the company's rolling stock moving.'

Jack raised an eyebrow. 'Don't you know there's a war on?'

'And that's why I've called you 'ere,' Ted said, jumping in as Wally drew breath. 'I suppose you've seen that the French are caving in?'

'Bloody frogs,' muttered Harry.

Prentice opened his mouth to speak but before he could utter a word someone rapped on the door briefly then it burst open again.

'Like Piccadilly circus in here today, ain't it, gov?'

As the door bounced off the rubber door stop screwed to the floor, a second lieutenant who looked as though he should be in school rather than in the army marched in.

However, the new arrival that caught Jack's attention was the sharp-faced individual with sergeant stripes on his upper arm. He'd last seen Billy Butcher in Cable Street four years earlier, clad in the black uniform of the British Union of Fascists and sporting a set of knuckledusters.

Although the lieutenant's uniform had been tailored and freshly pressed, he looked dishevelled compared to Butcher. His white-blond hair, which used to be fashioned into a curl over his forehead, had been trimmed to within an inch of his bony head. Always a flashy dresser, the creases in his trousers and down his sleeves could have sliced silk, his buttons positively gleamed and you could truthfully see your reflection in his steel toecaps.

Doing a double step and then standing at attention, Butcher's gaze flickered indifferently over the assembled men until it reached Jack.

Although Butcher's gaunt features remained impassive, recognition flared in his flat, grey eyes. The hint of a sneer curled his top lip as he stared across at him.

Jack matched the sergeant's adversarial stare for a second or two then the lieutenant cleared his throat.

Butcher's eyes snapped to the front as his senior officer took a step forward.

'H–have you briefed your chaps, Mr Prentice?' he asked, barely giving way to his slight stutter.

A flush coloured the supervisor's face. 'I'm afraid not, I—'

'Never mind,' cut in the officer, casting his pale, guileless gaze over the men. 'Probably better I do it anyway. Lieutenant Davenport's the name and this f-fine fellow here,' he indicated Butcher, 'is my right-hand man, S-sergeant Butcher.'

Wally and Harry mumbled a greeting while Jack held his peace.

'There's no point dressing it up, chaps,' the officer continued. 'The Germans could arrive any day. With this fine weather and the Channel like a bally millpond, it wouldn't surprise me if they weren't already piling into landing craft as I speak.

'We have batteries all along the south coast standing ready to repulse them, of course. However,' Davenport frowned, 'if they do manage to get a f-foothold we must do everything in our p-power to hinder their progress.'

'The men at Stratford are ready to play their part,' said Ted Prentice.

'That's the s-spirit,' beamed the lieutenant. 'England expects and all that … Now, I suppose you're all wondering what you railway chaps have to do?'

Thanks to the illuminating weekend at Coleshill House, Jack knew exactly what he was expected to do when the Germans invaded. However, as Colonel Gubbins and Major Beyts had been at pains to point out, the regular army weren't aware of this, so he played dumb.

'Sabotage, that's what,' Davenport went on. 'One of the Nazis' first objectives will be to take over the railways like they did in Belgium and the Netherlands to stop our troop evacuation and move their own troops inland. It's imperative we stop them, at all costs,' Davenport said. 'That's why we're here. I'm sure you've seen the Nissen huts and ack-ack guns being set up at the northern boundary of Stratford yard.'

'Couldn't very well miss it, could we?' said Harry. 'Spread across Hackney Marshes like that.'

'Well, that's the Fifth London Field Regiment, Royal Artillery,' explained Davenport, 'just back from France. Their job is to defend Stratford from aerial attack. In addition, my men in the Forty-seventh London Infantry, who are billeted alongside them, will be patrolling the yard. As Stratford is one of the main junctions and yards that armaments and troops have to pass through, I'm sure the Germans have it high on their list of crucial targets. Your job is to identify vital points and signals and disable them when the German troops arrive. Although I will be in command, the day-to-day running of the operation will be overseen by Sergeant Butcher. Any questions?'

'But our boys'll stop 'em before then, won't they?' asked Wally, looking wide-eyed at the young lieutenant as though willing him to agree. 'I mean, they have to. Right?'

The youthful commander's frown deepened. 'We will do our very best, but if the worst does happen then ...' He pressed his thin lips together, unable to utter the words.

As the men in the room stood silently, weighing the lieutenant's words, Butcher's gaze shifted across to Jack again.

After a long pause Davonport tucked his swagger stick under his arm. 'Carry on, Butcher.'

Butcher snapped to attention and gave a salute that looked as if it would take his eyes out, then, as his senior officer left, he turned his attention to Ted sitting behind his desk.

'Right then, Mr Prentice,' he said, in an accent very like Jack's own, 'I need someone to show me over the yard so I can see the lay of the land.'

'Quinn, you can do that, can't you?' said Ted.

'Not just now I can't,' Jack replied.

Butcher's eyes narrowed. 'Didn't you hear the lieutenant? Me and my boys are in charge now, chum.'

'Well, if one of your *boys c*an rehang the furnace door on the 0-4-6 in the locomotive shed then I'll be happy to take you on a little tour, Sergeant,' Jack replied, giving his erstwhile adversary a cool smile.

'It's all right, I'll show 'im around, Jack,' said Wally, stepping alongside him.

Butcher's gaze darted between them for a moment.

'Let's be 'aving you then!' he barked. Turning on his studded heels, he marched towards the office door.

'And don't forget to watch where you're going, Sergeant Butcher,' Jack called after him. 'We don't want you to be mowed down by the four-ten from Shenfield, do we?'

Chapter twenty-two

'So HAVE YOU heard the latest?' said the woman in a faded headscarf queuing in front of Prue.

'Wot, you mean 'bout shipping the Duke of Windsor and 'is floozy off to the Bahamas?' her portly, bespectacled friend asked.

'Naw, that they've scrapped the blooming penny bus fare,' the first women replied.

It was just after one thirty in the afternoon on the second Friday in July and Prue was at the back of the queue in Stepney High Street post office.

'If scrubbing floors for a couple of coppers ain't bad enough,' continued the woman in the headscarf, 'now it's going cost me another tanner a week for the privilege.'

Cyril Mason, the elderly postmaster serving behind the counter, slid a few coins and half a dozen green halfpenny stamps through the arched space in the wire grille and the young woman carrying a baby on her hips moved aside.

The queue shuffled forward.

Guessing she was likely to be some time, Prue considered the display rack containing birthday cards, boxes of stationery and wrapping paper. Not that there was much to choose from since paper production had been given over to the war effort.

'Oh, hello, Prue.'

She turned and for a split second the image of Jack flashed through her mind as she found his sister standing behind her.

A smile spread across her face. 'Hello, Rosie. No point asking what you're doing here on a Friday.'

'No, me and every other soldier's wife in Stepney Green,' Rosie replied, indicating the half a dozen young women in front of them in the queue. 'I did think leaving it until after dinner would be better, but it seems like everyone else had the same idea.'

'I thought the same,' Prue said, as the queue moved forward again. 'I only want a couple of stamps, but this is my only day off and I'm overdue replying to a couple of friends' letters plus one to my sister. Have you heard from Mick?'

'Yes, thank goodness,' said Rosie. 'He's been stuck down on the south coast somewhere so can't get home, but at least I know he's safe. Not like my poor friend Ella Jolly, and her with her baby son only four weeks old.'

'It's so sad,' agreed Prue, thinking of the young woman with her baby on her knee sitting stone-faced beside her mother-in-law in the pews.

'Did you hear about Stan Willman?' Rosie continued.

Prue shook her head.

'Fell down the belfry steps and broke his ankle two nights ago.'

'Poor man,' said Prue, thinking of the church's longest serving bell ringer. 'But we can't ring the bells so what was he doing up there?'

'Fire watch,' Rosie replied as they shuffled forward. 'With men getting their call-up papers the ARP are getting desperate. I'd do it myself but ...' She glanced down at her rounded stomach.

Rosie's eyes flickered past Prue and she let out a sigh. 'Thank goodness.'

Prue followed her gaze and saw that Bettie Mason, Cyril's daughter and post office clerk, had just removed the closed sign from the second gap in the grille.

'I've been meaning to thank you again for stepping up and helping Sister Martha with the Sunday school,' said Prue, as they moved forward.

'That's all right; it's the least I could do after what she's done for me and everyone else around here,' said Rosie. 'She really is a sweetheart.'

'She seems it and I've been very grateful for all her help with the refugees,' said Prue.

'I'm sorry I wasn't able to squeeze any of them in, but I've already got my own refugee,' said Rosie.

Prue looked puzzled.

'My brother, Jack.'

The image of Jack returned to her mind but this time it was of him as she'd glimpsed him crouched down beside a huge locomotive wheel while explaining to his young apprentice Tosh how to fit a piston securely.

'Do you?'

Prue blinked. 'I'm sorry, I ...'

'Do you see him much at Stratford yard, I mean?'

'In passing,' Prue replied.

Both counter positions became free so the two women in front of Prue stepped forward and Prue made a play of reading the notice on the wall of July's blackout times, while she waited for the slightly unsettling feeling in the pit of stomach to subside.

The woman being served by Bettie collected her change then waddled away, so Prue took her place then having bought her stamps stood aside. She waited as Rosie handed over her flimsy buff-coloured allowance book so she could receive the few pounds deducted from her husband's army wages each week, then they walked out together.

'Look, I don't know if you're busy, Prue, but would you like to come home for a cuppa?'

Pushing aside thoughts of the basket of ironing and her overdue letter to Fliss, Prue smiled. 'That sounds just about perfect, lead the way.'

Twenty minutes later, having passed a platoon of the Royal Artillery setting up a new ack-ack gun on the public park at the south end of St Winifred's graveyard, they reached Arbour Terrace. Stopping in front of the last-but-one door before the school at the bottom of the cul-de-sac, Rosie hooked her finger through the letter box and drew out a key.

'Aren't you worried that someone might use the key to break in while you're out?' ask Prue as Rosie opened the door.

Rosie shook her head. 'Too many eyes.' She indicated the half a dozen women sunning themselves in chairs outside their front doors, all of them with a scrubbed half-circle of pavement outside. 'You can't do a thing in this street without everyone knowing.'

Prue studied Rosie's neighbours for a moment then followed her inside and found herself standing in a square hallway about the size of the rectory's kitchen table with a narrow flight of stairs straight in front of her.

'Make yourself comfortable, and I'll put the kettle on,' Rosie said, leading her into the family lounge.

Putting her handbag on the floor next to one of the fireside chairs, Prue gazed around the room.

Her mother was always bemoaning the fact that because of working at Stratford Prue didn't help her in the parish; however, the truth was otherwise. Despite spending five days a week cleaning the detritus left by train passengers, Prue had visited at least two members of the congregation each week so was now familiar with the snug little houses in the parish. Nearly every one she'd visited in the past two months had been clean and tidy, but Rosie's home positively shone.

The leather sofa and two armchairs might have been made before the first war with Germany but they sported cream linen antimacassars and arm covers. Under the crochet dollies protecting the wood from the vases and figurines, the walnut veneer of the sideboard was polished like glass. The cast-iron hearth was blackened and swept and the glass peeking out between the gummed paper latticing on the window was without smears. However, although it was spotlessly clean, the box of toys tucked under the window and the Singer treadle machine sitting in the light of the window gave the room a warm domestic feel.

Her eyes came to rest on the picture frames that stood between the seaside souvenirs on the mantelshelf. Stepping closer, Prue studied the smiling faces of bygone events and family pride beaming out of them.

'There we are,' said Rosie, returning from the kitchen carrying a tray of tea.

Prue tucked her skirt under her then sat in the chair alongside her handbag as Rosie poured their tea.

'Some cake?' Rosie picked up a knife and indicated the golden-brown oblong on a larger plate.

'That would be lovely.'

'It's a recipe from last week's *Woman's Own*,' Rosie added, cutting a generous slice and plonking it on a tea place. 'It's got carrot in, which seems a bit queer but I suppose we should count our blessings it ain't potato. It seems to be in everything from scones to cheese tarts these days.' She handed the plate to Prue. 'Every recipe is mock this and mock that nowadays. *Woman and Home* even advised the housewife to use liquid paraffin as a substitute for fat. Mind you, whoever dreamed up that one hasn't got a lav in the backyard?'

Prue laughed.

'I don't know if you heard,' said Rosie, taking up her knitting needles, which had a square of lemon three-ply knitting dangling from them, 'but Sally Thompson had her baby on ...'

As they drank their tea the two women chatted easily. Rosie did her best to cheer Prue after she told her they had still not heard anything about Rob's whereabouts. Prue in turn congratulated Rosie for securing a pound of best stewing steak while commiserating with her for failing to find an onion for love nor money to go with it. As Rosie swapped her needles across to start another row, Prue told of her own ration triumph earlier that day when she happened to pop into the chemist just as a box of cold tar soap arrived. Rosie matched her good fortune by having nabbed three oranges at the greengrocer's.

Prue had just finished her second cup of tea when she caught sight of the dome-shaped clock on the sideboard.

'I should be getting home before my mother starts thinking I've been kidnapped by fifth columnists.' She picked up her handbag, but as she stood up the photos on the mantelshelf caught her eye.

'You really have some lovely photos,' she said, taking a step closer to consider them again.

'That's my mum,' said Rosie, pointing to a silver-framed photograph that took pride of place in the centre of the collection.

Prue studied the sepia photo of a young women with her hair swept up in a cottage-loaf bun, dressed in an ankle-length skirt and high-necked blouse. She was standing beside a majolica jardinière with a painted garden scene behind her and smiled out at Prue without a care in the world. 'It was taken on her twenty-first birthday, just before she married my dad.'

'You look very like her,' said Prue.

Rosie pulled a face. 'That's what everyone says. I only wish I had her grit and determination.' Her attention shifted from Prue to the portrait. 'Brought me, Jack and my older brother Charlie up single-handed she did after my dad was killed in the docks when Jack was three. Kept us all from the workhouse by scrubbing slaughtermen's aprons in the backyard and sewing shirt collars and cuffs for a couple of pennies, but we always had full bellies and a kiss goodnight. She died fourteen years ago last January. Jack was just fourteen. Of course, 'im being the brainy one of the family, Mum had hopes for keeping him at school so he could sit his school certificate but although me and Charlie were working we weren't bringing home enough to keep a roof over our heads and food on the table so Jack had to leave and start work.'

'Has your older brother moved out of the area?' asked Prue, trying to remember if Jack had ever mentioned him.

'In a manner of speaking,' Rosie replied in a flat tone. 'He's in the City of London Cemetery in Manor Park next to our mum.'

'I'm sorry,' said Prue.

'That's him,' said Rosie, indicating a smaller, grainy image of a young man with a cigarette in his mouth, slouching against the back wall of a yard. 'It was taken one year when we were 'opping in Kent – harvesting the hop vines,' Rose clarified. 'We used to do it like every other family in the area every year as kids. And that's me and Mick outside St Winifred's on our wedding day nine years ago.'

Prue studied the happy couple for a moment then her gaze settled on a young man standing beside Rose with wild curly hair and a familiar smile. Her eyes lingered there for a moment then shifted on to the last photo in the row. It was another studio portrait but this time of Jack, in a suit and tie, standing with his arms affectionately around the shoulders of a young girl. She had long dark hair and was wearing a party dress that any girl of the same age would wash up the family dishes for a month to possess.

'And this must be Jack's daughter,' said Prue.

'Yes, it is,' said Rosie, looking a little anxious.

Prue's gaze shifted back to the photograph.

This was Jack's child. His child by another woman, a woman he'd once kissed and held in his arms. A woman he'd once loved.

An odd emotion twisted through Prue. Reaching out, she picked up the photo and studied it more closely.

His love and pride for his child was written so large on Jack's face that a lump formed in Prue's throat in response.

'She is so lovely.'

'I think so,' replied a deep, resonant voice.

Prue raised her eyes and the breath caught in her throat as they rested on Jack standing in the doorway.

Jack had heard the sound of female voices as he came through the back door but only realised who his sister was chatting to when he stood on the threshold of the front room.

He'd actually been standing there for a few moments, enjoying the sight of Prue as she studied the portrait he'd had taken of him and Rachel together.

Like almost every other woman in the hot summer weather, Prue was wearing a flowery pink and green cotton dress and low-heeled sandals. However, although some might say there was a more beautiful woman in the world, with a shapelier figure and a brighter smile, Jack knew that could not be so. From almost the moment he'd laid eyes on Prue, his fate, along with his heart, had been sealed.

Smiling, Jack walked across the room to where she was standing. 'But then I'm a bit biased.'

'And so you should be,' Prue replied, smiling up at him. 'What's her name?'

'Rachel,' he said. 'I had that taken on her birthday in February when she was seven.'

Prue looked surprised. 'I thought she must be at least eight or nine; she's obviously got your long legs.'

As always, looking down at her Jack started to lose himself in her large hazel eyes but then, breaking from her gaze, he took the photo and returned it to its place on the mantelshelf.

'Both the tea and cake were delicious,' Prue said, adjusting her handbag on her arm. 'But as I said I was only popping out for half a dozen stamps, I don't want my mother sending out a search party.'

'Hold up,' said Jack. 'I'm going past the rectory to … fetch my boots from the menders so—'

'You've just got in, Jack,' said Rosie.

'I meant to do it on the way home,' he replied.

'Surely, have a cup of tea first,' Rosie persisted. 'There's still some in the pot.'

'It won't take five minutes,' Jack replied. 'And I need them for parade later. I'll have a cup when I get back.'

Rosie gave him a puzzled look but thankfully said no more and started gathering their mother's rarely used best crockery together.

'Thank you very much, Rosie, and I'll see you on Sunday,' Prue said, looking at his sister.

Darting in front of Prue, Jack opened the front door.

They walked to the bottom of the road chatting about mundane things, but as they turned into Oxford Street the church hove into view.

'Sister Martha told me you were once one of St Winifred's best choristers,' said Prue, as the passed Arbour Square police station.

'Did she now?'

She gave him what could only be described as a mischievous sideways look. 'She did. Said you had a voice like an angel.'

Jack laughed. 'I wouldn't go that far, but I was the boy soprano lead for "Once in Royal David's City" two years in a row.'

'She seems very fond of you,' she continued.

'And I'm very fond of her, too,' Jack replied. 'She was good to us when Mum was ill. Used to come around to sit with her until she died. She did the same for Rosie and me a few years later when Charlie was killed.'

'Killed!'

'Yes, he followed our dad into the docks and was found dead one day in an empty ship's hold,' said Jack, his brow furrowing slightly as the aching memory of his brother lying, white-faced and hands crossed in his coffin, flitted through his mind.

'I'm sorry, Jack,' she said, her expression matching her words. 'Did he fall?'

'That's what the inquest said.'

Prue frowned. 'Sister Martha was telling me about the shocking number of accidents in the docks.' Her serious expression lingered for a moment then her face brightened. 'They need my sister Fliss down there to sort out the wharf and quay owner.'

As they walked towards St Winifred's, Prue gave him a potted history of her radical older sister, allowing Jack to freely enjoy her ready smile and the graceful tilt of her head, oblivious to his gaze as she recounted the latest exploits of the Carmichael family's firebrand.

'Rosie was telling me how the church fire-watch team are very short,' said Prue, as they paused outside the Green Dragon to let a three-ton army Bedford truck pass by. 'I think I might volunteer to cover a couple of nights.'

'I'm sure you'd be a welcome addition,' said Jack. 'The whole roof's made of old dry timber so it wouldn't take much, and it would go up like a firework.' He grinned. 'And you can wave down at me on patrol.'

Looking up at its familiar square tower, Jack sighed.

'What's the matter?' asked Prue.

'I just hope that God is watching over it when the Luftwaffe arrive,' he said, as they strolled past the thousand-year-old church.

'So do I,' said Prue, 'because I'm just about to turn the crypt into an air raid shelter.'

'Good for you,' said Jack, nodding in appreciation.

Prue's cheeks flushed a little under his admiring gaze. 'I got the idea when Father David showed me around. As he pointed out, the vaults beneath the church have withstood a thousand years so they should keep us safe. Mrs Lavender's son says he can get some timber—'

'Tommy Lavender?'

She nodded. 'Do you know him?'

'We were in the same class at school and he's in my DLV patrol,' Jack replied, wondering which builders' yard would soon find themselves short of a few planks.

'And the churchwardens have collected names for the working party, so we should be making a start early next week,' she concluded.

'Well, I'll make sure I catch Ronny Mills in the Ship later so he can put my name on the list,' Jack replied.

'You'll help?'

'Of course,' said Jack. 'Rosie has got hers and the boys' names down for a space under the Congregational Church shelter in Dempsey Street, but St Winnie's is nearer and I'm sure she'd be happier with her friends.'

'Thank you,' said Prue. 'The more there are to help the quicker we'll be ready if the bombers come.'

Turning at the bottom of the High Street, they crossed the road and within a few paces were standing in front of the rectory.

'Well, here we are,' said Jack, turning to face her.

'Yes.' Her eyes flickered over his chest and shoulders then returned to his face. 'It seems strange to see you without grease smeared all over your face.'

'And it's nice to see you not dressed in dungarees,' he replied.

Yes, he was flirting but he didn't care.

And why should he? He'd just spent the past half an hour strolling along with the women who was in the process of capturing his heart.

They gazed at each other for a long moment then, heralded by a thunder of running feet, two boys barrelled between them.

'Sorry, Miss Carmichael,' said a tall girl with skin and hair like Rachel's. She was holding the hands of two little girls while another, who was obviously her sister, brought up the rear. 'I told zem not to run.'

Prue smiled fondly at them all, squeezing Jack's heart. 'Boys will be boys, Johanna.'

Acknowledging this universal truth with a sigh, Johanna led her charges up the path towards the rectory door.

'They're the children of the three families we've got living with us,' explained Prue, looking at the youngsters heading up the path.

'You've got quite a houseful,' Jack replied, trying to keep his thoughts away from how pretty her slightly turned-up nose looked in profile.

'Indeed, and quite noisy at times, but I don't mind. I love children,' she added. Her gaze lingered on them for a moment then returned to Jack. 'I hope I can meet Rachel some time.'

'So do I.'

'Why don't you bring her to church one Sunday?' she asked.

'Her mother wouldn't like it.'

'Some other time maybe.' She glanced towards the closed door then back at him. 'I ought to go in,' she said, not making a move to do so.

Jack stood, gazing down at her.

Knowing his hopes and desires were no doubt writ clear in his eyes, he expected her to look away.

After a few seconds she did, but not before he caught a glimpse of something that set his pulse racing and his hopes soaring.

'As you can see, our junior guests can be a bit boisterous when they return from school, so I like to be there to help their mothers with tea. Thanks for keeping me company.'

Giving him a hesitant smile, she walked up the path towards the rectory.

'I might see you at work tomorrow,' Jack called after her.

'Most likely,' she called back over her shoulder.

His eyes followed her.

Perhaps it was just as well the children had crashed between them, as had they not Jack wasn't certain he could have stopped himself taking Prue into his arms and pressing his mouth on to hers. A wry smile lifted his lips, and he went to turn away but then something snagged his eye.

Looking towards the casement window to the right of the front porch he found Father David staring back at him.

'You're dripping ink, Father David,' said Hugh.

Blinking, David looked away from the window and down at the half-written sermon on the desk.

'Sorry,' he said, adjusting the angle of his fountain pen to stop the flow. 'I was a little distracted.'

His mentor, who was sitting in one of the three easy chairs in the rectory's study reading one of the current Archbishop of Canterbury's weighty tomes, smiled. 'I often am myself when grappling with the words of Isaiah. It is indeed a struggle for us mere mortals to interpret his prophecies and visions.'

David gave a wan smile but didn't reply. After all, the vision he'd just witnessed through the window of two people gazing into each other's eyes didn't need any interpreting at all. The front door banged shut.

'Sounds like the wanderer has returned,' said Hugh.

A moment or two went by then there was a light knock.

'Come in,' shouted Hugh.

The handle rattled and then the door flew back, and Prue bounced in smiling.

'I'm back.' Crossing to her father she perched on the arm of his chair then planted a kiss on his high forehead.

'So I can see,' Hugh replied, looking adoringly up at his last born. 'But I was expecting you sooner.'

'I met Rosie Stapleton in the post office and she invited me around for tea,' Prue replied.

'And did you have a nice time?' her father asked.

'Very enjoyable,' said Prue brightly, a slight flush colouring her cheeks. 'In fact, I recruited a willing volunteer for St Winifred's air raid shelter, too.'

The memory of what he'd just witnessed through the window flashed through David's mind and his eyes narrowed.

'Have you heard about Mr Willman, by the way?' Prue asked.

'Yes, I heard at the vestry meeting yesterday, poor old chap,' said Hugh, shaking his head dolefully. 'Another parish visit for your dear mother.'

'I'll pop in tomorrow before work,' said Prue. 'His daughter Cora was a great help to me when the refugees arrived, so I've already met all the family. I also thought I might volunteer to take a couple of fire-watching shifts on the church tower.'

The rector's woeful expression deepened. 'I don't know what your mother will say.'

'I do,' said Prue. 'But someone has to do it. Talking of Mother, where is she?'

'She had to pop across to the church,' the rector replied. 'An ominous situation regarding flowers for Sunday, as I understand it.'

Prue laughed then she spotted David.

'I'm sorry, I didn't mean to interrupt,' she said. 'I'll leave you to it as the children will be waiting for their tea.'

'Yes, I heard them come in,' said David.

He had. It had been the blasted children thundering through the hall like a herd of rampaging elephants that had caused him to look up and out of the window. Gripping the arms of his chair, David started to rise.

'Would you like me to help?' he asked, hoping after one of the waifs and strays spilt orange juice down his linen trouser last week that she would not.

'No, I think we'll manage,' she replied. 'But do either of you want a cup of tea while I'm making a pot?'

'That's just the ticket,' her father replied, as David resumed his seat. 'I'm sure a hot Earl Grey will help Father David as he grapples with the Old Testament's metaphysical text.'

Prue hopped off her perch on her father's chair and retraced her steps to the door, but just as she reached for the handle a two-tone wail outside stopped her in her tracks.

'It's probably another false alarm,' said David. 'The Luftwaffe have been sending the odd plane over for months just to give the ARP the jitters. In fact, people have started to ignore the Moaning Minnies altogether.'

'Well, Cardiff was bombed last night so I suggest we go to the basement to be on the safe side,' said Prue. 'It'll be good practice, in any case.'

She left the room as the front door banged again.

Leaving their books and papers where they lay, David and his mentor followed Prue out. By the time they reached the hall, the refugee families were already filing out of the kitchen. Prue, now with her gas mask hanging from her right shoulder, was shepherding them down the stairs to the basement while her mother, who had just arrived, was taking off her hat.

'Ruddy Hun,' said Mrs Lavender, emerging from the dining room carrying an empty tray in one hand. 'Ain't got the decency to let a body go about their business in peace.'

'Aren't you going to join us in the basement, Mrs Lavender?' asked the rector, as the housekeeper marched past him.

'That's right kind of you, but I've a casserole in the oven and I ain't having it burn because of some bleeding siren, excuse my French, Rector,' she called over her shoulder as she headed towards the kitchen.

As the pregnant Jewish woman whose name he could

never remember and the skinny girl carrying a baby joined the end of the queue of children, David made his way across to Prue.

'Look here, if you don't mind me asking,' he said, using the excuse of a crowded hallway to get close, 'but is your new recruit to help with the shelter Mrs Stapleton's brother?'

Prue looked puzzled.

'I saw you standing with him at the rectory gate through the window,' David explained.

'Oh, well actually it is Jack, if you must know,' said Prue.

'Jack?'

'That's his name,' said Prue. 'Jack Quinn.'

David's chest tightened. 'Yes, I know his name, but clearly you know him better.'

'I wouldn't go that far,' said Prue casually as she lowered her gaze to pick a bit of fluff off her sleeve. 'I just run into him at work.'

'Regularly?'

'From time to time,' Prue replied. 'In the canteen mostly.'

The thought of Jack Quinn cosying up to Prue under the guise of being friendly clawed at David's chest.

'Perhaps it would be wise to avoid him in future,' said David.

'I beg your pardon?'

'I know men like Quinn have some rugged sort of appeal to women of the lower classes, but—'

Fury flashed across Prue's face for a second and, turning smartly on her heels, she marched towards the basement door.

David skirted around in front of her and down the first couple of steps then turned.

'The treads are a bit uneven,' he said, smiling fondly at her and offering his hand, 'so if you'd allow me.'

'Thank you,' she said, giving him a cool look. 'As I spend most of my days climbing in and out of railway carriages, I'm quite able to walk down a couple of steps by myself.'

With her face averted, Prue brushed past him down the remaining stairs. Weaving her way between empty wine racks and rickety shelves crammed with tatty books and papers, she headed towards her parents. They were sitting on a couple of old threadbare armchairs, next to a shelf containing their shelter provisions: tins of food, blankets and a primus stove still in its cardboard box.

David descended the final few steps then, pulling the front of his jacket down, he went over to join them just as Mrs Carmichael was complaining – rightly, in his view – about how the extra people in the cellar made it very cramped.

'Don't worry,' said Prue. 'Once we have the bunkbeds up and installed the amenities everyone will be able to use the St Winifred's shelter during an air raid.'

'Sound very jolly,' said David.

Prue gave him another chilly look and turned away.

David opened his mouth to say something more but then an infant wail echoed around the empty space.

'That's Peter,' said Prue, addressing her parents. 'He's been a bit feverish. I'll just pop over and see if everything is all right.'

Turning and without glancing at David, Prue made her way over to where the huddle of mothers and children were sitting.

David caught up with her halfway across and stepped in her path.

'I know, I know,' he said, raising his hands in gesture of mock surrender. 'It is utterly preposterous that a young lady with refined sensibilities like yourself would be attracted to some coarse fellow like Quinn.'

To his utter relief Prue smiled. 'Is it?'

'Yes, it is,' laughed David, gazing down at her. 'Believe me, I wouldn't have said anything, and I know you're only being kind to him, but you don't understand the way of men like Jack Quinn.'

Prue's lovely innocent eyes stretched wide. 'Don't I?'

He gave her an indulgent smile. 'If he had the chance, he'd try to take advantage of your innocence, I'm certain of it. And while I have no doubt at all you would rebuff him instantly, the damage would be done.'

She looked adorably perplexed. 'Damage?'

'To your reputation,' said David.

Prue's artless expression remained for a second or two then she glared at him.

'I've pointed out before, Father David, that this is nineteen forty not eighteen forty, so as well as showing their ankle and remaining unaffected by the sight of a

271

jacketless man, young women can now talk to whoever we like without seeking anyone's permission.'

David jolted back. 'But I'm only thinking of—'

The strident tone of the all-clear cut across him from above.

The children sprang off their seats and clattered towards the stairs while the adults followed after them.

Prue glanced at them then looked back at David. She studied him levelly.

Wrestling with the unbearable thought that Prue might desire such a man as Jack Quinn, David held her gaze for a moment then stepped aside.

She marched past and followed the rectory's houseguests up the wooden stairs.

David stared after her, his brain emptied for a moment, then a thought that could only have been sent from above filled his consciousness.

A slow smile spread across his face.

Of course, to ensure he was worthy of Prue, like all the men God destined for great things in His name, David would have to prove he was worthy.

Chapter twenty-three

'**O**W MANY MORE WE GOT to do, Prue?' asked Kate, as Prue emerged from the end of the passenger carriage, bucket and mop in hand.

'Just two more carriages and then we can go for our mid-morning cuppa,' said Prue.

'Fank Gawd for that,' said Maggie, putting her hands in the small of her back and stretching upwards. 'I'm desperate to wet my whistle. And it's so blooming hot, too.'

It was the third Monday in July, just before ten in the morning, and her friends and fellow LNER cleaners were halfway through an early shift and just finishing their second set of six carriages.

And Maggie was right, it was so blooming hot.

The barometer in the rectory had shown high pressure all week and the cloudless sky above confirmed the matter. England was not only in the middle of the war but in the middle of a heatwave. However, as much as the constant clear blue above them would usually have been a cause for celebration after a cold and prolonged winter, this year it brought dread. Many had wondered why, having reached the northern coast of France, the

Germans hadn't just sailed straight over, but in the past week the answer had become clear.

After Cardiff was bombed the week before, air raid sirens that had previously blared out only once or twice a week suddenly did so each day – and often three or four times. Also, rather than lasting half an hour before the all-clear sounded, now it could be an hour and a half, or even longer. And everyone could see why, as squadrons of RAF Spitfires and Hurricanes flew southward in that clear blue sky. With the Germans sweeping all before them, only an extreme optimist thought there wouldn't soon be Panzer tanks rolling along the Dover Road towards London.

Thankfully, because the carriage shed had been taken over by the army to store their equipment, all the carriages designated for cleaning were shunted on to a couple of tracks at the back of the yard where the LNER old Victorian warhorses were deposited while they waited to be decommissioned.

'How much did you find today?' asked Kate, retying her loosened headscarf, as Prue reached them.

Rummaging around in her pocket, Prue held out her hand. 'Just a threepenny bit and a couple of pennies.'

'I dug out a tanner between two of the seats,' said Maggie, showing them her morning haul.

'I've just got a couple of coppers,' Kate added, uncurling her fingers to show the coins on her palm. 'It's not much, but better than the false eye Ivy found last week.'

'Well, every little bit helps towards the Stratford Yard Spitfire,' said Prue. 'We'll put it in the jar when we go over to the canteen.'

A sound of male laughter rolled across from the other side of the perimeter fence and all three women looked through the wire at the army camp beyond, where half a dozen squaddies were kicking a flat-looking football about while their compatriots sat around on empty crates and upended boxes.

'I don't know why they are here,' added Maggie. 'They spend all day getting in everyone's way and making the place look untidy.'

'Jack says their orders are to defend the shunting yard while the engineers and signalmen destroy all the points and booby-trap the locomotives,' said Prue, recounting the conversation they'd had the day before when they'd met in the canteen.

Kate and Maggie exchanged looks.

Prue looked puzzled. 'What!'

'It's Jack this,' said Maggie, in a sing-song voice.

'And Jack that,' chipped in Kate, using the same tone. 'And you and 'im seemed very pally when I saw you yesterday sitting in the canteen together,' she added, nudging Kate playfully in the ribs.

'I'm friendly with his sister, and Jack is helping to set up the air raid shelter under the church. We were talking about that, if you must know,' said Prue, trying her best to appear nonchalant despite her warm cheeks.

'While gazing lovingly into each other's eyes,' said

Maggie, pulling a soppy face and fluttering her eyelashes.

'Not that we blame you, mind,' said Maggie, extracting the roll-up she'd stashed behind her ear and relighting it. 'Goodness, the man is temptation on legs and sweet enough to sink your teeth into. And you're not the only one who thinks so.'

She nodded towards the other set of carriages, where Gladys and her two friends, Pat and Gloria, had just emerged.

'I saw her making eyes at him yesterday when she caught him coming out of the paint shop,' said Kate.

'She practically pinned him to the shower-block wall last week,' said Maggie.

'I thought Gladys had hooked up with that loud-mouthed sergeant whose been swaggering about like he owns the place,' said Prue, trying to ignore the prickly sensation behind her breastbone.

'She 'as,' agreed her friend, puffing a cloud of smoke skyward. 'But she'd dump 'im like a hot potato if Jack Quinn looked 'er way.'

'Not that he's gonna,' added Kate, throwing her arms around Prue's shoulders. 'Cos 'e's only got eyes for our Prue.'

She squeezed Prue's shoulders and the uncomfortable lump in her chest dissolved a little.

Seeing Prue and her friends, Gladys muttered something and three pairs of heavily mascaraed and none too friendly eyes looked them over before the three women made their way along to the next carriage.

'Let's go for our well-earned cuppa before we start the last two,' said Prue, hoping to get past the carriage before Gladys and her team reached it.

Collecting their buckets ready to stow in the locker, Prue led the way. However, as they were halfway across the wooden walkway they spotted Knobby Clark, puffing and panting in the mid-morning sunshine, hurrying towards them.

'Oi, hold up a bloody minute, you lot,' he shouted.

Prue and her two friends stopped in their tracks.

'Where are you off to?' he asked as he reached them.

'To have our morning break,' Maggie replied.

'All right, but you three are being transferred,' he said.

'Where to?' asked Prue, as visions of the Plaistow yard popped into her head.

Knobby pulled out a grubby handkerchief and mopped his brow. 'The lamp shed.'

'I thought we were only allowed to work on the carriages,' said Maggie.

'Fings change,' Knobby replied. 'Three of my best blokes in Lamps have got their papers and that brainless bloody idiot Keith Hargreaves managed to walk between the St Vincent Dart and it's coal tender as it was backing up.'

'Is he dead?' asked Prue.

'By rights he should be,' their supervisor replied. 'But lucky for him he just had his left arm crushed to a pulp between the couplings. So, as I'm losing men to the army every day, you lot can take up the slack in the lamp shed.'

'What's all this about the lamp shed?' said Gladys as she and her two friends ambled over.

'Mr Clark is transferring us to work on the lamps,' said Prue.

'That ain't fair,' grumbled Pat.

'Why're they going and not us?' asked Gloria.

A sneer spread across Gladys's powdered face. She regarded Prue and her friends for a moment then turned to Knobby. 'I'll tell you why: it's bloody favouritism that's what. Miss Goody-two-shoes-vicar's-daughter and her chums here are everyone's blue-eyed girls around the yard.'

Prue's grip on the mop tightened and her eyebrows pulled together. She was just about to open her mouth and give Gladys a few home truths when Knobby beat her to it.

'I'll tell you why I'm moving 'em and not you, Miss Loudmouth, because you and your bloody crew spend half the day avoiding work and sliding around the back of the workshops with bloody soldiers. On top of that you're always the last to bloody clock in and the first to clock out, so that's why I'm promoting Carmichael and her crew to lamp cleaners.'

Knobby turned his attention back to Prue and her two friends, and fury flashed across the faces of Gladys and the women flanking her.

'Right, you three,' their supervisor continued, 'have your break then go and see Harry Pegg in the lamp workshop. ''E's expecting you and I 'ope you don't mind heights.'

He stomped away, leaving the two teams of cleaners standing next to the railway track facing each other.

There was a long pause then Gladys turned and, with her team members bringing up the rear, she stamped off towards the next carriage.

'Well, that told 'er,' said Maggie, grinding her roll-up stub under her boots and into the gravel as the other women reached the steps at the end of the carriage.

It certainly had; however, as Gladys grasped the metal rail to climb up, she half turned. Her scarlet mouth twisted into an ugly shape which told Prue that she would have to watch her step in future.

'So, Jack, how many do we have?' asked Sister Martha as Jack took a sip of his tea.

'Four,' Jack replied. 'Donny Duncombe, Georgie Murray, Isaac Morris and Freddie.'

It was just after four-thirty on the third Thursday afternoon and Jack was sitting in one of the two comfortable chairs in the nun's small parlour, where he'd been for the past half an hour.

St Winifred's elderly nun lived in King John Passage, a narrow walkway between the road of the same name and Stepney High Street. In contrast to the Victorian three-up three-down houses that lined the majority of the street in the area, the passageway had a neat row of tithe cottages on either side, with diamond leaded windows and low roofs, built in a much earlier period.

Comfortably furnished with a couple of flowery upholstered armchairs, a small sideboard and shelves either side of the chimney, the homely room carried the delicate fragrance of beeswax.

Although she was wearing her grey skirt and cardigan, Sister Martha removed her wimple to reveal a full head of silky grey hair trimmed in a bob below the ear. In contrast to her relaxed appearance, Jack was dressed in his old grey boiler suit with LDV armband, his cap stowed in his breast pocket, a leather belt, holster and recently issued revolver.

A wry smile lifted the nun's thin lips. 'A safe cracker, an underworld enforcer, a forger and a cat burglar. The perfect auxiliary unit. Well done.'

'All old playmates,' Jack explained. 'And we get two for one as Isaac is a watchmaker, too, with a workshop at the kosher end of Brick Lane. I did consider Tommy Lavender and Marty Summers, but I decided to hold them in reserve. Although some might say otherwise, they are all solid. I'd stake my life on it.'

'You will be,' said Sister Martha. 'Now following up on our plan, it took a bit of searching but I discovered the key to St Winifred's charnel house last week.'

'What's it like inside?'

'Not the place to be if you don't like creepy-crawlies, but the walls are sound enough. As you suggested, it's perfect,' Sister Martha replied. 'It's even got an escape route down the old passageway to the crypt. There's a gate with rusty bars to it but its arched roof looked to be intact when I shone the torch along its length, although you'll only know for certain when you go down there.'

'We need to change the locks at both ends,' said Jack. ' I'm helping to make the crypt into an air raid shelter so I can change the one that end of the passageway without anyone seeing and I'll have a word with Isaac to see if he can make us a couple that look as old as the ones they are replacing.'

'That's sounds sensible,' said the nun. 'As far as I know no one has gone inside the charnel house for years, but there's no point taking the chance that someone will. There is one thing that bothers me.'

'What's that?'

'Although there're several gaps in the roof tiling, there's not much air inside so if you use a gas lamp for more than a couple of hours you'll pass out from the fumes,' she explained.

'I know. That's why I don't plan to use it as a base like the country units. The ventilation will be fine for an hour or two's training, but even if the ventilation was up to it the charnel house is too visible so I propose we use it mainly as a weapons dump, which we can access once we've decided on a target. Any news?'

'There should be a consignment of guns coming soon,' Sister Martha replied. 'Plus a shortwave radio, TNT, pencil fuses and a couple of sub-machine guns. But, where are you going to train your unit until you've got it set up?'

Leaning back in his chair Jack grinned.

'Here,' he said, surveying her handkerchief-sized lounge with flowery wallpaper, chintz furniture and a collection of ancient bone-china ornaments. 'Just until we get the locks changed on the charnel house.'

Sister Martha stared at him for a moment then her wry smile returned. 'Very well, but I hope I can think of a plausible story as to why I have three local villains and a Jewish watchmaker visiting me as I doubt my neighbours will believe they've all seen the light.'

'Well, firstly we will be meeting after the blackout starts and me and Freddie shouldn't raise too many eyebrows because we've visited you since we were kids,' Jack replied. 'But if the others can't slip in via the back door without rousing suspicion, then I've recruited the wrong team.'

She smiled. 'I knew I was right to suggest you as unit leader to Colin.'

'Colin?' said Jack.

'Colonel Gubbins,' Sister Martha explained. 'What?'

'Well, that explains why he asked me on the QT to give you his regards,' Jack replied. 'I guess you've known each other a while.'

'Since October nineteen-sixteen when he was stretchered into a dressing station with a gunshot wound to the neck,' she said. 'I was a VAD with the Red Cross. I nursed him until he recovered sufficiently to return to the front.'

'Were you close?'

'We were, but I was closer to his friend. Much closer,' she added.

Jack raised an eyebrow.

'Well, Jack!' she said, laughter twinkling in her eyes. 'I haven't always been a nun.'

A broad smile stretched Jack's rugged features. 'As you're the area intelligence officer for goodness only knows how many auxiliary units, in your dark, distant past you've clearly been something other than a nun.'

She sipped her tea. 'I'm pleased to hear you've been helping Prue set up St Winifred's air raid shelter.' A fond expression spread across the nun's wrinkled face. 'She's such a whirlwind.'

'Who, St Winifred?'

'No, you silly boy,' said Sister Martha, giving him an exasperated look. 'Prue Carmichael. Such energy and fearlessness, too.'

'She certainly has all those things,' said Jack, mentally subscribing several more attributes of his own.

'She reminds me of me when I was young,' added the nun. 'Except, of course, I was just a couple of points above ordinary in the good looks stakes, whereas Prue Carmichael is very pretty.'

Jack's mind conjured up a picture of Prue, standing with a bucket in one hand and a mop in the other, and he laughed. 'She's stunning.'

With her cup suspended halfway to lips, Sister Martha gave Jack the same look she had given the ten-year-old Jack when she'd questioned him about the smashed vestry window.

'Do you see her a lot at work?' she asked.

'A couple of times a week,' Jack replied, trying to sound nonchalant under her needle-eyed scrutiny. 'You know, in passing. In the canteen at lunchtime or when I'm on my way between sheds we sometimes have a quick chat. And when we're just walking back to the changing rooms after a shift.'

Sister Martha studied him over the rim of her teacup.

'Actually, now I come to think about it, I see Prue most days,' Jack added, forcing himself to hold the elderly nun's gaze. 'Especially now she and her team have been transferred to the lamp shop; she's out and about fetching lamps back and forth all day.'

Sister Martha lowered her cup. 'Alma was stunning too.'

'She was and still is,' admitted Jack. 'But whereas Alma wore her looks like a crown and expected everyone to pay it homage, Prue isn't even aware of it.' An image of her smiling across at him while they sat at one of the canteen tables floated into his mind. 'And Prue's more than just a pretty face. Much more.'

The nun studied him for a long moment then opened her mouth to speak; however, the clock on the sideboard struck the first note of the hour.

'Is that the time?' said Jack, throwing back the last of his tea and rising to his feet. 'Thanks for the tea, but I should be on parade.'

'Well, you know you're welcome here any time, Jack,' said Sister Martha.

She went to stand up but Jack waved her not to. 'I can

see myself out. When can I tell the lads to report for their first training?'

'Next Wednesday,' she replied, as the clock chimed through the numbers. 'Hopefully I should have word about the weapons shipment by then.'

He nodded and turned towards the front door.

'Say hello to Prue if you see her tomorrow,' she called after him.

Jack raised his hand in acknowledgement and opened the door on the last strike of five.

In truth, he wasn't due to be on parade for another half an hour and under usual circumstances he would have quite happily whiled away that half-hour wallowing in Sister Martha's snug armchair, eating cake and drinking tea.

He didn't know the secrets of Sister Martha's past, but having spent a weekend under Gubbins' and Beyts' espionage and resistance tutelage, he suspected that she had once been involved in something very similar. One thing he did know was she was a skilled interrogator because in regard to his growing feelings for Prue, as with the broken vestry window all those years ago, there would be no fooling Sister Martha.

Standing next to Bill, Jack watched the fireman, a lanky chap with a haphazard set of teeth, swing the beam from his lamp back and forth on the gravel while the driver of the N Class 4-6-0 locomotive inched it back the last few yards.

It was Friday, a day after he'd updated Sister Martha on the auxiliary unit and a full three hours since his clocking-off time, because at five-thirty Ted Prentice had come puffing across the yard with a red-topped emergency chit in his hand.

The blackout had come into force a while back and since then, Jack and his crew had been forced to work on the neglected rolling stock using only their bull's-eye lamps.

He, Tosh and Bill had spent all afternoon in the carriage at the back of the yard, where the buffet and sleeper carriages that had been converted to ordinary passenger carriages when war was declared were housed.

Many of the carriages in the shed were well over sixty years old and had been destined for the scrap heap as part of the war effort to garner any useable metal. However, being its usual efficient self, the London and North Eastern Railway hadn't quite got around to signing whatever docket was necessary to wave them goodbye, so they had sat languishing until Dunkirk; they'd been used for moving troops ever since.

Thankfully, despite their age, when Jack inspected them other than one old carriage whose brakes had rusted, the rolling stock was in pretty good shape. So, after oiling all their wheels, checking the couplings and brakes, Jack was able to pass six of the sleepers safe to use.

Tosh had been fretting about meeting some girl he was sweet on, so Jack had sent him home an hour ago, telling him to stop by at the control room as he passed to let them know the carriages were all but done.

The fireman stopped swinging his lamp and let out a two-tone whistle. The iron wheels ceased turning and squealed to a stop. The clang of metal on metal echoed around the high-vaulted ceiling as two of the sleeping-car carriages juddered back along the rails.

Jack stepped forward to give the fireman a hand joining the couplings as Bill held a lamp aloft so both of them could complete the task of joining the carriage to the engine with the same number of fingers they started with.

'There're all yours,' said Jack, having secured the joint with a steel bolt through his side of the connection.

'Thanks, chum,' said the fireman, grasping the handrail and heaving himself into the train's cab alongside his driver.

Walking alongside the rolling wheels, Jack shone his lamp just in front of the engine as it glided along the tracks and out of the shed. Once clear, Jack and Bill took one of the tall folding doors on either side.

'Go home, mate,' said Jack, jamming the long bolt into it's designated hole on the ground. 'I'll finish up here.'

'You sure?' asked Bill.

Jack nodded. 'No point us both having a burnt dinner.'

In the glow of the railway lamp, Bill gave him a grateful look then, opening the small door in the right-hand gate, he left.

Gathering up his tools and checking everything was secure, Jack followed his friend out of the train shed and into the unlit shunting yard some five minutes later.

Even though it was nearly nine o'clock at night, the whole railway site was still a hive of activity. The air was filled with the sounds of wheels squealing as drivers applied the brakes and the slow clickety-clack of engines rolling over the points as they passed by. There was no hint of freshly mown grass or tree blossom on the breeze, just the tarry smell of the coal heaps and the aroma of industrial lubricant.

Jack paused for a moment or two until his eyes had adjusted. He took his dimmed torch out of his pocket and pointed it on the gravel beneath his boots, setting off towards the staff shower block.

However, as he turned the corner of the coal bunker, he spotted a figure lurking by a cargo wagon; whoever it was seemed to be fiddling with the tarpaulin covering it.

Placing his tool bag on the floor, Jack took out one of his larger spanners and advanced over the tracks. When he was within a few feet of the stationary wagon he lowered his improvised weapon.

'Found anything worth nicking, Billy?'

The one-time wingman of the Green Street Gang spun around, fists raised.

'Jack Quinn.' Billy's top lip curled. 'Fancy seeing you here.'

'Yes, fancy. Well, have you?"

Pulling a hurt expression, Billy placed a knuckle-scarred hand on the breast pocket of his combat jacket. 'I'm a changed man, Jack.'

'A sergeant, too, I see.' Jack indicated the stripes on his sleeves.

'Promoted under fire.' Billy dusted the three chevrons on his arm. 'Dunkirk, as it 'appens.'

'Well, you never were short of bottle, Billy, just brains and conscience.'

The ruthless back-street bruiser beneath flashed across the other man's face for a second then his lazy smile returned. 'I bet you were gobsmacked to see me, weren't you?'

'Too right,' agreed Jack. 'I thought you'd be banged up in Holloway with your mate Mosley by now.'

Billy's indolent grin widened. 'How's your bit of Yiddish skirt and that half-caste sprog?' he asked, as Jack somehow resisted the urge to swipe the spanner across his brutish face. 'Bet your old lady – 'scuse me, your ex old lady – is getting a bit jittery now with Hitler and his mob an 'op, skip and a jump away, eh?'

Although raw fear of Alma and Rachel's fate should Hitler make it across the Channel tore through him, Jack managed to smile.

'Oi, oi, Sarge!' cried a voice from behind them. 'Come, see wot—'

'All right, lad,' Billy shouted back without taking his eyes off Jack.

'I'll see you around then,' said Jack.

'You will, Jack. Mind 'ow you go.'

'You too, Billy.'

They eyeballed each other for a moment then setting his tin helmet straight on his thick-boned head, Billy sauntered off towards the end of the line of waggons.

Jack watched him go for a moment then went back to his abandoned tool bag and returned the spanner. Picking it up from the floor, he continued on towards the shower block.

It was dangerous enough working at Stratford railway depot, but in addition to having 150-ton locomotives criss-crossing his path, with Billy Butcher at large in the shunting yard Jack had never had sounder advice than to 'mind 'ow you go'.

Chapter twenty-four

'CAN YOU TELL ME where the post office is, please?'
Prue said to Ingrid Hass, who was sitting across from her.

'Yes, Prue, I can tell you where ze post office is,' Ingrid
replied, her fair brow furrowed with concentration. 'It is
in ze High Street ... naast ... ne ...'

'Next to,' prompted Prue.

'Next to ze baker,' repeated the young mother.

It was ten o'clock in the morning on the fourth Friday
in July and Prue was sitting at the dining-room table with
Ingrid and Marie Moleen and Beattie Hansen, two of the
young Dutch mothers whom Prue had found places for
in the parish.

Although it was her only day off, Prue had set her
alarm clock for seven as she had a full day ahead of her.
She had already washed her smalls and pegged them
on the line in the warm summer sunshine. She was now
halfway through her weekly English lesson with the three
refugee friends. She had a couple of letters to write, which
would take her up to lunchtime, after which she would
join those beavering away in the church's crypt. Thank
goodness, too, for although the RAF fighter pilots had
managed to hold their own against the Luftwaffe thus far,

Scotland and Wales had been bombed the previous week, so it looked as though St Winifred's shelter would soon be needed. She'd told Jack that much yesterday when she'd meet him on her way back to the lamp shop.

Jack was one of the workers hammering the bunkbeds and setting up a refreshment area today. Although she told herself it was of no consequence, knowing he would be there caused an unsettling feeling in the pit of her stomach.

Try as she might to remind herself that divorce was something the Church abhorred, she had to admit to herself that a small part of her was very pleased indeed that Jack Quinn wasn't spoken for.

The strident buzz of the telephone in the hallway cut across her thoughts. It rang a few times then someone picked it up.

There was a knock at the door then her mother's head appeared around the edge of the door. 'It's Mrs Shaw from the council for you.'

Excusing herself, Prue left the three women to practise the lesson so far and went out into the hall.

Her mother handed Prue the receiver. 'Just to remind you, Mrs Lavender will need to set the table for lunch in an hour.'

Prue replied with a sweet smile as she put the receiver to her ear.

'Good morning, Mrs Shaw,' she said, as her mother closed the door to the sitting room. 'What can I do for you?'

'Good morning, Miss Carmichael,' came the welfare

officer's tinny voice through the wires. 'I know you've already helped so much with the borough resettlement of refugees, so I'm loath to ask any more of you, but is it possible for you to squeeze a young single lady in somewhere? I wouldn't ask, but due to an unforeseen circumstance she's had to leave her billet.'

'Oh dear,' said Prue.

'It's nothing to do with Miss Kratz, you understand,' continued Mrs Shaw. 'But the daughter of the elderly lady where she had been placed has taken her mother to the safety of the country and the landlord has repossessed the house. I'm afraid I can't tell you much else about her as my colleague is dealing with her. He left a note on my desk asking for help, so other than that it's imperative she be found another billet in the area, I can tell you nothing more about her.'

'Of course I can help,' Prue replied. 'In fact, I think with a bit of shifting around I can make room for her here in the rectory. When should I expect her?'

'A couple of hours, I should think,' Mrs Shaw replied. 'And thank you, Miss Carmichael.'

The phone went dead.

Prue replaced the receiver then went to find her mother in the lounge.

She was sitting at the writing bureau, bent over her correspondence, but looked up as Prue walked in.

'I suppose she was just checking up on our lodgers,' her mother said, the nib of her fountain pen poised above the vellum paper.

'No,' said Prue. 'She rang to ask if we could take another refugee. I said yes.'

'Not more children,' Marjorie said, horror writ large across her face. 'I don't know how your father will be able to concentrate on his sermon with more of them running up and down the stairs.'

'No, this is a young single lady, Miss Kratz,' Prue replied.

'Well, I suppose that's something,' her mother replied. 'At least she'll be able to give a hand around the house. I'm just finishing a letter to Auntie Minnie, but I really could do with some help planning this week's menu for Mrs Lavender this afternoon.'

'I'm sorry, Mother,' Prue replied, 'but as soon as I've finished luncheon, I'm going over to St Winifred's to help in the crypt.'

Her mother opened her mouth to speak but Prue left the room. Crossing back to the dining room, she opened the door and peered around the corner.

'I'm sorry to ask,' she said, smiling at the three women, 'but as all the men are out, would you all mind giving me a hand upstairs shifting some furniture about?'

An hour later, after the four women had carried Fliss's bed into Prue's room and transferred the spare single divan from the poky box room into her sister's more spacious one, the faint sound of the rectory doorbell echoed up the stairs.

'It's all right, Mrs Lavender, I'll get it,' Prue shouted, hurrying downstairs and across the hall runner.

Stepping into the porch she opened the front door.

Standing on the step was a slender young woman a few years older and a few inches taller than Prue, wearing a mint-green, tailored dress of some quality and polished lace-up shoes. She was carrying a leather suitcase.

The long oval face was prevented from being regarded as too narrow by strong cheekbones and a firm but feminine jawline. Her hair, which had a hint of a wave through its ebony tone, was woven into two plaits secured into an arch across the top of her head.

'Miss Carmichael?' she said, her dark brown eyes looking unflinchingly at Prue.

Prue smiled. 'I am, and you must be Miss Kratz. Welcome and please come in.' She stood back from the door and the young woman entered the house.

'It's very good of you to take me in at such short notice,' she said, with only the faintest hint of an accent.

'Not at all,' said Prue. 'It's the least we can do. And as we are going to be living under the same roof, it's Prue.'

'And I'm Hester.' The young women offered her hand. 'It is very good to meet you.'

'And you,' said Prue, taking hold of it. 'We already have three families in what used to be the old servants' quarters at the top of the house, so I've moved a few things around and put you in my sister's room along from me.'

Miss Kratz frowned. 'Won't she mind?'

'Fliss lives in Pimlico and only comes home for a weekend every now and then, so she can bunk in with me when she does,' Prue explained. 'Mrs Lavender, our housekeeper, will be serving lunch in about an hour, so I just have time to show you to your—'

'Miss Kratz!'

Prue looked around to see her mother emerging in a flurry from the small parlour at the back and homing in on them.

'Welcome, welcome,' she said, beaming at the young woman standing beside Prue.

'Thank you,' said Miss Kratz. 'As I was just saying to your daughter, I'm very grateful for you and your family's generosity.'

'Think nothing of it.' Prue's mother's face formed itself into a pious expression. 'I'm sure you'll agree that our Lord himself said blessed are those who give succour to the poor?'

'I am afraid I would not, Mrs Carmichael,' said the young women, studying her levelly. 'I'm Jewish.'

Surprise flickered across Marjorie's face for a second then her magnanimous smile returned. 'I'm sorry, it was your almost perfect English that confused me.'

The corner of Miss Kratz's lips lifted in a faint smile, but she didn't reply.

'Well, no matter,' Prue's mother continued. 'The rectory housekeeper will show you the ropes.'

'Ropes?' said the young woman.

'Yes, where the mops and dusters are,' continued her

mother. 'That sort of thing. I'm sure you'll want to pitch in with the housework and—'

'I'm sorry, Mrs Carmichael,' their new lodger interrupted. 'Perhaps I should have introduced myself properly. I'm Dr Hester Kratz, paediatrician, and Professor Kleinman is already showing me the ropes in the children's department of the Jewish Hospital.'

Holding a cup of tea in her right hand, Prue knocked lightly on what had been until an hour ago her sister's room. After hearing a firm 'come', Prue turned the handle and walked in. Hester was folding a light blue jumper with flowers embroidered into the yoke into the second drawer of the chest of drawers. Through the open wardrobe door Prue spotted two tailored outfits with plain blouses, a couple of formal gowns and a long velvet evening dress with beaded trim.

Their new guest looked around as Prue walked in.

'I thought you might like another cuppa,' Prue said.

'That's very kind of you,' said Hester, lifting her soft, pink lipsticked lips into a smile.

Prue placed the mug on the cast-iron fireplace. 'How's it going?'

'Almost done,' Hester replied. 'Thank you again for offering a room.'

'Not at all,' Prue replied. 'I'll introduce you to the families who are also staying with us at lunch and I hope you don't mind children because we have quite a lot of them at the moment,' Prue concluded.

'Mind children?' Hester replied, giving Prue a wry look.

She cast her gaze towards the half a dozen books on the window sill, with 'Child Development', 'Modern Pediatrics' and 'Less Common Childhood Illnesses' embossed in gold leaf on their spines.

Prue laughed. 'Stupid question.'

She spotted the book at the end and wandered over.

'Are you an obstetrician, too?' she asked, looking at *Clinical Obstetrics*.

'Halfway through my training at the American Hospital in Paris when the Belgians surrendered,' Hester replied. 'I knew the Germans wouldn't stop there so … I'm hoping to complete my studies here.' She glanced around. 'It's a very nice room, especially as it has a sink; I hope your sister doesn't mind being evicted from it.'

'I'm sure she won't,' Prue replied.

Hester looked around the room briefly then back at Prue.

'Such kindness,' she said, her voice catching slightly in her throat. 'After so much …' Tears glistened on her lower lashes and she pulled the handkerchief from her sleeve and looked away.

'Well, I'd better go and see how Mrs Lavender is getting on with lunch,' said Prue, trying hard to imagine the hell that this slightly built young woman must have been through in the last few months. 'I'm not sure what it is, but if you can't eat it then—'

'As long as it's not pork pie I'm fine,' Hester replied, looking up at Prue with tear-bright eyes.'

'Good. I'll leave you to it then,' said Prue. 'And I'm sorry about earlier.' Hester looked up again. 'My mother, I mean.'

'Don't worry,' said Hester, waving her words away. 'I've been mistaken for worse.'

The telephone downstairs in the hallway rang.

As it had done each time the phone rang since Robert had been declared missing in action, a feeling of dread loomed up in Prue. 'If you'd excuse me ...'

She hurried out of the room and down the stairs to find her mother standing beside the ringing telephone.

They stared wide-eyed at each other for a moment then Marjorie snatched up the receiver.

'Good morning, St Winifred's Rectory,' she said, her eyes fixed on Prue.

The hall clock ticked off a couple of seconds then, putting her hand over the mouthpiece, her mother closed her eyes and her shoulders slumped.

Prue crossed the space between them in a couple of
_____ around her.

_____ asked.

With tears now streaming down her face, her mother nodded.

'Yes,' she whispered. 'He's been found.'

Dressed in her work overall, her hair covered by a scarf turban and a grin that would have rivalled any Cheshire cat, Prue practically skipped down the St Winifred's aisle before she grabbed the rope handrail and made her way down the worn stone steps of the crypt.

As she reached the bottom and her eyes adjusted to the muted light, Prue looked around at the dozen or so volunteers working away in the stone vault beneath the ancient church.

'Afternoon, everyone,' she called. 'How are we all today?'

There were mutterings of 'mustn't grumble', 'not so bad' and 'I've been worse'.

'Well, I've brought us all a little treat, for when we have a cuppa and to celebrate.' Placing the basket on one of the benches, Prue grinned at the working party. 'They found my brother Robert.'

Those in the crypt crowded around her to congratulate her, causing happy tears to pinch the corners of her eyes again.

After thanking everyone for their kindness, Prue got to work.

Since Father David had given her his ~~guidance~~ of the church's treasures, the saintly statues had ~~been~~ wrapped carefully in newspaper and cardboard and were now lying in the rectangular niches in the walls.

Tommy Lavender was as good as his word and had delivered a large consignment of newly cut timber two weeks ago. Now half a dozen male members of the congregation were sawing and hammering them into benches for the occupants to sit on while they waited for the all-clear to sound. Above their head and standing on a set of stepladders were a couple of men fixing a string of light bulbs to the ceiling.

Not to be outdone, members of the Mothers' Union were dusting away cobwebs and scrubbing floors. Rosie, who was brushing grit into a dustpan with a stiff brush, waddled over to Prue.

'Should you be doing this?' asked Prue as the heavily pregnant woman reached her.

'I'm only doing the alcove, so there's no bending or stretching,' Rosie replied. 'And I wanted to do my bit to help. What do you think?'

Prue cast her eyes around the crypt. 'I think you've all worked a miracle getting it ready.'

'We're not quite finished yet, but I reckon another week should do it,' said Rose. 'Just as well, with the Luftwaffe bombs getting ever nearer. Dropped a load on Kent last night, as far in as Tunbridge, they did. And along the coast in Eastbourne. It's only a matter of time before they drop some this way.'

Prue frowned. 'I must have missed that in the newspaper.'

'It wasn't there,' Rose replied. 'Jack heard it from a driver on the *Spirit of Dymchurch*. 'E says we don't hear the half of it.'

'I thought he'd be here today,' said Prue.

'He was supposed to be,' Rosie replied, 'but they found something else wrong with the engine he was working on yesterday so even through it's his day off he had to go in first thing to finish off.'

'Oh well, never mind,' said Prue, her heart sinking a little. 'Anyhow, what do you want me to do?'

'The Arbour family crypt needs a good sweeping out before we can set up the refreshment table,' said Rosie. Giving a sharp intake of breath, her hands went to her stomach.

'Are you all right,' said Prue.

'Just a practice pain,' she explained, between tight lips. 'I had them all the time with the other two.'

'Even so, perhaps you'd better sit down for a moment,' said Prue.

'No, I'm fine, honest,' insisted Rosie. 'You get on; I'll be as right as rain in a while.'

'All right, but give me a shout if you need me,' Prue told her.

Prue grabbed one of the stiff brooms and headed for the Arbour family's vault.

The recess, which was about as large as the rectory's box room, ran off the main crypt to the left but had been cleared out of the long-dead aristocrat and his decedents.

The ARP wardens had been handing out the *Your Air Raid Precautions* pamphlets for months, which advised people to bring with them to the shelter family documents and warm clothes, as well as a flask of hot drink and food. However, as no one knew how long they might have to take refuge during an actual bombing raid, Prue and the newly formed St Winifred's shelter committee decided to use the old family vault as a refreshment area so they could provide hot drinks.

Although there was an electric light dangling from the stone family crest fixed above the entrance, the interior was gloomy. Stepping inside, Prue continued past the empty coffin spaces to the back.

Gripping her broom firmly and throwing up little puffs of dust before her, she started in one corner, clearing the dust and grit that had accumulated over the ages. She went back and forth a couple of times, allowing her mind to wander off in no particular direction at first then, although it really should not, on to Jack, imaging him clambering over locomotives with his shirt collar open and sleeves turned back over his strong, hair-dusted arms.

'Hello!'

Prue gave a little cry and shot around, only to find the image in her head standing in the entrance of the antichamber in the flesh.

'Sorry,' he said, stepping over the threshold as her heart did a little tap dance. 'I didn't mean to startle you.'

'It's my fault; I was miles away,' Prue replied, hoping he couldn't hear the quiver in her voice. 'Have you come straight from work?'

He nodded and the lock of hair that never behaved flopped on to his brow.

'Yes,' he said, smoothing it back. 'I promised to give Ollie a hand with wiring up the generator.'

'Good. I'm just doing some sweeping.'

'I can see,' he said, indicating the yard brush in her hand.

They gazed at each other for a moment then Jack thumbed over his shoulder.

'Well, I'd better g—'

'Have you seen Rachel?' she blurted out.

'On Saturday,' he replied. 'We did story time at Whitechapel library and then I wanted to go for a trip up to see the King's house up West but she opted for going back to Rosie's so she could play with her cousins.'

'Sounds like the perfect childhood Saturday,' said Prue, imagining Jack and his daughter walking hand in hand.

A tender look crept into Jack's expression. 'She won this year's class prize for arithmetic and brought her workbooks with her to show me.' He gave her that quirky smile of his. 'She tells me she wants to be the first ever lady railway engineer. And knowing Rachel, she will be.'

'Oh, Jack, you must be so very proud,' said Prue.

'I certainly am. I only wish she could live …' An aching expression replaced Jack's loving one.

Something inside Prue echoed his emotion and she only just stopped herself reaching out and placing her hand on his arm.

Jack gave a heavy sigh then forced a smile. 'What about you? Any news of your brother?'

'Well, funny you should ask,' Prue replied, 'because two hours ago …' She told Jack about the phone call.

'That's wonderful,' he said when she'd finished. 'No wonder it took so long to find him.'

'Well, it's a bit of a walk from Belgium to St-Malo,' said Prue. 'He's down on the south coast somewhere, but as soon as he can he's coming home for a day or two.'

Jack stepped forward and looked down at her, his eyes almost black in the dim light.

'It must be a great relief for your mother,' he said, losing himself in her gaze.

Her words seemed to have got lost somewhere on their way to her throat, so she just smiled.

Their eyes locked for a moment – or it could have been an eternity – then Prue leaned forward. For a moment she had the distinct impression that Jack was doing the same, that he was about to put his arms around her, but then a shrill, two-tone whistle cut between them.

'Oi, oi, Jack, give us a hand, mate,' bellowed Ollie as they both straightened up.

Jack gave her little smile. 'I'd better …'

'Me too,' said Prue, cheerfully grasping her broom again. 'This floor won't sweep itself.'

Neither of them moved for a moment, then Jack turned and strolled towards the main part of the crypt.

'Oh, Jack, I meant to say …' He turned. 'We're having a party in the rectory garden for the parish children in a few weeks; why don't you bring Rachel? I'm sure she'd have a great time with all the others, and I really would love to meet her.'

'I'm sure she would,' Jack replied. 'But perhaps I ought to tell you my Rachel is half Jewish.'

'Is she?' said Prue. 'Well, I'm glad you told me because

305

I'll ask Mrs Leitner to make sure we have plenty of kosher goodies.'

An unreadable expression flitted across Jack's face then he smiled. 'I'd love to bring her along.'

'Good,' said Prue. 'I'll put you on my list.'

'Jack!'

'Coming,' Jack called back over his shoulder.

Jack gazed at Prue for a long moment then walked off to help Ollie.

Prue's eyes following his rolling shoulders for a moment, then humming 'It's a Lovely Day Tomorrow' quietly, she set to work with the broom again.

Chapter twenty-five

PASSING A DUST-COVERED coalman shouldering a half-hundredweight sack off the back of his wagon and sidestepping an uncovered coalhole, Prue continued along Belgrave Road.

Reaching a junction, she took the map her sister had sketched and studied it for a moment before turning right into Warwick Square and its elegantly proportioned Edwardian townhouses, many with sandbags covering their ground-floor windows.

Before the war, of course, the enclosed park at the centre would have had neatly manicured flower beds. Now, like everywhere else, it had been given over to the war effort, so at one end stood a hut with 'Warden's Post' painted in white on the side, and a blackboard fixed alongside it with a clock showing the blackout times. The rest of the plot had been dug over ready for planting, so now it resembled an allotment rather than a landscaped floral oasis. Skirting around it, Prue made for the far corner and turned into Westmorland Road, checking the door numbers until she reached the last-but-one house.

Climbing the three steps to the front door, Prue shaded her eyes against the early-morning sun and peered at the four doorbells. Having skimmed over Mr Fedorov, interpreter; Miss E Baird, seamstresses, and the imaginatively named Mademoiselle Tutti Belle, French teacher, Prue saw the one with 'F, Carmichael' and 'Flat 4' next to it.

Picking the milk bottle from the crate on the doorstep with the corresponding number, Prue pushed open the heavy Edwardian front door. Catching the faint sound of the nine o'clock pips coming from the ground-floor flat, Prue walked to the stairs and made her way up past the wallpaper burnished by countless shoulders scraping it, to the floors above.

Reaching the top of the house where the servants' quarters had once been, Prue stopped in front of the solid-looking pine door with a number four screwed to it.

As there wasn't a knocker on it and she could see no bell, Prue rapped on it with her knuckles.

There was a pause then the door opened and Fliss's head appeared around the edge.

Her sister, who still had last night's make-up smudged around her eyes, was barefooted and clutched the front of her dressing gown together and the phrase 'dragged through a hedge backward' didn't do justice to the auburn bird's nest on her head.

'Prue!' Fliss said, clutching on to the half-closed door. 'What are you doing here?'

'And a very good morning to you, too,' said Prue.

'Sorry,' said Fliss. 'I just wasn't expecting you. What time is it?'

'Just after nine.'

'Nine!'

Prue rolled her eyes. 'Yes, in the morning on Saturday the twenty-seventh of July nineteen forty; so now can I come in?'

Like a rabbit caught in the beam of a flashlight, Fliss stared blankly at her for a moment then stepped aside.

Handing her sister the milk bottle, Prue walked in.

The kitchen, if you could call it that, had a butler sink, with a cold tap and a sloping draining board on one side and an ancient stove on the other, with used saucepans and a frying pan with a layer of congealed lard covering its base on it. There was also a yellow painted country dresser that must have been carried out of the ark and a bleached wooden table with four mismatched chairs, all of which stood on lino with flagstones printed on it.

In contrast, the lounge area was covered with a large Turkish rug of some quality, although its once vibrant pattern had been bleached pale with age. There were two squat round armchairs upholstered in lime green and a worn tan-coloured chesterfield sofa.

'This is your little flat.'

'Yes, yes, it is,' said Fliss, running her fingers through her dishevelled hair. 'But what are you doing here?'

Prue smiled. 'I'm here to tell you that yesterday we had a telephone call to say Rob's been found.'

Fliss, despite her flirtation with atheism, looked skyward. 'Thank God.'

'We haven't got too many details but he's on the south coast somewhere and should be coming home soon. I rang as soon as we heard but there seems to be a problem with your telephone,' continued Prue.

'Oh … oh … yes, there's been a bit of a mix-up at the post office about the bill, that's all,' said Fliss.

'Mother was going to send you a letter,' continued Prue. 'But I said I'd pop over and tell you. Give me a chance to see you and your penthouse.'

Fliss glanced around the low-ceilinged room and snorted. 'Garret, don't you mean?'

'Well, anyway,' Prue laughed, 'can you point me towards your smallest room?'

Fliss pointed at one of the doors at the far end. 'The one on the left. The other's the bedroom.'

Although the slope of the roof restricted the headroom a little, the bathroom had all you'd expect including a drying rack over the bath with a selection of her sister's smalls drying on it. Putting down the toilet seat Prue did what she had to and returned to the main area.

'Well, as I've given up a lie-in and suffered a bone-rattling trip on the District Line to bring you the good news, am I going to get a cup of tea or are you just going to stand there hugging that bottle of milk?'

'Er …' Fliss glanced at the door next to the one Prue had just emerged from.

'Sorry,' whispered Prue, 'is your flatmate still asleep?'

'No …Th … they're … away,' said Fliss, putting the milk on the kitchen table as she went to fill the kettle.

Leaving her sister to make the tea, Prue took off her hat but as she shook out her hair, she noticed that hanging on the back of the door alongside a couple of her sister's lightweight jackets was a donkey jacket and a saggy tweed sports jacket with leather elbow patches.

Wandering idly around the room, she glanced at the handful of books with images of Karl Marx and hammers and sickles stamped on their spines sitting alongside her sister's collection of romantic novels. Careful not to knock over the half a dozen placards leaning against the wall denouncing capitalism, Prue moved a box full of pamphlets about workers' rights from the sofa to the coffee table then sat down.

'It's a nice little flat,' said Prue, as her sister placed a mug of tea on the low table in front of her.

'I like it,' said Fliss, perching on one of the lime-green armchairs. 'And I can catch a twenty-four bus straight to the *Workers' Clarion* offices.'

'Talking about work,' said Prue, 'I've been promoted to a lamp man.'

Fliss looked blank. 'What exactly is a lamp man?'

Prue told her briefly.

'Well done,' Fliss said when she'd finished. 'Although I feel sick at the thought of you climbing up on to a gantry.'

'I was a bit wobbly at first,' said Prue. 'But they are pretty solid and once you've done it a couple of times it's—'

Something thumped behind the door at the far end of the room.

Fliss's head shot around for a second then the door burst open and Giles, in socks and wearing a pair of rough cords and vest, staggered out of the room.

'Why didn't you wake me, Fliss?' he said, as he stumbled towards the bathroom clutching his shirt. 'I'm supposed to be in Clerkenwell at—'

He spotted Prue.

'Morning, Giles,' she said coolly, her cup hovering a few inches from her lips.

Urbane and articulate, Giles Naylor was a few months short of thirty and five foot ten or thereabouts; he was a lean individual with a high forehead, aquiline nose and slender hands.

Having been sent down from Oxford in his second year, after he led the university's Communist Society into a pitch battle with the university's British Union of Fascists, it was natural that, having already gained a reputation for his fiery letters in support of workers' rights, he became an editor on the *Workers' Clarion*, which is where Fliss met him.

He stared at her for a moment or two then an indolent smirk spread across his face.

'Prue,' he said. 'I didn't know you were here. How's that fairy-tale deity of yours?'

'God's the same as he's always been,' Prue replied, giving him her sweetest smile. 'And sends you his love.'

Giles snorted, then continued on his way across the room to the bathroom.

'For goodness' sake, Fliss!' hissed Prue, as the door clicked shut.

Fliss formed her features into an artless expression. 'What?'

'*What?*' snapped Prue. 'You're living in sin with Giles, that's what?'

'Sin is such a bourgeois concept,' her sister replied, waving Prue's words away.

'A bourgeois concept that could leave you holding the baby, literally,' Prue reminded her.

'We take precautions,' Fliss replied. 'And anyway, Giles and I are virtually engag—'

The bathroom door opened again, and the man at the centre of their heated discussion strolled out, now freshly shaven and with his shirt on.

He smiled at them in passing as he strolled back into the bedroom, buttoning his shirt as he went.

As he disappeared inside, Prue frowned. 'Are you saying that Giles has asked you to marry him, then?'

'Well, not in so many words,' her sister replied, struggling to hold her gaze. 'But I know he will. It's just that he and the rest of the Socialist Party committee are locked in negotiations with the Independent Labour Party and the Communist Party of Great Britain to oppose the curtailing of the fundamental rights of the workers in this country, but once they've agreed to form a united front then I'm certain Giles will propos—'

Giles walked back into the lounge now fully dressed wearing a pair of brown suede shoes and a red tie. Taking a cigarette packet from his trouser pocket, he extracted one and returned the packet from whence it came.

'What time do you think you'll be back?' Fliss asked him as he flicked his lighter into life and drew on the cigarette.

'I'm not sure, luv,' he replied, blowing a stream of smoke upwards. 'We're meeting at the Crown, and you know how some of the comrades go on sometimes. But you have Prue here to keep you company.' Taking another long drag of his cigarette, he curled it into his palm then stooping down he pressed his lips on to Fliss's briefly. 'I'll see you later.'

Straightening up, he crossed to the front door, Fliss's adoring gaze glued to him all the way. However, at the door he turned back into the room.

'Sorry to ask, darling,' he said, 'but I've only got two ten-bob notes and I doubt any cabbie will have change this early in the morning, so …'

'Take some silver out of my purse,' said Fliss.

Clamping his cigarette between his lips, Giles rifled through her handbag which was sitting on the kitchen table then jingling the change in his hand he left the flat.

Fliss stared longingly at the door for a moment then her attention returned to Prue.

'Don't look at me like that,' she snapped.

'I'm just worried for you, Fliss, that's all,' said Prue.

'Well, you needn't be,' Fliss replied. 'Giles loves me, and I love him, and I thought of all people you'd understand.'

Prue looked confused. 'Me?'

Fliss raised her eyebrows. 'Jack the engineer?'

'Oh, Jack,' said Prue, a familiar ache squeezing her chest as she spoke his name.

'Who, if I recall correctly, managed to put rather a

hungry expression on your face just thinking about him,' added her sister.

'Well, yes but …'

'But?'

'He's divorced.'

'So what?'

'What do you mean, so what?' Prue replied. 'A rector's daughter walking out with a divorced man! Can you imagine our parents' faces? Mother would take to her bed for a week with the shame! Not to mention I'd be the talk of the parish and diocese.'

'Who cares?' her sister said. 'Attitudes are changing, anyway.'

'Not that much; many churches still won't allow divorced people to take communion, and in case you've forgotten four years ago the King had to step down from the throne because he wanted to marry a divorcee.'

'Well, that proves my point, Prue,' said her sister. 'Believe me, when you love someone as much as I love Giles, you won't worry about what our parents, the congregation, the bishops or anyone else says.'

'Thank, luv,' said Jack, handing over a couple of coppers to the motherly woman in forest green manning the WVS mobile canteen.

'Are you sure you don't wanna bit of cake to soak it up?' she asked, sliding a mug of milky tea across the counter.

315

'No, ta.' Jack patted his stomach beneath his Home Guard battle jacket. 'Got to keep an eye on me figure.'

The WVS volunteer rolled her eyes as Jack took his tea and moved aside.

It was Thursday and just before ten o'clock in the evening and Jack was standing by the WVS mobile canteen in front of the gas board offices at the end of Ben Jonson Road.

He'd been allocated the Salmon Lane patrol that evening and had just completed his second three-mile circuit of it, so he reckoned he deserved a cuppa. Other members of the Civil Defence on duty that night seemed to have had the same idea: in addition to a couple of chaps from his own platoon there was an auxiliary fire brigade lorry parked on the corner with three men sitting on the tailgate slurping tea plus a Red Cross first-aid crew lolling against their ambulance. Well, ambulance was pushing it as their vehicle was in fact a double horse box hitched to an ancient Daimler, both of which were painted white with a red cross on the side.

Spotting a couple of familiar ARP wardens, Jack adjusted his newly acquired Enfield rifle on his shoulder and strolled across, mug of tea in hand.

'Wotcha, Jack,' said Jimmy Putnoe, whose prominent ears had earned him the nickname of 'wingnut' as a boy. 'Caught any Germans dressed as nuns lately?'

'Not so far,' Jack replied. 'Found anyone signalling to the Boche with washing on the line?'

'Joke, ain't it?' chipped in Doug Mercer, a well-padded

chap who was once the captain of the school football team. 'Parachuting nuns! Old ladies doing semaphore with their knickers!'

'Ridiculous,' said Jimmy. 'Sometimes I don't think the bloody government have got the sense they were born with.'

Jack raised an eyebrow. 'Just sometimes?'

They all laughed.

'Seriously, though, have you heard the latest?' said Doug. 'The bloody authorities are refusing to let people shelter in the underground during an air raid.'

'What for?' asked Jimmy.

'Because the toffs in charge of the show think that if they let us down into the tube during a bombing raid, we'll be too afraid to come back up,' Jack replied.

'Bloody liberty,' said Doug.

'Talking about toffs.' Jimmy indicated towards the shops on the other side of the road.

They looked around to see Father David strolling towards them dressed in his ARP warden's uniform, with a tin hat on his head and a white dog collar around his throat.

'Let's push off before he gets here,' said Doug.

'You're too late, mate,' said Jack. ''E's spotted you.'

'Bugger,' muttered Jimmy.

'Bloody Holy Jo,' added Doug, under his breath. 'Gave my missis a right telling-off last week, he did, cos the baby was a bit niggly during the service.'

The priest spotted them and displeasure flickered

across his face. With his eyes fixed on Jack, he came to a halt in front of them.

'Lovely evening, Father, isn't it?' said Jimmy, giving St Winifred's curate a jolly smile.

'Delightful.'

'And it's so light still you wouldn't know it was almost chucking-out time, would you?' added Doug.

Father David's attention shifted from Jack to the two men standing beside him. They suffered the curate's patronising gaze for an awkward moment then Doug threw back the last of his tea.

'Well, I s'pose I ought to crack on,' he said.

'Me too,' said Jimmy, following his friend's example. 'See yer round, Jack.'

'Not if I see you first,' Jack replied.

Doug grinned at him then he and Jimmy escaped.

Father David watched them head off down Ben Johnson Road then his cool, blue eyes returned to Jack.

'Can I buy you a cuppa, Father?' asked Jack, raising his half-drunk mug of tea.

'Thank you, no,' Father David replied. 'Actually, it's providential that I've run into you tonight.'

'Is it?'

'Indeed. I understand you were talking to Miss Carmichael in the church crypt the other day,' Father David went on.

'I was.'

'In the Arbour family's side vault,' added the priest.

Jack looked puzzled. 'So?'

318

'Well, I would have thought it was obvious, even to you,' he continued in his Sunday sermon voice. 'Being seen in a secluded place with someone with your dubious background could tarnish Miss Carmichael's reputation.'

'You mean because I'm divorced.'

Father David gave an exasperated sigh. 'Obviously because you're divorced, but also your marriage to a Jewess, links to the criminal underworld, but most of all your … your …'

'My class?' said Jack, somehow resisting the urge to clench his fist then smash it into the priest's superior face.

'I was going to say your station in life,' said Father David. 'But yes.'

'Oh, I see what you're getting at,' Jack said, giving the priest an artless look. '"Rich man in his castle and poor man at his gate", and all that?' said Jack flatly.

'Precisely,' Father David replied. 'I'm glad you appreciate my reason for bringing up the matter.'

'I certainly do.'

A smug expression curled Father David's top lip. 'Good, I'm glad you—'

'You've got your sights on Prue and you don't want any competition,' Jack cut in.

A flush crept above the curate's dog collar. 'That is *not* what I'm talking about.'

Jack feigned surprise. 'Isn't it?'

'Not in the least,' Father David snapped back.

Regarding the man opposite him coolly, Jack raised an eyebrow.

Fury stripped away Father David's tranquil façade. 'Don't flatter yourself, Quinn, that Miss Carmichael would ever give you a second look, because she wouldn't. But be warned, I will not stand by and let her reputation be sullied by the likes of you, so stay away from her. Do you understand?'

Answering the priest's furious look with a cool one, Jack didn't reply.

They remained eyeball to eyeball for a long moment then, pulling the front of his ARP warden's jacket down, Father David marched away, his blond hair glowing white in the last rays of the setting sun.

Studying Father David for a moment, the memory of Prue gazing up at him with those beautiful eyes of hers returned to his mind and a broad smile spread across Jack's face.

Chapter twenty-six

'I THINK IT'S A TAXI, said Marjorie Carmichael, stretching on her tiptoes to peer through the window. 'No, my mistake; it's just a police car.'

'Patience is a virtue, my dear,' said her husband, giving her a fond look from the fireside armchair.

'I know, Hugh,' sighed Marjorie, her eyes fixed on the street.

'And I'm sure he will be here at any moment,' said Felicity, who was sitting next to Prue on the saggy chintz sofa.

'You've been saying that for an hour,' their mother replied, without shifting her attention. 'He said he'd be here by mid-morning and it's almost noon.'

It was, in fact, just twenty past eleven on the first Tuesday in August and just over a week after they'd heard the news that Robert, who they were now waiting for, had been found.

Prue and her sister, who had arrived at the rectory from Pimlico just after nine, were sitting in the family lounge at the front of the house.

'What could have happened?' Marjorie asked, bobbing her head back and forth as each vehicle went past. Turning from the window, her eyes grew wide with dread. 'You don't think he's had an accident, do you?'

'I shouldn't think so; since the petrol ration was cut again, there's hardly a car on the road,' her husband assured her.

'And half the taxi drivers in London have been called up, so he probably had trouble finding one at Waterloo,' added Prue.

The clock ticked off another five minutes as Terence Casey played the final couple of tunes on the theatre organ in the background.

'He's here!' Marjorie yelled, leaving her lookout post at the window and dashing across the room to the door.

Prue and Felicity sprang from their chairs and sprinted after her, leaving their father to bring up the rear. The two sisters burst into the hall just as their mother flung open the door.

Standing on the threshold in his khaki battledress, complete with kit bag slung across him and a black beret sitting at a rakish angle on his corn-coloured hair, stood Prue's brother.

Like Fliss, Rob favoured their mother's side and had the long-boned limbs and fingers of their d'Apremont nobility, along with their finely sculptured features and firm chin.

He was thinner and had weariness writ large across his angular features, but his eyes still had the familiar spark of humour and wit in them. Their light blue gaze ran over them all for a moment and then he smiled. 'Hello.'

'Robert,' cried Marjorie, throwing her arms around him.

He held for a moment then released her and offered his father his hand.

'Welcome home, Son,' Hugh said, his voice heavy with emotion as he grasped Robert's hand firmly. 'It's good to have you back.'

'Thanks, Dad.'

Rob's attention shifted to Prue and Felicity. Unhooking his kit bag, he dropped it on the floor 'Hello, you two.'

'Rob,' they said in unison and they stepped forward to him.

Putting an arm around each of them, he hugged them close. Tight in his embrace, Prue closed her eyes and said a heartfelt thanks to the Almighty as Rob gave them both a peck on the forehead then released them.

Marjorie glanced past her son through the still-open door and her generous eyebrows drew together. 'I thought Lydia was coming with you?'

'She intended to but something cropped up,' he said.

Prue and her sister exchanged relieved looks.

'Her fashion house is involved in some tour in the Midlands promoting the Ministry of War fashions,' Robbie continued. 'You know, in factory canteens and the like.'

'How tiresome for her,' said Prue's mother. 'But I suppose it's part of the war effort and we will have to put up with it.'

'She promised to be here by Saturday at the latest.'

'Don't keep your poor brother standing there,' their mother said, bustling Prue and her sister aside. 'Let him come—'

The sound of laughter and feet clattering on the landing above drowned out Marjorie's voice as Nicolas Haas holding a football, hurtled down the stairs, closely followed by his sister Freda, plus Leah Leitner

Grasping the banister post at the bottom, Nicolas swung around then dashed towards the back door with the three girls in hot pursuit. Upstairs Peter, who Prue guessed had just woken up from his morning nap, started grizzling.

Rob looked at his mother.

'Don't ask,' she said. 'Now, my darling,' she slipped her arm through his, 'you've had a long journey up from wherever you've been on the south coast, so leave your kit where it is, and we'll show you your room after you've had a nice cup of tea. Prudence, would you pop and tell Mrs Lavender tea for five in the lounge?'

By the time she'd rejoined the family in the lounge, Rob had unbuttoned his battle jacket, loosened his tie and was sitting in the fireside chair opposite his father.

Marjorie had taken one of the other easy chairs. 'I would have thought after all you've been through these last few months your commanding officer would have given you leave as soon as you landed. Surely, he must have realised we were beside ourselves with worry. And you've lost weight. What kind of army camp is it where you don't get enough to eat? I tell you, Robbie, I've a good mind to phone cousin Jeremy.'

'Mother,' said Robbie, giving her a fond look, 'I'm not the only soldier who managed to make it back to England, and having traipsed across central France I had up-to-date information about the German advance and positions, so GHQ were keen to interview me while it was still fresh in my mind.'

'Even so ...'

'Peace.' Prue's father raised his hand. 'The boy's here now, Marjorie. So let him tell us of his adventure in France.'

Pain flashed across her brother's angular face briefly then a schoolboy grin, which didn't reach his eyes, replaced it.

'Adventure's the word, Dad,' he said. 'Dodging Germans, hiding in the woods with the Resistance fighters, then, under cover of the night, jumping aboard a Breton fishing boat and dodging through German costal patrols. Ripping stuff and straight out of the pages of *Hotspur*.'

'There,' said Marjorie, preening herself. 'Have I not always maintained that the military d'Apremont blood ran through Robert's veins?'

'You have, my dear,' Hugh agreed. '"Fight the Good Fight", as the hymn succinctly puts it, eh?'

'Our son is a hero, to be sure,' his wife agreed.

'I wouldn't go that far, Mother, after all—'

A knock on the door cut across her brother's words.

It opened and Mrs Lavender, swathed in a wraparound apron as always, pushed in a tea trolley.

'Tea,' she announced, parking it in the middle of the fringed India rug. 'And, I've taken the liberty of putting a couple of slices of Miss Prudence's seedy cake on as well.'

'Thank you, Mrs Lavender,' said Prue's mother. 'And this is my son, Robert.'

'A pleasure to meet you, I'm sure,' said the housekeeper.

'He's a captain with the King's Own Artillery Company and has just escaped the clutches of the Germans to arrive back to England safe and sound,' Marjorie added.

Mrs Lavender looked suitably impressed. 'I 'ope as 'ow you sent a couple of them buggers – pardon my language, missis – to meet their maker on your way.'

Unease flickered across her brother's face again.

'Thank you, Mrs Lavender,' said Marjorie.

'Lunch will be at one as usual,' the housekeeper said then toddled out, closing the door behind her.

'So,' said Robbie, relaxing back in the chair. 'The children?'

'Well,' said Prue, as her mother put the strainer on the first cup. 'It's a bit of a story ...'

She told him how they came to have the Haas, Leitner and Bakker family as lodgers.

'And Prue's running an English class each week, too,' added Fliss. 'Plus, she's helping Johanna to secure a place at Toynbee Hall for September so she can carry on her studies and take the school certificate.'

'Of course, although it's our Christian duty to offer these poor souls refuge,' said her mother added, 'I have to say this past couple of months might have been a little easier if we didn't have quite so many children in the house.'

'Oh, I don't know,' said Hugh. 'It's nice to watch them playing in the garden.'

'It is,' said Marjorie, her vicar's wife face sliding into place. 'I just worry that all the screaming and shouting might interfere with your studies, that's all.' She sighed. 'I suppose we should be thankful that Miss Kratz – or should I say Dr Kratz – at least is single.'

'Hester managed to get out of Paris just before the panzer divisions rolled in,' explained Prue. 'She's a paediatrician at the Jewish Hospital, which is a short walk from here.'

'She's of that persuasion herself,' chipped in her mother.

'To be honest, she works such long hours at the hospital we hardly know she's here,' added Prue.

'Well, at least if I run into a tweed-clad spinster wearing spectacle on the stairs, I'll know who she is,' laughed Rob.

'You won't,' said Prue. 'Because Dr Kratz is—'

'Well, Prue, I have to say you've certainly been busy,' Rob said, taking another sip of tea.

'And she's working on the railway at Stratford,' said Felicity.

'And Felicity is now the chief editor on the Trade Union news desk at the *Workers' Clarion*,' added Prue.

'Well, both of you can tell me all about it over lunch,' he said, 'as I ought to take my gear upstairs and freshen up. And by the way,' he raised the last portion of cake on his plate, 'this cake is delicious, Prue. Are you practising your cooking skills with someone in mind?'

A picture of Jack started to form in her mind.

'She certainly is,' cut in her mother, dispersing the image in an instance.

'I am not, Mother,' said Prue, looking pointedly across the room at her.

'Of course not,' simpered her mother. 'And quite right, too. A respectable young lady should not give the slightest hint at liking a young man.' Shifting her attention back to her son, Marjorie smiled. 'Now, Robbie, if you've finished, I'll take you up and show you your room.'

Robbie put his cup back in the saucer, stood up and followed his mother out.

'See, I told you,' said Fliss, leaning towards her. 'Mother's definitely got Father David earmarked for you.'

Chapter twenty-seven

'HOW YOU DOING?' asked Kate, as she scraped soot from the inside of one of the old Victorian lamps that was still dotted about the shunting yard.

'Almost finished,' Prue replied. 'Just got to top up the oil in this one. What about you?'

It was just after four on Wednesday, the day after her brother had arrived home. She and Kate were standing behind one of the wooden benches in the lamp shop, which was situated on the west side of the shunting yard.

Like all the other workshops on the site, the lamp shop was a cavernous space, but whereas the others had the smell of grease and hot metal, and the clatter of machinery, the lamp shop was an oasis of calm with just a faint whiff of oil from the paraffin drums stacked against the wall.

It was just over three weeks since Prue and her team had been set to work as lamp men and once they'd got used to climbing up the ladders to collect and return the lamps, the job was pretty straightforward. What's more, her move to the lamp shed meant she no longer had to clean up some of the less than savoury litter left behind by passengers.

Bending down, Kate plunged her hands into the soapy water of the bucket at her side. 'Just two more. Hi, Mags,' she added, as Maggie strolled into the shed carrying a pole in each hand with two lamps dangling on each.

Placing them on the floor, she put her hands in the small of her back and stretched. 'Peggy and her team gone?'

Unlike drivers, firemen and engineers, lamp men weren't regarded by the Government as a reserve occupation so after a spate of Stratford shunting yard's finest railway porters, ticket collectors and cleaners receiving their call-up papers in the past few weeks, Knobby Clark had been obliged to transfer Beryl, Peggy and Maureen's teams over to the lamp shop too.

'About ten minutes ago,' said Prue, wringing the dirty water from her cloth on to the earth floor of the lamp shed. 'They've got to walk halfway to Maryland station to fix the lamps back up on number ten signal.'

The shunting yard had over two hundred signal lamps dotted all over the site. As well as cleaning the lamps, the lamp men's job also involved climbing up to the signal to replace the dirty lamps with clean ones, topping up the oil then trimming the wick so the lamps gave an even glow through the coloured glass on the signal arm before returning them to their place on the gantries.

There were a dozen cleaning teams working in the lamp shop, each responsible for a particular patch. Peggy and her crew had been allocated the signals on the eastern side of the station on the Southend and Shenfield line.

'Give us an 'and, Prue,' said Maggie.

Running the duster around the bulbous glass of the signal lamp, Prue placed it on the bench then went over to help Maggie. Grasping the end of a pole, Prue took up the strain then she and her friend lifted the two lamps and rested them on the bench opposite, then they repeated the operation with the other two lamps.

'Are they the last ones today?' asked Prue.

'They are, but as they aren't needed until tomorrow, I'm going to leave it till the morning because I want to clock off on time for once,' said Maggie.

'Oh, yeah,' said Kate. 'Seeing that lieutenant on the ack-ack guns tonight, are you?'

A dreamy smile lifted the corners of Maggie's mouth. 'Might be.'

'That's the third time in the past week, isn't it?' said Prue, as she made her way across to retrieve the paraffin can from the storage area.

'Sounds like it's getting serious,' said Kate. 'What's 'is name?'

'Doug, but I don't know about serious,' Maggie replied. 'Still, it's grand to have a man taking you in 'is arms and getting you all 'ot and flustered, I can tell you.'

'Maggie, you're a right one, you are,' giggled Kate, pushing a wisp of blonde hair away from her face with the back of her hand.

'Well, it's true, ain't it?' said Maggie. 'And don't pretend you don't have a nice warm glow all day after you've been in the back row with your Malcom.'

'Well, maybe I do,' Kate laughed. 'But just you be careful, Mags, or you'll find yourself in trouble.'

'Don't worry, Doug knows what 'e's doing in that department,' said Maggie. 'He always pulls—'

'And don't say any more before you have me and Prue blushing like a couple of light bulbs,' said Kate.

'Don't you worry about me,' said Prue. 'I know all about the birds and the bees.'

Maggie pulled a face. 'The birds and the bees is just the mechanics. I'm talking about having a big, strong, hairy-chested man with plenty of energy to keep you awake all night.'

Once again, an image of Jack as he'd been working in the shelter, sleeves rolled up and a couple of shirt buttons undone, loomed large in Prue's mind.

'Don't take no notice of our Mags, Prue,' said Kate. 'She'll just lead you astray.'

'I won't,' said Prue, damping down the fluttering in the pit of her stomach that thoughts of Jack always provoked.

Running the cloth over the glass for the last time, Prue reached below the bench and picked up the paraffin can. After refilling the reservoir at the bottom of the lamp she screwed the cap back tightly and trimmed the wick.

Lining the lamp up on the floor next to the other three she'd cleaned, Prue took the two carrying poles Maggie had just set aside and threaded them through two of the lamps.

'Now, as my brother's only home for a couple more days I'll push off once I've brought the empties back,' she said. 'If you're not here when I get back I'll see you in the morning.'

'Not if we see you first,' her two friends called back in unison.

Grasping the middle of the pole firmly in each hand, Prue straightened up and after making sure the lamps were balanced, she set off.

Blinking into the late-afternoon sunlight, Prue emerged from the shed. She checked that the track was clear then crossed on to the wooden walkway and carried on alongside the track, her eyes peeled along its length for a locomotive heading her way.

Prue, Maggie and Kate had been given the signal lamps on the Dalston, Hackney and North London line to maintain. There were about fifty on their patch, which took the three of them all week to clean in rotation.

Unlike the Eastern line from Norwich, Felixstowe, Colchester and Southend, which travelled into Liverpool Street, the line Prue and her team were responsible for headed north across Hackney Marshes and wound its way across North London to Highbury and Gospel Oak.

Picking her way between the ends of the sleepers and keeping her eyes peeled for any oncoming trains, Prue continued towards the first set of signals straddling the tracks.

Leaving three of the lamps on the ground, she hooked the fourth one over her arm and reaching up pulled the ladder down. These were pushed upwards and locked into place each night to prevent thieves climbing up and pinching the lamps. Having ensured it was correctly positioned, Prue climbed up to the gantry above.

Walking along the narrow wooden platform, she nipped around to the back of the signal then unhooked the smoke-covered lamp behind it, putting the clean one in its place. Opening the back, she straightened the wick then took the box of matches from her dungaree pocket, struck one and relit the lamp.

Retracing her steps, Prue carried the dirty lamp down then repeated the process three more times; however, as she picked up the last lamp and headed back to the ladder, the cables attached to the signal rattled as the arms shot upwards.

Squeezing herself against the iron girder at the far end of the gantry, Prue closed her eyes and mouth tightly and turned away. Holding her breath, she waited as a T18 Class locomotive thundered over the tracks beneath her, belching a cloud of thick black smoke into the blue sky above.

As the ratter-ta-tar of the wheels going over the points faded, Prue opened her eyes and saw the last carriage weaving its way towards the number nine platform.

From her vantage point she gazed across the sea of rail tracks and workshops until her eyes came to rest on the engine repair shop at the far west side of the site. Jack would be working there now.

Of course, if she were sensible, she wouldn't think of him at all because no matter that he was handsome, kind and funny, and much as she was growing to like him, the fact was he was divorced, something her parents would never accept.

Pulling herself together and hooking the redundant lamp over her arm, she climbed back down the ladder. Pushing it up until it clicked into place, Prue reloaded her carrying pole and set off back to the lamp shop.

There were a few workshops around her at the back of the site, mainly dealing with fixtures and fittings such as upholstered seats, leather window straps and the elasticated basket-weave luggage racks, most of which had been given over to war work.

Behind them, supposedly at the ready to repulse any fifth columnists or disguised Nazi paratroopers intent on sabotage, but in fact just loitering about smoking, were half a dozen soldiers.

One of them spotted Prue and said something to his comrades and they looked across for a moment then three of them peeled themselves off the brick wall they were lounging against and sidled over.

The tallest one, with corporal stripes on his sleeves, untidy sandy-coloured hair and his hands in his pockets, stopped in front of her. 'Hello, little lady.'

Prue didn't reply; keeping her head low, she tried to walk around him but he stepped into her path.

'What's your hurry, sweetheart?' he said, displaying a set of uneven teeth as he grinned at her.

'Let me pass,' she said.

The corporal frowned. 'Now that ain't very friendly is it, lads?'

'No, it ain't, Len,' said the soldier with shaving rash standing beside him.

'Downright *un*friendly, if you ask me,' added a skinny youngster who was in the process of growing his first moustache.

Feeling the weight of the lamps dragging on her arms, Prue forced herself to look Len in the eye. 'Will you please move aside?'

The corporal's youthful sidekick pulled a face. 'Oh er, she's a bit of posh skirt, ain't she?'

'That she is, Sid,' Len agreed, and his eyes slid over her and came to rest on her breasts. 'Got a nice handful, too.'

Ignoring her heart hammering uncomfortably in her chest, Prue forced herself to remain calm.

The private with the pimply face moved across to stand at Prue's right side. 'P'raps she thinks she's too good to talk to the likes of us.'

'Has Barry got the right of it then, miss?' asked Len. 'You think yourself too grand, do you?'

He kneed the end of the carrying pole and the two lamps suspended from it swung back and forth.

'Careful, Len,' said Barry, looking at the ringleader with mock horror. 'You nearly made her drop 'er pretty lamps.'

Prue frowned.

'Tell you what,' said Len, 'you give us all a little kiss and we'll let you go about your business.' All three of them shuffled forward and loomed over her. 'What do you say?'

Tilting her head right back Prue summoned up all her courage and looked up at him. 'I say, get lost.'

An ugly snarl spread across Len's face. 'Now that ain't nice, is it, boys? I think maybe we should take you for a walk into one of the sheds and teach you some proper manners.'

He grabbed her arm and pulled her forward. Prue lost her grip on the pole and all four lamps cluttered to the ground.

She wrenched her arm free and stumbled back; however, as she prepared to fall into the cinders a pair of strong arms caught her and set her back on her feet.

'You heard Miss Carmichael,' said the deep voice that spoke to her in her dreams. 'Clear off.'

Placing her behind him, Jack picked up one of the carrying poles and squared his shoulders.

As his two sidekicks shuffled back, Len chewed his lips and eyed Jack.

'You can try, mate,' said Jack, twisting the pole in his hand. 'But you'll be the first on the floor.'

Prue held her breath, expecting to see Jack battered and bloody at her feet at any moment, but after what seemed like an eternity, Len flashed a toothy smile. 'No need to take on, chum; me and the lads were just having a bit of a laugh, that's all.'

'Yeah, we didn't mean no harm,' chipped in the lightly whiskered youth, his throat aflame with a nervous flush.

The muscles along Jack's jawline tightened in response.

Len shuffled on the spot for a moment then he turned. 'Come on, lads.'

Giving Jack a hateful look, and with as much bravado as he could muster, he swaggered away, his two sidekicks a couple of steps behind him.

Jack didn't move until all three had disappeared behind the disused sawmill, then he turned to Prue.

'Are you all right?' he said, his dark eyes searching her face.

Although her heart was still pounding ten to the dozen, Prue somehow managed to force a smile. 'Y ... yes, I ... I'm ...'

Her knees gave way and she staggered sideways.

Jack dropped the carrying pole and caught her.

'It's all right, Prue,' he said softly, gathering her into his arms. 'They can't hurt you now.'

Placing her hand on his chest, she looked up at him. 'It's not me but you I was afraid for.'

Jack pulled a face. '*Me?*'

'Yes you,' she replied. 'I thought you were about to get beaten to a pulp.'

'Oh, Prue. The day I can't take down a bully like that corporal, well ...' A rumbling laugh rolled through him then his eyes captured hers. 'But I'm pleased that you care.'

Swimming in the depth of his gaze, Prue became aware of his arms, the hardness of his body, the male scent of him, and her senses reeled. She would only have to raise herself on to her tiptoes to press her lips on his, but before she gave into temptation Prue stepped out of his embrace.

Jack's arms returned to his side, but his gaze remained intertwined with hers.

They stared wordlessly at each other for a moment, then Jack smiled. 'Perhaps we'd better get these lamps back.'

Prue blinked and brought herself back to the here and now. 'Yes.'

Scooping down, they picked up a pole each and reloaded the lamps.

Jack went to take hold of Prue's, but she held it firm. 'It's all right. I can manage and you must have been on your way somewhere.'

'Well, I was on my way to the paint shop but—'

'Honestly, I'm fine,' Prue insisted. 'Anyway, I don't want to give Knobby Clark the excuse to tell everyone that we women aren't up to the job.' She held out her hand and he passed the pole he was holding to her. Her hand brushed against his briefly, sending another rather pleasant sensation through her.

Taking the weight, Prue smiled. 'Thank you again. And I'll see you at the rectory party on Saturday.'

'You will.'

They stood looking at each other for a long moment, then Prue spoke again. 'I ought to get on.'

'Me too.'

Another moment passed then Prue gave him a quick smile and walked off towards the lamp shed.

'And any time you need a knight in shining armour, Prue, I'll be there,' he called after her.

She turned and looked over her shoulder at him. 'Perhaps next time I'll be rescuing you, Jack.'

He gave her that roguish smile of his and then she continued on her way.

Despite her mother telling her she would enlighten her as to what to expect on her wedding night when the need arose, Fliss, who was very up on such things, had lent Prue a well-thumbed copy of Marie Stopes' *Married Love* a couple of years ago so Prue thought she knew what Maggie had been alluding to earlier. However, now having found herself briefly in Jack's arm she had a fresh insight into what female desire, pleasure and satisfaction might actually mean.

Jack watched Prue for a few moments then he headed towards the paint shop. However, as he reached the end of the upholstery shop Gladys stepped out from the corner.

'Hello, Jack,' she said, blowing a stream of cigarette smoke skywards as she gave him the once-over. 'Fancy meeting you here.'

'You're a bit off your patch, aren't you?' he said, nodding towards the cleaning sheds on the far side of the site, a mile away.

'Just stretching my legs.' She took a long drag on the cigarette between her scarlet lips. 'And I wouldn't bother.'

'With what?' Jack asked.

'Chancing your arm with Miss La-di-da,' the blonde replied.

'And why's that?'

'Thinks herself very grand, does that one. D'you know she's a vicar's daughter?'

'I do.'

'Well then, Jack,' she laughed, 'you don't want to waste your time chasing around after some quivering virgin.' She stepped forward until she was just a few inches from him. 'You want to find yourself a woman who knows what to do with a strong, handsome man.'

She reached out and flipped his top shirt button with her varnished nail then, giving him a long brazen look, she wiggled past him and headed off towards the carriage sheds.

Jack stared after her for a moment then he turned to continue on his way to the paint shop.

The brassy blonde might well be right. Prue was certainly several rungs up the social ladder from a grubby railway engineer.

He knew the sensible thing would be to forget any thought of having Prue Carmichael love him, and he might have even considered it had it not been for the look in her eyes a few moments ago when he'd held her in his arms.

Chapter twenty-eight

'Now, ROBBIE, if you want anything, Mrs Lavender is in the kitchen,' said Marjorie as she pulled on her gloves.

'I'll be fine, Mother,' he replied, looking across at her from the comfort of the fireside chair.

'There's cake in the pantry and some ham in the chill box so you can have a sandwich if you get peckish,' she added.

She was off to some meeting at the church and so was wearing a navy dress with a white frilly bit around the neck and sleeves and a hat that could best be described as a ball of dark red feathers.

'I've just had lunch,' he replied.

Actually, as it was now two-fifteen, it was over an hour since the family had finished lunch, but as his mother had insisted on giving him a second helping of beef pie and dishing him up a portion of treacle pudding and custard that barely fitted in the dessert bowl, he was still full.

In fact, his mother had been plying him with food since he'd arrived home the day before yesterday as she maintained that he had lost at least three stone, instead of the one recorded by the army medic.

'Well, if you're sure you'll be all right,' she repeated.

'Honestly, Mother.' He sighed. 'I'm twenty-nine not nine, so I think I'll survive for a few hours by myself.'

She hovered by the door for a moment then, setting her handbag in the crock of her arm, she opened the door. 'I'm just going to remind Mrs Lavender that I'd like her to have a word with the window cleaner when he arrives and then I'll be off. See you later, then.'

'Have a good meeting,' he called after her.

The door closed and Robbie picked up that morning's early edition of *The Times* from the coffee table and settled back.

As his father was holed up in his study tacking a tricky passage in Judges for this Sunday's service and Father David was out for the afternoon visiting parishioners, he now had the house to himself.

Of course, the refugee families were still there, but as the sun was burning brightly in the sky above, they were outside in the garden.

Flicking open the paper, Robbie started reading a report about British bombers destroying Nazi and Italian aircraft works but abandoned it after a couple of paragraphs. He'd seen a couple of old newspaper reports about the retreat to Dunkirk while he was in the army camp outside Bournemouth, so now took any stirring tales of British success with a pinch of salt.

Letting the paper fall open on his lap, Robbie let his head fall back into the soft upholstery and with some soprano warbling away in the background he closed his eyes. However, just as his mind started to wander off, the door clicked open.

'Honestly, Mother, I'll be fine,' he said.

'I'm certain you will be.'

Robbie's eyes flew open.

Standing on the threshold was a tall young woman with braided black hair pinned like a crown on her head. She was dressed in a very understated, mulberry suit over a white blouse; however, while its plain cut would have seemed austere on most women, on the young woman standing on the other side of the room it only drew attention to her slim, shapely figure. Hugging half a dozen buff-coloured files to her chest, she looked across at Robbie out of a pair of very assured, very dark brown eyes.

Forcing his brain back to the here and now, Rob sprang out of the chair.

'Pardon me. I thought you were my mother,' he said.

'So I gathered,' she replied, with just a hint of amusement. 'I'm sorry; I didn't mean to startle you.'

'You didn't, not really,' he replied. 'I'm Rob Carmichael, by the way.'

'Hester Kratz,' she replied. 'One of the waifs and strays who your family have kindly given shelter to.'

Rob stared at her dumbly for a moment then the penny dropped.

'You're the doctor?'

'That's what my certificate from Vienna University tells me,' she replied, with a sweet smile.

'I'm sorry, it's just that I was expect you to be—'

'A *stara panna*.'

He frowned. 'I'm sorry, I—'

'An old maid,' she added. 'Perhaps I should have introduced myself sooner but we're a doctor down in the department and we've had a few children brought in with suspected polio, so I've spent the last two days at the hospital. I did pop back briefly for a change of clothes early yesterday morning, but I surmised when I passed your room that you were sleeping.'

'Gosh was I snoring that loudly?'

She gave him a quirky smile by way of an answer. 'Now, if it's not intruding on you too much, I have the notes from this morning's clinic to write up and I usually use the table under the window.'

'Yes, of course. I was just,' he snatched up the newspaper that he'd knocked on to the floor and held it aloft, 'catching up on the news. Are you all right with the wireless being on? If not I'm happy to … '

'No, it will not hinder my thoughts,' she replied.

She stared at him for a moment then lowered her gaze and headed over to the table. Robbie waited until she was sitting at the table then resumed his seat.

Opening the newspaper again he turned to the second page. He briefly read a report about a bomb landing near Southampton then his eyes drifted over the top of the sheet and across to Hester, pen in hand and head bowed over her work.

If he was going to be completely honest, although her

out-of-date hairstyle and simple, unadorned outfit were completely the opposite of the colourful summer dresses and oversized victory rolls most women were sporting, it was rather charming, as was her pale pink lipstick instead of the more common cherry-red.

She made some notes in a ledger then scribbled a signature at the bottom of the medical notes.

'Looks like it was a busy clinic,' Robbie said as she took another from the stack beside her.

'It always is,' she replied. 'Even more so as we're conducting a research study alongside.'

'Into what?'

'Into the effect of wartime rationing and food shortages on the growth and development of Jewish children whose families follow orthodox dietary rules,' she replied.

'Oh, do you think it will make any difference? I mean, as I understand it, children are given extra rations,' Robbie said.

'That is the question we hope to answer.' She sighed. 'It is not so much the rations themselves we – that is Professor Kleinman and I – are worried about but the shortages. When beef and lamb are in short supply you can eat rabbit or pork or even whale meat, but Jews cannot. And growing children need protein.'

'I never thought of that,' Robbie said. 'Sounds quite involved.'

'It is,' she replied.

A tennis ball hit the window and they both looked around for a second.

'It must feel a little strange to come home and find so many strangers living in your house,' she said.

'Not at all,' he replied.

'I think your mother finds it … uncomfortable,' she said.

He gave her an awkward half smile. 'It's a long time since she had young children in the house.'

'And what about you?'

'Me?' He shrugged. 'Other than once being one I know nothing about kids, but I don't mind them at all. Actually, in an odd way, seeing the children playing in the garden for the past few days has …'

'Helped you find peace?' she said softly.

Jumbled images of the dirt, hunger and fear of the past few months filled Robbie's mind and he nodded.

'I walked from Paris to Calais, carrying my weekend suitcase in one hand and a briefcase with my life's work in the other,' she said, in the same soft voice. 'I threw myself into ditches with sobbing women and children when low-flying Fockes and Dorniers strafed the fleeing columns of refugees, so you do not have to keep the stiff upper lip with me, Rob.'

'There were some days when—' His voice got caught in his throat.

'You didn't think you'd survive?'

'No. I didn't.'

'Neither did I,' she replied, her large dark brown eyes holding his pale blue ones.

They stared wordlessly across the room at each other for a moment then the bell rang in the hall outside.

There was a pause as Mrs Lavender made her trek through the house to answer it. A long moment of silence followed, then the lounge door burst open.

'Here's my very own hero!'

Rob turned to see his fiancée, Lydia Fincham, with her blonde curls bouncing on her shoulders and dressed in a tight green dress with matching bolero and a hat with a brim so wide it would have kept her dry in a downpour.

Looking as if she's just stepped off the front page of *Vogue*, she stood, arms raised and one foot forwards as photographers preferred, in the doorway.

'Surprise!' she cried, her red lips lifting into a dazzling smile.

'Lydia, I didn't know you were coming today,' he said.

Holding the pose for a second or two, she tottered across the room on her black patent six-inch heels.

'I know,' she said. 'But I told Maurice that I simply couldn't wait a moment longer to see my returning hero, so he moved my photograph session up the schedule yesterday and I caught the midday train from Birmingham back to London.' Her hurt-little-girl expression replaced her wide-mouth smile. 'Aren't you pleased to see me?' she asked, thrusting out her bottom lip.

'Of course I am, darling. Just surprised.' Forcing his dark memories back into the recesses of his mind, Rob gave her his best smile. 'Very pleasantly surprised.'

Throwing out her arms, she tilted her head so he could kiss her cheek without dislodging her headgear.

Rob stepped into her embrace and a cloud of Chanel No 5, pressing his lips to her powdered cheek beneath the stiffened brim of her hat.

Looking up, his gaze met Hester's for a moment, then she looked away. Gathering up her files, she hugged them to her and without glancing his way, she left the room.

'So you can imagine our surprise,' said Lydia, placing her hand on the exposed flesh above her sweetheart neckline, 'when I heard there was going to be a newsreel crew from the Ministry of Information at the factory.'

'Weren't you nervous, my dear?' asked Hugh Carmichael, slicing through the lamb chop on his plate.

It was just after seven on Thursday evening and Prue was sitting at the dining-room table. Her father was in his usual place at the head of the table and was flanked by his wife and Robbie. Next to her brother and across the table from Prue sat Lydia, who'd arrived that afternoon.

Father David was at the other end of the table from her father, his gaze never far from Lydia's quite considerable cleavage.

To be honest, it was difficult not to stare at Lydia. While Marjorie had spruced up one of her older gowns with pearls and Prue had pulled her crêpe de Chine cocktail dress out of the wardrobe, Lydia, in a figure-hugging, plunge-neck green evening dress, wouldn't have looked out of place waltzing up the stairs at the Ritz.

'I certainly was.' Lydia glanced around the table with

a look of wide-eyed astonishment. 'But I thought, Lydia my girl, you have to do your bit to win the war just like your darling Robbie is.'

Turning towards her fiancé, Lydia bestowed him with an adoring eyelash-fluttering look.

'Perhaps if you were in the ATS or WRAF I might agree, but I cannot understand how modelling clothes on a catwalk is in any way comparable with Robbie being shot at and bombed by the German army and then trudging for a hundred-plus miles across enemy occupied territory,' said Marjorie.

In contrast to David and Rob's obvious fascination with Lydia's décolletage, Prue's mother had spent the whole meal with her lips so tightly drawn together it was a wonder she'd managed to squeeze any food between them.

'Now now, dear,' said Hugh, who seemed to be the only person around the table oblivious to his son's fiancée's lavish display of flesh. 'Remember the widow's mite. Lydia is giving what she can.'

A sour expression spread across Marjorie's face but she refrained from arguing with her husband, whereas Lydia rewarded him with a syrupy smile.

'And you say the newsreel is to be shown in cinemas?' asked David.

'Yes, it will,' said Lydia, bobbing in her chair and causing Marjorie's lips to tighten further. 'I do hope you'll go and see it, Father David.'

'Well, I'm not one for the cinema as a rule,' he replied,

reaching for his half-drunk glass of lemonade. 'But perhaps I'll make an exception just this once.'

'And of course, it might even be Lydia's big break,' added Robbie.

Prue's mother looked puzzled. 'Break?'

'Into films,' Lydia replied.

'Yes, she's hoping to be spotted by a talent scout,' added Robbie, spearing a lump of potato.

'That's very exciting, isn't it, my dear?' said Hugh.

His wife's face didn't agree.

'Of course, if I do get offered a part in a film, I'll have to change my name,' she added. 'I thought perhaps Lydia Noble or Lydia Lord, or perhaps something continental like Lydia Beaufort.'

'So where was the factory that put on the show?' asked Prue.

'I'm afraid I can't tell you,' Lydia replied.

'Loose words cost lives, eh?' said Hugh, smiling indulgently at her.

'Well, no, I simply can't remember,' she replied.

'Lydia's been to dozens,' said Rob. 'And I'm sure one factory looks very much like another.'

'They do,' said Lydia. 'Drab little northern places where people speak oddly.' A bright smile lifted her Cherry Burst lips. 'But enough about me and my exciting job, what have you all been up to since I last saw you?'

'Well, obviously we have moved parishes …' As they finished their evening meal, Marjorie told her about

351

their terrible journey to Stepney, the appalling state of the rectory and how she was whipping the Mothers' Union into shape. 'And then, of course, we have our three families up—'

'And what about you, Prue?' cut in Lydia. 'Rob tells me you're working as something in a railway station.'

'I started as a coach cleaner but now I'm a lamp man,' Prue replied. 'And it's a shunting yard not a railway station.'

'What on earth is a lamp man?'

'The person who cleans the signal lamps throughout the yard,' said Prue, placing her cutlery together on her empty plate.

Lydia pulled a face. 'Isn't that very dirty?'

'Very,' said Prue. 'But someone has to do it now that the men have been called up, otherwise the trains wouldn't keep running. There's six of us girls working in the lamp shop now.'

'That's war work, Lydia,' chipped Marjorie.

'Just like yours, my darling,' said Rob, gazing adoringly at the woman by his side.

'Of course, it's only until Prudence gets married,' added her mother.

Interest returned to Lydia's blue eyes. 'You're getting married! Prue, why didn't you say something sooner? Oh, you must let me be your bridesmaid, but please don't have red dresses. Your sister might be able to carry it off, but that colour dies on me.'

Leaning forward, she rested her chin on her clasped

hands. 'Who's the lucky man? He's not a train driver or something at the yard, is he?'

'Certainly not!' snapped her mother.

'Do I know him?'

'I shouldn't think so,' said Prue, as the memory of Jack's arms around her faded from her mind, 'because I certainly don't.'

Lydia looked puzzled.

'I'm not getting married,' explained Prue.

'Not yet, perhaps, but ...' For a split second her mother's eyes flickered past Prue towards the end of the table. 'You never know. Now, as we all seem to have finished,' her gaze travelled around those sitting at the table, 'who's for dessert?'

Lydia patted her corseted stomach. 'Not for me, thank you. As Beaumont's top model I have to keep an eye on my figure,' she added, sending a sideways glance at both of the men who'd been doing pretty much that all evening.

'Nor me,' said Prue. 'I'm plane spotting tonight so I ought to be getting over to St Winifred's.'

'Couldn't you have swapped?' said her mother.

Prue shook her head. 'With the Germans shelling towns all along the south coast and the Luftwaffe flying nearer to London every day, we have to keep our eyes peeled.'

Taking the napkin from her lap she placed it next to her plate and stood up.

'Didn't you say you had to go over to the church for something, Father David?' said Marjorie.

'Did I? Oh yes … I did.' He too stood up. 'Maybe I'll walk over with you, Prue.'

'Why don't you have your coffee first?' said Prue. 'I'm sure Lydia would love to tell you about when she was chosen to be the lead model of wedding dresses on the Harrods' catwalk in front of the Queen and the two princesses.'

'Honestly, Father David,' said Lydia, 'it was the highlight of my first season as Beaumont's house model and …'

Prue made her escape.

Actually, the truth was she didn't have to be on duty at St Winifred's for another hour, but if she had to suffer another minute of Lydia's mind-numbing conversation or another not-so-subtle attempt by her mother's throw her and David together, she'd run screaming from the room.

Besides, yesterday morning in the canteen Jack had mentioned that he was on Home Guard duty tonight. He quite often grabbed a cuppa at the WVS mobile canteen in Ben Johnson Road, so perhaps she would too before climbing to the top of St Winifred's bell tower.

Chapter twenty-nine

'WELL, HERE WE ARE, Rachel,' said Jack, looking down at his daughter as they stopped in front of St Winifred's rectory.

With her hand in his she tilted her head back and looked up at the huge three-storey detached house in wide-eyed wonder. 'It's bigger than Bubbe's, Daddy.'

She was right: the rectory was larger than her maternal grandmother's semi-detached house in Mill Hill – and any other house in the area, for that matter.

'There must be hundreds of people living in there,' added Rachel. 'Maybe even a beautiful princess like Snow White.'

Jack suppressed a smile. He'd taken Rachel up to London to see the cartoon in April as a treat and it had clearly made quite an impression.

'Well, not quite a hundred but a few,' he replied. 'Shall we go and meet them?'

She nodded. He gave her hand a light squeeze and they walked up the gravel path. Someone had stuck a sheet of paper on the front door with 'PLEASE USE THE SIDE GATE' neatly written in capitals on it so they turned left and followed the noise.

The rectory's rear garden, enclosed within a six-foot-high wall, was about half the size of the pitch at West Ham's ground at Upton Park. However, although the lawn had recently been mowed and the flower beds surrounding it were a riot of colour, you could barely see either as a dozen small boys were dashing across the garden in pursuit of a leather football. To one side, a group of girls were jumping in and out of a long, swirling skipping rope. Their parents and other members of the congregation stood with cups and saucers in hand watching the fun, while older members of the parish sat in a hotchpotch of candy-striped deckchairs under the three laden apple trees by the south wall.

Although, apart from the Day of Prayer, Jack hadn't set foot in St Winifred's since the day he'd married Alma at Stepney Town Hall seven year ago, there were still a few faces he recognised, several of whom were looking his way and nodding a greeting.

Although members of St Winifred's congregation were mostly dressed in their smartest clothes as befits a visit to the rectory, there were a goodly number in Home Guard khaki, ARP warden black and the occasional air-force blue of the Royal Observatory Corp.

There were also a few new faces, including a tall chap with a mop of blond hair surrounded by a small crowd of young women. As he was wearing a Royal Artillery uniform with captain's pips on his shoulder, Jack guessed he was Prue's brother Rob.

The rector, dressed in a dark suit and stiff high-necked

dog collar, was chatting with his two churchwardens, Ronny Mills and Tim Hanson, who were a little fatter and a little balder respectively. Mrs Carmichael had cornered a couple of the women by the birdbath while Sister Martha was enjoying a cup of tea in the shade with a few of the older members of the church.

However, there was one member of St Winifred's clergy who wasn't having such a relaxing time at the rectory party. Dressed in a charcoal-grey suit, encircling dog collar and with a bored expression on his face, Father David was attempting to suppress a yawn. He was standing at the east wall by a trellis dotted pale yellow with nodding honeysuckle and talking to a young mother with a niggly baby, and although he was doing his best to feign interest, his eyes kept flickering past his audience towards the house.

Jack followed his gaze and smiled. On the patio, under the overhanging lilac-coloured laburnum, were three refreshment tables with a handful of women behind them, one of whom was Prue.

Well, Rachel was half right. Although she wasn't a princess, dressed in a pink candy-striped summer's dress and her auburn hair bobbing on her shoulder, Prue Carmichael certainly was beautiful.

However, he'd know many good-looking women, he'd even made the mistake of marrying one, but whereas theirs was often just the outer wrapping, Prue was beautiful to her core. Jack was still amazed that, as he'd remarked to Sister Martha, she was totally unaware of just how beautiful she was. But his attraction to Prue was more than just the physical. It was deeper than that. Much deeper. So deep that he knew she held all his hopes for happiness.

Perhaps sensing his gaze, she looked around and spotted him. Her smile widened instantly, and Jack's pulse galloped. It also set off the tightness well below his waistband, as the memory of feeling her in his arms earlier in the week flooded back to him.

She said something to the woman beside her then, leaving her fellow servers to carry on, she hurried over.

'Jack,' she said, her eyes capturing his. 'I'm so pleased you could come.' Her attention shifted on to the little girl standing beside him.

'Rachel, this is Miss Carmichael,' said Jack, feeling ridiculously nervous.

He shouldn't have been, because Prue's eyes softened as her smile widened still further.

'Hello, Rachel,' she said, taking his daughter's hand. 'Your dad's told me so much about you; it's lovely to meet you at last. And what a beautiful dress.'

'My mummy bought it for me,' Rachel replied, lifting the skirt a little to show its fullness.

It was true. Alma had dressed Rachel in a cotton dress with tiny blue birds fluttering over it and dazzlingly white ankle socks; she'd braided her hair in two long plaits fastened with the same-coloured blue satin ribbons. Say what you like about his ex-wife, she knew about looking good.

'How do you know my daddy?' added Rachel.

'We work together at Stratford,' said Prue.

'Are you an engineer too?'

Prue shook her head. 'No, my job is to clean all the lamps so the train drivers can see them properly.'

'I'm going to be a locomotive engineer like my daddy when I grow up,' Rachel announced.

Prue looked suitably impressed.

'Miss Carmichael is one of the ladies I was telling you about who have come to work in the shunting yard,' Jack explained.

Rachel considered this for a moment. 'Are you Daddy's special lady friend?'

Jack gave an inward groan.

Prue looked puzzled. 'I'm not sure what …'

'A special lady friend who will make him happy,' continued Rachel, oblivious of his discomfort.

Prue's gaze flickered on to him then back to his daughter. 'We are friends, but—'

'Because Daddy needs a special lady friend so he can be happy like Mummy is with Uncle Manny,' concluded Rachel, smiling artlessly up at Prue.

A slight flush coloured Prue's cheeks.

'Look, Rachel, Russell and Michael are over there; why don't you run over and say hello?' suggested Jack, never so pleased to see his nephews.

'But don't forget to come back for cake and lemonade,' added Prue as the little girl ran off, braids bobbing behind her.

Prue's gaze remained on Rachel for a moment longer, then she turned to Jack.

'She's absolutely lovely, Jack, and as bright as a button,' she said. 'I can see why you're so very proud of her.'

'I am,' he replied, feeling the truth of it as he watched his daughter, who having said hello to her cousins had now joined a group of girls swinging a long skipping rope.

Prue's gaze returned to the boys and girls playing on the lawn in the sunshine. 'I love the way children have such a straightforward way of looking at things.'

'Yes, being a parent gives you a very different perspective on life,' said Jack as his daughter leapt up to avoid the downward stroke.

'I hope to find out for myself one day,' she replied. 'I think I'd like three. Perhaps even four.'

Jack studied her averted face and he dared to imagine that the children she yearned for might be his.

She turned back to him. 'Let's get a cup of tea.'

Leaving the faint smell of her perfume, Prue walked off towards the refreshment tables. Jack turned to follow, but then caught sight of Father David on the far side of the garden, looking across at him with a less than saintly expression on his face.

Jack held the curate's belligerent stare with an unwavering one of his own for a moment, then smiled. Father David looked away and Jack continued after Prue.

'Thank you, Mrs Hanson,' said Prue, as the secretary of the Mothers' Union handed her two teas.

She turned to find Jack standing behind her looking very jolly.

'Thank you,' he said, his fingers brushing lightly against hers as he took his cup.

Cup in hand, they wandered away from the tea table to the other side of the paved patio and stood in the shade of the rhododendron bush.

Although Jack was wearing the same suit he'd worn to church on the National Day of Prayer, Prue noticed he'd brightened it up with a dark red tie. But as it was a hot day, he'd unfastened his collar and loosened the knot. Also, as his five o'clock shadow wasn't as noticeable as it usually was at this time of day, she thought he'd obviously shaved before setting out.

'You've got a good turnout,' he said, a faint whiff of aftershave drifting up as he moved.

'Yes, about sixty at the last count, plus at least two dozen children,' she replied.

'And it's a lovely garden,' he added.

'Well, it won't look like this soon,' said Prue ruefully. 'We'll be digging up the flower beds and the lawn in a few weeks to plant vegetables.'

'And I guess that's your brother over there by the hollyhocks,' Jack said.

'Yes, he's been with us on leave for the past week or so but he's travelling to Scotland on Monday to take up his duties there,' Prue replied.

'It looks like he's created a bit of a stir among the young ladies of the parish,' said Jack.

'Well, they'll be disappointed: he's engaged. His fiancée was down for a few days but she couldn't stay for the garden party,' she said, trying not to sound too relived that Lydia had left early that morning.

Jack took a mouthful of tea then rested his cup in the saucer. 'Look, Prue, I'm sorry about Rachel and the whole "special lady friend" thing.'

'Don't be silly,' Prue replied. 'I think it's lovely that she wants you to be happy.'

'Even so …'

'Honestly, don't give it a second thought.'

Jack's attention returned to the assembled crowed in the garden and Prue stole a quick look him, and her heart ached.

'So *have* you got a special lady friend?' she blurted out.

He turned and a faint smile lifted one corner of his lips.

'I know sometimes children pick up on things,' she replied, glancing down and straightening a non-existent crease in her skirt.

'No, I haven't.' An expression that threatened to melt her bones crept into Jack's eyes. 'But recently my hopes have been raised.'

Her eyes stretched wide in astonishment. 'You don't mean Gladys?'

A rumbling laugh rolled through him.

'I only ask because she seems very keen on you.'

Jack smiled. 'She may be, but I've already made one

mistake; I'm not going to make another. And truthfully, I'm not looking for a special lady friend.'

'You're not?'

'No, Prue,' he replied, his voice lowering half a tone. 'I'm looking for a woman who I can share my life, who will have my children and who I can grow old alongside.'

Emotions Prue had never before experienced tumbled over in her mind. Her breath seemed to still in her lungs as her lips parted.

Jack took a step forward.

'Daddy, Daddy!'

Prue lowered her gaze as Jack's head whipped around.

'You have to be on our team,' Rachel cried as she hurtled towards them.

'Team? What team?'

She grabbed his free arm. 'Our cricket team, of course.'

'Oh, Rachel, you know I'm a football man,' Jack said, pretending reluctance.

Rachel heaved an exaggerated sigh. 'It's easy, Daddy. Come oooon.'

Jack gave Prue that smile of his. 'Duty calls.'

She nodded. 'I'll take your cup.'

He gave it to her, and as his fingers brushed hers a wave of excitement rolled over Prue, stealing her breath yet again.

Jack's gaze lingered for a moment longer then, unable to resist his daughter, he allowed her to lead him over to the far side of the garden with Prue's eyes following him all the way.

Finding herself with two empty cups, she returned them to the refreshment tables, intending to take up her post again. However, finding there were more than enough women pouring tea and dishing up cake, Prue replenished her drink and ambled back across the lawn.

Stopping under the ornamental cherry tree a little way from where Rob was setting up his old cricket stumps, Prue's eyes returned to Jack and her heart did a little double step in her chest.

He'd taken off his jacket and tie and was in the process of rolling back his cuffs, revealing his muscular, hair-dusted forearms while Rachel and the rest of her team jumped excitedly around. Rob, who was on the other team, had Leah and Nicolas Haas plus a couple of choir boys.

Having set up the pitch, Rob, also down to his shirtsleeves, strode over to Jack and the two men shook hands and seemed to have a bit of a discussion, after which Rob shouted for David to join them.

Looking somewhat reluctant, David did. There was another short discussion, then, looking as if he'd rather be anywhere else than on the improvised cricket pitch, David took up position as umpire.

Jack rummaged around in his trouser pocket for a moment then flipped a coin. Rob called it and chose to bat first, leaving Jack's team to field. Hunkering down on his haunches so he was at their level, Jack had a quick chat with the children huddled around him then they dispersed around the field. The game began, with Rob helping Ernie Leitner to hold the bat and Jack explaining to Johnny Bird, whose left leg was supported by a calliper, how to throw underarm.

The first ball was lobbed and with Rob's guidance Ernie, who wasn't the best coordinated little boy, managed to hit it.

Rob sent Ernie off towards the other set of wickets as a couple of the girls fielding scurried off towards the herbaceous border.

But Prue's eyes didn't follow the ball. They remained on Jack.

'He's very handsome, isn't he?' said her mother.

Prue turned to find her standing beside her.

'He is,' said Prue, more than a little surprised by the observation.

'And he'd make a wonderful husband, too.'

'Would he?'

'Of course,' her mother replied. 'I've heard that a couple of influential bishops at Lambeth Palace have Father David earmarked for a very comfortable parish when he finishes his curacy next year and,' she continued with a conspiratorial expression in her eye, 'he's clearly sweet on you. In fact, I wouldn't be surprised if he asks to speak to your father very soon.'

Prue stared incredulously at her then her mother's gaze shifted to something behind her.

'For goodness' sake,' snorted Marjorie. 'How many times have I told Mrs Lawless to cut the slices of cake thinner? I'll have to sort it out.' Pressing her lips together and with her eyes fixed on her quarry, she stomped off towards the tea table.

Prue's gaze returned to the cricket match.

Leah, who at twelve years old needed no help to throw a ball, was now bowling to Nicolas, so Jack was a little way away from David.

In contrast to David, who barely glanced at the game or the children playing it, Jack smiled and cheered them on as he swung the bat or jumped to catch the ball.

Watching him, an emotion that she'd been vaguely aware of hovering around for a little while suddenly burst through her. A few moments ago, Prue had had the wildest notion that Jack was about to take her in his arms, so Rachel's interruption was divine intervention because had he done that, and pressed his lips on hers, Prue couldn't honestly say she wouldn't have kissed him back.

Chapter thirty

D AVID KNOCKED LIGHTLY on the door to the small parlour. There was a moment's pause then he heard 'come'. Grasping the brass handle, he did just that.

Mrs Carmichael was sitting at the writing bureau in front of the window; she looked up as David entered.

'I hope I'm not disturbing you,' he said. 'It's just that I'm off to have lunch with an old school pal who is in town in a while so …'

'No, please come in,' she replied. 'In fact, after spending an hour and a half with Mrs Gordon, Farmer and Weston while they went through their inventory of the church's altar linen, I welcome the distraction.'

Actually, he knew that she'd been holed up in the rector's study with the three matrons of the parish. Of course, he should have been exploring a passage from Colossians ready for tomorrow's mid-week communion service, but ever since the garden party three days before, something far less spiritual had dominated his thoughts.

'St Winifred's can be a little challenging,' he said, oozing sympathy.

Mrs Carmichael raised one of her substantial eyebrows. 'Challenging! I could think of a few more apt descriptions.'

She sighed. 'I know the Lord has called the rector to minister to His poor and lowly flock here in Stepney, but …' She forced a smile. 'But you haven't come to hear about the crosses I have to bear, so what can I do for you?'

'Well, the truth is, Mrs Carmichael, I'm a little uncertain how to approach the matter,' David replied.

Placing her fountain pen alongside the inkwell on the pen tray, she swivelled in her chair to face him. 'I'd recommend head-on might be best.'

'Indeed.' He swallowed. 'And I would have come to you yesterday, but you were busy seeing your son off.'

Fussing would be a more accurate description of Mrs Carmichael's farewell, so much so that Robert must have heaved a great sigh of relief when the taxi finally arrived.

'It's rather delicate.' David drew in a long breath. 'It's about Prudence.'

The rector's wife frowned. 'What about her?'

'I don't know if you're aware that Rosie Stapleton's brother Jack Quinn attended the garden party on Saturday.'

Marjorie looked confused. 'I'm not sure I know him.'

'I doubt you would as he's not one of the faithful at St Winifred's,' David replied. 'He was the tall chap with untidy black hair playing cricket with your son.'

'Oh, yes, I recall him now,' she said. 'Rob said he seemed like a decent chap. What has this to do with Prudence?'

David gave an urbane smile. 'She and Jack Quinn work together at Stratford.'

'I don't see ...'

'Quinn didn't come with his sister,' said David. 'Prudence invited him and his half-Jewish daughter herself.'

'Mrs Stapleton didn't mention her brother was a widower?'

'He isn't. He's a divorcee,' added David, struggling to conceal his relish.

A look of horror spread across Marjorie's face.

'I wouldn't have raised the matter,' continued David smoothly, 'if it hadn't been for the fact that he's one of those rough, earthy types that young women seem to find irresistible. I've also heard that he was the guilty party in his divorce and since then he hasn't exactly been – how can I put this? – celibate?'

Of course, that wasn't strictly true. Although it was common knowledge that the divorce was granted on the grounds of adultery, David hadn't heard any such thing about Jack having women friends. However, he was pretty certain Jack Quinn was the sort of man who would make a hobby of putting notches in his headboard.

The rector's wife's nostrils flared as she drew in a deep breath. 'Father David, I hope you are not suggesting that my daughter—'

'Not at all,' David cut in, looking suitably horrified. 'But ...'

'But!'

'Although I hate myself for bringing you such distress, Mrs Carmichael, I've seen them alone together now on several occasions.' David forced a deeply pained expression on to his face. 'And they do seem to be becoming increasingly friendly.'

'In what way?'

'Standing close together. Laughing at intimate jokes and ...' He tightened his agonised expression. 'And on Saturday, in front of everyone at the party, they were gazing dreamily into each other's eyes. Of course, I may not have taken much note of Jack Quinn and his designs regarding your daughter if it were not for my own hopes in that direction. However, as you know yourself, one of the main prerequisites for a clergyman's wife is a blameless reputation and ... Well, need I say more?'

A red flush crept up Marjorie's neck as she stared unseeing ahead.

The elderly carriage clock in the middle of the mantelshelf ticked off half a minute then she gave him a brittle smile.

'Thank you for bringing this matter to my attention, Father David, and I hope you have a lovely lunch with your friend.'

Prue was just packing her clean overalls into her holdall ready to set off to work after she'd had lunch when her bedroom door burst open and her mother, throat aflame and eyes glaring, burst in.

'Is it true that you and Jack Quinn are romantically involved?'

Panic fluttered in Prue's chest. 'What?'

'You heard?' her mother replied.

'We work together at Stratford, that's all,' she said, trying to stop her mind from spinning.

'And I suppose that's where you see him, then,' her mother spat back.

'From time to time in the canteen and around the site,' Prue replied. 'And I've seen him a couple of times at his sister's house.'

'Was she there at the time?'

'Of course she was.'

Marjorie's eyes narrowed. 'Are you sure?'

Prue gave her mother a hard look. 'Yes? What's all this about, anyhow?'

'I have it on good authority that you have become too familiar with this man,' her mother replied.

'From whom?'

Her mother's steely gaze wavered a little, but she didn't reply.

'I suppose it was Mrs Farmer?' continued Prue. 'She was giving me funny looks on Saturday and I saw her come in for your meeting. So what did she accuse me of: having a torrid affair or planning to elope with Jack?'

'Don't be tiresome, Prudence,' her mother replied. 'No one is accusing you of anything other than being too innocent to recognise a seducer.'

'A seducer! For goodness' sake.' Prue gave a mirthless laugh. 'We're not living in a Victorian melodrama, Mother.'

'And you invited him to the garden party.'

'Yes, I did, with his daughter Rachel, who had a wonderful time,' Prue replied. 'What of it?'

Her mother fixed her with a hard stare. 'Did you know this Quinn is divorced?'

'Yes, he told me himself,' Prue replied.

'Did you also know that his wife divorced him for adultery and that he has women all over the area?' her mother asked.

Unhappiness dragged on Prue's heart, but she forced herself to maintain her unflinching expression.

'Prudence, darling,' said her mother in a softer tone, 'you know the Church's teaching on divorce, adultery and carnal relationships, so why let your reputation be damaged by being seen to be friendly towards this man? Think of your father's position, at least. After all,' her mother gave a tinkling laugh, 'it's not as if marriage to someone like Jack Quinn would ever be possible. Apart from the obvious reason of his unsavoury past, you're the daughter of a clergyman with noble ancestors and he's a railway worker whose grandparents probably arrived barefoot on these shores from Ireland half a century ago with not a penny to their name.'

Suddenly weary of the battle, Prue's shoulders sagged. 'Look, Mother, Jack Quinn and I happen to work together and I've seen him around the parish from time to time. We are just acquaintances, nothing more,' she replied. 'Now if you don't mind, I have to get ready for work.'

Her mother hovered in front of her for a moment

then headed for the door, but after a couple of steps she turned back.

'Prudence, darling, all I want for you is what every mother wants for their daughter: to see her walk down the aisle in a lovely white dress to marry an honourable young man who will make her happy. And Father David, who I know has a great fondness for you, fits the bill in every way. He's under your own roof, so please don't waste your time on a man like Jack Quinn.'

Turning again she headed for the door; this time, mercifully, she went through it.

As the handle clicked shut, Prue sat down heavily on her bed and stared unseeing at the swirls on her bedside rug. From nowhere the urge to burst into tears welled up in her, but she cut it short and stood up. Stuffing a clean handkerchief and her headscarf alongside her dungarees, she grabbed the door handle and, reminding herself that, in her own words, she and Jack were 'acquaintances, nothing more', Prue pulled back her shoulders and followed her mother out of the room.

Thankful for the breeze on her face on what must have been one of the hottest August days ever recorded, Prue turned left out of Stepney Green just as a squadron of Spitfires, probably from Hornchurch or South Weald airbases, stretched overhead southward, no doubt to battle yet another Luftwaffe incursion over the green fields of Kent.

Dodging around a couple of small boys, arms outstretched and dashing across the cobbles as they imitated their heroes flying overhead, Prue coasted to a stop outside Sister Martha's small cottage in King John Passage.

Stepping off her bicycle she secured it to the boot scrape set into the brickwork and took her workbag from the front basket.

Like every other door in the street, the elderly nun's dark green front door was open, so Prue stepped over the threshold and into a neat little parlour.

'Sister Martha, are you in?' she called, standing uncertainly on the half-circle coconut mat.

There was a noise in the scullery and Sister Martha's head minus her wimple appeared around the edge of the door. 'Oh Prue, what a nice surprise.'

'I hope you don't mind me popping in,' said Prue. 'But I thought if you weren't busy—'

'I'm never too busy for you, my dear.' The elderly nun's wrinkled face lifted in a kindly smile. 'Just give me a moment and I'll make us both a nice cuppa.'

The nun returned to her kitchen.

To be honest, she usually pitched up on the doorstep of Sister Martha's snug little home at least once a week, knowing the elderly nun's kettle had always just boiled.

Dropping her holdall on the floor, Prue flopped into the soft upholstery of the nearest chair, let her head fall back and closed her eyes. With the homely smell of lavender and beeswax filling her nose and listening to the slow tick-tock of the grandmother clock in the corner, Prue felt sleep edge towards her. Hardly surprising really, considering she'd barely had a wink of sleep for the past two nights.

The rattle of crockery brought Prue back to consciousness and she opened her eyes as Sister Martha walked back in with a tea tray.

'Sorry,' said Prue, yawning.

'Don't apologise,' said Sister Martha, setting the tray on the coffee table in front of the unlit grate. 'I'm not surprised you're tired; I don't think anyone can sleep in this heat.'

Prue gave a wan smile. That was true. The temperature at night barely dropped below sixty degrees, but that wasn't the reason for her insomnia.

Sister Martha poured their tea and handed Prue a cup and a plate with a generous slice of fruitcake.

'So, did your brother get back to his camp without a hitch on Monday?'

'Yes, once my mother actually let him out the door,' Prue replied. 'He telephoned yesterday evening saying he'd arrived after getting stuck in Glasgow when his train was requisitioned at the last moment to move an infantry battalion south.'

'At least, after all he's been through, he had some time with his family before returning to duty, which is a blessing,' said Sister Martha. 'And he certainly seemed to be enjoying himself on Saturday at the garden party. I was pleased to see Jack Quinn there with Rachel. I—'

'Can I ask you something about Jack?' Prue blurted out.

The nun looked surprised. 'If you like.'

'Is it true that his wife divorced him for adultery?'

'How do you know that?'

'May Farmer's told my mother,' Prue replied, the scene in her bedroom two days before replaying itself yet again in her head.

'And she told you,' said Sister Martha.

'She also said that he was … friendly with women all over East London,' Prue added, trying to ignore the sharp pain jabbing at her breastbone.

Sister Martha smiled. 'Well, Jack's had a goodly number of women set their cap at him since he was old enough to shave, but he's not some sort of Cockney Casanova, Prue. Would it bother you if he was?'

'Of course not, but for some reason my mother's got it into her head that I'm becoming romantically involved with him.' Prue forced a light laugh. 'Which is ridiculous, I know.'

'Is it?' asked Sister Martha, raising her cup to her lips.

'Of course it is,' Prue replied. 'And even if I wanted to I couldn't because the Church condemns divorce.'

'Well, the bishops certainly do,' said Sister Martha. 'But I don't think a God who loves us as He does would want anyone to live a life of misery because we made a mistake. You look surprised.'

'Only because I've thought the same for ages.' Prue sighed. 'But even so, there's my father's position to

376

consider; and as my mother pointed out, I wouldn't be able to have a white wedding.'

Aware of Sister Martha's sharp grey eyes scrutinising her closely, Prue lowered her gaze and took a bite of cake.

'And anyway,' she went on, 'my mother thinks Father David would make a perfect husband.'

'What about you?'

'Well, he is very good-looking, and he is fond of me,' said Prue.

'And of course, as a clergyman's daughter, you'd make the perfect vicar's wife,' said the nun. 'You could run a parish and parsonage with your eyes closed.'

Prue laughed. 'Well, I've had a good teacher in my mother, that's for sure.'

'You certainly have,' agreed Sister Martha.

Prue placed her empty cup on the tray and stood up.

Reaching down to pick up her handbag, Prue caught sight of the photos on the small mantelshelf. Most were family portraits from half a century ago, but one at the end caught her eye.

It was a head-and-shoulders studio portrait of an army officer. His cap was set at a slightly jaunty angle on his fair hair. A pencil moustache hugged his top lip, which had a hint of a smile hovering on it, and he looked out of the sepia image with a confident gaze.

Leaving her handbag where it was, Prue took a step closer. 'What a handsome young man.'

'Giles McCloud certainly was,' agreed Sister Martha, taking the portrait from its place and looking down at it. 'He died on the seventh of March nineteen eighteen. I was a VAD working in a hospital at Amiens and he was in the intelligence corps attached to command headquarters there,' she continued, her eyes soft as she gazed at the portrait. 'We were engaged to be married as soon as the war was over, but it wasn't to be.'

'I'm so sorry,' said Prue.

'Oddly, whereas many people lose their faith in God after the death of someone they love, Giles's death strengthened mine,' the nun continued. 'I couldn't believe that the Almighty would have been so cruel as to have cut short his life and the lives of thousands of young men just like him unless it was part of a larger plan, and I still believe that even now, as young men stand ready to sacrifice their lives for our freedom once again. I have to or nothing in this world makes any sense.'

'But did you never meet anyone ...? Forgive me, I shouldn't have ... '

'That's all right, my dear,' said Sister Martha, turning and smiling at her. 'It's a question I've been asked before and yes, since Giles died, I have met several men, good men, who would have been wonderful husbands and fathers, but from the first moment Giles took me in his arms I knew I would love him for the rest of my life.' Putting the portrait back on the mantelshelf, she turned to face Prue. 'And believe me when I tell you that the most important thing about any man you marry is that you love him exactly the same way I loved, and still love, Giles.'

Chapter thirty-one

GIVING HIS SUPERVISOR'S office door a cursory knock, Jack reached for the handle, but before he was able to grasp it the door opened, and Billy Butcher stood on the threshold.

The two men eyeballed each other for a moment then Butcher stood aside and Jack strode in, expecting to see Ted Prentice sitting behind his desk; instead, there was a military police captain.

Squashed in beside him was PC McMann from West Ham nick. This was a bit unexpected, because at this time most afternoons McMann was either slurping tea in the shunting-yard canteen or propping up the bar in the Two Puddings on Stratford Broadway. In addition, standing behind them to their right was a regimental sergeant major.

'I'm Captain Hargreaves of the Royal Military Police and you are?' he asked.

'Jack Quinn.'

He ticked off Jack's name. 'And it says here you're a locomotive engineer.'

'I am,' Jack replied. 'And that's why I've got the Felixstowe flyer over one of the pits waiting to be fitted with a new firebox, so I'd like to know what this is abo—'

'Theft,' PC McMann supplied, 'of army supplies.'

'More correctly: treason under the new Emergency War Powers Act,' added the RMP captain.

'What sort of army equipment?' Jack asked.

Hargreaves chewed his lips for a moment then spoke. 'Guns and ammunition.'

'Disappeared they did,' chipped in Billy Butcher, a gleam in his eyes as he looked at Jack, 'from freight trains parked overnight in this yard.'

'Were you on late duty last Thursday?' said the RMP officer, looking at the workshop rota.

'I was,' said Jack.

'And can you explain,' said Hargreaves, 'why you've been on a late shift each time a box of weapons and ammo has gone missing?'

'Your guess is as good as mine,' Jack replied. 'But I'm sure I'm not the only one who happened to be working on the same night that army firearms have gone missing.'

'No, you're not, but PC McMann, who is assisting us, has come up with some interesting information about you, Quinn,' said Hargreaves. 'Well, more particularly your brother, Charlie Quinn, who ran a protection racket in London Docks.'

'Wrong 'un he was, and no mistake,' muttered the local bobby.

'My brother who died ten years ago,' snapped Jack, glaring at Hargreaves.

'And you were seen lurking around the armament wagons by corporal Stone last Tuesday,' said the RMP captain.

'Well, Captain, he's either mistaken or a liar,' said Jack.

'Stone's a good man, sir,' said Butcher. 'Adamant he was and said that he thought that Quinn looked like he was up to no good.'

'This squaddie who is so certain he saw me wouldn't happen to be Corporal Len Stone, would it?' asked Jack.

Although his expression remained noncommittal, Billy Butcher's eyes narrowed as he looked across the head of his senior officer at Jack.

Captain Hargreaves glanced at the sheaf of papers in front of him. 'Well yes, it is.'

'Well, the reason he's probably so adamant that it was me is because two weeks ago I stopped him and his ugly mates harassing one of the female lamp cleaners,' Jack replied, matching Butcher's hard stare, 'and dragging her into an empty work shed to teach her "some proper manners"?'

Captain Hargreaves turned to look at the man in the doorway. 'Is this true, Sergeant Butcher?'

The RMP officer glared at Butcher. 'Well?'

Butcher swallowed and snapped to attention.

'I'm afraid I know of no such incident such as Mr Quinn is referring to, sir!' he barked, a red flush creeping upwards from beneath his pristine khaki collar.

Captain Hargreaves studied his subordinate for a moment or two longer, then turned back to Jack.

'If that's all, Captain,' Jack thumbed over his shoulder,

'I'll go and get on with putting that ancient locomotive back into service.'

Hargreaves and McMann exchanged looks then the captain gave a small nod.

'All right, Quinn, you can go,' said PC McMann.

Jack headed towards the door but before he reached it Billy jumped forward and opened it.

'Be seeing you, Jack,' he said, under his breath.

'And I'll be seeing you too, Billy,' Jack replied in the same low tone.

With the dirty lamp from number six signal hooked over her left arm, Prue stepped off the bottom of the ladder. Setting it next to the one she'd already taken down, Prue loaded them on to the carrying pole. Grasping it firmly in the middle and then making sure they were evenly balanced, she started off along the railway tracks towards the lamp shed.

She'd only gone about two hundred yards when she spotted Gladys loitering by the carriage shed with one of the soldiers. Unfortunately, Gladys had clearly spotted her, too. Grinding her cigarette stub under her toe, she peeled herself off the wall and stomped over.

'Oi!' she said, pony-stepping over the tracks that gleamed in the late-morning sunlight. 'I want a word with you.'

Prue carried on walking, but Gladys planted herself in front of her.

'I know it was you who told Knobby,' she said, the blonde curl on her forehead bobbing as she spoke.

'Told Knobby what?' asked Prue wearily.

'About Pat clocking me in on Tuesday when I overslept,' Gladys replied.

'Firstly, I didn't know Pat clocked you in,' Prue replied. 'And secondly, even if I had I've got better things to do than to tell tales on you.'

'That's a lie,' Gladys spat back. 'I know it was you and now I've got another bloody written warning.'

'Perhaps you didn't hear me, Gladys,' said Prue, looking the other woman square in the eye. 'I just said it wasn't me. Perhaps if you concentrated more on your work and less on flirting with anything in trousers you wouldn't find yourself hauled into the office all the time.'

'I graft as 'ard as any of you,' Gladys replied, her bright red mouth turning down at the corners.

'Oh, I know you do,' laughed Prue. 'In fact, I've never seen anyone work so hard at avoiding doing what they're being paid for as you. And is there a soldier you haven't been caught smooching with behind some shed or another? Part of the war effort, is it, to keep up the troops' morale?'

Outrage flashed across Gladys's face for a second then she delved into her boiler-suit pocket and pulled out a packet of Senior Service.

'I know why you want to see me get the sack,' she said, grasping a cigarette between her lips and lighting it.

Prue sighed. 'And why would that be, Gladys?'

'Jack Quinn.' Smoke snorted from her nostrils like a horse on a frosty day.

Prue's heart did a little double step of excitement. 'I don't know what he has to do with anything?'

'Don't try and play Little Miss Bloody Holy-holy with me. I've seen the way you look at him. I bet you get a right fizz in your knickers, don't you?' Gladys sniggered. 'Not that I blame you. Jack Quinn's the sort of man who'd get the Virgin Mary all hot and bothered.'

Maintaining her cool expression, Prue didn't reply.

A sly look crept into Gladys's eye. 'I suppose you dobbed me in to Knobby because someone told you about me and Jack getting friendly round the back of the Rotunda last week.'

Prue's heart lurched uncomfortably as an image of Jack with his arms around Gladys loomed large in her mind.

Seeing Prue's bleak expression, Gladys laughed and blew a stream of smoke from the side of her mouth.

'I haven't got time to hang around here listening to you; I've got to get these lamps back to the shop.' Sidestepping, Prue tried to walk past but Gladys blocked her path again.

'Just you wait,' Gladys said, jabbing her cigarette at Prue's face. 'I'll get you back proper for dobbing me in to Knobby.'

Flicking the ash off the end of her cigarette, Gladys took another long drag, gave Prue a hateful look, then sashayed back across to the carriage shed.

Renewing her grip on the pole, Prue continued towards the lamp shed.

After her mother berating her about Jack the week before, Prue teetered on the edge of believing Gladys about the Rotunda but then she recalled her conversation at the garden party with Jack under the shade of the rhododendron bush. Remembering the unguarded softness in his eyes and the clear tone of truth in his voice when he spoke about finding a woman to share his life and love with, Prue knew that Gladys was lying. Her quest to capture Jack's affections were doomed to fail just like Prue's hope of ever being able to reconcile herself to the fact that Jack was a self-confessed adulterer.

'So, once you've prepared your explosives,' said Jack, holding two fat sausages of plasticine bound together with gaffer tape in the palm of his hand, 'and you're ready to place them, all you have to do is prime them.' He slid half an HB pencil between them. 'And then set the timer.' He indicated the rubber on the top.

''Ow long should we set it for?' asked Isaac Morris, sitting across from Jack on a case of Springfield rifle ammunition.

''Ow fast you can run, Isaac?' said Freddie Fouke, his teeth flashing in the gloom as he grinned at his comrade in arms.

Donny Duncombe and Georgie Murray, perched on

either side of Freddie on a crate of grenades and a first-aid box respectively, snorted.

It was the first Wednesday in September, and five days since Jack had been questioned about the missing ammunition at Stratford.

Now, along with the four other members of his auxiliary unit – or the Artful Dodgers, as Colonel Gubbins had christened them – he was in St Winifred's charnel house, and had been for the past three hours.

Around them, secured in metal cases, were a range of weaponry, from two Tommy guns through to knuckledusters, which was why he was demonstrating how to construct a car bomb with plasticine and a pencil rather than with gelignite and a detonator.

As he was on the twilight patrol with his Home Guard unit at ten, Jack was dressed in his newly issued khaki uniform. Freddie, who'd volunteered as an ARP warden, was wearing something similar in navy, while Isaac, Donny and Georgie were dressed in rough working clothes.

In addition to the auxiliary unit's tools of the trade, so to speak, squashed into the corner were boxes of tinned food and two canisters of fresh water, plus a short-wave radio. Although they were some thirty yards from St Winifred's, Sister Martha, under the pretence of tidying around the graves, had managed to sink a wire into the ground linking their hideaway to the church, which Jack then attached to the drainpipe at the rear of the church to act as an aerial.

It was probably about nine in the evening by now, although it was a little difficult to know. A few streaks of light cut through the gloom where Jack has shifted the roof tiles to increase ventilation, but the men had been working by the light of a paraffin hurricane lamp for the past hour.

'You'll have to judge that according to where you're going to place it,' said Donny Duncombe, the deep scar down the left side of his face at odds with his cherub-like features.

'And remember: the Nazis marching through our streets have already run up against Resistance fighters in Belgium and France, so they will be on their guard against the same here,' said Jack. 'As I've said before, when the Germans get here each of us may have to work independently. If this place is discovered, you might have to stash explosives and guns in lofts, down the bog in your backyard or in the coal holes. Now, are there any questions?'

No one replied.

'Well, the last thing to tell you tonight is that the top brass took my point and they've reprinted the training manuals.' Reaching into his bag, Jack pulled out four magazines and handed them out. 'They'll probably blend in a bit better with your decor.'

Taking his 1939 racing almanac, Freddie laughed. 'A darn sight better than that blooming fertiliser diary they sent us.'

They all laughed.

'Well, if there's nothing else?' They shook their heads. 'Right, push off then and remember: the balloon could go up tomorrow so when it does ...'

'Don't worry, we know what to do,' said Isaac.

'Good, check your message drops each day and I'll be in touch,' Jack replied.

Rising to their feet, the four men in Jack's auxiliary unit slipped silently into the glooming one by one.

As Jack tided away, the charnel house's handle rattled.

Grabbing his rifle, he leaned on the wall next to him and pointed it at the ancient door. The door creaked open, and Jack let out a long breath as Sister Martha's wimpled head appeared around the edge.

'Good, I'm glad I caught you,' she said, as she struggled into the hideout lugging an old carpet bag.

Resting his rifle back against the wall, Jack crossed the space and took the bag from her.

'How on earth did you manage to carry this from your cottage?' he said as the weight of it dragged on his arm.

'Divine intervention,' she replied, smiling up at him in the yellow glow of the hurricane lamp. 'These arrived today.'

Resting the bag on a box of ammunition, Jack opened it to see half a dozen Mark III Sten carbines inside.

'The ammunition's underneath and there'll be more coming next week,' she said as Jack gazed down at the unscratched barrels of the sub-machine guns.

Jack took one out and, holding it at hip-height he flicked the safety lock then snapped the trigger a couple of times.

'We were trained with these on my last visit to Coleshill but were told it would be months before we'd get our hands on them,' said Jack, turning it over in his hands. 'How did you manage it?'

A mischievous smile hovered on Sister Martha's lips. 'Let's just say I have friends in high places.'

'Well, thank God for that,' said Jack. 'The *Sketch* had a report about some towns up north being bombed, so it looks like we're going to need these and *Him*,' he glanced skywards, 'soon.'

'You may well be right,' she replied, her smile vanishing. 'Did you hear there were three air raid warnings around here yesterday?'

Jack nodded. 'Rosie told me; plus, there was an almighty air battle with the Luftwaffe over New Cross and Blackheath.'

'Yes, Prue Carmichael was up on fire-watch patrol and said she saw everything,' said Sister Martha.

An image of Prue alone on the top of St Winifred's tower as a squadron of Dorniers or Junkers raged overhead loomed in his mind.

'Is it?'

'I'm sorry, I ...'

'I said, is your unit ready?'

'As we'll ever be,' said Jack, cutting short the panic rising in his chest.

The nun gave a rueful smile. 'I suppose that goes for all of us.'

Her perceptive grey eyes studied his face for a moment then she let out a long breath. 'Blast!'

'What's the matter?'

There was another long pause then the nun gave a heavy sigh. 'You, Jack.'

'What have I done?'

'Nothing,' Sister Martha replied. 'But I'm fond of both you and Prue Carmichael, which is why I'm going to break my golden rule of not gossiping. She came to see me last week quite upset—'

'Is she all right?' Jack raked his fingers through his hair. 'Has someone hurt her? Because if they have, I'll—'

'No one's laid a finger on her,' she assured him. 'But they have been telling her tales about the reason for your divorce.'

'Who?'

'That doesn't matter,' she replied. 'But I know you well enough, Jack, to know that friendship isn't how you feel for Prue, so unless you want her to be pushed into Father David's arm you need to do something.'

Chapter thirty-two

AS A SLUGGISH BUMBLE BEE droned around the apples in the branches above, Prue, who was sitting on a garden bench in the shade of the trees, turned the page of her book.

It was the first Friday in September and as it was about ten minutes since the signature tune heralding the start of *Music While You Work* had drifted out from the open kitchen window, it was just after ten-thirty in the morning.

Reaching the bottom of the page, Prue was just about to begin the next when Father David stepped through the French doors and started across the lawn towards her.

'Ah,' he said as he reached her, 'your mother said you'd be out here.'

Damping down the irritation that bubbled up in her chest, Prue smiled. 'Yes, as I'm not due at work until two I thought I'd take advantage of the good weather while it lasts.'

'Yes, it has been unseasonably warm, hasn't it?' said David, his Adam's apple rising above his dog collar as he surveyed the forget-me-not-blue sky above them. 'What a blessing this summer has been; wall-to-wall sunshine since June.' He shifted his attention to the herbaceous border. 'And with the summer flowers in full bloom, the garden looks particularly lovely at this time of year.'

'Well, enjoy it while you can,' said Prue, 'because the parish Dig for Victory working party is arriving in two weeks to dig up the lawn and borders to plant vegetables.'

David shifted his weight from one leg to the other, then spoke again. 'I wonder if I might speak to you about something.'

'Of course,' she replied. 'But if it's about the intersession's rota then—'

'No, no,' he cut in. 'it's not a Church matter. Well, at least not in the usual sense of the word.'

Prue placed her book face down on her lap and rested her hands on the cover.

Father David cleared his throat.

'Prudence, I do not think it will come as too great a surprise when I tell you I have admired you from almost the first moment I saw you,' he said in his Sunday sermon voice as his blue eyes looked down at her. 'Since that time, it has become clear to me that you are, as St Matthew puts it in the Good Book, "a pearl of great price". Although I am the humblest of God's servants, it seems I have found sufficient favour in His eyes for Him to place you before me. You, Prudence, are not only a delightful vision of loveliness but, and more importantly to one in my position, a woman who personifies the Christian values of gentleness and compassion,' a knowing smile lifted the corners of David's lips, 'attributes which I'm sure you will agree are essential in a clergyman's wife.'

Prue's heart thumped painfully in her chest. She opened her mouth to speak, but Father David hurried on.

'I know at present I am only a humble curate,' he continued, with more than a trace of smugness. 'But as I'm sure you are aware, my godfather is the Bishop of Rutland so I have an influential advocate in the House of Bishops. In addition, thanks to Great-uncle Eustace, who made a pile in Rhodesia after the Boar War, I have a not inconsiderable income, so I will be able to provide you with the comfortable lifestyle you have become accustomed to as well as ensure that any children that God blesses us with will have a good start in life. Now, although etiquette dictates that I should speak to your father before asking you,' an indulgent expression slid across Father David's face, 'you are, as you often point out, a very modern young woman so ...' Tugging up his right trouser leg an inch, he knelt on one knee in front of her. Taking her hand, he looked earnestly at her. 'Prudence, darling, will you do me the greatest honour and consent to be my wife?'

He looked beseechingly at her and the moisture in Prue's mouth evaporated.

'I know it is rather sudden,' he said, wobbling slightly because of his narrow centre of gravity. 'And if we were living in ordinary time I would have declared myself at the end of my curacy so we could marry at St Winifred's next summer before I take up my own living, but with things the way they are I decided it would be expedient for us to marry as soon as the banns can be read.'

'Father David, I don't know what to …'

His indulgent smile morphed into a condescending one.

'Your modest surprise does you credit, my sweetest darling, so I'm happy to wait until you've had a chance to speak to your mother about the duties of a wife before you say those blessed words that will make me the happiest man on earth.'

Rising to his feet, Father David brushed down his trousers then giving her the sort of look you might bestow on a puppy who'd fetched back a ball for the first time, he walked back into the rectory.

Feeling as if she'd suddenly become a character in an am-dram production of a Regency play, Prue stared after him and then, right on cue, her mother appeared. With her heels sinking into the lawn, Marjorie Carmichael practically sprinted across.

'Are my eyes deceiving me or did I just see Father David down on one knee in front of you from the spare-room window?' she asked, breathless with excitement.

Prue nodded.

Her mother clasped her hands together and looked heavenward. 'I am so thrilled, my darling. He's such a fine young man and destined for high office in the Church, I'm sure. Who knows, one day you could be a bishop's wife or even an archbishop's.' She gave an oddly girlish giggle. 'When is the wedding?'

'According to Father David, we're to be married as soon as the banns are read,' Prue replied.

Pressing her lips together, Prue's mother frowned. 'All these shortages are very tiresome, but never fear. No daughter of mine will be wearing anything but white when she walks down the aisle.' Her dour expression brightened in an instant. 'I know. I have my mother's wedding dress stored in mothballs upstairs. It was made in Paris by Worth and has yards of fabric, so I'm sure there's enough to make a lovely gown for your special day, Prudence.'

'Well, Mother, perhaps you should wait a bit before you get your dressmaking shears out,' said Prue, 'because I haven't agreed to marry him yet.'

Having marched back from Mile End Road along Stepney Green, Jack reached the clock tower at the junction with Redmans Road and turned left. He passed Redcoat School's redbrick Victorian building and reached Stepney High Street a minute or two later.

With the sun high above and temperatures hovering around the mid-seventies, you'd be forgiven for thinking it was the height of summer, but in fact it was just after four on the first Saturday in September.

Pausing on the corner, Jack studied St Winifred's square bell tower for a moment then, shouldering his rifle, he let an ARP van pass before marching across the cobbles and through the church's stone gateposts.

A couple of Boy Scouts with black ARP armbands and a large white 'M' for messenger painted on the front of their tin helmets were lolling about, smoking and playing pitch-and-toss against the flint-stone wall. Sitting at a school desk by the open church door was a well-padded ARP warden, with a roll-up dangling from his lips. He was supposedly keeping an eye on the youngsters, but was in fact reading the paper.

He gave Jack a cursory look as he approached then returned to studying the runners and riders.

Leaving the balmy air behind, Jack entered the cool interior of the tower and as his eyes adjusted to the dim light he headed for the door to his right. Squeezing through the narrow medieval entrance and careful to place his size tens squarely on the outer edge of the spiral staircase, he ascended into the loft. The brass bells forged in the Whitechapel foundry centuries before hung in open-mouthed silence from the oak beams overhead. Praying they wouldn't soon be ringing out warnings of German troops on English soil, Jack crossed to the metal ladder fixed to the wall and began to climb upwards.

Emerging on to the top a few moments later, he gazed across at the reason he'd climbed the tower: Prue.

She was diagonally across from him, standing by a picnic chair with her elbows resting on the top of the parapet and holding a pair of ancient binoculars to her eyes. She was peering southwards between the cigar-shaped silver barrage balloons and into the cloudless clear blue sky stretching way off into Kent. She was dressed in a pair of trousers, her gas mask case slung across her and a 'Fire Guard' armband on her upper arm, and her long hair swirled up under her tin helmet.

Jack's chest swelled with love and desire at the sight of her, and he longed to slip his arm around her and place his lips on her slender neck. But if he was ever to have a chance of doing that and more, he needed to tell her about Alma.

With his heart thumping and knowing that any chance of future happiness lay in her hands, he squared his shoulders, but as he was about to take a step a pigeon flapped past and Prue yawned.

'Anything interesting?' he asked.

She looked around and her eyes lit up. 'Jack. What are you doing here? I thought Saturday was your day to have Rachel.'

'It usually is, but she's at her grandmother's house in North London for the weekend, so as two of our platoon got their call-up papers this week, I stepped in to cover,' he replied. 'Anything happening?'

Prue shook her head. 'But as the City, Hackney and Plumstead have been bombed in the last week, I'm keeping my eyes peeled.'

Jack looked out over the grey-tiled terraced houses and past the Victorian warehouses lining the river at the expanse of clear sky over Kent.

'Everyone should,' he said, his mouth pulling into a hard line as he studied the vast stretch of blue before him.

He turned his attention back to Prue and found her gazing up at him with such a look in her eyes that he almost took her in his arms.

They stayed like that for a moment or two then Prue lowered her eyes and reached into the wicker basket at her feet. Pulling out a fern-green canister, she held it aloft. 'I was just about to pour myself a cuppa; would you like one?' she asked. 'That is if you're not in a hurry or going to get court-martialled for dereliction of—'

'No, I'd love a cup,' he replied. 'But only if it doesn't leave you short.'

'This is our family picnic flask,' she said, 'so there's enough for your whole platoon.'

He laughed. 'Well, if you put it like that.'

Resting his rifle against the stone, he pulled across the spare picnic chair and set it alongside Prue's.

'There you are,' she said, handing him a Bakelite mug with whirls of steam escaping from it.

'Thanks.'

He took a sip but before he could speak, Prue did.

'I saw Rosie this afternoon at the butcher's,' she said.

'Did you?' he replied.

Prue nodded. 'She'd just come back from seeing the midwives at Munr—'

'Prue, I need to tell you about me and Alma,' Jack burst out.

Her mouth dropped open in surprise.

'You're not going back to her, are you?' she asked, a slight tremor in her voice. 'I mean, people do try to patch things up for the sake of the children and—'

'No, no, it's nothing like that.' He forced out a light laugh. 'And besides, she's remarried.'

'Oh, has she? Good. I don't mean … well, you know … I …'

Still holding her tea, Prue snatched up the binoculars with the other hand and scanned the horizon again.

Jack raked his fingers through his hair and waited. After a moment she lowered them again and with a slight flush colouring her cheeks her gaze returned to him.

'The thing is I met Alma when we were both very young. She was the girl every bloke wanted to dance with and to cut a long story short when I discovered she was in the family way, despite her parents' objections, I insisted on doing the right thing and marrying her.'

Prue looked puzzled. 'Her parents' objected?'

'Yes, they wanted to make other arrangements,' Jack replied, as the horror of discovering they'd organised a private clinic flashed through his mind. 'Anyway. We weren't happy and after Rachel was born things went from bad to worse until her parents got their solicitor involved and Alma sued for divorce on the grounds of adultery.' He took another deep breath. 'But that's not the full story—'

'What's that?' cut in Prue.

Jumping to her feet, she snatched up the binoculars and pressed them to her eyes. Shading his vision with his hand, Jack followed her gaze.

In the distance, probably over New Cross or Catford, and in a V formation like a flock of metal geese, were hundreds of aircraft glinting in the late-afternoon sunlight.

As the Luftwaffe planes drew nearer, the ack-ack guns in Woolwich and Bermondsey punctuated the space around them with little puffs of white.

A low buzz pulsed through the still air as the planes flying high overhead drew nearer.

Prue span around, her eyes wide with dread. Neither of them moved and they stared wordlessly at each other for a long moment then the bloodcurdling wail of the air raid siren tore between them.

The German planes soared over them, releasing thousands of tiny cylinders in their wake. The incendiary bombs found their targets in the warehouses filled with flour, rubber and sugar in Limehouse Basin and the main London Docks half a mile away, and flames like the very fires of Hell burst skywards.

The church tower rocked as incendiary bombs fell from the sky and ignited houses and factories all around them and the piercing screams of people in the streets below joined the ominous hum of engines above.

Jack snatched up his rifle. 'You have to go to the shelter.'

'No, I'm on fire watch,' Prue replied.

'But it's too dangerous up here,' he protested.

'No more than it is down there,' she replied. 'And are you going to the shelter?'

'Of course not.'

'Then neither am I,' Prue snapped back. 'My duty is to make sure the central control at the Town Hall know where the fire crews need to go.'

'But—'

Prue's determined expression stopped his words.

Jack wanted to beg her to go to the safety of the church's crypt, to make her promise not to do anything silly or put herself in danger, to tell her that he loved her so much that his heart would likely stop beating if anything happened to her, but …

He gave a heavy sigh. 'You're right, of course. We both have to do our duty.'

'We do,' Prue shouted, as frantic fire-engine bells joined the bedlam of noise around them.

Pleading silently with God to keep her safe, Jack shouldered his weapon and dashed towards the trapdoor.

'Yes, the ladies are still serving tea in the shelter, Mrs Pearman,' said Prue.

'Fank Gawd for that,' said Stanley, who was standing next to his wife. 'Bloody Hun dropped one of those insendi-wotsits two streets down and the fire brigade blokes have plugged themselves into the mains so our water's off.'

'Just go straight through the church and the door to your left,' said Prue, pointing through the open doors of the church towards the far end.

Leaning on their respective walking sticks, Elsie and Stanley Pearman, the elderly couple who lived in the row of almshouses on the other side of the church grounds, shuffled off down the aisle.

'But be careful on the stairs,' Prue shouted after them. 'They are very worn.'

It was just after eight in the evening and Prue had been relieved from her duties on the church roof when the nightshift arrived just as the all-clear sounded. Although that was almost two hours ago, people were still seeking comfort and shelter in St Winifred's.

Prue didn't blame them.

The blackout had come into force half an hour ago, but the wardens and the rest of the Civil Defence personnel had more to worry about tonight than someone forgetting to draw their blackout curtain.

Although there were several black columns of smoke coming from a few streets away, the houses and shops in the High Street by the church seemed to have escaped most of the incendiary bombs. As people wandered around, dazed by the destruction and coughing with the smoke, appliances from all over London raced to join the local crews.

Although officially off duty, Prue was standing just outside the front door of the church ready to help if needed. To be honest, she was pleased to have something to keep her mind from returning to the conversation she'd had on the bell tower with Jack.

Her mother was right! Alma divorced him because he was unfaithful. What was there to explain? she wondered, as the hollow feeling she'd had ever since made its presence known.

'I just heard the paintworks next to the kiddies' hospital

in Shadwell's gone up,' said a familiar voice, cutting into her unhappy thoughts.

She looked around to see Rosie with her youngest son on her hip.

'My goodness, were the children all right?' Prue asked.

'As far as I know,' Rosie replied.

Spotting a couple of friends playing chase, Michael slipped his hands from his mother's and ran off.

'Stay where I can see you,' Rosie shouted after him.

Rosie pulled a face.

'He's a bit big for you to be carrying around in your condition,' Prue asked.

'I know but 'e won't let me put him down,' Rosie replied.

'I'll hold him, if you like,' said Prue.

'Give Auntie Prue a cuddle, Russell?' Rosie smiled encouragingly at her youngest offspring.

The little boy replied by winding his arms around her neck and pressing his face into her shoulder.

Rosie sighed and rolled her eyes.

'I'll let you look through my binoculars,' said Prue, holding them out for the child to see.

Russell studied them for a moment then stretched his arms towards her. Prue took him and, slipping the strap around his neck she settled the little boy on her hip.

'Oh, that's better.' Placing her hands in the small of her back, Rosie stretched.

'Are you all right?'

'Just a bit of cramp,' Rosie replied. 'I've had it before.'

'How long have you got to go?' asked Prue, casting her gaze over Rosie's huge stomach.

'A couple of weeks,' Rosie replied.

As Russell peered across the graveyard through his new toy, a wall of black smoke billowed skywards, blotting out the last rays of sunset.

Prue wrinkled her nose. 'What on earth is that smell?'

'The Orient and Colonial warehouse,' Rosie replied. 'Filled to the rafters with rubber and it went up like a box of matches, according to Elsie over the road whose husband was in a pub nearby.'

Another fire engine hurtled past the stone pillars at the church entrance, its brass bells ringing frantically. Then its clanging was blotted out as the air raid siren on the top of the memorial hall in Ben Jonson Road burst into life.

A collective moan went up from the handful of people milling about outside the church.

There were murmurs of 'for Gawd's sake' and 'can't they give it a bleeding rest?', along with a few less savoury comments.

Prue hurried over to one of the centuries'-old flat-top tombs lining the church's main path. Placing Russell on top she climbed up alongside him.

The little boy, who had the binoculars pressed to his small face, lowered them and pointed towards the horizon.

Prue scanned the evening sky above the clouds of acrid black smoke.

'There's more planes coming,' she shouted above

the siren's two-tone drone as Rosie waddled over and stopped on the pathway below.

'Probably ours,' Rosie said. 'The stuff earlier's made the observers down at North Woolwich a bit jumpy, I expect.'

Starbursts of white from the ack-ack guns punched hole in the gathering darkness.

'It's not. It's the Luftwaffe.' Picking up Russell, Prue handed him down to his mother. 'Get the boys to the crypt.'

Rosie nodded and hurried as best she could towards the church's open door, collecting Michael along the way.

Others had now realised what was happening so Prue jumped off the memorial into a wave of screaming men and women surging up the path towards the church, clutching babies or dragging children behind them.

'Don't run!' Prue's voice was lost in the pandemonium of sirens, fire bells and screams.

Pushing her way through the crowd, she reached the front doors. Ducking inside, she cut through the Lady chapel and reached the narrow doorway leading to the crypt just ahead of the panicking throng.

Prue spread out her arms across the medieval stairs. 'The stairs are too narrow so—'

'Get out of the way,' roared an unshaven, roughly dressed man who had elbowed his way to the front.

'Let the children go down first,' shouted Prue.

'Bugger the kids,' the man said, barging past a blonde woman with curlers in her hair.

'Oi, who you pushing?' she yelled, shoving him back.

'Yeah, get to the back,' shouted an old man dressed in his dressing gown. 'We was here first.'

'That's enough!' shouted Prue, glowering at the crowd. 'Women and children first and one at a time.'

The unshaven individual stepped forward and shoved his nose within an inch of hers. 'Who d'you think you're talking to, Miss La-di-da?' he shouted, as stale beer, pickled onions and halitosis wafted into her face.

'You, Sid Munday,' hollered Jack, squeezing his way down the side of the press of people.

Jack planted himself in front of the interloper and glared down at him. 'Now do as Miss Carmichael said and get back.'

With a belligerent expression on his face, Sid sized up Jack for a moment then sloped away, swearing under his breath.

Prue stepped away from the door and the women and children started to file down into the crypt. Jack took up position alongside her.

Although his khaki uniform was heavily dusted with soot and his angular face streaked with dirt, to Prue he'd never looked so handsome.

'Thank you,' she said.

Jack gave a hard laugh. 'I wouldn't have stepped in but Sid's brain doesn't work when he's got a couple of drinks inside him.' His attention returned to the loosely formed queue and he frowned. 'I can't see Rosie and the boys.'

'They are already below,' Prue replied. 'I sent them down when I realised it was the Luftwaffe not the RAF heading our way.'

'Thank you, Prue.' He sighed. 'And thank God that Alma took Rachel to visit her mother in Mill Hill this weekend or …'

Jack pressed his lips together and took a couple of deep breaths and the tension in his broad shoulder ebbed away.

As the last few stragglers made their way through the arched Gothic doorway to the crypt, Jack turned to Prue.

'About Alma,' he said in a low voice, his dark eyes capturing hers. 'As I was saying earlier, adultery was cited in our divorce, but only because—'

Fear and a glimpse of death sparked through Prue as a burst of multicoloured light flashed through the stained-glass window, cutting across the stone-vaulted interior as the foundation of the medieval church rocked and her knees buckled.

Wrapping his arms around her, Jack lifted off her feet and carried her a couple of paces, then, tucking his head into her shoulder he wrapped his body around her, shielding her from the blast. Without thinking, Prue grabbed the fabric of his battle jacket and pressed her face into his chest as plaster, grit and dislodged debris showered down on them.

Loosening his embrace a little, Jack looked down at her. 'Are you all right, Prue?'

Giddy from the heady smell of his body and the

hardness of his chest beneath her fingertips, Prue looked up at him and nodded.

With fire-engine bells echoing all around them, Prue stood gazing into Jack's captivating dark eyes for what seemed like an eternity before another flash of intense brightness slashed across the pews, vaulted ceiling and altar as another German bomb crashed to earth somewhere nearby.

Jack released her from his embrace.

'You'd better get below, Prue,' he said, tightening the chin strap of his tin helmet.

'Aren't you coming?'

One side of Jack's mouth lifted in that quirky smile of his. 'Look after Rosie for me.'

Jack turned to go but as his boot studs scraped against the flagstones beneath them Prue caught his arm.

He half turned and as the church gave another shudder Prue forced a brave smile. 'Please be careful, Jack.'

Smiling back at her, he ran down the aisle and out of the church.

Raw fear clogging her chest, Prue stared into the empty space until another blast brought her back to her senses.

Ducking her head, she went through the crypt door and down the stairs, but as she got to the bottom one of the ladies who did the church flowers hurried over.

'Now there's nothing to be alarmed about, Miss Carmichael,' she said, as another blast shook the ground beneath their feet, 'but I thought you ought to know that Rosie Stapleton's waters have just gone.'

Chapter thirty-three

GIVING THE BOLT another half turn to be sure, Jack rested the spanner on his chest and studied the firebox he was halfway through reattaching to the ancient 0-6-0T to check its alignment.

"Ow's it looking, Jack?' called Bill from the footplate above.

'Ready to do a run from Land's End to John O'Groats,' Jack called back.

It was Saturday and at about six-thirty in the evening and he was lying on his back on a gurney at the bottom of an inspection pit in shed three, where he'd been all afternoon.

It was the end of a long week full of split pistons, unstable couplings and buckled suspensions, all of which he and the team had somehow put back together. That was nothing new. What was new was that for the past week everyone in Stratford's shunting yard and beyond had arrived to clock on for another day's hard graft bleary-eyed and yawning thanks to the nightly visits from the Luftwaffe.

Since last Saturday, as soon as the sun disappeared behind the houses in the western sky, the siren would start as droves of Heinkel and Junkers, their engines throbbing in the sky above, advanced across the Kent countryside towards East London.

'Fank Gawd for that,' Bill replied.

'I 'ope you don't mind me asking, Jack, but we done?' asked Tosh, who was standing beside Bill on the footplate.

Bending his knees, Jack dug his heels into the dirt beneath him and rolled the inspection trolley backwards until he was clear of the engine.

'You got a date?' he asked, moving his safety goggles on to his forehead and looking up at his two team members standing five foot above him.

Tosh shook his head. 'I want to get me ma to the shelter before … Well, you know.'

Jack did.

Now when the sirens went off, the population, blankets under their arms and clutching briefcase filled with life insurance papers and bankbooks, trudged towards the public shelters with only the promise of six hours or more of bombs dropping and very little sleep.

'Which one?' asked Jack.

'The Tilbury,' Tosh replied.

In the gathering gloom of the shed, Bill pulled a face. 'Gawd, I heard that place is a right shit hole.'

'You're not wrong,' Tosh replied. 'But at least it's underground – well, mostly – and if you get a billet in one of the bays near the door and can ignore the smell of the rancid marge in the sub-basement below it's not so bad. Ma likes it because she's with the neighbours and they cheer themselves up by 'aving a sing-song.'

411

Jack had heard about the Tilbury shelter – who hadn't? But it wasn't alone in being disorganised and grim. He was just thankful that Rachel didn't have to shelter in one of the public shelters. As the German air force's mission seemed to be to wreak death and destruction on the docks and industries on either side of the river, Alma had decided that for the time being Rachel would be safer staying with her grandmother in Mill Hill.

'Go on, lad, sling your hook,' said Jack, as the ache of missing his daughter rose in him again. 'We'll see you Monday.'

Tosh grinned then jumped down from the footplate, spraying Jack with grit as the youthful apprentice's size nines landed on the cinders.

'You can push off too, Bill,' said Jack as Tosh hurried towards the shed's open doors.

'You sure?'

Jack nodded. 'I'm all but done, so there's no point you hanging about, too.'

Slinging his tool bag over his shoulder, Bill climbed down from the footplate. 'Ta, mate, but I thought you wanted to skip off to see your Rosie.'

'No, visiting time's been over for hours; I can pop in tomorrow,' Jack replied. 'Go on and give Lena a peck on the cheek from me.'

'Not likely,' said Bill. 'She's already too sweet on you.'

Jack forced a smile and Bill strolled away.

Repositioning his goggles, Jack rolled the trolley back under the engine.

Actually, he'd seen Rosie and his new niece in the East End Maternity Hospital that morning before he'd set off for work. She and her baby daughter were well, even after several nights in the hospital basement listening to the bombs landing all around them.

But he had wanted to finish before now to catch Prue before she went off duty. However, he'd seen her and her crew heading for the changing block at five, so he knew he'd already missed her.

He'd seen her since they'd parted company on Saturday night, but it had always been in the canteen or in the yard with others milling around. They'd even arrived at the same time to see Rosie two days ago, but he couldn't very well explain to her about his divorce with Rosie sitting in the bed between them.

Sighing, Jack grasped his spanner and fixed it around the next bolt. But as he turned it the top snapped off and the edge of the metal plate he'd fixed into place two hours earlier fell down on one side.

Swearing, Jack reached for the electric drill, ready to drill out the embedded bolt.

However, as he rolled back and positioned the bit against the severed end of the bolt, the nerve-jangling wail of the air raid siren on top of the main offices rattled through the shed.

With the drill poised in his hand, Jack stared up at the flapping metal sheet.

Of course he should head over to Stratford station to take shelter in one of the underground passageways between the platforms, but this locomotive was due to pull the recently harvested wheat and barley arriving from Norfolk in the morning across to the flour mills in Putney.

It was cutting it fine, but the warning was usually twenty minutes before the aircraft arrived overhead; if he got a move on he could have that bolt back in place before the first bomb landed.

Shifting up on to his elbow, Jack pulled the OXO tin out of his tool bag and flipped open the lid. Having found the correct size replacement, he dropped the tin back in the canvas bag and grasped the bolt between his lips.

Rolling back, Jack wriggled on the gurney to relieve his shoulders and backbone pressed into the hard wooden surface, then resumed his task.

However, as the damaged bolt fell out, a flash of light burst into the shed and the earth shook all around him.

Another bomb crashed nearby, setting the equipment in the shed rattling. Forcing himself to remain calm, Jack took the bolt from his mouth and after giving it a couple of turns to anchor it, he picked up his spanner.

A flash of white light cut beneath the engine, dazzling Jack, and another explosion rocked the earth. The wheels of the locomotive above him squeaked as it shifted on the rails either side of the pit where he was lying, then another explosion shook Jack's world.

The hundred-and-fifty-ton steam engine lurched to one side then back again before jumping off the two six-inch rails it was resting on. Lying helplessly beneath it,

Jack watched in disbelief as the massive cast-iron wheels crashed down into the inspection pit.

With her Girl Guide sleeping bag under her arm and the final notes of the all-clear jangling in her sleep-deprived brain, Prue trudged down Stepney High Street towards the rectory.

It was the second Saturday in September and a full week since what the press had christened the Blitz had started. She wasn't alone; she was surrounded by yawning adults and niggly children who like her had spent the past eight hours trying to snatch a bit of sleep between the relentless bombing.

The first couple of nights had been a bit of a scramble into the shelter, but now people were falling into a routine. As soon as the sun started to dip behind the factories and tenements to the west, a steady column of people would make their way to one of the shelters now dotted throughout East London. They'd even bring deckchairs and baskets with food and drink. Mrs Kemp and Miss Sanderson, who ran St Winifred's Sunday school, had started reading the children in their shelter a bedtime story each night. Someone always started up a sing-song, too, and women often kept each other company with a set of knitting needles in their hands.

Prue slogged along, a column of weary humanity all around, and as far as the eye could see was evidence of the previous night's destruction: glassless windows with curtains flapping out of them in the early-morning breeze; billowing black smoke and flames licking skywards; exhausted heavy rescue, ambulance and fire crews whose work was not yet done even though the German bombers had returned to their bases.

So many thousands of bombs had landed on each of the past seven nights, Prue was surprised each morning to find that the shops and houses around St Winifred's were still standing.

With the acrid smell of cordite from spent German armaments and charred wood clogging her throat, she finally reached the rectory. Dragging herself the final few yards she put the key in the lock but as she did so, a voice called her name. Suppressing a sigh, she turned to see Father David hurrying up the path towards her.

'Morning, Father David.'

'Morning, my dear,' he replied, smiling down at her as he stopped in front of her. 'I spotted you at the end of the High Street and waved but you didn't see me.'

Thankfully, she hadn't.

Not only was it a week since the Luftwaffe had started their nightly visits to East London, it was also a week since David's proposal, and she still hadn't given him an answer.

He gave her a coy look. 'You could call me David, surely. When we are alone.'

Prue forced a smile. Pushing open the rectory door, she dragged herself over the threshold as the hall clock struck four in the morning.

'Your parents must have gone up to their beds as soon as the all-clear sounded,' whispered David, as he closed the door behind him.

'I'm sure,' Prue replied, in the same hushed tone.

Unlike Prue, who had headed off to the shelter for the past week, her parents – well, her mother actually – had declared their intention to shelter in their basement during air raids. The reason Marjorie gave was that it would free up space for others, although Prue suspected it was so she didn't have to spend the night lying head to toe with St Winfred's parishioners.

'I'm going to make myself a cocoa; would you like one, Fa— David?' asked Prue.

He shook his head. 'Thank you but no. I'm taking the eight o'clock Eucharist so I might try to get a bit of shut-eye before then.'

Turning, he headed for the stairs.

'Sleep well,' Prue called after him.

He turned back, and the coy expression returned to his face. 'Dreaming of – if I might be so bold – you beside me.'

As thoughts of what David's words inferred loomed large in her mind, Prue stared at him until he reached the top of the stairs.

The jangle of the rectory telephone sitting on the hall table cut across the silence and brought her back to reality. Not wishing to wake her parents, Prue snatched it up off its cradle before the second ring.

'St Winifred's Rectory,' she said softly.

'Is that Miss Prudence Carmichael?' asked a gruff voice at the other end.

'Yes.'

'I'm Sergeant Taylor at Bow Street Police Station,' said the officer. 'It's about your sister Felicity. She's been arrested.'

'I'll be there right away.' She put down the receiver and saw Father David standing at the top of the stairs.

'I heard the telephone,' he asked. 'Is there a problem?'

'N–no … not as such,' Prue replied, pushing aside the cloud of weariness clogging her brain.

'What is it, my darling?' he asked, starting down the stairs. 'You know I'll do any—'

'It was … was work for me,' Prue said, raising her hand and halting his descent.

He frowned. 'On a Sunday?'

'Yes, there's been a problem,' said Prue.

David puffed out his chest. 'Even so. Have they no respect for the day of rest ordained by the Almighty himself?'

'Well, there is a war on?' Although her head pounded, Prue forced a smile. 'I'd better get going, but could you tell my mother I've gone out?'

Before he could answer, Prue picked up her handbag and gas mask and hurried out the door.

Chapter thirty-four

'THANK YOU,' said Prue, handing over a ten-shilling note to the cab driver as her sister tumbled out of the back of the taxi behind her.

'Ta, luv,' the cabby replied, giving her back half a crown and a couple of coins. 'I 'ope as 'ow your sister's all right after her run-in with the law.'

Prue gave him a tight smile but didn't reply.

Flipping his *For Hire* sign up again, the cabby sped off towards Pimlico High Road, the early-morning sunlight glinting on the bonnet of his black cab as he went.

Prue turned and marched up to where her sister, who was wearing a pair of trousers and a block shoulder jacket, was jiggling the key in the front door of a grand Victorian house.

'I'll give you the cab fare back as soon as I get paid, Prue,' said Fliss.

She gave her a sisterly smile, which Prue didn't return.

Pressing her hand on the flaky paintwork to unstick the door from its surrounding frame, Fliss led the way into the house.

Squeezing past a weary-looking bus driver on his way to work, Prue followed her sister up the narrow stairs to the servants' quarters at the top.

Fiddling with her keys again, Fliss finally fell through the door into the lounge-cum-kitchen with Prue a couple of steps behind her.

'Home at last,' sighed Fliss, trying her sisterly smile again with the same result. She frowned. 'For goodness' sake, say something.'

'All right, I'll say something,' Prue snapped back. 'What on earth were you thinking of?'

Glaring at her, Fliss dug her fists in her hips. 'I was thinking of all the working people's children who are prevented from sheltering in the underground while the Establishment and their cronies knock back champagne and caviar safe underground, that's what.'

'I don't mean you and the socialist workers' thingy – or whatever they are calling themselves this week – occupying the Savoy,' said Prue. 'But assaulting that policeman.'

'I didn't assault him,' her sister replied. 'He tripped over a chair.'

'Only because you were advancing on him clutching an upended bottle,' Prue replied.

'I wouldn't have hit him.'

'He didn't know that. Anyway,' Prue looked pointedly at her sister, 'after I've trudged across London, bailed you out of a cell and covered up for you, are you going to offer me a cup of tea?'

Fliss gave her another fierce look then snatched the kettle from the hob and marched over to the sink.

Prue slipped off her jacket and then, her brain barely

functioning, collapsed on to the sofa. Resting her elbow on the arm she pressed her hand to her forehead and closed her eyes, listening to her sister making the tea.

She must have drifted off because she woke with a start as Fliss placed a cup of tea on the table. Prue looked through the steam rising from it at her sister.

'Thank you, Prue,' said Fliss softly.

'I should think so, too.' Prue raised an eyebrow. 'The night bus I caught at Stepney had to detour around half of London because of last night's bombing and even then it couldn't get any further than Holborn, so I had to suffer being wolf-whistled at by the porters in Covent Garden Market as I walked through.'

'Lucky we got a taxi straight away, then,' said Fliss, sitting down at the other end of the sofa.

'Lucky you were let off with a caution,' Prue replied.

Her sister looked smug. 'That's because Giles made sure we had the press there.'

Prue took a sip of tea. 'And where is Giles?'

'He's probably back at HQ,' Fliss replied.

Prue looked perplexed.

'Oh, yes,' her sister replied. 'But ... Well, as he says, the police and the court system are rigged against the proletariat so, as a matter of principle, he avoids them at all costs especially as—' Fliss bit her lip.

Prue looked expectantly at her sister. 'Especially as ...?'

Her sister drew in a long breath. 'Well, if you must know, he's up in front of the magistrate next week for marching with the Trade Union Congress to the Ministry of Labour over the plan to trample workers' inalienable right to withdraw their labour.'

'So obviously the "Cause" means more to him than you, his fiancée, sitting in a police cell. And I say fiancée,' continued Prue, 'as I assume Giles has now done the decent thing and asked you to marry him.'

Studying the toe of her shoes, Fliss didn't reply.

'Oh, for goodness' sake! Fliss!'

'Marriage is an outdated patriarchal Judo-Christian concept,' said Fliss, 'designed to treat women as property to be owned by men.'

'Is that what Giles says?'

Fliss frowned. 'That's what all revolutionary thinkers say. Giles and I are married as far as we are concerned; we don't need a piece of paper to prove it.' A rapt expression lit her sister's face. 'Giles is so brave and completely focused on building a new world.'

So selfish and completely focused on himself, more like, thought Prue.

'I love Giles and that's all that matters,' continued Fliss. 'Just his look sends shivers up my spine, and when he takes me his arms ... Perhaps one day, Prue, when you meet a man who is everything you ever dreamed of, you'll understand.'

As always at the slightest reference to love and marriage, several images of Jack Quinn loomed in Prue's mind.

'Well, Fliss,' said Prue, struggling to keep several arousing images at bay, 'you're home now and no real harm done.'

Fliss raised her teacup in salute. 'Thanks to you, little sis.'

'And don't do it again; you might not be so lucky next time,' said Prue.

'You're right.' Fliss sighed. 'Next time the police might actually charge me with something.'

'No,' said Prue, fixing her with a meaningful look, 'I mean next time Mother might answer the phone.'

When Prue emerged from Stepney Green Station just after five o'clock in the evening, Mile End Road looked like a Saturday morning. A year ago, at this time on a Sunday afternoon, any street in the kingdom would have been all but deserted, but now it was filled with men, women and children, loaded down with provisions, making their way to underground shelters in anticipation of the Luftwaffe's unwelcome arrival.

She had left Fliss's flat just after three-thirty feeling a great deal better than she had when she'd arrived. This was due mainly to the fact that she'd had a full eight hours of uninterrupted sleep alongside her sister on Fliss's double bed. It was just like old times, in fact, as she and Fliss would often sneak into each other's beds as children.

Thinking about not very much, Prue made her way down White Horse Lane towards the rectory. As she opened the front door and stepped inside, she came face to face with her mother, wearing her electric-blue shot-silk dress and jacket.

'Oh, Prudence, thank goodness! I was just about to write you a note,' said Marjorie, pulling on her gloves.

'Note?'

'Yes, Cousin Jeremy is in town and staying at the Carlton Club – he's being sent off somewhere tomorrow. So as Father David is taking evensong, your father and I are going to join him for a couple of drinks,' she replied. 'Your father's just gone to warm up the car. You don't mind sorting something out for yourself in the kitchen, do you?'

'Of course not,' said Prue. 'What time will you be back?'

'I'm not sure,' her mother replied. 'But don't worry; if there's an air raid, Jeremy assures me they've set up a very comfortable shelter in the basement. Oh, and did you hear about the incident in the Savoy last night? A bunch of communist ruffians forced their way into the shelter under the hotel and refused to leave. It was all over the Sunday papers.'

'I did hear something,' Prue replied.

'Disgraceful. Makes you wonder what we're fighting for.' Her mother peered into the hall mirror and patted her feathery cocktail fascinator into place then picked up her handbag. 'Anyway, I'm sure that after a day at work – especially as you were called in unexpectedly – you could do with a quiet evening in. How was it?'

Prue looked puzzled.

'Work, darling?'

'Oh, the usual.' Prue forced a laugh. 'You know: too many lamps and not enough time.'

Her mother's face formed itself into its sympathetic vicar's wife expression. 'Poor you. Still,' she continued in a jolly tone, 'you can give it all up, can't you, once you marry Father David. Bye!'

The horn of the Austen Seven tooted and Marjorie hurried out of the house in a swirl of fluttering feathers and a cloud of Elizabeth Arden Blue Grass.

The door banged shut and blessed silence returned to the rectory. Placing her handbag and gas mask on the hall table, Prue shrugged off her jacket and after hanging it on the coat rack, made her way to the kitchen.

She relit the gas under the still-warm kettle and decided to squander her cheese ration on a couple of slices of Welsh rarebit. She was just retrieving the last quarter of loaf from the bread bin when the back door opened and Mrs Lavender walked in.

'Oh, Miss Carmichael, thank Gawd you're back,' the housekeeper said. 'Only, with you 'aving been called in to the shunting yard, like, I was wondering if there's any news?'

Prue frowned. 'News?'

'About Rosie Stapleton's brother,' said Mrs Lavender.

Something akin to ice trickled through Prue. 'What about Jack Quinn?'

''E was one of the poor sods – pardon my French – caught in last night's air raid on Stratford,' said the housekeeper. 'I thought you might have heard at work if the rescue party have found 'im.'

As the Moaning Minnie on top of the memorial in Ben Jonson Road wailed out the all-clear, people in the bunks around Prue stirred. Not that she needed the siren to bring her back to the here and now, for she'd hardly slept a wink all night.

In the dim light of the dangling forty-watt light bulbs, Prue looked at her wrist watch. Six-thirty.

Letting her arm fall back on the bed, she gazed up at the rough wooden struts of the bunk above hers for a moment then, pushing away the crushing fear that had kept her company all night, Prue swung her legs out and sat up.

'Morning, Miss Carmichael,' said Doreen Hayes, as she joined the queue for the exit carrying her sleepy two-year-old daughter.

Although her heart was like a lead weight in her chest, Prue forced a bright smile. 'Morning.'

'A bit lumpy last night, wasn't it?' the young mother said. 'I thought we were all goners when the ground started shaking.'

'I think that was the ack-ack guns in the park,' said Prue.

'That's wot Pop Harris said,' Doreen replied. 'Said it was like that when 'e was in the trenches during the last caper. You at work today?'

Prue shook her head.

'Well, have a nice day off and I'll see you tonight.' Adjusting the weight of the sleeping child in her arms, Doreen joined the crowd heading for the exit.

The clock in the church tower chimed the hour as Prue emerged from the crypt into the cool stone interior of the chancery.

Although the central area of the church was empty, Father David was standing behind the altar in the Lady chapel on the far side of the church. Kneeling in front of him in the pews were a dozen or so members of the congregation, including many who'd just emerged from the crypt.

Father David preferred to sit out the air raid in the basement of the rectory with Prue's parents. Because of this, instead of looking somewhat dishevelled after sleeping in his clothes all night, he was freshly shaven and sported a clean dog collar above the grass-green of his embroidered vestments.

In the diffused sunlight streaking through the criss-crossed gummed side windows, Prue watched him for a moment then walked across the main aisle to join the small knot of worshipers in the side chapel. Slipping into one of the pews, she unhooked a kneeler and placed it before her and lowered herself into an attitude of prayer.

With her head resting on her clasped hands as they gripped the moulded wood of the pew in front, Prue muttered 'Amen' in the appropriate places and let the ancient liturgy wash over her as she prayed the one heart-felt and constant prayer that had been in her head ever since Mrs Lavender had walked into the kitchen yesterday. However, regardless of whether the Almighty in his great mercy granted her request, she had come to a decision.

Reaching the end of morning prayers, Father David raised his right hand in a final blessing before the weary-eyed parishioners filed out into the bright sunshine of the September morning, each wondering as they went if they would find a pile of rubble where their home had been.

Prue remained seated until the last worshiper had gone, then she rose to her feet and made her way to the altar.

'This is a pleasant surprise,' said Father David, as she reached him. 'We don't often see you at morning prayers.'

Prue drew in a long breath. 'I'm sorry, David, but I can't marry you.'

He looked puzzled. 'Would you mind telling me why?'

'Because I don't love you.' Prue replied.

'Oh, my dearest Prue,' he said, as a patronising expression slid across his face. 'The basis of a successful marriage is mutual respect, companionship and shared interested.'

'I'm sure you're right that a happy marriage needs all those things, but above all it needs love,' Prue replied. 'And the truth is I don't love you.'

A crimson flush crept above his waxed dog collar and his mouth drew into an ugly line. 'It's Jack Quinn, isn't it?'

Prue held his furious gaze but didn't reply.

'I thought so. I know that, despite the fact he married outside his faith and is a self-confessed adulterer and divorcee, you invited him to the garden party. Then when he had the audacity to turn up, the two of you did nothing all afternoon but bill and coo in front of the

428

whole congregation. If you choose to throw away your good name, so be it.' A pious expression slid across his face. 'I can't pretend I'm not bitterly disappointed. Not so much in your turning your back on the respectable life I am offering you, but because you're allowing your head to be turned by a man such as Quinn, which clearly shows me that you would never ever be a suitable wife.'

Slamming the leather-bound prayer book closed, Father David gave Prue a withering look then turned and marched out of the chapel, his vestments billowing behind him.

Chapter thirty-five

'OW YOU DOING DOWN THERE?' Bill yelled down.

'Not so bad,' Jack shouted back, his voice echoing around the inspection pit and the tangle of metal wedged in it.

'Breakfast all right?'

'The best I've ever tasted,' Jack replied, resting his hand on the empty greased paper bag and thermos flask that had been lowered down to him by a rope half an hour before. 'What time is it?'

'Almost eight-thirty,' his engineer replied. 'You just hold tight. The Heavy Rescue boys are just getting the crane in place and then they'll have you out of there in no time.'

The first night had been the worst because although the locomotive looked as if it had come to rest within an inch of crushing him, each time the ground shook as another bomb crashed to earth, Jack feared it would slide further and that would be the end of him. Having survived what could only be described as Hell on earth trapped at the bottom of the inspection pit, when the all-clear sounded in the early hours of yesterday morning he'd expected to be found.

However, it wasn't to be and it wasn't until close to six o'clock on Sunday evening, when the Heavy Rescue teams had finally removed enough of the rubble surrounding the engine shop, that they'd located him, by which time he was almost delirious with dehydration.

Having established he had no bones broken, the rescue party had lowered much-needed food and drink to him, but just as they slid stout wooden support beams beneath the dangling locomotive, the air raid siren went off again.

Thankfully, although he had heard the odd boom and felt a slight shudder beneath him in the past hours, the Luftwaffe seemed to have been aiming at targets away from the shunting yard. The first pink light of dawn had just started to filter into Jack's black tomb when the all-clear sounded and the rescue teams returned.

However, lying in a pool of stinking engine oil, with bombs dropping around you as you stare up at death certainly is wonderful for concentrating the mind. And Jack's mind had been concentrating. In fact, more than just his mind, because for every minute of the last thirty-six hours Jack's head and heart had been focused on just one thing: Prue.

'Right mate, 'ow you doing?' shouted an unfamiliar male voice from above.

'Not so bad,' repeated Jack.

'Good, now listen up. We've got the crane in place and pretty soon we're going to take up the slack. There might be a bit of creaking when we do, so don't panic,' explained the rescuer. 'Once we're happy everything's in place we'll start lifting the bugger and you climb out. Get it?'

'Loud and clear,' Jack yelled back.

There was a pause then someone gave a strident two-tone whistle, and the jumble of metal suspended a few feet above him squealed as the crane took the load.

Although the massive wheel that had come to rest only a foot above his chest had only just been raised an inch or two, Jack was able to roll over, then, keeping low, crawl to the end of the six-foot-deep inspection pit. Holding his breath, he flexed his stiff muscles as the crane lifted the locomotive inch by agonising inch, then finally, after what seemed like an eternity, the locomotive lifted free. With the morning light almost blinding him, Jack grasped the ladder and heaved himself up, collapsing exhausted between the rail tracks.

Looking up at the clear blue sky visible through the broken roof of the engine shed, Jack did something he hadn't done for a number of years. He thanked God.

A cheer rang in his ears as Bill lumbered towards him and offered his hand.

'I never thought I'd be so glad to see your ugly mug,' said Bill, helping him to his feet.

'The feeling's mutual,' said Jack.

'Although he looks like 'e's been down a mine, don't 'e, Bill?' said Tosh, as he arrived with others to congratulate Jack.

Jack looked down at his oil-soaked clothing and laughed.

A tall well-built chap of about his own age with dark curly hair and wearing a set of overalls almost colourless with age and a tin helmet with a big white 'R' stamped on the front strolled over.

''Ow you doing?'

Jack grinned. 'Never better.'

'The ARP have set up a first-aid post in the station's booking office so go and get checked out by the doc,' the rescuer said.

'I will.' Jack extended his hand. 'And thanks, mate.'

The rescuer took it in a firm grip. 'No problem.'

A shout went up outside and the man hurried off. Jack turned to Bill and Tosh.

'You sure you're all right, Jack,' said Bill in a softer voice.

Jack nodded. 'Although I could eat a horse and I ache in places I never knew I had, I'm better than all right because when that locomotive came crashing down on top of me, everything became crystal clear.'

Prue stared at the dining-room door for a moment then, squaring her shoulders and taking a deep breath, she went in.

Sitting opposite each other at the long table eating their lunch were Father David and her mother, who both looked up as she walked in.

Father David looked very much as he had some four hours before at morning prayers except now, instead of warmth, there was a hard glint in his eyes. Not rising as he usually did, his disdainful gaze ran over Prue for a moment then he looked away.

'Well, a very good morning to you,' said her mother, as the clock on the mantelshelf ticked its way towards a quarter past one.

'Sorry,' said Prue. 'I didn't have much sleep last night.'

'I'm sure none of us did with eight hours of bombing,' her mother replied. 'But we've still managed to get ourselves out of bed before noon.'

'Where's Dad?'

'At the monthly deanery lunch,' her mother replied, spearing a floret of cauliflower with her fork. 'I thought you were at work today.'

'I was, but Maggie wanted Friday off so I swapped,' Prue replied, as she crossed to the sideboard where Mrs Lavender has set out lunch. Lifting up the tureen lid she studied the four kidneys sitting in gravy. Although her stomach was in knots of anxiety, she ladled some of the stew on to a plate then carried it over to the table and sat down next to her mother.

Father David's icy-blue eyes fixed on her for a moment then, throwing his cutlery down on his half-eaten dinner, he rose abruptly to his feet. Ripping his starched napkin from its anchorage between two shirt buttons he threw it on the plate.

'If you'll excuse me.'

'Whatever's wrong, Father David?' asked Marjorie.

'I've lost my appetite, Mrs Carmichael.' He cast Prue a loathsome look then marched out of the room.

Marjorie started after him for a moment then turned to Prue with a frown. 'What, may I ask, was all that about?'

'I turned down his proposal.'

Her mother's eyes stretched wide with astonishment. 'You did what?'

'I told Father David I couldn't marry him,' Prue replied. 'This morning. After morning prayers.'

'Why?'

'Because I don't love him,' said Prue.

'Don't be absurd,' her mother snapped. 'You don't even know the meaning of the word.'

Jack's smile, his laugh, the shape of his mouth and his liquid brown eyes set an aching in Prue's chest that made a lie of her mother's words. Feeling tears pinching the corners of her eyes, Prue pressed her lips together.

'I blame all those romance books you girls read,' continued her mother, oblivious to Prue's soul being torn asunder. 'Love isn't all beating hearts and flowers, you know. Do you think I was in love with your father when we married? No, I wasn't, not in the soppy way it is portrayed in those sentimental Hollywood films,' she continued. 'I was fond of him, naturally, but I trusted my mother's judgement that your father was the right husband for me. She knew that a couple being likeminded and having respect for each other was much more important than some fleeting passion.'

Clutching her knife and fork until her nails dug into her palms, Prue didn't reply.

'Is it that you're nervous about ...?' Although they

were the only people in the room, her mother glanced briefly over her shoulder. *The wedding night,* she mouthed soundlessly. 'Let me assure you that it's not half as unpleasant as you might imagine,' she added in her normal strident voice.

An aching chasm of unhappiness opened in Prue's chest and a fat tear rolled down her right cheek. Putting down her knife, Marjorie placed her hand on her daughter's forearm.

'Oh, my dear,' she said, in an uncharacteristically sympathetic tone. 'You're just overwrought. We all are. It's these tiresome German bombs. Once you've calmed down you'll realise that Father David is everything you could ever want in a husband.'

Prue wiped her eyes. 'No, Mother, he's not. And no matter what you or anyone else says or thinks, I am not marrying Father David.'

Her mother stared at her for a moment then resumed her meal. 'I'm not going to listen to another word because you're clearly too emotional to think straight. All couples have the occasional lovers' tiff, but I'm sure, once you're feeling a bit more like yourself, you and Father David will sort out this silly misunderstanding.'

Prue stared at her mother's profile for a moment then, placing her cutlery together on her plate and her napkin beside it, she stood up.

'Where are you going?' asked her mother.

'To the lying-in hospital to see Rosie Stapleton and her new baby,' Prue replied. 'Her brother's missing after

Saturday night's bombing raid so I thought she might be in need of a friendly face.'

'But you haven't touched your lunch,' her mother replied.

'I've lost my appetite, too.'

Leaving her mother sitting open-mouthed at the table, Prue marched back across the room. When she reached the door she turned.

'And you're wrong about love, Mother,' she said, tears gathering on her lower lashes. 'You don't love someone because you come from the same background, or you believe the same things, or even because of what they look like. You love them because they are who they are and for no other reason. I just wish I'd realised that two days ago.'

Holding open the door for a chap on a set of crutches and clutching half a dozen chrysanthemums from the rectory garden wrapped in pages from yesterday's *Times*, Prue walked into the lobby of the East End Maternity Hospital.

The square five-storey building sat on Commercial Road more or less opposite the south end of Jamaica Street. Although it had been run by the council for the past twenty years, its origins stretched back to the middle of the last century when Miss Robina Munroe, who founded the St Dunstan and St George's Nursing Association, acquired a house from a local philanthropist and set up the Stepney Lying-in Hospital.

However, rather than being a calm oasis of maternal bliss, the foyer of the nursing facility looked more like a battle zone. Like every other hospital, clinic and doctor's surgery in the area, the main maternity facility for the poor of the area for almost a hundred years was now part of the war effort.

Even though it was a few minutes before two in the afternoon and over nine hours since the all-clear had sounded, there were still dozens of people caked with dirt and with shredded clothing, holding bloody gauze to their foreheads or hobbling about with the aid of an upended broom wedged under their arm.

Passing a young mother cradling a crying child with a raw red patch of flesh on the side of his face, Prue made her way up the central stairs.

A young nurse in a pale pink uniform and skilfully folded frilly cap had just opened the door to Marigold Ward to allow the afternoon visitor in, so Prue took her place at the back of the small queue of women shuffling in to see daughters, sisters and friends.

The ward was very much the same as St Peter's cottage hospital in Bedford where she's worked, with beds at neatly spaced intervals running along each wall. However, instead of windows flooding the space with light, a fine metal mesh had been hung in front of the panes of glass to prevent flying glass, which bathed the whole area in a haze. There was an unlit central boiler and a nurses' desk in the middle of the ward.

Passing a couple of nurses, head bowed over their

paperwork, Prue made her way towards her friend, who spotted her halfway down the ward and waved.

As was expected from a hospital patient when you had visitors, Rosie was sitting up in bed under a pink bedspread. She was wearing a button-fronted nightdress with her dark hair neatly tied back.

'Hello, Prue,' she said, smiling up from the cocoon of pillows. 'Good of you to come.' She spotted the blooms in Prue's hand. 'And flowers, too.'

'The last from the garden before we start digging it up to plant vegetables.' Prue placed the bunch on the locker next to the palm-sized Sunday school photograph of her two sons. 'How are the boys?'

'Right enough,' Rosie said. 'And Dolly Methven who's minding them says they've been no trouble.'

Prue walked around to the cradle on the other side of the bed and gazed down at the infant who was lying in it.

For a child that had been born in a thousand-year-old crypt, with Miss Robertson, a retired fever nurse in attendance, and death and destruction raining down all around her, Rosie's baby daughter looked the picture of peace and tranquillity.

'And what do they think of their new sister?' she asked, gazing down at the sleeping baby.

'Not a lot,' laughed Rosie.

'Have you decided what you're going to call her?' asked Prue, studying the child's soft skin and delicate features.

'Ellen, after my mum,' said Rosie.

As if knowing she was the object of attention, the baby girl gave a little cry and opened her eyes.

'Would you mind if I held her?' asked Prue.

'No, give her a cuddle if you like,' Rosie replied.

Prue gently scooped the baby up and cradled the tiny infant in her arms.

Gazing down at Rosie's baby daughter Prue's heart ached, as she imagined herself holding a baby with the same mop of black curly hair.

'She's so beautiful,' she whispered, as tears once again clouded her vision.

'She is, isn't she?' agreed Rosie, a doting expression on her face.

Prue's attention returned to her friend. 'How are you?'

'Bit tired,' Rosie replied. 'But I'll be up back to me old self in no time.'

Wriggling in Prue's arms, Ellen started to niggle.

'I expect she wants feeding.' Rosie stretched out her arms and Prue handed Ellen back to her mother.

Unbuttoning her nightdress, Rosie offered the baby her breast and her daughter latched on immediately.

'They say,' said Rosie, a look of motherly contentment spreading across her face, 'that if you feed a baby as soon as it cries, you'll spoil them, but I don't care. Mind you,' she laughed, smoothing her finger over the nursing baby's soft cheek, 'when it comes to spoiling, I shall have to keep an eye on your Uncle Jack, Ellen, for he's the one for—'

'Jack,' cut in Prue, the blood pounding through her ears. 'What? Is there any news?'

Rosie looked up, puzzled. 'I thought you'd have heard. They found him last night. He phoned the ward two hours ago; once he'd been checked over, had a good scrub and a fry-up he was heading home.'

Prue stared open-mouthed into space as a myriad emotions threatened to burst from her chest.

'Prue, what's the matter?'

'Nothing,' Prue replied, as a smile she could not have held back even if she'd wanted to spread across her face. 'Absolutely nothing, Rosie, nothing at all. Sorry, I have to dash but I'll see you again very soon.'

Snatching up her handbag, Prue turned and all but sprinted out of the ward.

Chapter thirty-six

Twisting his mouth to the left, Jack scraped the razor along his right jaw, flicked the bristles and suds into the enamel sink in his sister's kitchen, then raised his chin and repeated the process on the underside.

As the signature tune for *Music While You Work* had just started, Jack didn't need to glance at his wristwatch sitting on the kitchen window sill to know it was three o'clock in the afternoon, some six hours after he'd dragged himself out of the inspection pit that was very nearly his tomb.

Having joined the queue of walking wounded in Stratford station's first-aid post, who were still being treated from the previous night's air raid, he had been pronounced fit for release by the weary-looking doctor in charge. Jack had then phoned the maternity hospital and Alma to ensure that both Rosie and Rachel knew he was alive. After scrubbing himself raw in the showers and donning a clean boiler suit, he felt almost human again and had devoured a plateful of cooked breakfast, after which he went in search of Prue only to find that she had swapped with another girl so was actually having a day off.

Perhaps it was just as well because what he was planning to say couldn't very well be said in a busy workshop or the works canteen. Finally, as the factory whistles were sounding the midday break, Jack had retrieved his bicycle from the rack and cycled home. Having arrived home half an hour later he'd fallen asleep on the sofa waking only twenty minutes ago. Swapping the rough overalls for a clean vest, pants and socks, he'd grabbed a fresh shirt, his suit and TWU tie and returned to the kitchen.

He was now just a couple of strokes away from removing the last few bristles. After all, he couldn't very well turn up on the rectory doorstep with the intention of asking for the rector's daughter with three days' worth of stubble on his chin.

Flicking the last razor-load of shaving foam into the sink, he grabbed the towel from the draining board and dried his face. After a quick check in the mirror, Jack reached for the bottle of Old Spice Rosie had given him last Christmas; he poured a little into his palm then dabbed it over his newly scrapped cheeks.

Stowing his washbag and sluicing water around the sink, Jack headed for the parlour. He'd just fastened his flies and buttoned his trouser waistband when there was a knock at the front door. Thinking perhaps as it was Monday it was the rent man calling for his money, Jack went to answer it but as he opened the door his heart practically burst from his chest.

There, standing on his sister's scrubbed doorstep, in a light green dress, with her hair curling on her shoulders was the sum of all his happiness and hope for the future. Prue.

However, as her eyes flickered across his chest then travelled down his bare arms before returning to his face, there was an expression in her eyes that he'd not seen before but that set his pulse galloping.

They stared wordlessly at each other for a long moment then Jack found his voice. 'It's you!'

'Yes.' She frowned. 'Were you expecting someone—'

'Sorry, no,' Jack said. 'I'm not. I'm just surpri— pleased. Very pleased to see you.'

'I just heard.'

He looked puzzled. 'Heard?'

'That you'd been found alive.'

He forced a laugh. 'Oh, yes, they got me out this morning.'

They stared at each other for a long moment then Jack remembered his manners.

'Sorry,' he repeated. 'Come in.'

He stepped aside and Prue walked in, a faint hint of violets in her wake.

Closing the door, he followed her through to the parlour where she was standing in front of the criss-cross taped window. She turned as he walked in, and that lovely smile of hers lit up her face and his soul.

The urge to cross the space between them and take her in his arms almost overwhelmed him, but he forced his feet to remain where they were.

'Actually, I was coming to see you,' he said.

'Were you?'

'Yes to tell you the truth about Alma—'

'I know, but it doesn't matter—'

'But I wasn't,' he blurted out. 'Unfaithful that is. Alma and I wanted different things out of life and after Rachel was born our marriage just fell apart. She went back to her parents, who were overjoyed. They offered to foot the bill for the legal costs for our divorce as long as I agreed to be named as the guilty party. They arranged everything, including a seedy hotel room in Southend and red-haired professional co-respondent for me to be found in a room with. That's the truth.'

She smiled. 'I believe you, Jack.'

Relief swept over him.

'Thank goodness,' he laughed. 'I've wanted to tell you—'

'I'm glad you did but ...' She took a step forward.

Prue's gaze flickered over him again then on to his clothes hanging on the back of the door.

'I'm sorry,' he repeated yet again, grabbing his shirt. 'I should have put a shirt on before answering—'

'Oh, Jack, I thought you were dead.' Dropping her handbag Prue threw herself across the space between them and into his arms.

'I love you, Jack,' she sobbed, burying her face in his chest.

With her small hands pressed on to his back and her soft breasts against his chest, Jack's senses were reeling. He let go of his shirt and with his whole world suddenly in perfect harmony, enfolded her in his arms.

Prue had spent the twenty minutes between dashing out of the maternity hospital and arriving on Jack's doorstep rehearsing in her head what she was going to say. However, seeing him, alive and well, had stolen her words. Now, with his arms encircling her and her face pressed into his hard chest, she sobbed helplessly for a few moments then pulled herself together.

'I'm sorry,' she said, wiping her eyes with the heel of her hand as she stepped out of his embrace. 'And I know young women aren't supposed to … to say this sort of thing … but … but I do … I love you.' She shrugged and forced a smile. 'You don't have to say anything. It's all right if … I just had to tell you, that's all.'

He stood motionless for a moment then, reaching out, he took her hand.

'You know something?' he said, drawing her back into his arms. 'I'm really glad you did.'

Placing her hands on his chest, she raised her head. His dark gaze ran slowly over her face for a moment then, moving a stray lock of hair from her forehead, he looked deep into her eyes.

'Because, my sweetheart,' he said, in a vibrant voice laden with love and desire, 'I was just on my way to the rectory to tell you the very same thing.'

His liquid brown eyes slowly ran over her face for a moment then he did what Prue had wanted him to do almost from the first moment she'd laid eyes on him, Jack lowered his lips on to hers.

Prue's mouth opened instantly under his, as desire

446

surged up in her. The only kisses she'd experienced before had been the tight-lipped ones that had lasted a second or two; Jack's kisses were very different.

With his arms clasping her tight to his hard, muscular body, and his lips and tongue exploring her mouth, emotions and desires she'd never felt before coursed through Prue. Gone was the clergyman's daughter, replaced by a woman deeply in love with the man who set her senses reeling with his kisses.

Prue found herself matching his passion with her own as love and desire mingled together within her.

After a heart-pounding moment, her needs matching his and excitement tingling up and down her spine, Jack released her lips.

'And,' he said breathlessly, looking down at her, 'I was coming to ask you to marry me. Will you?'

'Yes, yes,' laughed Prue, flinging her arms around his neck. Rising on to her tiptoes, she recaptured his lips briefly.

'And I'm sorry I can't give you a white wedding, Prue, but—'

'I don't care. I don't care!' Prue cried, holding him tighter. 'I don't care about anything but being your wife, Jack. Now just love me.'

An emotion flickered across Jack's eyes for a second then, spreading his stance, his dextrous hands slid down her back to lock her hips against his. Feeling his hardness, Prue's passion ignited again.

Her right hand smoothed back and forth over his skin before sliding down to his chest, beneath his vest then up again, allowing her fingertips to tangle amongst Jack's springy chest hair.

He let out a low groan then tore his lips from hers. Planting kisses across her cheek as he went, he buried his mouth into the sensitive area just below her ear.

Some would call it wrong, wanton and sinful, but Prue didn't care. The man she would love into eternity and beyond loved her, so closing her eyes she surrendered to the exquisite pleasure of Jack's embrace.

Prue moulded herself into him, feeling his hardness pressing into her, and excitement curled downwards from her navel. Jack's hand stroked her waist then moved up and closed around her breast, his thumb grazing lightly over the tip.

Prue let out a low moan.

'Make love to me, Jack,' she whispered, ripping his vest out from his trousers and sliding her hand up over his bare hair-covered chest.

For a moment, his arms tightened around her, and his kiss became demanding, but then he released her and stepped back.

'We should wait,' he replied, breathing heavily. 'So an I have a chance to—'

Prue put a fingertip to his lips, stopping his words.

'Jack,' she said, 'two days ago you nearly died and I could die under a German bomb in two days' time, so I don't want to spend another day without you.'

Winding her arms around his neck, she stretched up to kiss him but he moved his head back. 'I will love you,

Prue, for as long I have breath in my body, which is why I want to do this right.' His hungry dark eyes locked with hers for a long moment then he gave her that quirky smile of his. 'But as I don't want to spend another day without you either, we need to make plans, so we're going to speak to your parents.'

'You're going to do what?' asked her mother, staring incredulously at Prue, whose hand rested in the crook of Jack's arm.

She and Jack were standing at the edge of the fringed Indian carpet which covered most of the rectory lounge's parquet floor. According to the grandmother clock in the corner, it was now almost five o'clock and just two short hours since Prue had thrown herself into Jack's arms.

After a blissful while curled up in each other's arms on the sofa and making plans, Jack, who was on parade at six, had ditched his best suit for his Home Guard uniform.

Then, arm in arm, they'd walked to the rectory, arriving fifteen minutes ago, and announced to her parents their intention to marry.

'Marry your daughter, Mrs Carmichael,' Jack replied, his friendly expression being answered with a hostile one.

Marjorie, dressed in a tweed skirt and twinset, was sitting on the sofa next to her husband opposite Prue and Jack.

'Don't be ridiculous,' she snapped. 'Her father would never consent. Would you, Hugh?'

She turned to her husband, in his clerical garb, who had returned from taking Compline a few minutes ago to find his family, that's to say his wife, in uproar.

'I'm afraid, my dear, as Prudence is past her majority, I don't believe my consent is required,' he replied.

'I know this is a bit unexpected,' Jack continued, placing his hand over Prue's and starting a warm glow in her chest. 'But—'

'Unexpected!' snapped her mother. 'I should say so. One moment I'm enjoying a string quartet on the wireless, the next I'm listening to you,' her disapproving gaze slid over him, 'someone who spends his days covered in grease in a railway yard, casually informing me that you're marrying my daughter. Yes, I'd call that *unexpected.*'

'Certainly, a little out of the ordinary,' Hugh agreed.

Prue gave Jack's arm an encouraging squeeze as he squared his shoulders.

'A bit unexpected,' he repeated firmly, 'but I love Prue and I swear I will take care of her and any children we are blessed with.'

The three or four dark-haired children they were hoping to have hovered around Prue and her heart swelled with happiness.

'Well, children are indeed a blessing, are they not, my dear?' the rector said, patting his wife's hand. 'And our Lord Himself was very fond of them while He was here on earth.'

Her mother shot him an exasperated look before

returning her enraged attention back to Prue and her fiancé of a few hours.

There was a long silence as the clock ticked away the seconds, then Jack cleared his throat. 'Prue and I are going to the Town Hall to—'

'A registry office!' wailed Marjorie, covering her eyes somewhat theatrically with her hand.

'We're hoping to book for next Saturday,' Jack continued. 'But we might have to settle for a weekday slot as there're so many couples tying the knot.'

Her mother's eyes narrowed. 'Tying the knot! Tying the knot! Marriage is a blessed sacrament ordained by God Himself—'

'"Is honourable in all", so sayeth St Paul in his epistle to the Hebrews,' muttered Prue's father, steepling his fingers as if in prayer. 'And as he also points out in—'

'Although, clearly not to you, Mr Quinn,' her mother cut in.

Jack's jaw visibly tightened.

'You're referring to my previous marriage,' he said, giving his future mother-in-law a frosty look.

A syrupy smile lifted Marjorie's face. 'You're a widower, then?'

'You know full well I'm not, Mrs Carmichael,' Jack replied.

'Well, as I believe you were once a communicant member of St Winifred's, Mr Quinn, *you* also know full well that the Church of England only recognises a previous marriage if the first spouse has died,' she replied.

'Well, Mrs Carmichael,' Jack replied, coolly, 'fortunately for my seven-year-old daughter, her mother is very much alive.'

Prue's father's face lit up. 'You have a little girl.'

'I have, sir,' Jack replied. 'She's called Rachel. However, I am no longer married to her mother.'

'Because she divorced you for breaking the seventh commandment,' said Prue's mother with more than a trace of satisfaction in her tone.

Jack frowned. 'It wasn't like that—'

'You don't have to explain anything, Jack,' Prue cut in, hugging his arm and looking defiantly at her mother.

'For goodness' sake, Prudence!' barked her mother. 'Your father is the rector of this parish.'

Prue's father nodded. 'I am indeed.'

'He has been appointed, Prudence, to uphold the Thirty-Nine Articles of the Church, one of which is the sanctity of Holy Matrimony,' shrieked her mother. 'So tell me, how he can possibly do that if his own daughter—'

'I know it might make it difficult for you, Dad,' cut in Prue, looking beseechingly at her father. 'But Jack and I love each other.'

A sentimental look stole across Hugh's face. 'Do you?'

'Very much, sir,' Jack chipped in. 'I'm sorry this has been a shock, but as none of us knows if we will see another day or just be another name on the list of deceased pinned up in the ARP warden's office …'

'Which is why we are getting married next week,' Prue added.

Her father frowned. 'I don't know what the archdeacon will say.'

'Or the bishop,' added her mother. 'But obviously the problems this will cause us are of no concern to Prudence.'

Turning away, she fixed her eyes on the far wall.

Prue and Jack exchanged glances.

'Given everything that is going on,' continued Prue, 'Jack and I have decided we are only going to invite close family so—'

Mrs Carmichael's head whipped around and she rose to her feet. 'Well, I can tell you, Prudence, which member of your family will not be at your wedding. Me. And I will tell you something else. If you do marry this,' she jabbed her finger at Jack, 'this … man, you will never again set foot in this house.'

Giving both Jack and her daughter a contemptuous glance, she marched out of the room and slammed the door behind her, setting the china in the glass-fronted display cabinet rattling.

With a hollow feeling in the pit of her stomach, Prue stared after her for a moment then felt Jack's strong arm around her shoulder.

He gathered her into his embrace and kissed her forehead. She smiled up at him then turned her head and looked across at her father.

'What do you say, Dad?'

Grasping the arm of the chair, the rector rose to his feet and shuffled over.

With a mixture of love and sadness in his eyes, he studied his daughter for a moment before reaching out to place a hand on her shoulder.

'I think I should go to see how your mother's faring,' he said.

His watery grey eyes shifted to Jack for a couple of seconds then back to Prue. Giving her a melancholy smile, he followed his wife out of the room.

As the door closed again, Jack's arms tightened around her.

'I'm so sorry, Prue.' His lips pressed on to her forehead again. 'I knew your parents wouldn't exactly be delighted about us getting married, but I never thought…'

With tears shimmering on her lower lashes, Prue smiled. 'Unlike my parents I can't remember chapters and verses, but I do know somewhere in the Bible it says that charity – that is to say love – bears all things and always hopes. So, Jack, I'll *bear* my parents' displeasure and *hope* that one day they will agree that I have married the most wonderful husband.' And sliding her hands up and around his neck, she pressed her lips on to his.

Love and desire mingled together in Jack's dark eyes for a moment as she relished his kisses, wishing it was this Saturday not next that they were taking their vows.

Prue was so lost in Jack's embrace that it took her brain a moment to register that someone was in the room. Reluctantly releasing his lips, she turned and found David standing in the doorway. Raising his head, Jack followed her gaze, then keeping his arm firmly around her, he straightened up.

Something she couldn't interpret flashed between the two men then a smile spread across Jack's face. 'Father David. Good to see you again and you're just in time to congratulate us.' He hugged Prue to him. 'As we're getting married.'

Chapter thirty-seven

WITH HIS MUTED torch pointing at the pavement, David, dressed in his black warden's uniform with dog collar beneath, turned into White Horse Street. Holding his nose as he passed the public urinals on the corner, he crossed over at the Little Star public house and made his way along the row of eighteenth-century almshouses.

Stopping in front of the black-painted door of number three, David grasped the knocker and brought it down, imagining as he had every time he'd kicked a stone, slammed a door or punched a cushion into shape in the last two days that it was Jack Quinn's grinning face.

To be honest, if he hadn't heard it from the scoundrel's own mouth, he wouldn't have believed that they were actually getting married. But to see him standing there in the middle of the rectory lounge brazenly kissing Prudence Carmichael, who until Quinn enthralled her in his roguish charms, David had thought the perfection of Christian womanhood ... However, like Eve, Prue Carmichael had been tempted by the devil and succumbed.

A bolt rattled behind him, bringing David back from his painful thoughts to the matter at hand. He turned as the door opened and Miss Lavinia Hartman's aged face appeared around the edge of the blackout curtain draped behind it.

'Who is it, Vinia?' called a warbly woman's voice from within the house.

'It's that nice young man Father David, dear,' Miss Hartman called back to her sister Nancy.

The Hartman sisters, both unmarried, were the daughters of a local horse fodder merchant whose business and income had declined when mechanical horsepower took over from the hoof kind. As lifelong members of St Winifred's, when they found themselves financially embarrassed some ten years ago the sexagenarian sisters were offered one of the almshouses in White Horse Street.

'Well, ask him in for a cup of tea then,' Nancy trilled.

'Thank you, dear, I do know what to do when someone calls,' Lavinia replied testily over her shoulder. Her pale gaze returned to David. 'Would you like to come in for a cup of tea, Father?'

'I'd love to, Miss Hartman, but I'm on duty.' He touched his tin helmet with the white 'W' painted on the front. 'And that's why I'm here. I just checked in with Bill who oversees St Winifred's shelter, and he told me you and your sister weren't there so I'm wondering why.'

'We thought we might go over a bit later as the BBC theatre orchestra are in concert tonight,' Miss Hartman replied. 'They are playing ballet music, which Nancy is particularly excited about.'

'Sounds sublime,' said David. 'But promise me if the siren goes off before the concert's finished, you'll head off to St Winifred's shelter.'

'Of course we will, Father. I have to say, when I heard that Miss Carmichael was proposing to set up an air raid shelter beneath our dear little church, I was a little apprehensive and I said as much to my sister.' Miss Hartman's wrinkled face lifted in a fond expression. 'These past two weeks we've been so thankful for it and her, Miss Carmichael that is. She's such a lovely young lady. Everyone says so and she'll make some young man a wonderful wife one day.' A twinkle sparkled in the old woman's watery eyes. 'Perhaps even a wonderful vicar's wife?'

Despite his teeth grinding together, David forced a smile.

'It's starting, Vinia,' squealed Nancy excitedly.

'Coming!' shouted her sister. 'Goodnight, Father, and we will see you on Sunday.'

She closed the door.

Taking a couple of deep breaths, David turned and resumed his patrol.

The blackout had been in force for the past three hours because there had been a full moon just two days before and tonight the sky was still clear. He could clearly see St Winifred's bell tower across the public park that butted on to the south side of the graveyard. A bomber's moon, the locals were beginning to call such an evening; they didn't need the siren's wail to tell them to go to the shelter.

Having regained his equilibrium, David continued along White Horse towards ARP post number three. However, halfway down he noticed a movement among the headstones at the back of the churchyard. Father David's lips pulled into two tight lines. A courting couple, no doubt, intent on sullying the church's sacred ground with their fornication.

Stepping over the low wall, and with his torch pointing at his feet, David made his way between the granite tombstones and monuments. However, as he reached one of the large family mausoleums he realised it wasn't a couple but a single individual, with a knapsack on his back.

David was just about to stroll over and challenge the man when he stepped into a beam of moonlight for a second, before disappearing into the shadows again.

Jack Quinn! What the …?

Fury surged through David as the memory of seeing Prudence in the blackguard's arms returned, then a malevolent smile spread across his face.

Maybe his initial thoughts about the graveyard's interlopers weren't wide of the mark. Wouldn't it be a turn-up for the books if he discovered Quinn meeting one of the dockside trollops who plied their trade in local churchyards and squares?

It would be a devastating blow to poor Prudence, of course, but then perhaps it would finally make her realise the godly life she could have had as Mrs Harmsworth.

Dodging between the tombstones, David followed Jack as he made his way silently across the open space.

However, when he reached the old charnel house at the far end of the graveyard, Jack stopped for a second then disappeared.

Puzzled, David skirted around the old bone repository in a wide arc, trying to see where Jack had gone.

He'd just come to the conclusion that he must have scaled one of the garden walls that butted on to the church's land when he heard a faint squeezing and the scrape of metal.

Ducking behind a plinth with a weeping angel standing on it, he was in time to see Jack slide out of the charnel house's sunken doorway, minus the knapsack.

David pressed his lips together.

He really should march over and confront the villain but ...

The memory of the countless times he'd ended up bruised and bloodied on the canvas of Winchester College's boxing ring flashed through David's mind.

Safe behind his granite shield, he watched as Jack slipped silently back across the graveyard.

When he was certain Quinn was gone, David left his hiding place and picked his way between the slabs underfoot to the sunken medieval building. He saw nothing of note at first, but when the beam of his torch illuminated the wrought-iron grille covering the door it sparked his interest.

Taking the padlock in his hand he turned it over in the beam from the torch then let it fall. And at that moment the ear-shattering wail of the air raid siren went off.

Blast! Ten minutes, if that, to get to the safety of the rectory.

Biting his lower lip, David stared at the ancient brickwork of the bone house for a moment then turning, and with the pale light from his torch on the floor just in front of him, he ran back across the graveyard. Jumping over the low wall, and with the grating two-tone sound of the air raid warning jangling in his ears, he sprinted towards Ben Jonson Road. Stopping on the corner and looking in both directions, he heaved a sigh of relief as he spotted two police constables.

'Officers, come quick,' he yelled over the noise of the siren, waving frantically at them. 'I've just seen Jack Quinn stashing black market contraband in St Winifred's charnel house.'

An almighty crash as his bedroom door smashed against the wall brought Jack awake and sitting bolt upright in a split second.

The light from the bulb overhead cut painfully through his vision, causing Jack to squint as his pupils adjusted to the sudden brightness.

Blinking the sleep from his eyes he found three burly royal military policemen squeezing through his bedroom door with hateful expressions contorting their bovine-like features.

Through half-closed eyes, he glanced at the alarm clock beside his bed.

Three-thirty! He'd only collapsed into bed half an hour ago after the all-clear sounded.

'What the—'

Two of the squaddies sprung forward and grabbed him, dragging him from under the covers.

Stumbling, Jack managed to find his footing and then spotted Rosie, wide-eyed with horror and with her hands clasped over her mouth, standing in the hallway outside his room.

Yanking himself free from the soldiers' brutal grip, Jack glared at them. The third soldier, a sergeant, who seemed to have missed out in the neck department, stepped forward and smiled, revealing a set of oversized, tobacco-stained teeth.

'Jack Quinn?'

'Yes, but—'

'Sergeant Tugman, Royal Military Police, and I 'ope you ain't going to come quietly,' he said, bouncing the business end of his truncheon lightly on his other hand.

'Come where?' asked Jack, matching the sergeant's bold stare as best he could, standing in his underpants.

Scooping up the clothes Jack had laid over the end of the bed ready for the morning, the sergeant threw them at him. 'Get dressed.'

'Not until you—'

Tugman's truncheon collided with his left cheek, knocking his words away and setting off myriad bells in Jack's head.

Pushing away the blackness crowding into his peripheral vision and tasting blood, he raised his hand to his face and found his cheekbone unbroken. Clearly, the MP knew how to inflict pain without causing lasting damage.

Glaring at the three intruders, Jack dragged on his clothes and had only just fastened his top fly button when his arms were forced behind his back and handcuffs bit as they fastened around his wrists.

Shoving him into the corner of the room, the two squaddies then upturned his bed, pulled out the drawers and discarded them and their contents on the floor. Nearly tearing the doors from their hinges, one of the soldiers ripped the contents of his wardrobe off their hangers and dumped them on the rest of his belongings. Another tipped his bookcase forward, scattering books and Rachel's photograph on the fringed rug.

Having practically destroyed the twelve-by-fifteen room without discovering whatever it was they were looking for, the two squaddies resumed their position on either side of Jack.

Chewing his lips, the RMP sergeant gave them a brief nod and they grasped Jack's arms again.

'Where are you taking me?' he asked, as they marched him towards the door.

'That's for us to know and you to find out,' replied the squaddie gripping his right arm.

'At least tell me why?' pleaded Jack as they shoved him through the door.

Chapter thirty-eight

'So IT'S ALL BOOKED then, Prue?' said Maggie, as she wheeled her bicycle through the Angel Lane gate behind her friend.

'Yes, we were really lucky,' Prue replied. 'Jack went to the Town Hall yesterday first thing and managed to get the last slot for next Saturday.'

It was just after seven-thirty on Thursday morning and they, along with dozens of railway workers, were streaming into Stratford yard at the start of an ordinary working day. It was also three days since she'd thrown herself in Jack's arms and her world and future had changed for ever.

'Next Saturday? That's quick,' said Kate, who was walking next to Maggie.

Maggie winked. 'Would you want to wait any longer if you were marrying Jack Quinn?'

Prue lowered her eyes as her stomach fluttering.

'Stop it, Mags,' said Kate. 'You're making our Prue blush. Is your mum still upset?'

'A little,' Prue replied.

This, of course, was a complete lie because her mother wasn't still a little upset, she was still incandescent with rage and hadn't spoken one single word to Prue since Monday.

'She'll come round,' said Maggie.

Clearly her friend didn't know Prue's mother.

Thankfully, a N1 Class locomotive hissing steam rattled by, the noise putting paid to their conversation. It was heading towards one of the engine sheds, and Prue's gaze followed it as it clickety-clacked across the tangle of rail tracks gleaming in the early-morning sunlight. Jack's shift had started at six, so he was probably already hard at work bolting or welding an engine back into service. As it always did when she thought of Jack, her heart did a little happy dance.

When they kissed goodnight before he left for Home Guard duties and she went to St Winifred's shelter the night before, they'd agreed to meet at midday in the canteen, which by Prue's reckoning was just over four hours and fifteen minutes away.

A handful of their fellow lamp men were already going through the changing-room door so, stowing their bicycles in the rack, Prue and her two friends strolled in.

Passing the lockers, they pushed open the door to the shower and the larger room behind, which now after four months of female occupancy smelled a great deal sweeter than when Prue had first entered it. Before them, in various states of undress, were at least a dozen women all pulling on grey boiler suits, fastening leather belts or securing their hair beneath multicoloured scarves.

'Oi, oi, girls,' said Maggie, who was bringing up the rear. ''Old up the chatter for a mo cos our Prue's named the day. Next Saturday.'

A squeal of delight echoed around the white-tiled room as the women turned as one in Prue's direction and smiled.

'Can't wait eh, Prue?' called Maureen, one of the other lamp cleaners.

'Can you blame her?' came a reply.

'Lucky girl,' called another.

'Where you going for your honeymoon?' shouted Beryl, shrugging on her boiler suit at the back of the room.

'What does it matter?' laughed someone at the back. 'I doubt she'll see much other than the bedroom ceiling.'

Prue's cheeks felt warm again as everyone laughed and added their own suggestions to what her honeymoon would be like.

'Wot's so bleedin' hilarious?'

Prue turned to see Gladys with Pat and Gloria, all overly dressed up for a day scrubbing carriages, standing by the door.

Of course, it didn't take long for the news that Prue and Jack were getting married to whip around the yard, and while most of the comments they'd received from their fellow workers were light-hearted and good natured, there were a few notable exceptions, three of whom were standing in front of Prue now.

'Well?' demanded Gladys.

'Go on, Prue,' said Maggie. 'Tell her your news.'

'Jack and I booked our wedding for next Saturday,' Prue replied, holding the other woman's hateful stare.

From beneath her clogged mascaraed lashes Gladys stared at her for a moment then her scarlet lips pulled back into a wide smile. 'Well congratulations, but you might wanna 'old fire on the invitation because I 'ear Jack Quinn's been arrested.'

Prue turned her key in the rectory's front door and stumbled inside, dropping her bag by the coat stand. Somehow she had managed to propel her bicycle the three and a half miles home, but now she felt that her legs were about to give way. Bracing herself against the wall, Prue stared unseeing across at the oil painting of some long-dead family member's prize cow.

'Whatever's 'appened, Miss Carmichael?'

Dragging her mind back from the vast tangle of confusion it was mired in, Prue looked around to see Mrs Lavender, a tray loaded with her parents' mid-morning coffee in her hand, standing beside her.

'I'm just a bit breathless, that's all.' Prue forced a smile.

The lounge door opened and Prue's mother appeared. 'I wondered what all the commotion was.'

'It's Miss Carmichael,' said the housekeeper. 'Says she's just a bit puffed out, but she looks right queer, if you ask me.'

Marjorie's unsympathetic gaze flickered over Prue. 'You'd better come in.'

Prue crossed the hallway and went into the lounge, where she and Jack had announced their intention to marry only three days before.

Her father was sitting in one of the fireside chairs with his eyes shut and his hands clasped together in front of him.

He looked up as she came into the room. 'Prudence, my dear, this is a pleasant surprise; I thought you were at work.'

'I was but—'

Prue flopped on to the sofa as Mrs Lavender bustled in behind her and laid the tray on the coffee table then left.

'But what, my dear?' her father asked, as his wife poured the coffee.

'I felt unwell and had to come home,' Prudence replied.

Her father looked concerned. 'Unwell, how?'

'I was sick and felt dizzy,' said Prue, recalling how she'd only just made it to the toilet before losing her breakfast.

Her mother, who was pouring the coffee, looked up sharply. 'Sick and dizzy? Dear God, don't tell me that—'

'No, I'm not,' snapped Prue, glaring at her mother. 'I just had a shock, that's all.'

With her mother's hard eyes and her father's sympathetic ones fixed on her, the second hand of the clock ticked halfway around the dial then Prue took a deep breath.

'Jack's been arrested.'

'Oh, my dear child,' muttered her father. 'What for?'

'I don't know,' Prue said, the horror of the past hours washing over her again. 'I went to Stratford police station, but they said under the Emergency Powers Act they weren't allowed to tell me anything. But whatever it is, I know Jack's innocent.'

'*Innocent,* ha!' snorted her mother.

Feeling as if her head was about to burst, Prue rested it on the back of the sofa and closed her eyes. In the darkness behind her eyelids Gladys's sneer and the face of the tight-lipped police officer staring across the counter at her jostled each other in Prue's mind.

Breathing deeply to contain the sob sitting at the back of her throat, she listened to the chink of china as her mother poured out the coffee. After a few moments, she opened her eyes and looked across at her parents.

'And you have no idea why your fiancé has been apprehended by the police, Prudence?' her father asked, coffee cup in hand.

Prue shook her head and wished she hadn't as another wave of nausea swept over her.

'What does it matter?' asked her mother with an undisguised glint of satisfaction in her eye.

There was a knock on the door and Mrs Lavender came in carrying a cup. Father David followed her in, his top lips curling into a smug smile when he spotted Prue.

'I know you're not too fond of coffee, Miss Carmichael, so I've made you a hot sweet tea just as you like it,' the housekeeper said, placing it on the table in front of Prue before shuffling out.

'Thank you, Mrs Lavender,' said Prue. 'Everyone says a strong cuppa is good for shock.'

An expression of utmost sympathy formed itself on David's long face. 'You've had a shock, have you, Miss Carmichael?'

'Yes, she has,' said her father. 'Jack Quinn has been arrested and the police won't tell her why.'

'Oh, well then, Miss Carmichael, let me enlighten you,' said David, smiling pleasantly at her, 'as I'm the one who had him apprehended.'

'You did what?' said Prue, looking incredulously at him.

An undisguised smirk replaced Father David's compassionate expression. 'I spotted him lurking around the ancient bone house at the back of St Winifred's graveyard when I was on patrol last night. Naturally, I thought perhaps he was hiding stolen goods to trade on the black market, so I called the constables.'

'Didn't I tell you Jack Quinn was a villain the moment I laid eyes on him, Prudence?' interjected her mother, looking straight at Prue.

'And your instinct has proved to be right, Mrs Carmichael. However,' Father David's self-satisfied smirk widened further, 'it wasn't illicit merchandise he was hiding in the old charnel house, but guns.'

'Guns?' gasped her mother, covering her mouth with her hands.

'Yes guns, Mrs Carmichael,' Father David continued. 'Along with high explosives and detonators.'

471

'But why …?' whispered Prue, the blood pounding through her ears almost deafening her.

'Well, as far as I can see, there are only two plausible explanations,' continued Father David in a matter-of-fact tone. 'Either Jack Quinn was intending to sell the weapons to criminal gangs or he is a member of the fifth column who, once the Germans land on our shores, will rise up and assist the invaders. Either way, Miss Carmichael, you are planning to marry a crook or a traitor.' His hateful gaze locked on Prue's astounded one for a moment then a glacial smile slipped across his face. 'Is that the time? Sorry, Father Hugh and Mrs Carmichael, I have to dash. The archdeacon's sister and his niece, Miss Alton-Banfield, a children's nurse, are staying with him for a few days and he's kindly invited me to join them for lunch.'

He marched across the room with three pairs of eyes glued to his back and as the door closed behind him Prue's mother turned to face her.

'Well, I hope you're proud of yourself,' Marjorie snapped, 'because instead of preparing for a white wedding and a secure married life with Father David, you've thrown your family's good name away by becoming involved with Jack Quinn. Your so-called fiancé is "a crook or a traitor".'

Looking across at her mother's furious face, Prue didn't speak for a moment. Finally she stood up. 'Jack is neither.'

'For goodness' sake!' her mother replied. 'Didn't you hear what Father David said?'

'I did,' Prue said, her love slicing through the jumble in her head. 'I confess I don't know why Jack has guns and explosives, but I do know Jack, so I don't care what Father David or anyone else says. I know that Jack is neither a crook nor a traitor.'

Chapter thirty-nine

JACK GASPED AS ice-cold water smashed against his all but naked body, then gritted his teeth to stop them chattering.

'Morning, Jack,' said the brigadier. 'And how are you today?'

Shivering and with water dripping from his forehead and nose, Jack peered through his swollen left eye at the lean-faced brigadier sitting behind the desk.

'Oh, you know,' Jack replied, through his busted lower lip, 'mustn't grumble.'

He'd felt as if he'd only just fallen asleep when the raw electric light sliced into his eyes and rough hands dragged him from the wooden bench, forcing his sleep-deprived mind back to consciousness. In truth, it could have been five hours or five minutes since two gorilla-like royal military police officers threw him into the windowless, white-tiled cell after his last little 'chat' with the plummy-toned but nameless officer.

He didn't know where he was either as a sack had been placed over his head the moment he'd been dragged into the RMP van outside Rosie's house. As far as he could guess he was about an hour's drive from

London, but that could have been in any direction. The improvised hood had remained in place until he'd been stripped and shoved into the bare cell two, perhaps three, days ago.

Now wearing only his Y-fronts, he was in a long room with dirty light grey walls and a concrete floor that dipped slightly in the middle where the grate covering the drain was situated. There were a set of iron manacles fixed to one of the walls, a couple of battered buckets and a rusty-looking garden tap sprouting from the wall opposite. There were a series of long windows high up with bars at them, but as they overlooked the corridor he'd just been frogmarched along they gave Jack no clue as to whether it was midday or midnight.

'That's the spirit,' said the officer jovially. 'How's the old bruising?'

'I've survived worse,' Jack replied.

In addition to being left naked in a cell with a bucket for a toilet and a blanket-less wooden bench for a bed, Jack had been professionally beaten just enough to have it hurt like hell but without inflicting serious injury.

'Splendid,' the officer replied, as if congratulating Jack on hitting a winning six.

'Now, let's go over this again.' He glanced down at the sheet on the desk in front of him. 'You were seen going into and coming out of some ancient tomb in a churchyard that on closer investigation was found to contain six brand-new Enfield rifles plus half a dozen Winchester 61s, a quantity of explosives and fuses. We are still checking with the Ministry of War which armaments have been stolen while on transit through Stratford shunting yards, but even if they don't tally up then it still begs the question why you should have such an arsenal of weapons, doesn't it?'

Jack didn't reply.

The officer tutted. 'Jack, Jack,' he said, shaking his head dolefully. 'What have you been up to?'

Jack remained silent.

As many in the Government and army command were ignorant of very existence of D Division for fear of Nazi sympathisers and collaborators in their ranks, and with the Germans expected on Britain's shores at any time now, Jack knew it was absolutely vital that the existence of the auxiliary units remained secret, so he held his peace.

'Your daughter is half Jewish, isn't she?' continued the brigadier. 'Are you hoping to curry favour with the Germans to protect her?'

Although the horror that might be inflicted on Rachel should the Germans conquer England threatened to overwhelm him, Jack held his tongue.

'Or perhaps you've fallen in with that gang your brother used to head up,' continued the interrogating officer. 'You cockney types are all a bunch of thieves.'

'What, just like you toffs are a bunch of inbreds?' Jack replied.

The senior officer narrowed his eyes. He nodded at the RMP standing on Jack's right, who stepped forward, dragged Jack to his feet, and punched him in the stomach.

Doubled over, Jack collapsed back on the chair, coughing and desperately drawing breath into his lungs while the brigadier sat dispassionately watching him.

As the white stars popping at the corner of Jack's vision started to disperse, the officer behind the desk sat forward.

'Let me put it plainly, old bean.' He rested his elbows on the desk and clasped his hands in front of him. 'As you refuse point-blank to give an explanation as to why you were seen hiding a quantity of weaponry, you are either a thief or a fascist spy getting ready to aid the Germans when they land on our shores. Either way, under the new War Powers Act you will be judged a traitor. So unless you tell me where you got those guns and explosives and what they are for, you're for a short rope and a long drop. You do the sensible thing and tell me the truth and it's possible we might be able to swing it so you just get a life sentence. Come on, Jack. What do you say?'

With only the sound of the two squaddies on either side of him breathing punctuating the silence, Jack studied the man sitting at the desk in front of him for a long moment then he spoke. 'All right, I'll talk.'

The brigadier gave an audible sigh of relief. 'At last.'

'Well, it's like this …' said Jack, taking a deep breath. 'Mary had a little lamb, his fl—'

The punch knocked the nursery rhyme from his lips and he was hauled to his feet again and ceremoniously half-dragged half-carried out of the room, back down the corridor and then dumped in a heap on the floor of his spartan cell.

Crawling across to the six-by-three bench fixed to the wall, Jack dragged himself up and curled into a ball to conserve heat and ease his aching flesh.

Part of the training at Coleshill House was to teach them how to resist revealing the identity of other members of the secret army if they were captured and interrogated; but to be honest, Jack had never for a moment thought he'd have use what he'd learned to resist cracking under questioning by his own side.

'Are you all right, Prue?' asked Maggie, who was loading up a carrying pole with the four lamps she'd just finished cleaning on the other side of the workbench.

'I'm fine,' said Prue, wiping a stray lock of hair off her forehead with the back of her hand.

That was a complete lie, of course. She wasn't in any way, shape or form fine and hadn't been for the past four days.

Looking up, Prue forced a smile. 'I've just got to finish this one and I'll be ready to take it …' From nowhere tears sprang into her eyes. 'I'm so … sorry … I …'

Throwing down her rag, Maggie hurried around to Prue's side of the bench.

'Come on, luv,' said her friend, hugging her shoulders.

'Four days, Mags …' said Prue, taking her handkerchief from her pocket. 'Four days and the police still can't tell me anything other than Jack's being questioned.'

'Bloody law unto themselves they are,' said Maggie, rolling her eyes. 'But your Jack's innocent so they'll have to let him go eventually.'

Blowing her nose, Prue forced a smile.

'That's the spirit,' said her friend. 'Now you'd better crack on,' she indicated the lamp still caked with soot in front of Prue, 'or you'll be 'ere all night.'

Giving her another small squeeze, Maggie returned to her side of the bench and picked up her carrying poles.

'It's almost six, so once I've done these, I'm off; see you tomorrow,' said Maggie. 'And cheer up; you're getting married on Saturday.'

With the lamps jingling on the poles, Prue's friend headed out of the lamp shed into the gathering gloom of the mid-September afternoon.

Praying that she would be Mrs Quinn in five days' time, Prue plunged her cleaning cloth in the bowl of soapy water next to her and started on her task.

However, it wasn't just being confronted by a tight-lipped station sergeant each day at Stratford police station that brought tears to her eyes, nor the fact she'd hardly slept since she heard Jack had been arrested. It was also her mother. Although she was still barely speaking, Marjorie felt it her duty to remind Prue at every opportunity not only that she had warned her against becoming entangled with Jack Quinn but also that Prue had thrown away her chance of a respectable life with Father David. Prue had tried to talk to her father but although he'd been sympathetic and kept quoting Bible verses about endurance and faith, he'd pleaded ignorance about domestic matters, fearful of making matters worse.

'Ain't you got no 'ome to go to?'

Prue looked up to see her supervisor Harry's jolly face peering around the edge of the shed door.

'Just finishing, Mr Pegg,' said Prue.

'Which gantry they from?' he asked, nodding at the four lamps on the bench.

'Number five on the Hackney and Gospel Oak line,' Prue replied. 'I've just got to refill the last one and I'll be off.'

'Right you are, but don't 'ang about; it's only 'alf an hour until blackout,' he replied.

Prue wiped the final few smears off the bulbous glass, tided her equipment away, then loaded the four newly cleaned lamps on to her pole.

As always at this time, the station to the south of the shunting yard was busy with passenger trains taking office workers home after a long day's work, but as most of the routine maintenance was done in the daylight hours to save power, only the workshops dealing with emergency repairs still had mechanics working in them.

Keeping to the safety path, Prue passed a couple of soldiers lounging around by a ten-wagon army supply train awaiting its locomotive, and continued on her way until she reached number five gantry that straddled the northbound line.

Pulling down the ladder and carrying the lamp, Prue climbed up, replaced the grimy lamp with the clean one and climbed back down. She repeated the process twice more, and by the time she had got to the top of the gantry with the fourth lamp the sun had almost disappeared behind the factories and warehouses that lined the River Lee. Although the summer had been glorious there was now, in mid-September, a decided nip in the air, especially on a cloudless night such as this.

Mulling over whether to go straight to St Winifred's shelter rather than having to sit across the dining table from her stony-faced mother and self-righteous Father David, Prue had just hooked the fourth lamp in position when the scrape of metal on metal cut through her wandering thoughts.

She looked over the edge of the gantry and saw Gladys, dressed in her overalls and turban, standing by the ladder.

'What are you doing?' shouted Prue, running back along the gantry.

'Getting you back, Miss Nose-in-the-air, for grassing me up to Knobby about clocking in,' Gladys yelled, looking up.

'But I told you I didn't,' Prue called down.

'Well I don't sodding believe you,' Gladys replied. 'And that's not the only thing. I wanted to get my hands on Jack Quinn but you, all sweetness and light, got 'im, so this is for that, too. Still, it don't matter now, does it, seeing 'ow handsome Jack's going to be banged up inside so won't be marrying anyone.' She slammed the ladder's holding peg into place. 'Don't worry; I ain't put the lock on so whoever finds you won't have to search out a key. But perhaps you'll think twice now about telling tales to the bosses. Enjoy the view.'

Giving Prue a wave, she strolled off down the track.

'Gladys! Let me down!' Prue screamed after her, which was greeted with another wave of the hand as Gladys disappeared into the long shadows between the rows of stationary army wagons.

Gripping the girders of the gantry, Prue looked towards the main working area of the yard. There was a group of men over by the paint shop; they might be too far away but …

Cupping her hands around her mouth, she drew in a breath. 'Help! Someone help!'

The railways workers didn't react.

'I'm stuck up here,' Prue shouted again. 'On the gantry.'

The clickety-clack of an eastbound train some way off was the only reply. Leaning over the parapet, Prue looked down at the ladder. The securing bolt was six feet below her so there was no way she could reach down and pull it out. Even if she climbed down on the top half of the ladder and removed it, the lower half would likely take her fingers off as it fell.

The wires connected to the signals buzzed as the arms clicked up and down. Tucking herself into the corner, Prue pressed her lips together and shut her eyes as the train past beneath, belching smoke upwards and over her.

Looking out again as the rattle of the rails faded, Prue prayed silently that she would spot someone who was within earshot. However, instead of seeing people milling about she saw only the lights of the station and buildings nearby extinguished as the blackout came into force.

Panic rose up in Prue's chest but she held it at bay. It would be fine. It might be a tad chilly, and with wooden running boards underfoot it was hardly a comfortable perch, but she was quite safe up here. The station's ARP wardens would be making their rounds soon to check the workshops still operating weren't showing a light and they would get her down.

Just as she was about to make herself comfortable to wait it out, a nerve-grating sound filled the air as the air raid siren on top of Stratford's main station wailed out it's chilling two-tones warning across the shunting yard.

With her heart practically leaping from her chest, Prue looked south towards the river to see the searchlights scanning the sky. Ack-ack rounds peppered the sky as a burst of fire stretched upwards, announcing the Luftwaffe's arrival.

Wedged into the corner of the upright girders with her arms around her knees, Prue shut her eyes tightly as another bomb screamed downwards somewhere close to the gantry. The ack-ack guns on Hackney Marshes sent up another spray of shells while the searchlights alongside them tried desperately to pinpoint the German planes high above.

With the low thrum of hundreds of Heinkel engines pulsing through the air, Prue opened her eyes, then twisting her wrist towards the red light glowing over West Ham she looked at her watch.

One-thirty! Seven hours.

Her throat was on fire, choked with the cordite-laced air she was breathing and with each blast sucking the breath from her lungs. And although it was the least of her worries, she must be filthy too, as each bomb strike sent debris flying through the air, covering everything with coal dust and earth. And goodness, what she wouldn't give for a glass of water!

The Luftwaffe focus tonight seemed to be along the River Thames. This was hardly surprising really because although the moon was on the wane it still sat high and bright in the sky. Unfortunately for those living in the crowded streets around the docks, this meant the pilots in the aircraft above would have no problem finding their targets.

However, as the Germans no doubt knew that one of the Thames' main tributaries, the River Lee, brought vital supplies like coal from the Midlands, they had also targeted the waterway a mile to the west of Stratford yard.

A bloodcurdling shriek cut through the sound of ARP warden whistles and fire-engine bells. With her mind a jumble of prayers to the Almighty for herself and for Jack, Prue put her hands over her ears and shut her eyes.

The blast from the latest bomb as it struck the earth flashed red light through her eyelids and the heat from it stung her face. The vacuum created by the blast tugged at her clothes and hair, while the metalwork beneath her feet shook so violently that Prue had to cling to the nearest girder to stop herself from slipping between the iron latticework.

Please God, let it be over. She sobbed silently as gravel and shards of glass ricocheted off the signal arms and the gantry's metal frame.

As the wave from the bomb subsided, Prue slumped, exhausted, on to the wooden running boards.

The droning sound above changed at last: having dropped all their bombs, the enemy aircrafts were turning back to their bases in France. The explosion that had almost torn her from her perch had thankfully landed on the row of disused Victorian outbuildings on the yard's perimeter. They now blazed so bright that Prue could have read a book by their red and yellow light.

Forcing herself to move, Prue hauled herself to her feet and praying that a patrolling fire marshal would appear, she looked at the silent rails and stationary rolling stock.

However, as her gaze passed one of the tarpaulin-covered army wagons she spotted two soldiers inching along towards it. She was about to shout and wave when one of the soldiers released a rope from the wagon, lifted the tarpaulin and had a quick look inside. Letting it fall, he signalled back along the tracks.

Prue crouched down and watched them through the diagonal bars of the gantry's walkway.

In the reflected red glow from the burning sheds, Sergeant Butcher stepped out of the shadows, with half a dozen men on his heels. On reaching the wagon, Butcher ripped off the tarpaulin and two of the men with him leapt inside and started passing rifles to those waiting below, followed by some solid-looking boxes. Having got what they came for, two of the soldiers quickly secured the covering back in place. Shouldering a couple of weapons each and carrying the boxes between them, the men hurried along the track then cut across the Hackney and Gospel Oak line just a few hundred yards from the gantry where Prue was hiding, then carried on towards what remained of the Tudor windmill that gave Windmill Lane its name.

She stared after them for a moment then the blare of the all-clear sounded across the yard. Prue dashed along the rickety planks to the ladder and kicked it with the flat of her foot.

'Drop, damn you,' she shouted, stamping on the top rung. 'Drop!'

It rattled against the frame but didn't budge. Clenching her fists, she stomped on it again then hurried back to the middle.

Desperately summoning moisture into her mouth, Prue cupped her hands around her lips again.

'Help!' she screamed.

She spotted a couple of ARP rescuers with the white

'R' stamped on their helmets making the way down the track.

'Help. Over here,' she yelled again, jumping and waving her hands wildly.

Mercifully, they spotted her and ran over.

'The bolts stuck on the ladder,' she shouted, leaning over the edge and jabbing her finger towards it.

It took her rescuers a minute to figure out the problem, then the ladder crashed to the ground and Prue scrambling down seconds after.

'Thank you so much,' she said, as she hurried towards them.

'Wot you doing up there?' said the taller of her two rescuers.

'I got stuck when the air raid warning went off,' she replied. 'Have you seen any police officers around?'

'There's a couple milling about trying to look busy in the main office,' his mate replied. 'But you've got a nasty gash on your cheek; you need to get to the first-aid station.'

'I'll do that later,' said Prue, already hurrying past them. 'I've got something much more important to do first.'

Chapter forty

'MOVE IT, CHUM,' said the red-faced police officer as he shoved Jack towards the open door. 'You don't want to keep 'is Lordship waiting.'

Squaring his shoulders, Jack marched forward and found himself in a wood-panelled courtroom, with the two guards who'd escorted him from his cell half a pace behind him.

Although he was still sore from the casual beatings, since he'd been transferred from the anonymous army base to Holloway Prison two days ago the cold-water interviews had ceased, and he was now being fed on a regular basis. This had been the last of four cells he'd been thrown in since being dragged from his bed five days before. After being arrested by officers from Arbour Square he'd been transferred to West Ham police station for questioning before being handed over to the army for interrogation.

Thankfully, on arrival Jack had been given a set of the coarse grey canvas prison clothing, which was just as well because sitting on the other side of a long mahogany table at the far end of the room sat three judges in their red crown court attire, including full-bottomed horsehair wigs.

On either side of the table were two smaller desks; along with the black-gowned lawyers there were an assortment of khaki-clad army officers behind each. Jack's appointed solicitor, Reginald Skinner, and his barrister James Oliphant, resplendent in his gown and small wig, were among their number. Oliphant was a pleasant enough chap but he didn't look old enough to be taking his school leaving certificate let alone defending a man charged with high treason.

Although they had clearly taken over the prison boardroom to serve as a court room, they had tried to give it a judicial feel by mocking up a platform with a lectern in front of it on the left to serve as a witness box and another platform directly in front of Jack with a high railing on three sides to act as the dock. However, one thing that was notable by its absence was a jury. Jack wasn't about to stand trial in front of twelve good men and true in open court but behind closed doors by the Establishment's judiciary.

The three justices, whose combined age hovered somewhere around two centuries, raised their heads from their papers as Jack stepped up into the improvised dock.

The judge sitting in the middle, a flesh-faced individual with crow's feet across his cheeks and a bulbous nose, studied Jack for a moment and a disdainful expression settled on his heavy jowls. He signalled to the clerk of the court, who rose to his feet.

'Under the directive of the Wartime Government, this court, held in camera as stipulated under the Special Powers ratified by the Supreme Court under the direction of the Wartime Coalition, is now in session with Sir Algernon Holland presiding and with Sir Cicero Moncrief and Mr Reginald Fox-Unwin also in attendance.' The clerk looked down his long nose at Jack. 'Prisoner at the bar, is your name Jack William Quinn?'

'It is.'

'And do you reside at number thirty-one Arbour Terrace?'

'I do.'

The clerk looked at the chief judge.

'Read the charge to the prisoner,' Sir Algernon barked, flicking his blunt fingers at the whey-faced clerk.

The clerk cleared his throat. 'Jack William Quinn, you are charged under the War Power Act with obtaining and having in your possession illegally ...' The clerk listed the entire contents of the clandestine stash of armaments found in St Winifred's charnel house. 'How do you plead?'

'Not guilty,' said Jack.

'Who is acting for the prosecution and defence?' asked Sir Algernon, glancing around the court at the clerk behind one of the smaller desks.

Having established which cluster of lawyers was doing what, the senior judge leaned back and rested his hands across his considerable stomach. 'Get on with it, then.'

A fresh-faced barrister wearing what appeared to be his older brother's court gown stood up for the prosecution. 'On Wednesday the eighteenth of September constables Kemp and Perkins from Arbour Square police station were going about their duties when their attention was drawn to …' The barrister outlined the events of the evening and Jack's subsequent arrest.

'Witnesses, Crisp?' barked Sir Algernon when the army barrister had finished.

'Yes, m'lord,' Crisp replied. 'I'd like to call Constable Kemp.'

The barrister signalled to the chief clerk, who in turn signalled to one of his underlings by the side door. The man popped out for a moment and returned with a well-padded police officer with grey mutton-chop whiskers, who looked as if he'd stepped out of a Victorian crime novel.

He lumbered on to the stand and holding the Bible excessively high, was sworn in by the grey-haired, matronly court official. Having stated his name, rank and number for the records, he looked expectantly at the prosecutor.

'Tell the court in your own words about the events on the night of the eighteenth of September,' said the slender Crisp.

Taking his notebook from his uniform top pocket, the constable opened it and cleared his throat. 'Myself and Constable Perkins were proceeding in a westerly direction along Ben Jonson Road when …'

Over what seemed like a wet Bank Holiday weekend but was actually an hour and a half, Jack listened to PC Kemp's long-winded account of finding the auxiliary unit's stash of weapons followed by his fellow officer Perkins' recount of the same thing almost word for word.

Perkins was followed by Detective Sergeant McKay from West Ham police station, who told of Jack's refusal to answer questions but had to admit when questioned that the fingerprint department could not find Jack's or anyone else's prints on the guns. Next, a captain from the Royal Military Police took the stand and, after listing once more all the munitions found in the charnel house, he had to acknowledge under questioning by Jack's barrister that none of the serial numbers matched any that were stolen from the supply wagons at Stratford.

'So it seems that although no one doubts that a quantity of arms were discovered on the night of the eighteenth, none of the evidence so far links that to my client,' said Skinner, addressing the three ancient judges chewing their gums.

'Any other witnesses?' barked Sir Algernon scowling at the assembled lawyers and barristers.

'Father David Harmsworth,' replied Crisp.

'Catholic?' sneered Fox-Unwin on Sir Algernon's right.

'Church of England, sir,' Crisp replied.

'Good,' grumbled Fox-Unwin. 'Not cricket to hang a man on the word of a left-footer.'

Sir Cicero huffed and puffed his agreement.

'Well then, Crisp, let's hear what this priest has to say, shall we?'

The court officer popped out of the side door again, returning this time with Father David in his wake.

Freshly shaven, with his fair hair anchored in place by copious amounts of Brilliantine and wearing his high, waxed dog collar and long black cassock, Father David looked the epitome of a devout member of the clergy. However, the hatred in his pale blue eyes as he looked across the court room made it clear to Jack that St Winifred's curate was not there seeking divine justice but revenge.

Lifting the front of his cassock, Father David stepped up into the witness box. One of the female assistants to the clerk of the court handed him a Bible.

'Good grief, Miss Wickers,' snapped Sir Algernon. 'The man's a priest so I think we can take it as read he'll tell the truth.'

'It's all right, My Lord,' said Father David smoothly as he took it. 'I'm here as his ARP warden not a priest.'

Miss Wickers held up the card and Father David, black Bible held aloft, recited the oath in his plummy nasal tone.

'Thank you.' Crisp grasped his lapels theatrically. 'Now, Father David, you are a part-time ARP warden, are you not?'

'I am. Attached to post three in Ben Jonson Road,' the curate replied.

'And will you please tell the court in your own words what happened when you were on duty on the night of the eighteenth of September?' asked the prosecuting counsel.

'I was on patrol in Whitehorse Road at just after nine when ...' Father David gave the court an overblown account of ARP his duties that night and how he came to be in the graveyard concluding with, 'halfway across, I noticed some movement at the back of the churchyard. Thinking it was a courting couple engaged in an immoral congress amongst the oldest gravestone, I made my way over but instead it was Jack Quinn who was acting very suspiciously.'

'Suspicious how?'

'He seemed to be carrying something heavy,' Father David replied.

'And then what happened, Father?' asked the prosecutor.

'I was about to go over and ask him what he was playing at when the air raid siren started,' said Father David. 'Naturally, as an ARP warden my primary concern was getting people into the shelters before the bombing started. However, thinking perhaps he was hiding stolen goods, I ran off to call the police before continuing with my warden's duties. Thankfully, I found two constables who I took back to where I'd last seen Jack Quinn.'

'Then what happened?' asked Crisp.

Father David forced a light laugh. 'To be honest, I was a bit baffled when I got back to the charnel house because the door was slightly open.'

'And why was that baffling, Father?'

'Because the iron gate that secured the entrance has been rusted together since I arrived at St Winifred's two years ago,' Father David replied. 'But one of the constables shone his torch on the gate and although the metalwork was rusted with age, the chain and lock securing it were not. In fact, despite being covered with black paint like the rest of the structure, they appeared to be of a more modern design.'

'Then what happened?' prompted the barrister.

'Well, the constables forced the lock and went inside,' Father David replied. 'No doubt they told you what they found.'

'They did,' Crisp agreed. 'Can I ask how you know the accused?'

'His sister is a member of St Winifred's congregation,' Father David replied.

'Do you know him well?'

'Well enough,' Father David replied flatly. 'Although he hasn't felt the need for God's comfort or blessing for many years, in the last few months he has frequented some church events. He is also a member of the Stepney Home Guard platoon who parade in the church hall, so I have seen him there on numerous occasions recently.'

'Let us be clear, Father David, there is no doubt in your mind that you saw the accused around the charnel house on the night of the eighteenth?'

'None whatsoever,' Father David replied firmly.

'Thank you, Father,' said Crisp, resuming his seat.

Jack's barrister rose to his feet. To give Skinner his due, he tried his very best to throw doubt on Father David's testimony, especially as Jack himself had been less than forthcoming about the events of the night, but finally he, too, resumed his seat. Father David stuck to his story, which to be fair to him, was totally true. However, although his expression remained impassive throughout, Jack could hear the relish in the other man's voice.

Father David stepped down and joined the CID and RMP officers and a couple of army types sitting on the row of seats at the back of the room.

Jack watched him for a couple of seconds then turned his attention back to the court proceedings, where Crisp was already on his feet and pacing back and forth in front of the bench.

'So, in conclusion, the accused has been clearly identified by a credible witness – a priest in the Church of England, no less – who linked him to a huge quantity of guns and ammunition. Although the weapons in question are not those stolen from Stratford shunting yard, they still beg the question: Why has the accused got them? And what, indeed, are they for?' His knuckles white as he gripped the front of his black gown, Crisp cast his eyes over the three red-coated justices. 'Despite questioning by both the police and the intelligence service, the accused refused to give any explanation. Therefore, with the German army sitting across the Channel and our counter-intelligence officers discovering Nazi plots each day, we must draw our own conclusions. I put it to the court that the evidence points to the accused being part of a cell of Nazi fifth columnists who will rise up and join the Germans if they invade. I therefore ask that Your Lordships find the defendant guilty of treason.'

The prosecution's barrister sat down.

Despite his situation, the corners of Jack's mouth lifted slightly. The prosecution barrister was absolutely right, of course, except for one crucial detail, which having given his oath at Coleshill House, Jack couldn't supply.

The youthful Mr Skinner stood up and argued the wisdom of convicting Jack on the testimony of one person, but Jack could see the three old men who would decide his fate weren't swallowing it. Finally, Jack's barrister sat down.

The two judges on either side of Sir Algernon inclined their be-wigged heads towards their senior colleague.

There was a mutter of discussion with much nodding of heads, but after only a few moments they straightened up. Sir Algernon beckoned the clerk of the court forward and said something and she handed him a small wooden box. Opening it, Sir Algernon took out a square of black fabric and, with fingers gnarled with arthritis, he placed it on top of his wig.

'The prisoner will stand,' announced the clerk of the court.

Jack rose to his feet.

'Jack William Quinn,' said Sir Algernon, his voice booming around the otherwise silent room.

'You have been found guilty of treason, which is a capital offence under the Emergency Powers Act 1940.' Ice replaced the blood in Jack's veins, and he had to lock his knees to stay upright. 'Therefore, from this court you will be taken to a place of execution where you will be hanged by the neck until you are dead. And may God have mercy on your soul.'

Imagining the bristly hemp rope chafing his throat, Jack's breath stilled in his lungs as his bowels constricted. With jumbled images of Rachel and Prue colliding in his mind, he stared blindly ahead as the three justices stood up and shuffled out.

Skinner's youthful face swam into Jack's vision muttering his apologies for not having won the day. Jack murmured something in reply and his barrister disappeared from view.

Something gripped his upper arm. 'Come on, chum. Let's get you back.'

Dragging himself back from the horror in his mind, Jack found a prison officer standing beside him.

Mutely, Jack nodded. However, as he turned his gaze came to rest on Father David, his black cassock pooling around his feet, as he stood motionless by the row of chairs.

The curate's cool blue eyes meet Jack's brown one. They stared at each other for a moment then, as the prison officer led Jack away, the merest hint of a smile lifted the corners of Father David's thin lips.

Chapter forty-one

'BUT I DON'T UNDERSTAND,' SAID Prue, looking at the police sergeant who was standing on the other side the polished teak front desk.

'Well, it's easy enough, miss,' said the ginger-haired officer in charge of the day-to-day running of the establishment. ''E ain't 'ere.'

She was in West Ham police station and although it was now almost eleven o'clock in the morning, they were still dealing with the aftermath of last night's nine-hour raid, so there was a small crowd of walking wounded being tended to in the reception area that Prue had just come through.

Prue was confused. 'But the officer I spoke to yesterday said he was still in your—'

'And who are you, if you don't mind me asking?' the officer cut in.

'I'm Mr Quinn's fiancée,' said Prue.

The officer's eyes flickered on to her bare left hand.

'We've only recently decided to marry,' said Prue. 'In fact, we're supposed to be getting married this Saturday, so I'd really like to know where Mr Quinn is.'

'Well, we don't usually give out information about

prisoners unless it's to family members,' the sergeant replied.

'Well, I'm coming on his sister's behalf as she's only just come out of hospital after having a baby,' Prue explained. 'And we're both worried sick, as is his seven-year-old daughter.'

'I'm sure you are, miss,' said the police officer, 'but the truth is Quinn hasn't been here since Saturday.'

Prue stared at him in astonishment. 'Saturday!'

'That's right,' confirmed the sergeant, ''bout seven, just after the early relief clocked on, some army types pitched up, frogmarched him out and bundled him into a truck.'

Prue stared blankly at him. 'I've been here each day trying to see him since last Thursday; why didn't someone tell me?'

'National defence, that's what we were told,' he said.

Prue looked aghast.

'This is completely ridiculous.' Pinning her arms to her sides, she clenched her fists. 'Jack Quinn is innocent.'

The station sergeant chuckled. 'That's what they all say.'

'But he is,' insisted Prue. 'The real culprits who have been stealing from the army wagons in Stratford shunting yard were caught red-handed and have been arrested. I saw the RMPs march them away myself. And after spending half the night stuck up a signal gantry, I was here yesterday morning with Detective Sergeant Rawlings and his counterpart from the military giving a witness statement. I expected to hear that Mr Quinn

500

had been released, but when he didn't come to see me last night, I went to his sister's first thing and he wasn't there either.'

The officer raised a pair of bushy, carroty eyebrows. 'Sorry, miss, I wish I could help you, especially as you say he has a daughter and a sister just come out of 'ospital, but—'

'Is there someone who could at least tell me where he's being held?' she asked.

'I'm afraid not, but don't worry,' he said and gave her a condescending smile, 'British justice is the best in the world, so if this is all a mistake, as you say it is, then no doubt the army will let your fiancé go soon. Now if you don't mind, miss …'

He nodded at the small queue that had gathered behind her.

Pressing her lips together, Prue stepped aside and avoiding the buckets of sand and stirrup pumps stacked next to the police station's entrance, she made her way down the steps on to West Ham Lane.

Feeling utterly confused and helpless, Prue stood motionless as people passed back and forth before her for a moment then she turned left and with her head buzzing and her feet feeling like two lead weights, she trudged along the pavement towards Stratford Broadway.

Cradling a cup of hot sweet tea, Martha eased herself into her favourite chair. She put her feet up on the pouffe and gave a small prayer of thanks that she was finally home. Old bones didn't rest easy in lumpy hotel beds, wedged into overcrowded railway carriages or standing for hours in connecting corridors.

As Leonard's funeral had been on Friday, she'd kissed her sister Judith goodbye the next morning, intending to be back in the parish late Tuesday afternoon but what with cancelled trains and damaged railways lines, she'd only arrived into Waterloo at ten o'clock that morning. People had been kind as ever, offering an elderly nun their seat, and a couple of soldier's kitbags to sit on in the waiting room at one of the little village stations where she'd had to change trains, but she had to conclude that it was a blessing to be home.

She rested her head back and thinking she would call in at the rectory later to see what had been happening while she was away, she closed her eyes.

However, she was mentally going through the list of parishioners she needed to visit when her front door burst open and Prue Carmichael staggered in.

'Sister Martha,' she sobbed. 'Thank goodness you're here. I just couldn't face going home, so I don't know ...'

Putting her tea aside, Martha stood up and hurried over to her.

'My dearest child,' she said, putting her arms around the young woman's shaking shoulders, 'what on earth has happened?'

'It's Jack,' Prue replied, with tears streaming down her cheeks. 'Oh, Sister Martha, they told me he was in the cells, but he wasn't because they took him last Saturday.'

Sister Martha looked puzzled. 'What cells and who took him, Prue?'

'West Ham police station,' she replied, wiping her eyes with the heel of her hand. 'He was arrested on Thursday and the army took him on Saturday but no one will tell me where and why.'

Dread gnawed at Martha. Taking hold of Prue's upper arms, she turned the young girl to face her. 'Now, Prue,' she said firmly, looking her straight in the eye. 'I want you to start at the beginning and tell me exactly what's happened?'

Prue nodded and took a deep breath. 'I went to see Rosie last Monday and that's when I found out that Jack had been rescued so I …'

Martha listened intently as Prue recounted how she and Jack had discovered they loved each other and the less-than-joyful reaction to the news of their forthcoming wedding at the rectory before moving on to the events that had brought her sobbing to Martha's small cottage.

'I'd heard that army equipment was being stolen from wagons in Stratford, but I couldn't believe it when Jack was arrested for it,' said Prue. 'I knew Jack didn't do it but then I found out that Father David was involved in Jack's arrest.'

Martha looked puzzled. 'How?'

'Apparently, he was on warden duty last Wednesday night and spotted Jack in the graveyard "acting suspiciously", whatever that means. He called the police and they found guns and ammunition and they arrested Jack,' Prue explained, dabbing her eyes again with her handkerchief. 'But then ...'

Prue recounted her night stuck on the gantry and the subsequent arrest of the real thieves two days ago.

'What I don't understand is now that the police have the real thieves in custody why haven't the army released Jack,' she continued, oblivious to the cold hand of fear tightening around Martha's heart. She sighed. 'I'm sorry, I didn't mean to drop all this in your lap, especially as you've only just got back from a funeral. Is your sister all right?'

'Yes, she's fine. She and her husband have hated each other for years. Did Father David say where they found these guns?' asked Martha.

'In the old charnel house,' Prue replied. 'Oh, Sister '

'Now now, my dear,' Martha replied absentmindedly. 'You make yourself comfortable and I'll put the kettle on.'

Leaving Prue in her parlour, Sister Martha headed through to the kitchen. Refilling the kettle, she put it on the back ring and lit the flame beneath it.

Rinsing out the teapot, she set it on the draining board then rested her hands on the edge of the enamel sink and stared unseeing out at her handkerchief-sized backyard.

Unfortunately, unlike Prue, she had a pretty good idea why the army had not released Jack.

For fear of betrayal by Nazi sympathisers, the auxiliary units were ultra-top secret. Martha doubted more than a handful of the Cabinet knew about them and probably even fewer in the War Office. To maintain this there was a strict directive against divulging anything about the auxiliary units or even acknowledging their existence to anyone. Jack had sworn to uphold that protocol and he obviously had or there would have been knocking at her door by now. She'd sworn the same oath of secrecy, but this was Jack!

Images of him as a little lad singing in the choir, reading a Bible verse aloud in Sunday school and sobbing his heart out at his mother's funeral floated into her mind. It wasn't in God's eternal plan for her to be blessed with a family of her own, but the Almighty had graciously sent her a succession of children to love and cherish over the years. She loved them all. But Jack Quinn, with his cheeky smile and sharp mind, had a very special place in her heart. In all the ways that counted, he was the son she and Giles should have had.

The kettle's shrill whistle cut through her thoughts. Turning to flip off the gas she caught sight of Prue, open-hearted, generous and lovely with her auburn hair sitting lightly on her shoulder, as she gazed out of the front window.

Martha's aching heart shattered.

Leaving the kettle to cool on the stove she marched back through to the parlour.

'Follow me,' she said, snatching her purse and keys from the sideboard and shoving them in her skirt pocket.

'Where are we going?'

Martha handed Prue her handbag and took hold of her arm.

'I'll explain on the way,' she said as she ushered her through the front door.

Closing the door behind her, Martha, with Prue hurrying to keep up, strode across the street to the open door of number seventeen.

'Nora!' she shouted. 'It's Sister Martha!'

Wiping her hands on a tea towel, mother-of-six Nora Pollard hurried out.

'Is Wag about?' Martha asked.

''Es in the Fish and Ring, 'aving a lunchtime pint,' Nora replied.

'Can you send one of the nippers to fetch him?' said Martha. 'I'm in urgent need of his taxi.'

Thirty minutes later, having detoured down Kingsland Road because of an unexploded bomb in Shoreditch High Street and swerved around piles of rubble in City Road, Wag swung his taxi right into Baker Street then slowed to a stop outside Berkley Court, a nondescript four-storey office block.

Prue stood mutely on the pavement while, despite Wag's protestations, Sister Martha paid her neighbour, adding a hefty half-crown tip for his troubles.

'What is this place?' asked Prue as the taxi sped off.

Sister Martha tapped the side of her nose by way of

an answer then guided Prue through the entrance, letting the door swing behind them.

A doe-eyed receptionist with a large chiffon bow at her throat, who was perched behind a curved ash reception desk, looked up as they walked in.

'Can I help, Sister?' the young woman asked as they marched across the stylised art deco foyer towards the cage lift.

'That's very kind of you, my dear,' Sister Martha replied brightly, 'but I know exactly where I'm going.'

Looking alarmed, the receptionist rose to her feet. 'I'm afraid you can't just go up—'

Grasping the brass handle of the lift door, Sister Martha wrenched it open and ushered Prue inside. She slammed the metal outer and inner lift doors shut then pressed one of the buttons with her bony finger. The floor beneath Prue's feet glided upwards a second or two before the young woman whose job it was to prevent such things as unknown visitors wandering around in the building reached them.

Fury screwed the delicately featured face on the other side of the metal grille for a moment then she dashed back to her post and her voice echoed up the cavernous shaft as she spoke to someone on the telephone.

The lift juddered to a metal-jangling halt on the third floor. Sister Martha pulled back the lift doors and they stepped out into a sparse corridor with a concrete floor, dirty white walls, and several half-glazed doors running along both sides.

Without pausing, Sister Martha strode off towards the door at the far end with Prue trotting to keep up with her. Without pausing or knocking, the nun grabbed the handle and went in. Prue followed.

A map of the south of England covered one wall, beneath which was a bench with almost a dozen telephones on it in a variety of colours. To the right was another with a khaki-coloured shortwave radio with two sets of earphones on it. In the middle of the room were two women at typewriters who both looked up as Sister Martha and Prue burst in.

'Afternoon, ladies,' said Sister Martha. 'Is the guvnor in?'

'Yes, but you can't—'

'Oh, I think I can,' the nun replied, heading for the half-glazed door on the other side of the room.

The women behind the desks rose to their feet and stepped out from behind their desks but not quickly enough because Sister Martha had already opened the door.

'After you, my dear,' she said, nodding Prue into the room.

A man with a scrubbing-brush moustache and wearing a colonel's uniform raised his eyes from the document he was studying and his mouth dropped open.

'What the blue blazes …? Mattie McPherson, what are …?'

'Afternoon, Colin, I hope you are well.'

Yes, I am, very, but what—'

'Jack Quinn is sitting in a prison somewhere, probably waiting to be hung for treason, and this lovely young lady,' she looped her arm through Prue's, 'is his fiancée, Prudence Carmichael. They have their wedding booked for Saturday at eleven o'clock, and I want you, Colin, to do whatever you have to do to make sure Jack is there.'

Chapter forty-two

WITH HIS BACK AGAINST the hard wall behind him and his feet resting on the lumpy mattress of his bed, Jack studied the rows of oblong white tiles on the opposite wall. Since he'd been returned to his cell after his trial the day before, Jack had counted them horizontally and vertically a couple of times; now he just used them as a blank canvas for his thoughts.

As the beam of pale light through his high window had moved downwards as the sun rose, Jack guessed it must be close to seven in the morning. Not that it mattered to him; he'd been awake for hours. Having been condemned to eternal sleep some time in the not-too-distant future, Jack was happy to be so. It gave him time to think. And oddly to do something he hadn't done for many years: pray.

Despite his quarrel with St Winifred's clergy, Jack had always believed in the Almighty. Now, knowing he was soon to be coming face to face with Him, Jack found himself praying to God as you would to a friend. Not so much for himself but about those he loved. Rosie and her three children and Rachel.

The pain of knowing he would not live to see his daughter grow into a woman near cut him to the marrow. Jack worried, too, that if the Germans did finally decide to set sail across the Channel, he would not be there to keep her safe. So as this was now beyond his control, he handed her future over to the Almighty.

Alongside his daughter, only one other person filled his mind: Prue.

A lesser man might regret not taking her up on her offer and tasting the sweet fruit of making love to her, but although he'd had a mighty struggle with himself, Jack was glad he'd held firm.

Prue deserved a wedding ring and a wedding night. And as he was not going to be the man who could give her those things now, she could accept some other man's proposal with good conscience. Even though Jack's heart tightened painfully at the through of Prue in the arms of another man, he hoped in time she would find love again and have those children she yearned for.

Perhaps a lesser man, too, would have saved his own skin but if the anonymous captain who'd questioned him at length surrendered to the Germans if they arrived in a few weeks, then all would be lost. Knowing that the lives of all the men in auxiliary units throughout the south-east of England depended on the utmost secrecy, Jack had kept his oath. Even through it cost him everything.

The echo of marching boots heading in his direction along the corridor filtered into his cell then came to a halt outside his cell.

Swinging his legs around, Jack stood up as the gunmetal grey door opened and two prison wardens marched in.

'This way, chum,' said one of them with hands like shovels.

'Where are you taking me?' Jack asked.

'You'll see when you get there,' the other guard, with atrocious acne, replied. 'Now get a shift on.'

With one guard on either side, Jack was led along the rows of metal doors on the prison wing then down the enclosed iron staircase and along a corridor. They stopped in front of a light oak door at the far end, with the word 'Governor' etched on a brass plate fixed to it.

The spotty guard knocked then opened the door and marched Jack in.

In contrast to the grey-painted brickwork he'd just been marched along, the room Jack entered had walls covered with light oak panels, the window had net curtains rather than a grille and there was a desk with a man in a baggy grey suit sitting behind it.

But all these things barely registered because the only thing that captured his attention was Prue, in a tartan skirt and jacket, auburn hair curling over her shoulders and tired but still beautiful hazel eyes on him.

She dashed across the room and threw her arms around his neck. 'Jack!'

Struggling to believe Prue was actually in his arms, Jack enfolded her in his embrace, the flowery fragrance of her perfume wafting over him. Holding her tightly, Jack closed his eyes briefly only to find when he opened them that he was looking at Sister Martha, who was smiling, and Colonel Gubbins, who was not.

'Thank you, Governor.' Jack's most senior officer gave the man behind the desk a meaningful look from beneath his eyebrows.

Rising from his chair, the prison governor left swiftly.

Releasing Prue, Jack stood to attention.

'Stand at ease, Quinn.'

Jack adjusted his stance and stared at the other two people in the room.

'I don't understand,' he said, his attention shifting between them.

Gubbins cleared his throat. 'Well, the fact of the matter is, Quinn, that Sister Martha called in a favour I've owed her since nineteen sixteen. However, me flourishing Winston's written order for your release under the RMP brigadier's nose didn't go down too well, to say the least, and Sir Donald, the Attorney General, wasn't too pleased that a judicial verdict was overruled by the King's pardon but ...'

'Thank you,' said Jack. 'I really thought ...'

He covered his eyes with his hand for a second as the enormity of the moment washed over him, then clasping his hands behind his back again Jack squared his shoulders.

The senior officer's moustache waggled back and forth as he studied Jack. 'Of course, this does cause a bit of a problem. After all, guns were found that can't be accounted for and there're enough rumours flying about without giving them more so I can't just release you back into your old life. You understand, Quinn. Secrecy and all that.'

'Yes, sir.'

'But, Quinn,' continued the colonel, 'I'm putting together another little operation which I think you would fit into very nicely. However,' his frown deepened, 'before we move on to such things, there is a situation that needs to be addressed urgently.'

'And what's that, sir?' asked Jack, praying it didn't mean a return to the cells.

A half-smile lifted the corner of the colonel's lips. 'I believe for some reason of her own, the young lady at your side is keen to make a respectable man of you, on …'

'Saturday,' Prue supplied, squeezing Jack's arm and smiling up at him.

'Well then, I suggest, Martha, that we leave the future Mr and Mrs Quinn to get on with their plans,' said Gubbins.

Picking up his hat from the desk, he flipped it on to his head, then, tucking his swagger stick under his arm, he marched across and opened the door.

Sister Martha came over and Jack put his arm around the diminutive nun and hugged her.

'Thank you,' he whispered.

Stepping out of his embrace, Sister Martha finely lined face lifted in a smile. 'I'll see you both at the Town Hall.'

She and Colonel Gubbins left the room and as the door clicked shut Prue threw her arms around Jack's neck.

Jack gazed down into Prue's eyes with dark smudges

beneath but brimming with love, then savouring every curve of her body pressed into his he lowered his mouth slowly on hers.

Chapter forty-three

'Ready?' asked Fliss, slipping her arm through Prue's.

Prue smiled at her sister, who was holding her weekend case and standing next to her at the top of the rectory stairs.

It was ten-fifteen on Saturday morning and two days since she and Jack had walked out of the front gates of Holloway Prison.

After his release, they'd headed to Rosie's. On arrival, Jack's sister had sobbed for a full five minutes then the air raid siren had sounded so Prue and Jack had spent a romantic night in the shelter. She'd kissed him goodbye at first light then headed off to work, where she strong-armed Knobby Clark into granting her special leave until Tuesday. She arrived back at the rectory to find Fliss, who she'd phoned before leaving for work, already there. Jack arrived soon after and told her that his call-up papers and his reserved occupation release documents had arrived in the afternoon post.

But Prue wasn't going to dwell on the future; she would focus on today, because in less than an hour's time she would be Mrs Quinn.

Therefore, smiling through the short veil of her broad-brimmed hat Prue nodded. 'Yes I am.'

They exchanged warm looks then, arm in arm, they descended the stairs to the hallway to find Mrs Lavender, minus her wraparound overall and headscarf, waiting in the hall, alongside Dora and Johanna, babes in arms, and Ingrid, with their children in front of them, the girls bobbing with excitement and the boys doing their best to look interested.

'Here comes the bride,' said Mrs Lavender, as Prue stopped in front of her wellwishers. 'And what a lovely bride you are too, Miss Carmichael.'

'Isn't she?' said Fliss, who looked pretty good herself in a Navy box-shoulder suit with a dusky-pink blouse beneath.

Prue had found a lovely shamrock-green dress and bolero-style jacket on the Waste market the day after she and Jack had booked their wedding. It was shot silk and probably made in one of the local clothing factories for an upmarket shop in Oxford Street or Bond Street so it was better not to ask how it had ended up in and East End market stall.

'I'm so pleased for you,' said Dora, squeezing Prue's arm.

'I hope that your new husband knows how lucky he is,' said Ingrid.

'Don't worry,' chipped in Mrs Lavender, 'if he doesn't, I'll soon tell him.'

Everyone laughed.

The lounge door opened and Hester Kratz, reading glasses on the tip of her nose and a smile on her face, came over to join them.

'Here is our lovely bride,' she said, putting her arms around Prue and giving her a quick hug. 'I hope you and Jack are very happy.'

'Thank you,' said Prue. 'I know we will be. Who knows, one day I'll be saying the same on your wedding day. Perhaps to some handsome doctor?'

Hester rolled her eyes.

'And have many *kinder*,' added Ingrid.

'Ready, girls,' said Fliss, a mischievous twinkle in her eye. 'One, two, three.'

Dipping their hands in their pockets for a moment, the women showered Prue with tiny fragments of white tissue.

'It is a tradition, no?' said Ingrid.

'Yes, it is,' laughed Prue as confetti fluttered down on her hair and shoulders.

'Ve made it ourselves,' said Johanna. 'As they've stopped making confetti because of the war.'

Looking at them all smiling at her, a lump formed in Prue's throat. 'Thank you. Is Mother in the lounge, Fliss?'

'Yes, she is, but Dad has gone to meet the churchwarden,' her sister replied. 'I told her you were—'

'I'll just pop in before I go,' said Prue.

'All right. I'll go and keep an eye out for Wag's taxi.' Fliss squeezed her arm. 'And don't let her upset you,' she added softly.

Forcing a smile, Prue patted her sister's hand then turned to the door on her right and went in.

Her mother, dressed in a plain navy dress and pearls, was sitting at the bureau under the window writing. She looked up as Prue walked in.

'Hello, Mother,' she said. 'I've just come to tell you I'm off to the Town Hall.'

'So you're going through with this disgrace of a marriage, then?' her mother replied, her gaze flickering over her.

'Yes, I am,' Prue replied.

'I meant what I said, you know,' sniffed her mother. 'So I hope you haven't come thinking I'll relent.'

'No, I don't expect you to,' Prue replied. 'I've come out of respect before I leave.'

'I suppose you know that Father David is transferring to a parish somewhere in Buckinghamshire,' she said, giving Prue a hard look. 'Which means until your father can find a replacement, he'll have to shoulder the pastoral burden of St Winifred's alone. I, in turn, will have to help him more alongside everything else I have to manage in the parish and—' Running feet thumped across the ceiling. Her mother glanced up briefly. 'And in the rectory.'

'I'm not sure what you expect me to say?' said Prue.

'Well, sorry would be a start,' snapped her mother.

'Sorry for what?'

'For putting your father and me in this position,' her mother replied.

'This so-called position your in is of your own making, Mother,' Prue replied. 'Of course people would have muttered about me marrying Jack, they always do. But think what the ladies of the parish will say now when word gets around that the rector's daughter has been thrown out because she married for love. Goodness, that will keep the gossips going for months – longer if my waistline starts to expand in a couple of months.' Horror spread across her mother's face. 'So, I'll be off now to marry the man I love and I'll see you in church next Sunday.'

Smiling, Prue turned and headed for the door and her new life.

Although the morning light was only just creeping under the plum-coloured chenille curtain, Prue was awake and had been for an hour or so, resting her head in the dip between Jack's left shoulder and neck. The hotel they'd booked into for their two-night honeymoon was just off Bloomsbury Square, so instead of the sound of milk bottles rattling in their crates or boots crunching over cobbles, there was birdsong, so she guessed it was probably somewhere close to six in the morning. It also meant that for the first time in a month they'd been able to spend the whole night in an actual bed rather than in St Winifred's crypt, as the Luftwaffe was still concentrating their nightly raids on the docks, factories and warehouses along both sides of the Thames.

With its nondescript wallpaper and tasteless menu, the hotel itself had seen better days. However, in contrast to the elderly chambermaids and waitresses who shuffled about the place, the guests were almost without exception like her and Jack: just married and with the groom soon departing to do his duty. Of course, probably only Jack was doing so after receiving the King's pardon for treason.

In the muted light from the window, Prue glanced down at her left hand resting among the tangle of dark hair on Jack's chest. Lifting her third finger slightly, she smiled. Such a small band of gold but such a huge and very happy change to her life. Her gaze travelled upwards to the face of her sleeping husband.

Jack was sprawled next to her, the sheet only just covering his hips, one leg sticking out of the side and his right arm flung over his head. Unlike her he was fast asleep but that was to be expected as he'd been quite energetic over the last two days.

Having enjoyed running her eyes along his firm, bristly chin, well-defined lips and straight nose, Prue allowed her gaze to drift downwards. Slowly she contemplated his broad hair-covered chest then followed the line that tracked down the centre of his firm stomach to his navel before spreading wide and disappearing beneath the sheet.

Studying the raised area beneath, a little fizz of excitement below her navel, which she hadn't understood properly until two nights ago, made its presence known again.

To be honest, once they closed the door of the hotel bedroom on their wedding night, Prue hardly knew herself. It only took a couple of moments of Jack's dextrous hands exploring her body before she was responding in kind, practically ripping the buttons off his shirt in order to feel his bare skin under her fingertips. Although some would regard it as shameful, the lacy nightie she'd brought with her was still in her weekend case, as she and Jack had slept entwined in each other's arms naked. And it had been her who told Jack to leave the bedside light on. So much for her mother's warning about the wedding night not being too 'unpleasant'. It was very much the opposite.

After enjoying the feel of Jack's steady heartbeat under her hand for a moment and with her eyes on his face, she moved her hand downwards. A faint smile lifted the corners of his mouth then his hand closed over hers, stopping its progress.

Opening his eyes, he gave her that crooked smile of his. 'Are you trying to wear me out?'

Prue raised an eyebrow. 'No, I'm giving you something to remember me by.'

'As if I could ever forget you,' he replied. 'Especially after all that moaning you've been doing.'

Prue pulled a face and jabbed him in the ribs. Jack laughed and hugged her to him, pressing his lips on her forehead. 'Happy?'

'Very,' she replied, snuggling up to him.

'Even though it wasn't the wedding you probably dreamed of?'

Hugging the sheet to her, Prue sat up. 'It was exactly the wedding I'd always dreamed of because I married the man I love,' she replied, looking down at him. An image of her absent mother and father started to form in Prue's mind but she cut it short and focused on the man beside her. 'It would have been my perfect wedding if we'd both been standing in rags in a swamp because now you, Jack Quinn, are my husband. And, I might say, a very handsome one you looked too when you came down the Town Hall steps when I arrived.'

Jack gave a rumbling laugh. 'Well, you looked pretty good yourself, wife, in that snazzy little green number with your perky red hat.'

'And everyone was happy,' said Prue.

'Which is why, I suppose, Rosie and your sister were crying all the way through the ceremony,' said Jack. 'I even saw Sister Martha dabbing her eyes.'

'Tears of happiness,' said Prue. 'Rachel looked lovely, too, in that organza lemon dress.'

A look of pride spread across Jack's face. 'She did, didn't she? And I don't think I've seen her grin so much.'

'She's happy for you,' said Prue. 'And she's already planning what we're going to do when I pick her up next Saturday. I've promised to teach her how to knit, so you might get a scarf for Christmas.'

Jack laughed and taking her hand he pressed his lips on her knuckles. 'God, I do love you, Prue.' He kissed her hand again then his eyes softened. 'I wish I'd been able to take you dancing, to the flicks and on Sunday-afternoon walks in the park and do all the other things a courting couple do instead of—'

Letting go of the sheet, Prue leaned forward and stopped his words with her lips.

'We will do all those things and more in the years to come,' she said, running her fingers through his hair. 'But for now, there is a war on so we must be content with this.'

Prue gazed deeply into Jack's eyes for a moment then gripping his thick black curls, she covered his mouth with hers. Jack's arms wound around her instantly as the love and desire for him deepened her kiss.

Shifting over, Prue stretched herself along the length of him, her breasts pressing on to his chest and his hardness against the top of her thigh.

The familiar slow pulse of need started deep within Prue as Jack's hands ran up and done her back and over her bottom.

Breaking free from his lips, she raised herself up. 'Do you know what else Rachel said to me on Saturday?' she asked, idly twirling his chest hair with her index finger. 'She said, "Now you and Daddy are married, Auntie Prue, I hope you have a baby like Mummy."'

Amusement flickered across the strong planes of Jack's face. 'And what did you say?'

Prue gave him a sideways look from under her lashes. 'I said, "So do I."'

Jack's jaunty expression was replaced by one that set Prue's pulse racing. His arm tightened around her, then in one swift move her rolled her over.

Enjoying his weight on her and the hardness of his chest against her breasts, Prue looked up at the man who would hold her heart into eternity and beyond. She smiled.

'I love you,' she whispered, her gaze flickering over his face to burn it into her memory.

'I don't just love you, Prue,' he said, in a low voice. 'I totally adore you.' His lips then planted small kisses along her cheekbone.

'Babies seem to arrive when they will,' he whispered, as he reached her ear, 'but if Rachel doesn't have a little brother or sister by this time next year,' he continued, his lips sending shivers of excitement through her as they progressed down her neck, 'you can't say it's for want of effort on my part, my beautiful, gorgeous, wanton wife.'

Prue let out a low laugh and then closed her eyes. Although the chances were that Rachel would be out of luck on the baby front and she might never again be welcomed into the Carmichael family home, Prue was totally happy with her lot.

When she'd walked into St Winifred's rectory less than six months ago, she believed love stole over you softly accompanied by sweet words and innocent glances, but she was wrong. Love came at you full pelt from nowhere, knocking you off your feet and stealing your every thought. It made you strong and reckless and wholly complete when the one you loved loved you in return.

It hardly mattered that the war raged around them or if, God forbid, the Germans invaded, because wherever life took her Prue had Jack, her love, her anchor and her husband in this life and then for eternity.

Acknowledgements

As always, I would like to mention a few books, authors and people to whom I am particularly indebted.

In order to set my characters' thoughts and worldview authentically in the harsh reality of the Spitfire summer of 1940, I returned to *Wartime Britain 1939–1945* (Gardner), *The East End at War* (Taylor & Lloyd), *The Blitz* (Gardener), *Living Through the Blitz* (Harrison),*The Blitz* (Madden), *The Wartime Scrapbook* (Opie) and *London's East End Survivors* (Bissell).

I also revisited *The British Homefront 1939–45* (Brayley & McGregor), *Put that Light Out* (Brown), *Raiders Overhead* (Nixon) and *The Real 'Dad's Army'* (Scott)

To bring Prue and Jack's war work at Stratford railway locomotive works and shunting yard to life, I delved into *Britain's Railways in Wartime* (Lambert), *Female Railway Workers in World War II* (Major), *The Fair Sex: Women and the Great Western Railway* (Matheson), *Steaming into the Blitz* and *Steaming into the Firing Line* (Clutterbuck), *The Great Western at War 1939–1945* (Bryan) and *London's Engine Sheds Volume 2 The East and South* (Griffiths & Hooper).

I was greatly helped in creating Jack's role in Churchill's secret army by studying *Churchill's*

Underground Army (Warwicker), *Fighting Nazi Occupation* (Atkin), *Forgotten Voices of the Secret War* (Bailey), *Churchill's Ministry of Ungentlemanly Warfare* (Milton) and lastly *Gubbins and SOE* (Wilkinson & Bright Astley). In addition, the British Resistance Archives https://www.staybehinds.com/ and WW2TV https://www.youtube.com/watch?v=Xr1E5FaG1oU on YouTube were both enlightening on what was, until relatively recently, still a well-kept secret.

I would also like to thank a few more people. Firstly, my very own hero-at-home, Kelvin, for his unwavering support, and my three daughters, Janet, Fiona and Amy, who listen patiently as I explain the endless twists and turns of the plot.

A few friends of my tribe: Carole Matthews, Fenella Miller, Sue Merritt, Lynda Stacy, Janet Gover and Rachel Summerson have each walked alongside me on this very personal journey and supported me in their own unique way.

Once again, a big thanks goes to my lovely agent Kate Burke, whose encouragement has seen me through the always uncertain task of starting a new series. My lovely editor Sarah de Souza who turned my 400+ page manuscript into a beautiful book and lastly, but by no means least, a big thank-you to the wonderful team at Atlantic Books for all their support and innovation.